1

Sullivan came out of his house and banged the door behind him. He was eating a large slice of bread and jam and it was staining the sides of his mouth.

He scuffled his bare feet on the pavement. His feet were white. It was the first day he had left off his shoes and stockings. He decided that the pavements were barely warm. It was early May. It was a long street. Sullivan's house was in the middle of a row of about twenty houses, two-storeyed, with wide windows and nearly all of them containing pots of geraniums in front of lace curtains. There was another row facing him. It was early morning. The streets were deserted, except for a bread van down below, the horse already drooping although he had barely started his work. He must be tired, Sullivan thought, and then turning left he went towards the Gardens.

He walked cautiously there because the nettles were thick and beginning to grow strong again. He got one sting despite his best efforts, so he searched for a dock-leaf, licked it and stuck it to the sting and sat down on a stone.

He finished eating the bread and jam. He guessed that his mouth was stained, so he rubbed the stains off with the sleeve of his jersey. The jersey was navy blue, so the stains didn't show too much. Sullivan sighed as he surveyed the deserted Gardens. He wondered where all the fellows were. This was a holiday. No school, so where were they? He was bored. He propped his narrow chin on his thin hand. The Gardens must have been named by a cynic. It was a rectangular bit of spare ground that would one day be built upon by the Corporation, but at the moment it served as a playground for the children. All the middle parts of it where they played football were smoothed earth where even the nettles had no chance to grow, but thistles and nettles grew in profusion all around the bare ground.

5

Thistles are all right, Sullivan was thinking, watching the bees sucking at their purple heads, and there were nice smells too. He raised his head in the air to smell better. The sky was a hazy blue with cotton-woolly-looking clouds drifting lazily across it.

It seemed to Sullivan that he was being overpowered with this particular scent. Then he remembered and looked behind him at the high walls of the orchard. That was it. From there the smell was coming. He got up from the rock and made his way out on the road and ran around the high stone walls. They were really high, the walls that enclosed the orchard. Over twelve feet high, built of snugly fitted stones and smooth cement so that a sparrow would have a job getting a foothold in the cracks. The walls enclosed a space of about two acres. There was only one entrance to the orchard; that was a small wooden door up by a lane. Sullivan came to this door and put his nose to the cracks and smelled. It was wonderful. There was one small crack where you could put your eye and see a small sliver of the place inside. Just trees you saw, absolutely bothered with blossoms. Trees and green grass. Sullivan felt that he would have given all he possessed to be able to open the door and go in and walk under the apple trees.

He knew that an old man lived in there. People respected him but were slightly afraid of him. In the autumn if you knocked loudly on the door he would come and sell you a pennyworth of apples. Peer out at you and take your penny and go away closing the door and coming back with a handful of apples. Why any man should have come and built an orchard here and shut himself away was more than the people of the street could understand. But he did. So he was peculiar. So leave him alone. He was cranky too. When he had built, the place was all open fields. Now on all sides he was enclosed by houses, so it was a funny thing to have an orchard in the middle of the streets in a town.

I'll get Pi, Sullivan thought suddenly, and we will go into the orchard. That was Sullivan, impulsive. His green eyes were shining as he turned away. He ran down the lane again and turned right around the back of his own row of houses and

6

into another lane. It was a forgotten spot. Progress had not caught up with this lane, called Paradise, but it would. There were four thatched cottages there, dating from the Flood, people said, but they were condemned. One was decayed with the thatched roof fallen in, and you could see the smoke-stained gable-end and the green stains from the rain. The other three were occupied. Sullivan halted at the half-door of the one in the middle and rattled it.

'Mrs. Clancy!' he called. 'Mrs. Clancy! Where's Pi?'

'Come in, amac,' said Mrs. Clancy, appearing out of the gloom of the place. She held the door open, then turned her head and screamed: 'Pius! Pius! Young Sullivan is here for you.'

Sullivan didn't want to go in, but he went. He sat on a stool. The open fireplace was smoking. There were bits of boxes burning in it. 'Can't get them to do a thing,' Mrs. Clancy was grumbling. 'Not a damn thing, and how could you with their father lying on his backside in bed yet like a duke in the middle of the day?' Then she shouted again, 'Get up, Tom! Out of that, you lazy bastard, and get something done.'

Sullivan closed his eyes and thought of his own nice house at home, the almost surgically clean kitchen, the brightness. But then there was Pi. Pi was all right. Mr. Clancy drank, people said, and so did Mrs. Clancy, people said; when it was all added up they were no better than one degree above tinkers. She was grumbling away. 'Yeer all well up there, I hope,' she said, sitting opposite him, rubbing her eyes with the back of her hand. 'Well for ye with yeer nice house and yeer steady jobs, and what have we? In and out like jack-in-boxes. Sometimes better to be dead I say.'

Pi came in. He was carrying broken wood.

'It's all bruk, mother,' he said, and put it on the hob. 'Can I go now?'

'Yes, yes,' she said. 'Go now, go now. Not a thought for yeer poor mother. No thought. But go on. You'll be young once and dead when you're old, and in between what have you? Not a bloody thing, a bloody thing. Hey, Tom, Tom, you hear me? You hear me?'

By then Sullivan was outside with Pi.

'Phew!' he said, and grinned at Pi.

Pi was small for his age. He was as old as Sullivan, eight. He had spiky hair standing up on his head, white, it was so fair, and extraordinary blue eyes, and very regular features. His trousers were a hand-down from a big pair of his father's, the legs were very wide, and Pi's limbs were very skinny. His bare feet were not white. Sullivan never remembered Pi wearing shoes or stockings. He had braces on the trousers and a patched shirt that was a bit too big for him, but Pi was as clean as a pig's bladder, like they say. He always was.

'Where we going, Sullivan?' he asked.

'I'll tell you,' said Sullivan. 'We're going into the orchard.'

'Is it Morgan Taylor's?' Pi asked.

'Yes,' said Sullivan, turning away. Pi had to trot after him. Sullivan's legs were longer.

'But why?' said Pi. 'Ther's no apples in it now. Not until later on. Why do you want to go in now?'

Sullivan stopped. He put up his face.

'I want to walk under the blossoms,' he said, 'and feel my feet on the green grass.'

'Janey, you're cracked, Sullivan,' said Pi.

'Do you want to come or don't you?' Sullivan asked. 'You don't have to come if you don't want to. I can go in myself.'

'Oh, I will,' said Pi, 'but you won't be able to get in.' He said this decisively but with a note of doubt, because he knew that Sullivan was determined.

'You wait,' said Sullivan, starting to run. He didn't go directly to the orchard. He went up by the back of his own house and opened the back door and went in and shortly appeared. He was carrying two broken forks of a bicycle.

'You see these,' he said. 'I had these all ready to go into the orchard in the autumn. We can still use them then, at night, but now I want to go in, in the daylight.'

'But he has a dog,' said Pi, trotting beside him.

'I don't mind,' said Sullivan. 'All I want to do is get in, that's all.'

Pi wished that he could be like Sullivan, not counting the

8

cost until afterwards, or not having the imagination to see yourself being beaten by the stick of the old man or bitten in the bottom by the sharp teeth of a dog. Pi suffered all these indignities as he followed Sullivan in the circuit of the place. Sullivan was cute enough. There was one place around the far side near the posh people's houses where the land rose beside the orchard wall cutting half the height of it. Sullivan paused here and started to dig at the cement between the stones with the battered fork. He was about twenty minutes getting it sufficiently cleared, then he forced the fork into the crack. It held fairly well, so he stood on that and started digging another hold farther up. Pi was looking at him with his mouth open. Now Pi would never have thought up a thing like that. When he had a second hold made, Pi handed him the first one, levering it out of the crack; he stood on the second and started making another hold above him. In about fifty minutes Sullivan was leaning on the top of the wall peering into the orchard.

'Wow,' said Sullivan. 'Wait'll you see this, Pi; just wait'll you see this.'

The orchard was spread before his eyes. There were hundreds of trees bursting with white and pink blossoms. The scent arising from them was overwhelming. They were all low-spreading, carefully pruned over years and years. You could hardly see the ground under them, and what grass you could see was festooned with fallen blossoms, and the gravelled paths in between were the same. Farther back on his left, Sullivan thought he could see the path that led to the house. He had never seen the house. He had an overpowering desire to see it.

'Come on, Pi,' he said, 'get up here and we'll get moving.' He threw down the two forks and Pi, very reluctantly, started to fit one into the bottom crack. In front of Sullivan's nose there were iron stanchions, holding barbed wire. The stanchions were old, had never been painted and were rusting badly at the holes that held the wire. Sullivan caught hold of the top of one of them and bent it and it broke off like a rotten branch. He did the same with the one next to it, so they had only one strand to get over.

Pi got up on the wall beside him, shakily, and looked with wonder at the scene below him. He snuffed in the smell of it. 'Janey mac,' said Pi, 'oh, janey mac!'

'I'm going in now,' said Sullivan. He crossed the wire, caught the edge of the wall with his hands, let his body down its full length and dropped. It was a long drop. He fell on his back and sat there on the grass looking up at Pi and grinning. 'Come on, Pi,' he called, 'I'll catch you.' Pi was very hesitant. 'But how'll I get out again, Sullivan?' he asked. 'Easy,' said Sullivan; 'we'll just open the gate and go out that way.'

They could have done that too but for unforeseen circumstances. First, Pi became suspended on the barbed wire, and, second, an enormous black Labrador dog came running from the house, his fangs looking fearful as they were the only white thing about him. Pi was hung up on one of the broken stanchions. As he was turning to slide down the wall, it pierced the loose trousers and hung him up like a coat on a nail.

'Oh, Pi,' said Sullivan in exasperation, and then he turned and attacked the dog. He walked and then ran towards the dog. This was unusual. The dog had collected more samples of the seats of trousers, protecting this orchard, than a multiple tailor's would put out in a year, but no boy had ever before run towards him. He backed snarling. 'Good dog, nice dog,' said Sullivan and grasped him firmly by the loose fur of the neck. The dog subsided. Pi, uncomfortable, thought if that wasn't just like Sullivan. Sullivan talked to the dog. 'That's a grand fellow. That's a great dog,' and I declare to God if the dog was a cat he would have started to purr.

'You are very good with dogs,' said a soft voice above Sullivan's head. That startled him. He looked up and half stood up but he didn't let go of the dog.

There was a young girl there looking gravely at him. Sullivan's mouth dropped open for a minute as he looked at her. They had heard of Morgan's girl all right, but nobody that he knew had ever seen her much. The fellows trying to raid the orchard might have heard her, but they would have been too busy trying to save their meat to pay any attention, and then it

10

was mostly in the night that the raiding was done. She was a tall girl, but it was the way she was dressed that surprised him. A long dress, well below her shins it was, of white sort of stuff, and a blue ribbon around the waist of it. Like something out of an old picture. So far as Sullivan up to this knew, all girls wore long black stockings and blue knickers and they grew out of their skirts so that the hems of them were always being let down for the sake of decency.

'What are you doing here?' she asked him. She had brown hair. It was cut in a fringe across her forehead. She would be about twelve or so, he thought.

'Oh, miss, it was the smell,' said Sullivan. 'We're two country boys. Only last year our people came to live in this town, and we do be after missing the smell of the apple blossoms. At home we would walk under them in April. And now we have to live in small poky houses in the town and our hearts breaking, and we are walking by and we get the scent of the blossoms through the wall and nothing can stop us. I say to my friend: "We will climb the wall and walk among the apple blossoms, and I'm sure nobody will mind." '

She was fascinated. His green eyes were gleaming; his copper-coloured hair was shining in the sun. He was on one knee looking up at her. His voice seemed to have deepened and become mellifluous as he talked to her. My God, Pi thought, Sullivan is acting again.

'You don't look like country boys,' she said.

'That's what they have done to us in a single year,' said Sullivan.

'Hadn't we better do something about your friend up on the wall?' she asked.

'Oh, he's all right,' said Sullivan, 'he's used to it.' Now that he thought of it that was true. Pi seemed to be always hung up somewhere.

'His leg is bleeding,' the girl said.

Sullivan looked up at the hanging boy. The trousers were pulled right up under his crotch and a thin stream of blood was edging down one of his legs.

'Oh, for goodness' sake, Pi!' said Sullivan in exasperation. Pi looked hangdog. The girl laughed and clapped her hands at the look on Pi's face. Pi blushed.

'I'm sorry,' she said quickly, 'I didn't mean to laugh. There's a ladder up there by the wall,' she said to Sullivan. 'You needn't be afraid of the dog,' as he hesitated. She put her hand on the dog's collar. 'Quiet now, Satan,' she said. Satan growled and lay down, her hand patting his head. She watched Sullivan. All his movements were swift. His body was thin and lithe. His clothes were good. They were far better than Pi's clothes. She looked again at Pi. He was hanging patiently. She put a hand over her mouth to hide her smile. Pi wasn't looking at anybody. He was sweating with embarrassment. He tried not to think of his predicament. He wished the ground would open up and swallow him. Sullivan came back with a ladder and propped it against the wall. He climbed the ladder.

'I never saw anyone like you, Pi,' he said, as he climbed. 'You can't go nowhere that something doesn't happen to you.'

'I'm sorry, Sullivan,' said Pi. 'Janey, how could I help it. The ould yoke caught me up when I was turning.'

'Hold tight now,' said Sullivan. He got Pi's legs on the steps of the ladder and made him walk up backwards. He had a bit of trouble freeing him from the stanchion and two strands of barbed wire. A bit of his trousers gave with the strain. Pi put his hand back to cover his flesh.

'You better come down this way,' the girl said, 'and I'll let you out the gate.'

'Come on, Pi,' said Sullivan. Pi came down but he came down frontwards. It was a bit of an effort, but he felt ashamed with the hole in his trousers. They stood at the bottom of the ladder and looked at the girl.

'You must be cut, Pi,' she said. Pi plucked up courage when he heard her saying his name.

'Ah, it's nothin',' said Pi.

'All the same,' she said with a furrow on her forehead, 'we better look at it.' Pi backed away terrified. 'No, no,' he cried, 'it's fine. Honest, miss, there's nothing wrong with it. It's fine.'

'Let's look at it,' said Sullivan and pulled up the leg of his trousers. There was a hole in his thigh, where a barb of the wire

12

had caught him, a sort of blue-lipped hole.

The girl had come around to look even though Pi was backing away.

'I'll get some iodine,' she said, but before she could move the old man was on them. He was waving a blackthorn stick. Pi felt his mouth going dry.

'You little demons,' the old man was crying, 'what brought you in here? Why are you talking to them, Bernie? Get the police. You hear! Get the police! You saw the notice on the wall. You are trespassing, you hear that! Trespassing!'

He wore a beard, close clipped to his face. Sort of grey-black. He was dressed in a black suit with narrow trousers and a sort of swallowtail coat, and a hard hat that was a bit green with age.

'It's all right, father,' Bernie said, going to him. 'They didn't mean any harm. They are two country boys. They were attracted by the smell of the apple blossoms.'

'They were, heh?' he asked. Then he came close to Sullivan. He looked closely at him. Sullivan looked at him with a frank open gaze. Sullivan was interested in the way his eyes were lined at the side and the deep fissures by the side of his nose and the permanent furrow between his eyebrows. 'Your name?' he asked.

'Sullivan,' said Sullivan.

'That's what I thought,' he said, 'and you told a pack of lies. Didn't you?'

'Well, no, sir,' said Sullivan. 'They weren't lies really. We were attracted by the smell of the blossoms.'

'Are you not country boys?' Bernie asked.

'We are not, miss,' said Pi in a rush. 'Sullivan is always tellin' tales like that. He doesn't mean it, miss, it just runs away with him. He didn't mean any harm.'

'Your father is Tim Sullivan,' the old man said. 'I'd know you out of him. What kind of a misplaced liar are you at all? Your father is a good man. Didn't you know he prunes my trees?'

'Yes,' said Sullivan. 'He spoke so much about the beauty of the orchard that I had to see it.'

'Another lie,' said the old man. 'Go on now, pack off to hell with the pair of you and don't let me ever see you here again. What would you think if I broke into the privacy of your homes because I liked the smell of cooking meat? This is my home. All of it, you hear, all about it, walls and all, and when you break in here it's the same as if I broke into your houses, without rhyme or reason. You mustn't come back. Just go away and you mustn't come back, you hear, or I'll set the dog on you. You hear that?'

'Yes, sir,' said Sullivan.

There was a little spittle at the corner of the old man's mouth. His eyes were blue, but sort of washed blue. For no reason at all Pi suddenly felt sorry for the old man, and sorry that they had broken into his peace. The old man was looking over their heads.

'Yes,' he said suddenly. 'In November two of the Irish peach will have to go. There's canker on them, Sullivan. You hear? We'll have to cut them at the roots and fell them. That will have to be done and then we must get an auger and bore a deep hole in them and fill the hole with paraffin oil. That will kill them. They have mighty roots. They are as old as the orchard. But they will have to go. Remember that. A terrible thing, Sullivan, that a tree can live longer than a man and that it doesn't. That's terrible. And we must burn the canker away.'

He was looking at them and didn't see them.

'Remember that,' he said and turned away. Then he saw Bernie. 'You won't forget, Bernie.'

She said, 'No, father, I'll remember.'

He put a hand on her head. It was a thin hand with long fingers. Sullivan was remarking the blue shadows between the tendons. That's what makes hands look old.

'I don't mind about them, I have you,' he said. 'You are an Irish peach, Bernie. While I have you I have the peaches. That's right?'

'Yes, father,' she said, smiling at him.

Then he looked again at the two boys. Clarity came back to his eyes. 'These,' he said, 'get rid of them, Bernie. For God's

14

sake get rid of them.' Then he turned away and went back to the house.

'Your father is not well?' Sullivan asked.

'Sometimes he is forgetful,' she said.

'I'm sorry we broke in like that,' said Sullivan. 'Honest.'

She smiled.

'Maybe I'm glad,' she said. 'I don't see a lot of people. I'll get the iodine for Pi.' She turned and walked away swiftly towards the house. They couldn't see the house through the trees, just the grey lower part of it.

'Jay, it was a cruel thing to do, Sullivan,' said Pi. 'I knew we shouldn't have done it.'

'I didn't know the old man was a bit loopy,' said Sullivan. 'Imagine that girl living here all alone with a loopy old man, Pi.'

'He's not loopy,' said Pi. 'He's just old, that's all. Everybody forgets a bit when they get old. My oul Grannie couldn't remember the time of the day or nothing. She always thought I was me oul fella.'

The girl came back. Pi lifted the leg of his trousers carefully. He let her dab the cut with iodine. She noticed that he winced but didn't cry out. She noticed that his clothes were pitifully shabby but that his flesh was remarkably clean.

'Now, Pi,' she said, smiling at him.

'Thanks, miss,' said Pi.

She walked with them to the gate.

After all, thought Sullivan, feeling the petal-strewn grass under his feet and the smell of the blossoms wrapping him around, I got to walk on the grass under the apple trees.

At the gate he turned back and looked at the orchard once more and sucked the smell of it into his lungs.

'It's real nice,' said Sullivan.

'Even if you're not country boys?' Bernie asked.

Sullivan shrugged that away.

'Listen,' he said, 'Sunday night I'm having a film show in my backyard. It will be good. Why can't you come? Penny entrance but we won't charge you anything. Eight o'clock. You'll enjoy it. Can't you come?'

She hesitated.

'Ah, do come, miss,' said Pi. 'It won't be like to-day. Everything will be fine.'

'I'll try,' she said.

'Number eighteen,' said Sullivan. 'Around by the back door. We'll be waiting for you.'

Then they were outside and the door closed behind them. Sullivan had to shake himself a bit.

'It's like a different sort of world, Pi. In there and out here.'

'What are you going to have for the show, Sullivan?' Pi asked. 'What kind of fillums did you whip? Where are they?'

'They will be good,' said Sullivan. 'All my shows are good.'

2

'Sullivan! Sullivan!' his father was calling.

'I'm out here, father,' said Sullivan.

He was setting up the magic lantern in the yard. He got the thing for his last birthday. His father grumbled a lot. He said it cost him more than two weeks' wages and wasn't that a nice to-do? His father's average earnings were two pounds ten a week. The yard was small. It was surrounded by a wall pierced at the end by the wooden door with a latch. It was a concrete yard. Half of it was covered in with an iron roof. It was a sort of scullery, and at its far end held the lavatory. The rest of the yard was open to the weather and contained a lot of pots and boxes with plants and seedlings growing in them. Sullivan's father loved all these things.

Sullivan had a sheet hanging from the roof covering the sink and he was setting up the yoke on an upended orange-box. He was very intent on it.

He heard his father coming from the passage behind him.

'What's the idea?' his father was asking him.

'I'm putting this thing up,' said Sullivan. 'Going to have a show tonight, penny a skull.'

'I don't mean that,' said his father, 'I mean what's the idea going in and disturbing old Morgan Taylor?'

'Oh, that,' said Sullivan, walking back into the kitchen and shoving his head into the cubby-hole under the stairs searching for the flex and the bulb.

'What made you do it?' his father was asking him. 'If I knew you were going to do that I'd make your skin tingle, I'm telling you.'

'I didn't know I was going to do it myself,' said Sullivan, coming out again with the flex and going back into the yard.

'Stand still, dammit, until I talk to you!' his father roared at him.

'But I'll never be ready in time,' he said.

'I don't give a damn!' shouted Sullivan's father. Sullivan stopped then and looked at him. He was a massive man. He had his Sunday suit of navy blue on him. He had a broad clean-shaven face, with wide-spaced eyes and heavy black eyebrows. He looked very fierce, but he wasn't. His large hands were clenched. They were very delicate hands when they were handling young plants.

'How did you get in?' he asked. 'Even a cat shouldn't be able to get in over that wall.'

'We just climbed in,' said Sullivan.

'Now listen, Sullivan,' his father said. 'You are not to go in there again. Do you hear that? You mustn't go in there again.'

'All right,' said Sullivan, 'I won't go in there again unless I'm invited in.'

'You won't go in there at all,' his father told him. 'It took me twenty years to get to know Morgan Taylor. He's a decent man, and if I catch you spreading any tales about him it'll be the worse for you.'

'What kind of tales?' asked Sullivan. 'You mean about him being dippy?'

'He's not dippy,' said his father. 'Just because a man builds a wall and keeps himself to himself, he's supposed to be queer. Listen, that fella could blind you with knowledge. He's a well-educated man. You hear that?'

'All right,' said Sullivan, 'but he still has a slate loose.'

Sullivan's father turned his back. 'God give me patience,' he said, 'so that I won't strike you.'

Sullivan grinned. It's a good job he wouldn't strike me, he thought. One blow from him and I'd end up in the middle of next week.

'Ah, I'm only joking, father,' he said then. 'I wouldn't say anything abroad about him.'

'He's a good man, you see,' said his father, relaxing.

'Who was Bernie's mother?' Sullivan asked.

'There you go again,' said his father. 'Questions, questions! You're as bad as the women. Leave them alone, I tell you.'

'He's not her father,' said Sullivan. 'She called him "father". He couldn't be her father. He's a hundred years old.'

'He's not her father. He's her grandfather. But he likes to think that she's his daughter. His daughter died having her. Is there anything wrong with that, tell me?'

'No,' said Sullivan, 'just so long as I know.'

'Well, you know now,' said his father. 'He must be out there now for thirty years. Something happened, I don't know what. Away back. He was something in a university. He has many books. He's a good man. Just you leave him alone, Sullivan, and get all the other young monsters around the place to leave him alone, not hounding him.'

The voice from upstairs was calling: 'Tim! Tim!'

'There's your mother,' he said. 'I'll go up to her. Remember what I told you.'

'I will,' said Sullivan, turning back to meddle with his contraption.

Tim went into the kitchen and up the stairs. The kitchen floor was red-tiled and the range was gleaming. All the pots hanging on the wall beside it were burnished. It was mostly Tim's work. He sighed a bit as he mounted the stairs. The stairs were covered in linoleum. He worried about his son and Morgan Taylor. It would be all right. He knew his son. Once he spoke to him it would be all right. Tim thought of his friendship with the old man. It meant a lot to him to go behind the walls of the orchard and feel shut off for a while from the life outside.

His wife was in bed in the front room. The light was on. She was a thin-faced woman with copper-coloured hair and green eyes. Like his son, but his son had more chin on him. She didn't look well all right. Her face was a bit drawn and there were dark circles under her eyes. Her hair was flecked with grey ribs. He threw his cap on the bed, sat down beside her and took her hand.

'Feeling better, Mag?' he asked her.

'No,' she said. 'I have that tearing headache. It has me crippled. Would you get me another few aspirins? There on the table.'

'Are you taking too much of them things?' he asked her.

'No, no,' she said. 'Do you want me to die?'

He sighed and rose and turned a few tablets out onto his hand. Was there ever a time, he wondered, that she didn't want them? He poured water from the ewer into a glass and handed them to her. He looked closely at her, remembering. She had not always been like that. What? Nearly twenty years ago now. Up behind in the big place outside the town. He used to do the garden for her father. The garden was gone now. The town had crept up and engulfed it with houses, like a creeping disease the spread of a town was. She was a different girl then. Spry, dreamy-eyed. Not much work in the house. Three maids there. Time to help him to prune the trees; to watch over him in the greenhouse, until she became part of him, without hope, something you might never possess, like a blue rose. But her father died and he had been very fond of the drop, and when he went all went with him. And Meg was left like a ripe fruit to fall into the arms of the gardener. It would have worked out, maybe, he thought, if they had gone away altogether to another town. But here she had her memories of the good days, when she was bowed to in the shops and greeted on the streets and went to many parties here and there. She lost all that of course. He felt sorry about that. But she shouldn't have taken it so hard. It was nearly ten years before their son was born and he came hard too and she said, 'Never again, oh, never again, it would kill me', and so it was. Never again. Well, all that teaches you something, he thought. Patience and forbearance. Anyhow being in a garden prunes you in a way. You learn to put up with disappointment and frustration, and hope for next year.

'Where's Terence Anthony?' she asked. 'What is Terence Anthony doing now?'

Tim had to grin, thinking of Terence Anthony. Since his son had reached the age of reason and had been asked his name he would say, 'Call me Sullivan'. And so it was. How could any man live under the burden of his names?

'He's below,' said Tim. 'He's having some of the kids in to a show.'

'These dreadful children,' said Meg. 'Why does he encourage them?'

'It's his business instincts,' said Tim. 'Making a bit of money.'

'I don't know where we got him,' she said. 'Honest to God I don't know where we got him.'

'He's all right,' said Tim, 'he's not a bad boy.'

'What would my father say if he were alive?' she asked. 'If he saw him mixing with the children of this street. My father was particular.'

Tim thought her father wasn't so particular near the end. He'd drink with the devil, not to mind all the corner boys bumming around him for drinks. He had seen him, staggering down the town late at night, very well dressed in his black clothes and his starched stiff collar and black bowler, sometimes mouthing obscenities, hanging on to the arms of a bowsey. Meg never saw that, or if she knew about it she had put it away from her mind as she put every other unpleasant thing. If they were too unpleasant she went to bed and got rid of them with aspirin tablets. He chided himself for his thoughts. She was a good wife. She kept the place well when she was well herself, and even if the neighbours were awed by her standoffishness, she wasn't a bad woman. That was the way she was brought up. She had never been brought up to live in or with the mixem-gatherum of Duke Street.

'Send Terence Anthony up to me, Tim,' she said. 'He hasn't been near me at all since I got the head. Are you staying in?'

20

'I might go out and see old Morgan for a few minutes,' he said.

'Well, don't be too late,' she said.

He went then and called his son. The son was very reluctant. He was sticking two bits of film together with horrible-smelling stuff.

'What's up, father?' he asked.

'Your mother wants to see you,' Tim said.

'Ah, for goodness' sake,' said Sullivan. 'I'm shocking busy, father, and I'll never be ready.'

Tim clipped him on the head with his fingers.

'Go on, do what you're told,' he said. Sullivan looked at him. His voice was sharp. It was always that way when Meg was in the picture. He was very patient, very forbearing about everything else, but nobody must say a word about Tim Sullivan's wife, or disobey a command of hers or say the slightest thing about her.

Sullivan sighed.

'All right, father,' he said and started to mount the stairs, still holding the two bits of film in his fingers, pressing them to make them stick.

'And be careful with all those young villains out in the yard,' his father called after him. 'And don't let them make too much noise. Remember that your mother is not well. You hear?'

'I hear and obey,' said Sullivan, going out of sight.

Tim grunted. He put coal on the fire in the range, tidied Meg's apron on the back of the kitchen chair and then went out of the front door into the street, closing it softly after him.

'Why didn't you come and see me of your own accord, Terence Anthony?' his mother asked him as soon as he came through the bedroom door. 'Do I have to beseech you to come and see me?'

Sullivan wondered why he didn't come of his own accord. It seemed to him that his mother was a lot in bed. Sullivan discovered from reading a book one time, where he got the big word hypochondria, which at first he thought meant that you were bitten by a mad dog. He used the word in an essay at school. He remembered it well. The reason he remembered it was because the teacher thought it was amusing and read it out loud so that everybody could hear it. 'The snarling foaming animal bit him on the thigh and he got a bad dose of hypochondria.' After the laughter Sullivan looked it up in the dictionary and read that it meant a nervous malady, often arising from indigestion, and tormenting the patient with imaginary fears. He thought then, That's like my mother, and killed the thought, and had to tell it in Confession the next time he went and the priest read him off a long strip about the fourth commandment.

'I didn't think, mother,' he said. 'I have a big do on to-night. It will take a lot to be ready in time.'

'I think your mother is more important,' she said. 'After all you won't have your mother long. You know that? I might be here myself all the night and when you came to see me I might be cold and dead on the bed. You know that?'

Sullivan got cold prickles on the back of his neck. His mother, ever since he could remember, talked a lot about death. It always frightened Sullivan; the thought of coming up the stairs and into the room and seeing his mother stiff and cold in the bed.

'I'm sorry, mother,' he said.

'Don't forget to keep the fire going in the range,' she said, 'and don't let any of those dreadful children into the kitchen.'

'All right, mother,' he said, and stood there holding the film, not meeting her eyes, waiting to be dismissed.

'Go on back to your boys,' she said then, petulantly. He went. He will be hardly outside the door, she thought, when he will have forgotten me. She thought how different he was to the way she had been with her own mother. She had lavished attention on her mother until she died and afterwards she had spent her life on her father, pressing his clothes, starching his collars, waiting up for him at night when he would come home very late (he would be dead tired, poor thing, not helplessly drunk, as they said – he only drank a little wine with his meals) and she would undress him and get him to bed. There was devotion for you! Perhaps it was a pity that Terence

Anthony wasn't a girl. Sons would never treat their mothers well. They would go away and leave them.

Pi was below when Sullivan got down.

'Are you ready, Sullivan?' he asked. 'Is everything set?'

'All ready, nearly, Pi,' said Sullivan. 'Just to stick this last bit of film.'

There was just one reel for holding film on top of the lantern. There was a crank to turn the film in its grooves, but what was shown would just snake down and lie on the ground and would have to be tediously rolled again with the fingers. Sullivan stuck the last bit of film on to the last bit in the reel and pulled it through the catches. Then he switched on the bulb in the lantern. It threw a fairly good rectangular light on the sheet. Sullivan had earned the bits of film. He usually went to the cinema down there at the matinees on Sunday and turned the crank of the big machine for an hour. His payment was a free look at the films and all the spare bits of film that the operator cut off when he was patching up the broken reels.

'All ready now,' said Sullivan, 'except for seating accommodation.'

He went into the kitchen followed by Pi and they brought out the four kitchen chairs. With two to a chair that made eight, and they set on end a few of his father's seed-boxes and with those they could seat twelve.

'Now,' said Sullivan, 'we'll go to the back gate and wait for the customers.'

It was quite dark now. Their only illumination came from the light in the shed. Sullivan stood at the back door. He was a bit nervous. Suppose after all his preparations that nobody came at all? Nonsense then, his ego said, a Sullivan show is always appreciated and looked forward to. This was the first time he had shown films. The other times he had done shadowgraphs for them and spoken a few funny ballads like *Sarah Tinker's Turkey* and *Raftery's Pig* and *The Night of the Big Wind*, and as well he had sung a few things like *The Boys of Wexford* and *Skyball* and the *Wedding of Ahhy McGraw* and a few patriotic tear-wipers. The kids liked the show. That one had only had an admission fee of one halfpenny, however.

With the film show he had upped his prices one hundred per cent and he was wondering how they would take that.

They started to come. Small nippers, the little brother holding the sister's hand or the other way round, with their pennies clenched in their hot hands. One or two wise characters tried to get in for a halfpenny but Sullivan insisted on full prices and they duly paid up. The parents were glad to get rid of them for an hour or two and they knew they would be safe enough in Sullivan's place. It was well worth a penny.

There were eighteen of them altogether, but they were so small in the main that they could get three at a time sitting on the chairs. Sullivan was beginning to enjoy himself until Badger turned up with Porky and presented his penny with a smile. Badger was big and antipathetic to Sullivan. He was well built, coarse of features, and gave promise of being an excellent prospect for pugilism when he got a bit bigger.

Sullivan said: 'This is a show for kids, Badger.'

'I'm a kid,' said Badger. 'I'm oney twelve, Sullivan, and Porky is oney eleven. Two poor little kids. But we are not small enough, is that it? Will you prove that be comin' out the back here and having it out, coats on or off, take your choice?'

Sullivan summed up. He wouldn't mind a fight, but after all what was the use? And he was expecting Bernie, every minute wondering if she would come. He wouldn't like her to see him in a brawl.

'All right, Badger,' he said, 'but no funny business or you'll go out again on top of your head.'

'That goes for me too,' said Pi.

'Out of the way, maggot,' said Badger, pushing past Pi. Sullivan caught Pi by the back of his shirt and pulled him back as he went after Badger. Porky passed by. Badger went into the shed and brushed three kids off the chair and sat down on it and took out a Woodbine butt and lit it.

Bernie came.

'Hello,' she said.

Sullivan had been contemplating Badger when she spoke.

'Oh, hello,' he said. 'You came.' He didn't realise until now how much he had been looking forward to seeing her again.

She was wearing a dark coat of some kind. 'I'm glad you came,' he said.

'I couldn't,' she said, 'if your father hadn't come over.'

'That's good,' he said. 'Come on in.'

They went inside. Badger whistled, brushed three more kids off the seat near him and said: 'Sit down, Apples.' She behaved well. She said, 'Thank you' and sat there and took two of the kids up on her lap. 'Have a smoke,' said Badger, presenting her with a rancid butt taken from behind his ear. 'Thanks,' she said, 'I don't smoke.' Sullivan was furious. Is everything always to be spoiled by people, he wondered? He speculated about having a row with Badger. He thought what it would mean: the upsetting of all the chairs and the machine and the kids screaming. He went over to Bernie. 'I'm sorry a couple of rats got into the place tonight when we weren't looking,' he said, 'but say the word and we will exterminate them.'

'Don't bother,' said Bernie. 'Please go on with the show.'

'That's right,' said Badger. 'Let's have some action. Brighten the fillum.'

Sullivan doused the main light and switched on the bulb in the lantern and the film started. Pi had to keep pulling it and letting it lie on the ground. It was an entertaining film even if it didn't make much sense. First you saw a big tall house and smoke coming out of the windows and then the scene switched to a fire station with all the fellows dropping down the pole and rushing to the engines, then back to the house again and a lady leaning out the window enveloped in smoke and then a blank and the words 'Save me! Save Me! SAVE ME!' written on the screen, and then you saw the fire engine racing, and then there was a click and you saw a girl walking in a field picking some kind of flowers and you couldn't see her face at all on account of a big floppy hat she was wearing, and then the words on the screen said: 'The birds were singing in the pastures of Nebraska', and then you saw the pastures again and an enormous bull pawing the ground and setting off, and you saw another picture of the girl bending over the flowers, and another sight of the bull racing, and then there was another click and you saw a train with furious wheels turning,

turning, and the words on the screen said: 'Nearer! Nearer! Nearer!' but nobody ever got to see what was nearer because there was another click and you saw a fellow on some kind of a farm chasing another fellow with a pitchfork, and all the kids were delighted with this and screamed and screamed, but it didn't last very long because you saw a lassie in a very long dress hanging on a rope over a cliff and below her, hundreds of feet below her, the white waters thundered in a gorge and then just a lot of white lights.

'Well, that's it,' said Sullivan.

There was a silence in the shed. Even to Sullivan, now that he thought about it, the show seemed inadequate. It had only lasted about twelve minutes.

'Fraud! Fraud!' Badger started shouting. 'We want our money back.' All the little kids were inclined to agree with him.

'The film show is over,' said Sullivan, thinking quickly, 'but the stage play has yet to come.'

'Fraud! Fraud!' Badger cried. 'We want our money back.' He threw away his butt.

'You keep out of this, Badger,' said Sullivan. 'You can have your money back and get out of here. I've had enough of you.'

'It's about time this thing was broken up,' said Badger, getting to his feet, and then behind them there was a sizzle and a sheet of flame as the sprawled film exploded. Sullivan drew back as the flames spewed into his face. There was a sound of all the boxes falling and the kids screaming. Sullivan fell back. He thought he was blinded; his arm was over his eyes. Then he lowered his arm and looked and blinked his eyes and found he could see, so he raced around the fire towards the sink behind the sheet. The sheet was down and there was Bernie with a basin in her hand. He grabbed at children then and threw them away from him towards the back gate. The flames were licking up as far as the tin roof of the shed. They doused briefly as she threw a basin of water at them. Then she filled another one. Sullivan was beating at the fire with a box. The box was smouldering. What have I done? he thought. And there was his mother upstairs. The second basin arrived and the flames died even more and then they were black and out, with Bernie stamping at them with her shoes.

Sullivan looked at her.

She had smudges of black on her face. His own eyes were streaming with tears from the fumes.

'You're a g-g-good girl in a f-f-fire,' said Sullivan, 'but the show was a f-f-flop. I wanted it to be good and it was a f-f-flop.'

He saw her eyes widening as she listened to him. He didn't know why. Not for the moment.

Then he heard the voice of his mother calling from upstairs in a terrified voice: 'Terence Anthony! Terence Anthony! Come here to me! Come here to me at once!'

He moved to go.

'I'm s-s-sorry, Bernie,' he said. He walked towards the kitchen. Then he heard the way his voice had behaved. He turned back to look at her. My God, they are back again with me, he thought. He put pressure on his voice, dragging it up from his chest, exploding the beginning of every word. 'But next time, wait'll you see, I'll put on a POWerful show for you. Wait'll you see.'

He listened carefully to that. It was fine. No hesitation in it. Then he nodded his head and went in.

'Lord,' said Pi, at Bernie's shoulder, 'the stuts are back again with him. That bloody Badger!'

3

Sullivan was in a dilemma.

Here he was in this gigantic theatre, the biggest probably in the whole world. Thousands of people had their eyes glued to his form. He was tall and his chest swelled, and his arms were as thick as the thighs of a common man. He was dressed in chain mail and over that the flowing robes of the great king became him well. His own hair over a noble head only it wasn't

27

copper-coloured but fair and he wore a fair beard. There was a tense silence in the house. On the couch lay the form of his dead Queen whom he had just strangled with his own hands. Skewered to the floor with the blade of a great sword, that could only be wielded by the sinews of a really strong man, lay her lover, the Grand Duke of Spiddal, Connemara. Outside could be heard the raving shouts of a rebellious people. The audience waited breathless on the words of the doomed king. He spoke. *I will not yield*, said the king, *though each and every one of my veins was filled with the blood of cowards. I will go out and face the people and I will tempt them from their great betrayal by the glory of my unconquerable spirit.* The trouble was that when he reached the end of that speech it came out *g-g-glory* and *s-s-spirit*.

'Dammit,' said Sullivan, and stamped his foot on the ground. That hurt his foot because he was still in his bare feet, so he had to curse again and hop a bit. Then he heard the town clock striking four, and he started to run. He was carrying a can of tea for his father and the sandwiches rolled in paper. Not that his father would chide him but all the same it was well not to be too late.

He was crossing the bridge over the river on his way to the Docks. Gardening had fallen on bad times. Sometimes there was no gardening that required the services of his father, so at these times when extra help was needed down at the Docks Tim went down there. His mother didn't like his father working at the Docks, but then they had to eat.

He stood up on the bridge and looked down at the swirling water. He waved his hand in the air, twirling a great sword. He was the ferocious captain of the Gaelic fleet raiding into England, the prow of his long-boat churning the waves from the massed oars of the muscle-knotted arms of his great crew. 'Death and destruction,' Sullivan shouted, 'and spare none, no woman, no man, no new-born child!'

He heard somebody laughing and saw a man with a fisherman's jersey and long boots passing on the bridge. He didn't say anything. He just put a hand over his mouth, laughing. Sullivan ignored him and came down from the bridge. How

can the passer-by understand greatness? he asked. That satisfied him. As long as greatness doesn't stutter, he said to himself then. Immediately he started toward the enemies on the
ship with his leaping sword. He was hacking his way through
them, his eyes gleaming, his footwork wonderful to behold.
Stab and hack and retreat and advance, stabbing, blood flowing
down his great arm over his chest, the smell of blood on all
sides. He was wading through blood and the piled bodies of the
enemy when he saw six of his real enemies coming up from
the Long Walk near the river. They were the boys from down
there and they didn't like the boys from where Sullivan came
from, and if Sullivan or his friends saw one of them up in their
bailiwick they would do to them what these six running enemies were now intent on doing to Sullivan. They ran towards
him screaming. 'Here's Sullivan, men,' they said. 'Here's Sullivan from the West,' they cried. 'Get him, men! Get him!'

Sullivan had two courses of action. He could advance or he
could retreat in safety. His father wanted his tea. When you
were unloading coal all day at the Docks you could do with
tea. Of the six boys Sullivan could lick five in single combat.
The tallest of them might be a match for him. But Sullivan was
thin and at fourteen his legs were long and his wind was good,
so he raced madly to get through the closing space. Once he
got to the Docks he would have protection. It was a tight fit.
The whole six of them spread out, started obliquely to run
towards the one narrow opening between the tall buildings that
led down to the dock. Sullivan ran in a straight line. His flying
feet raised powdered dust into the air. He was laughing. This
was good. This was better than dreams. He was in danger. The
enemy was all around. Their screams of destruction loud in his
ears. But he was Cuchulain that could outrun the fastest
hound of Banba. He beat them to the opening with about six
yards to spare. He could nearly feel them breathing on his
neck. The can of tea was a handicap to him, but the lid was
tight and it couldn't spill so he could let it go with the waving
of his arms.

They flew into the next opening. There was a horse and cart
right in the middle of the road loaded with coal. Sullivan

shaved by it into the path. The horse reared, the driver cursed loudly, and as the other six followed Sullivan the horse reared more than ever and the small man, his purple face suffused, aimed blows at them with the whip as they passed by. They had to swerve to get away from him and Sullivan gained a few more yards and ran into the opening of the Docks with his heart soaring.

They were still behind him, but well strung out, he saw, as he looked over his shoulder, the smallest little fellow pounding along at the end, with his face red and scalded-looking, a little midget of a chap who was hampered in his running by the trousers he wore which came too far below his knees.

There were two long coal boats there, taking up almost one whole side of the dock. There were four great black baulks erected beside the ships, and the four donkey engines of the ships were screaming and groaning as they hauled out the coal in the steel buckets, guided them to the black-faced man on the baulk who directed them into the maw of the heavy horse-carts waiting below. There was apparently great confusion, with empty horse-carts milling about, and others being loaded, and others trying to get into line, and others crossing the road loaded or unloaded through the gates that led to the coalyards.

Into the middle of this confusion raced the seven boys, shouting and swerving and dipping under horses' heads and under wheels, and the drivers shouting and cursing and threatening. When he was well into the middle of the confusion, Sullivan halted and suddenly darted back the way he had come in order that the enemy would be completely foxed. So it was that he saw what had happened near the first baulk.

The little fellow that was bringing up the rear was running right near the edge of the water, pounding along with the heart of a lion, but from the confusion of milling horses and carts, one horse and cart had broken away, its reins trailing on the ground. These carts were very heavy. Their sides were built up with about four feet of inch-thick heavy timber to bear the burden of the falling coal. The horse was snorting and rearing and running, its eyes rolling in its head, and it was running directly for the little chap with the too-long trousers. Sullivan stopped, petrified. What could he do? He was too far away. There was nothing anybody could do. Sullivan's hand was up to his mouth. Oh my God, Sullivan was saying. The man who was directing the tubs at the first baulk did something about it. He levelled himself and jumped onto the cobble-stones. It was a long drop, but he landed safely. Sullivan noticed that his hob-nailed boots knocked sparks from the cobbles. He had just time to straighten himself and reach for the trailing reins of the horse. He grabbed them, drew himself close to the head of the horse, turned him, but they were too near the water and the horse had too much impetus and the cart was too heavy and before anybody could say or see, the man and the horse and the heavy cart were into the litter-ridden waters of the Docks.

Sullivan threw down his can and his package and he ran, and he ran straight towards the water. Other men were running too and shouting, but Sullivan got there first. The water was boiling. Just a great white boil was on the water, that was all, and before anybody could stop him Sullivan went feet first into the water, because he had seen the man from the baulk and that man was his own father, and Sullivan was terrified.

He went down, down, and he couldn't see anything, just the dirty dock water in his eyes. And he must have opened his mouth saying, 'Father', because it went into his lungs and it was dirty stuff, and he went down far enough to feel the wheel of the cart under his bare feet and then he couldn't hold himself because he was grabbed and hauled up and up with a terrible strong hand on his jersey.

It was a half-naked docker who had hold of him, shouting 'You bloody young fool! You bloody young fool!' as he hauled him towards the stone steps that led down into the water. Sullivan couldn't talk, just inside, My father is down there, he was shouting, but he could get nothing out, nothing out at all. Then he was lying above on the cobbles and they were squeezing water out of his body, and over where the cart had gone man after man was diving down, with shirts on or off, or trousers on or off, and the struggling head of the horse came above the filthy water and a docker swam beside him, guiding him over to the side of the ship where one of the donkey engines was swinging a great crane with a sort of hawser instead of a rope tied to it. But Tim Sullivan didn't come up. He's under the cart, Sullivan seemed to hear a voice say at one time. Pinned under the cart. But they got the cart up, and they got Tim Sullivan up. Sullivan didn't see this happening because he wasn't there. He had been swiped away, up somewhere, that was forever afterwards like a dream to him.

Just a long room with beds in it with white covers on them and a white ceiling. Everything was white, the women who were there, and there was nothing black about it, except the priest who sat beside his bed and held on to his hand and said: 'Listen, Sullivan, you'll have to be brave. Your father was a brave man. You will have to be as brave, because he died so that somebody else could live. You must remember that.' But all Sullivan could do was turn his face to the wall and leave it there.

4

Pi walked up and down in front of the door many times before he could bring himself to go and raise the knocker. The endeavour made him sweat even though it was a fairly chilly day. He was well dressed, if a bit loosely fitted. He was working as a messenger boy and his employer had presented him with cast-off clothes and shoes of his son. Otherwise there would have been a bit of a scandal if the boy that delivered the messages for him were to appear at people's doors with bare feet and trousers showing the scenery. His fair hair was still very fair and very spiky.

He hadn't seen Sullivan since the business, you know, and he was worried about him, glimpses he would get of him sometimes coming from school maybe, and he would go to run after him but Sullivan would have disappeared. Pi felt this and was sad about it. It often kept him awake for ten minutes at night. He didn't know how he could help Sullivan, but if he was even there beside him saying nothing maybe, just that.

So he raised the knocker and let it fall. He knew there were people in there, but he was hoping that Sullivan himself would be in.

His heart failed a bit when Sullivan's mother opened the door and looked at him.

'Is Sullivan in, ma'am?' he asked her quickly.

She was dressed all in black. Sullivan could see the other women sitting by the range in the kitchen. They were wearing black shawls and snuffing from Colman's Mustard tins. They were nice women. Mrs. Kelly and Mrs. Barrat. Two ladies that went to six-o'clock Mass every morning, had never anything bad to say about their neighbours, and were always there when they were needed, to help children whose mother might be up in the hospital, or to console you in sorrow, or to wash and lay out the corpse of your father.

'I don't know where Terence Anthony is,' said Meg. 'I know where he should be. He should be here at home helping his mother in her great trouble. He wasn't even at his father's month's mind Mass. What kind of a boy is that, tell me?'

Pi didn't think he was expected to answer this. He just shifted uncomfortably from foot to foot and persisted.

'I wonder where he might be, ma'am?' he asked.

'I don't know where he is,' she repeated, 'and if you find him tell him to come home to his mother. You hear that?' She had a handkerchief in her hand now and was blowing her nose and rubbing at her already tear-reddened eyes. Pi dropped his own eyes to his shoes. He couldn't bear looking at her because he didn't feel sorry for her. He felt sorry for Sullivan but he didn't feel sorry for Sullivan's mother. He just thought that quickly and then put it away from him.

'All right, ma'am,' he said. 'If I find him I'll tell him.'

'What way have I ever failed him?' Meg asked as she closed the door and sat on the chair out from the range. 'I brought him up with care. Wouldn't you think he would be with me when I need him? What kind of a son did I rear at all, Mrs. Kelly?'

'You reared a good boy, ma'am,' Mrs. Kelly said decisively. 'A biteen wild maybe, but then, God knows, boys are no good unless there's a bit of wildness in them. His father's going was a bad blow to him.'

'It was a bad blow to me too,' said Meg, 'but I have to put up with it. I haven't my one child beside me to comfort me when I am lonely. You would think that the boy hated his father. I had to force him to go into the room behind and look at the body of his father laid out on the bed.'

Mrs. Barrat sucked in air between her teeth and shook her head.

'You shouldn't have done that, ma'am, begging your pardon, because I told you at the time. Young people are very afeard of death. They don't know any different. The sight of a dead body is very foreign to a child, ma'am.'

'But he had to say goodbye to his father before they put him in the grave,' said Meg. 'Everybody must kiss their beloved goodbye.'

And you kissed the corpse enough, God forgive me for thinking it, thought Mrs. Kelly, remembering her, wailing in the room and then coming down and drinking tea, and as soon as a knock came at the door rising again and wailing and going back and kissing the dead face and crying: 'Why did you leave me, Tim, oh, why did you leave me?' This sort of way was very foreign to the people of the street. You wept all right but you put a good face on it, and you could laugh too; that was what people came for, to take your mind off things, to make you laugh.

'He has avoided the house,' said Meg. 'I see him at meal-times and sometimes not even then. After a whole month. And he won't open his lips to me. What am I to do? Who will look after me?'

You'll find somebody, thought Mrs. Kelly. Your kind always finds somebody. Oh, God forgive me, she thought then, is there no breath of charity left in me? She rose.

'We must be going now, Mrs. Sullivan,' she said. 'Our men will be in for their meals.'

'It was very kind of you to call,' Meg said, 'and to go to the month's mind Mass. The people were very good to go.'

'The people loved Tim Sullivan, ma'am,' said Mrs. Barrat.

'He was one of themselves. He was a father to the street, we could say. They called him the Duke of Duke Street, he was that good and thoughtful. I'm sorry, ma'am,' she said hurriedly then, as Meg started crying again. The women were exasperated with her. Sure you would have to talk about him, but how can you talk about him if she bursts into tears every time his name is mentioned? Not that they weren't sorry for her. They were, but it was hard to comfort someone like this. You didn't get a chance. And so you would have to start running around corners when you saw her coming.

They closed the door behind them.

'Phew,' said Mrs. Kelly.

'God help her,' said Mrs. Barrat.

'God help her son,' said Mrs. Kelly emphatically.

'Amen,' said Mrs. Barrat.

'God forgive us,' said Mrs. Kelly.

Pi ranged far and wide. He had the bicycle with the big carrier on the front of it so that he could go places in a short time. He did a great circle around the town, at all the places where he and Sullivan would go when things were normal. Out up by the railway and across it where the soldiers in the barracks above dug trenches near the sea, for their exercises. Sullivan was the Major-General up there. Further in near the Docks (he might be there, morbidly) on the old rotting hulk that had once been a proud fishing-boat, where Sullivan had been Henry Morgan. No sign of him there. Across the lock and up by the river and over the bridge and around by the sea over there where the silver strand gleamed beyond the dumped refuse of the city, out there across the sand where the big four-masted schooner was tilted and rusting away, stuck fast on the rocks and the sand. This was where Sullivan had been Commodore Barry, where they had climbed the rotting ratlines right up the mast, and seen the helpless city below under their guns. Pi went in there and called, climbing laboriously over the steep sides, slightly afraid of the wicked-looking rats that scurried and scampered away from him, or glared at him hungrily from the roof of the deck cabin. No sign of Sullivan.

He tried the coast road farther out and swung into the country, along by the woods and the deep brook up which they had travelled to sack Panama, sparing the nuns, unlike Morgan. He did a circle then by the old graveyard. He went in there. He didn't like this, the hair was freezing on his neck even though it was daylight. There was one tomb where you could slide the slab off the front of it. There was nothing in there except one half of a skull. Everything else had rotted away many years ago. Sullivan went in there with a candle, hauling Pi with him, and they played a game of twenty-five, just to show that Sullivan wasn't afraid of anything on earth. Pi, who was very much afraid, didn't want to prove anything but he had to go anyhow. He slid back the slab now and looked into the earthy darkness, and then got out of there very fast with wraiths on his heels.

That left the Sliding Rock and the Quarry. He found him at the Quarry.

This was a place where many years ago they had run a railroad and scooped rock out of the earth down a hundred feet nearly. One side of it was open where the railway line had run; the rest of it was encircled by the jagged rocks. Here and there wind had blown earth and the birds had brought seed on their legs, and very green grass and flowers grew in these nooks. One special one was hidden from above by an overhang and it was there that Pi found Sullivan. He was stretched full length, resting his chin on his arms, looking down twenty feet at the quarry water below which was the colour of Connemara marble.

Pi knelt at the top. His heart was beating fast. He felt very pleased that his search had had a reward.

'How yeh, Sullivan?' he asked in a soft voice.

He saw the body of Sullivan jerking as if it had been pierced with an arrow, and then he turned on his back and looked up at him.

'G'way, Pi,' said Sullivan.

Pi ignored this. He started talking in a louder voice.

'Where were you? All the lads were looking for you. I've been all round, Sullivan, up and down and back at the Docks

and the ship and all around. What's wrong with you, Sullivan? What have we done to you?'

'G'way, Pi,' said Sullivan, turning on his face again. He
would have dismissed him more emphatically, but there were
very few words in him now that he could say without stuttering.

Pi thought of all his searching, the way he had worried. He
suddenly got angry.

'Sorry for yourself, aren't you, Sullivan?' he asked. 'The
only one in the world that ever lost anybody. All the other
people, mothers and fathers they lost, not going around being
sorry for themselves. Bloody oul cissie Sullivan. Most important man in the world. The whole world must stop still
because that's the way Sullivan wants it. Sullivan gets a kick in
the belly and he's squealing like a rabbit. Make everybody miserable. Not even helping his own mother at home. Running
away, Sullivan. The great general. You know you're no general, Sullivan. I resign from the army. You hear that, Sullivan?
I'm out of the army.'

He was shouting this because Sullivan had suddenly leaped
up and gone scrambling down the rocks towards the water,
shutting his ears to the voice of Pi above him. It was a dangerous climb down. He could have fallen. He ran along by the
ledge below and over to the far side where the two railway ties
were strapped together by two pieces of nailed timber. He
launched these furiously and rode them out to the middle of
the grey-green water, paddling with the stave off a barrel. He
looked up then at Pi. Pi was standing up above, his face red
and he practically dancing on the eminence. Sullivan at the
picture had to smile, but it didn't last long, the smile, before the
cloud came down inside him again.

'Home, Pi,' he called. 'Home, home, gogogo home!' – sorry
that he had tried to say a g.

'I'm going home, Sullivan,' Pi was shouting, 'and to hell
with you. You hear that? I'm not sorry for you, Sullivan.
You're a pain in the neck, Sullivan. You hear that? You're
oney water inside. You hear that? I'm finished. You can cross
Pius Clancy off the strength. You hear that, Sullivan, and to
hell with you!'

He glared furiously at the figure below looking up at him. Then he turned away and was gone because there was something very sorrowful in Sullivan's face, and he seemed such a small thin figure down there, so that up here Pi felt very big and full of health and unhurt, and that's why Pi turned away before he might start crying or something. He put his hands in his pockets and slouched away across the fields towards the road and his bicycle, kicking at the dying daisies.

Sullivan watched the empty skyline. For a moment or two he hoped it would fill again with Pi, but it didn't. First he was sad and then he was glad. He thought: Is there something in what Pi says? Am I this way because I will never see my father again, or because I am sorry for myself? Am I ashamed to meet people because of the terrible stutters that have tied me up so completely?

They came very bad that time, when his mother was saying: 'Your father is back in the room. He looks like he was sleeping, Terence Anthony, you must go back and kiss him farewell.' He shook his head. No, he didn't want to. Why would he do a thing like that? He didn't want to see his father; his father was dead. She got him in. There were people there. He should have run away, run away and maybe never come back, but she got him in there and he couldn't close his eyes because they were looking at him. He got the knot in his throat and his chest there, just then, he knew that. And when he had cause to speak again his words came out like balls of ravelled wool. So he didn't speak. He would act like a dumb man. Even at school when he went back to school. He would be asked a question and he would shake his head. He wouldn't open his mouth for them. He just opened it once and what came out was so mixed that they started to laugh. He ran out of the class. But he went back because he wasn't afraid of anybody, like he had proved over and over again. The Brother put up with him, but he became exasperated, like Pi, even Pi. You say, talk to somebody about it. Who are you going to talk about it to? When you can't talk at all. Not at all. His mother's bosom was empty. His mother had too many tears of her own to take a few from anybody else.

When the makeshift raft reached the far shore he pushed back again and paddled it into the middle. He couldn't see through the water. It was mucky, grey sort of mucky. It was dead-looking water with green scum around the edges. It was very deep. If you dropped in there you would go forty or fifty feet before your feet touched the rocky floor.

He felt cold. He hugged his body with his elbows. The sky was peculiarly green too, like the colour of the water. The sun would soon be going. There was deep shadow in the quarry. All around the rim he could see the faded saffron in the sky. He felt very alone.

Until he heard this voice saying, 'Hello, Sullivan.' He turned, startled, and looked at the open part of the quarry where the railway ran out of it. She was standing there looking at him. She still had a school bag slung on one shoulder. She was wearing a dark-blue coat, opened and showing the gym frock and the white silk blouse with long black stockings on her. He thought: That's Pi, I'll swear my oath that's Pi. He shouted that angrily, he didn't care how it came out. 'It's Pi! That P-P-Pi,' he shouted. 'W-w-w-wait'll I g-g-get that f-f-f—'

Bernie thought of Pi. She was coming down from the school with the other girls, walking, and then the bicycle passes and humps and starts as the brakes are applied and Pi comes rushing back to her calling: 'Hey, Bernie! Bernie!' He was doing a sort of dance on the road. Bernie couldn't help blushing as the other girls looked at her with raised eyebrows. They didn't know Pi. Bernie went to him smiling. 'Hello, Pi,' she said. 'What is it?'

'Oh, I'm glad to see you,' said Pi. 'I'm glad to see you. I never thought of you at all until now. It's Sullivan. Will you come with me, Bernie, will you, will you come with me?'

'Of course I will, Pi,' said Bernie immediately. 'Excuse me, girls,' she said to the others and turned back the way Pi was indicating. She knew they were looking after her wondering what on earth she was doing with this little shoddy fellow with thick socks pulled up over the bottoms of well-worn trousers.

Pi was filled with glee.

'He'll listen to you, wait'll you see,' he told her. 'I bet you what you like he'll listen to you.'

She calmed him and heard him. He led her to the way in and then he went away whistling. It would be fine now, Pi thought. Wait'll you see. I bet it'll be fine now and maybe it's me who should have been the general all along.

5

Bernie wasn't sure that Sullivan would come near her. He stood out there on the makeshift raft, clenching the stave, his face very angry, in the middle of the green water with a green sky over him.

'May I come out with you?' she asked.

He looked at her and then he looked down at his feet. She thought he wouldn't. If he just stayed there where he was, that would be the end of it. But he suddenly dug in the stave and sent the unwieldy thing over towards the landing. As he came nearer she looked closely at him. His face was very pale. His body seemed to be thinner than she had remembered. His lips were tightly closed and his eyes were burning. The water had slopped up and wet his shoes and stockings up to the ankles. The thing bumped against the bank.

'Aboard,' said Sullivan. He made no effort to help her. Bernie was terrified. She didn't feel like trusting herself on such a frail craft over a deep hole. She was just doing it because she didn't see any other way to get near him. She swallowed and put a foot on the slippery plank. He noticed that the foot was small and the shoe highly polished. There were neat darns on the black stockings. She wavered as she brought her other foot beside the first. She dropped her eyes. She didn't want him to see that she didn't like it at all.

''ight?' he asked. He sometimes found that if he dropped the first letter of a word he wouldn't stutter. Sometimes.

'Yes,' said Bernie, gripping her bulging school-bag tightly.

He sent the craft away from the bank. He was watching her

40

sardonically. He knew she was afraid, but he admired the way she hid it. He didn't joggle. He just drove it smoothly to the middle of the hole and there it remained. She let her breath go when it finally stood still.

'I tried to see you before,' she said, 'many times. But you were never there. I didn't even see you at the funeral,' she said.

He turned his face away from her.

'My father was very hurt,' she said. 'He loved your father.'

He said nothing to that either.

'My father said he would like to see you,' she said. This intrigued him a little. He thought of the orchard with the house behind the trees that he had never seen in full. He grunted.

What am I going to do, she wondered, if I go on saying things and nothing comes out of him? How far will that get me? Besides, it was very cold out here on the water. She shivered a little and pulled her coat around her. Sullivan saw that at least.

'Hold,' he warned her, and started to propel the raft towards the far shore. 'Up here,' he said, pointing. Bernie looked up at what was practically a vertical height. How do I get up there? she wondered. 'Up,' said Sullivan. So she passed him. He held her arm and took the bag from her. She got a foot on a jagged rock and held on with her hands. It was all one gigantic piece of granite from which rough hunks had been blasted before being polished. She could imagine the great hunks, and she wondered if they had been blasted long ago to build the sides of the canal. She was surprised to find that it was easy to climb. If she expected Sullivan to assist the delicate sex, she was mistaken. She had to climb by herself. Bernie had to laugh when she thought of it. She would like some of her friends to see her crawling up the face of a quarry like a fly, a delicately nurtured girl like her. She giggled and then blasted when her stocking tore on a jagged bit. That meant another hour of darning. She couldn't go to school and explain to the Reverend Mother that she tore her stocking climbing a quarry with a boy.

She was surprised to see the flat nook above. It was a nice place. It was away from the wind and the weather. The grass in it was as soft with moss as the down of a good rug. Then her bag came flying up to land with a soft plop and after that Sullivan's face appeared. It was high enough up now to catch the rays of the dying sun. Bernie was hurt to see the suffering in it. He was only a boy. His hair was falling over, almost covering one eye. She could see the bones of his cheeks under the skin. Then he heaved himself up and sat beside her, turned away from her. Bernie was alarmed for a moment. What am I doing? Why did I do this so impulsively? I don't really know this Sullivan. I have spoken to him twice, three times, maybe four times in my life. Then she remembered his father, sitting big on the chair in front of the fire, arguing with her father. He had his own point of view. Morgan Taylor could try and convince him about something from a hundred books, but if Tim had a different view on it he would remain unimpressed. His son would be like him that way too, she thought.

'We loved your father,' she said.

'L-l-l-eave it,' said Sullivan, pounding his fist on the grass.

'I will not,' she said. 'We were so sorry, so sorry. He meant a lot to us, and to a lot of people. So he meant much more to you. You cannot keep running away when people tell you how much they loved your father. I can't see him running away like you are. Even if it hurt him he would take people's sympathy from them. He wouldn't run out on his mother like you are doing. He would put up with things. He was such a good man.'

There was silence from beside her, and then that ordinary silence turned into the tensed silence that comes with great moments of love or sorrow, that away-awareness, when the mind seems to float free from the body. One like that. Bernie tensed, hugging her knees, suddenly aware that there was sweat on the palms of her hands.

Sullivan was crying.

He made no sound. She was listening. He was lying on his face. He must have been biting the back of his hand. She knew that was the only way to stop the sound of your crying when you had the back of your hand stuffed into your mouth, with your teeth leaving marks on it. The trembling of his body was translated to her along the sod that covered the rock. She felt the quick sympathetic tears rising to her own eyes, but she blinked them back by grinding her teeth. She just sat there then and waited.

These things can't last for ever. The real intensity of them lasts only for a fraction of time. If that fraction was longer than it is, it is doubtful if human beings could sustain it.

Sullivan's mind was filled with pictures of his father, always smiling. That was his father, always gentle unless he was furrowing his forehead so that he could try and impress his son with his anger, roaring threats at him that both of them knew would never be carried into effect. He could see him bending over plants in a garden bathed with sunshine, his big hands soft and probing. Like that when Sullivan would come up to him with a can of tea. His father loved gardens.

That's what Sullivan started babbling about now, spitting out the words, gagging on them, but exploding them nevertheless, every word he spoke involved with the dreadful intensity of his feeling and none of them coming clearly. Bernie's fingernails were biting into the palms of her hands as if she could help him to talk that way. It was terrible to listen to the effort of his speaking.

About the only thing that crucified him was that Tim should have been where he was the day he was. What was a man like him doing down in the dirty ships, with filthy coal plucked by slaves out of the bloody bowels of the earth, when he was always above ground, in the sun or the rain, nursing the growth of flowers or plants? What kind of unfair existence was it that that should have to happen to him, when he was out of his setting? If he had to be killed, then let them kill him in the garden among banks of flowers, or near potato pits, impaled on the branch of a fruit tree, or dying from lockjaw from a cut of the dirty earth, or from sniffing the poison of weedkiller. Any way at all but the way it had to happen. Down in that place. You see the water. Scum and muck and dirt, coal dust and orange peelings and bits of paper and oil, that vile place. All unfair, because life was a bitch. Sullivan would never be that way. Sullivan would never die in or out of Duke Street. Sullivan was going to make up for all that. Out of Duke Street, where a man could love a garden and work in a garden all his life and never leave it if he didn't want to. Not to have to go down there and be killed because he had no other work. The curse of hell on Duke Street and on the people who made Duke Street, and the sons of bitches who fixed things so that nobody in Duke Street knew from one week to the next if they would be working or starving.

Bernie shouted at him.

'Tim Sullivan was happy with what he was.'

Happy, is it? What kind of happiness? Did she know anything about it, shut up inside her orchard wall, with her father to provide the groceries, unfailingly? What did she know about it?

'Your father was a happy man,' she insisted. 'No matter what he was at, he was a happy man. He didn't care. He found happiness that way. Didn't you see him? Didn't you know that about him?'

Is it happy to be dead? What kind of happiness was that, tell me? Not through your own fault either.

'Your father was a hero. How many men are there in the world that will give their own lives for the life of a child?'

That maddened Sullivan. He shouted at her. If he wasn't down there, there would be no need for him to be a hero. Hero my eye! He's dead and they say what a brave man he was and whip around a collection for his wife and write him off, when he should never have been down there in the first place.

'It was a very nice collection. You should be proud of the regard people had for your father. There will be enough money to rear you and keep your mother in modest comfort. Have you no gratitude?'

Spit in their faces. Throw their filthy money back in their teeth, the bloody pack of hypocrites. What did they care? All the time his mind nagging away that it was Sullivan's fault. If Sullivan had not dawdled going down he would not have had to run from the boys. If he hadn't run from the boys

44

the horse would not have run away, the little fellow would not have to be saved from death and Tim would be alive. That's what was getting Sullivan, eating into him, filling him with terror, tying up his guts. Oh, Tim, Tim!

She sensed it.

'I'm sorry, Sullivan,' she said. 'I can't help you. I don't know about it. All I know is that I liked your father. He was a good man. You always felt better in his company. It was ordained that he should die as he did. That's the way I look at it. I'm so sorry.'

There was silence then for a time.

I know, he told her. You helped. No one much to talk to, see. Not Pi. Pi was as soft as liver. Let Pi look at you with the big eyes and you would go down a drain from the sympathy of them. Not my mother. You don't know my mother.

'Do you know her?' she asked.

That stopped him again. He answered her. Maybe he didn't. Yes, maybe he didn't. 'Your father liked her.' That's right. 'Will we go now?' Yes, we will go now.

He helped her over the ledge. He had to hold his hands braced under her shoes so that she could scramble up. She shivered up there. The air was cold. The sun was gone, just leaving drab reminders in the sky behind it.

'Will you come home with me?' she asked him. 'My father would like to see you.'

He thought it over. Yes, he would go with her. He was glad it was dark so that his face was hidden. Sullivan thought: If only I could start thinking phantasies again, I would be all right. If only I could get back that old braggadocio, I would be all right. But he had only two memories. The sight of the cart and the horse and his father going into the vile water, and the sight of his father lying whitely on a bed with a brown habit covering his body, and the nails of his clasped hands blue intertwined with a white rosary beads.

There were no blinds or curtains on the windows. That struck Sullivan as a fabulous thing. Why should there be curtains, Bernie asked, when nobody could look into the house? That's all blinds and curtains were for, so even though we seem shut in, we have more freedom in the long run than the people outside the walls.

Morgan Taylor was in this room off the hall, sitting in front of a coal fire he had forgotten to stoke, until Bernie stoked it up for him, chiding him about it. The room was all books. There were shelves built up to the ceiling containing all sorts of books. The small tables were covered with them, and they were piled on the floor.

'I don't keep here tidy,' Bernie apologised. 'He won't let me. I just dust it off when he's asleep.'

'Hah,' said Morgan. 'So! Young Sullivan. Yes, sit down. Can you prune fruit trees?'

Sullivan couldn't.

'Pity,' Morgan said. 'Great pity. Miss your father. Don't know what I'll do. I suppose you couldn't *learn* to prune fruit trees?'

No, Sullivan couldn't. Muscles tight on his jaws. Remembered coming into the house. It was autumn. The smell of windfalls rotting on the ground, the smell of ripening fruit all around. In the harvest the fruit is gathered. Like Tim. No, he had no interest at all in fruit or gardens.

'Well, you should,' said Morgan, shaking a finger at him. He had a high forehead, Sullivan saw, very white hair growing long. Bet Bernie cuts it for him. Bernie was out somewhere getting the tea. 'What use is life if you are not dealing with the things of life? Hah?'

Sullivan didn't know.

'You're not like your father. Your father would argue about that. Have you no knowledge? What class were you in?'

In final intermediate.

'Omnia Gallia est divisa in partes tres,' said Morgan. 'I suppose you hate Latin?'

No, Sullivan liked Latin.

Morgan is surprised. What else did Sullivan like? Sullivan liked English and French and history. Nothing else. That was all Sullivan liked.

'Where did you get the stutters?' Morgan asked.

Sullivan felt like getting up and running away. All this on top of the other!

But he stayed. The pale-blue eyes were watching him keenly. Morgan was slumped down in his chair, his hands joined, his long forefingers tapping at his lips.

Sullivan didn't know where he got the stutters. They just came naturally, he supposed.

Nonsense, Morgan told him. How in the name of God can unnatural things come naturally? You didn't have the stutters the day you climbed in here, did you? No, I was clear then. When did they recur? He remembered that well. When he had to go in and look at his father. He didn't say that. When my father died, he just said. I see. When did you get them first? Do you remember that? Kind of. Way back. You remember when you had no stutters and then you suddenly had stutters. You remember that? I think so. When was it? I'm not sure.

'Come, come, come, you are a bright enough young man,' Morgan said. 'Your father had a brain as bright as a button. If he had had higher education he would have been a brilliant brain. You don't know that. None of the young scuts that are getting higher education flung into them now ever stop to realise that there are thousands of people who would really benefit if they got the chance. One day you were not stuttering. The next day you were stuttering. When was that day? Come now!'

Sullivan remembered but he had never spoken about it, not to a soul. He clamped his lips now. He wouldn't tell this old inquisitive bastard either. What was it to do with him? Anger flared up inside him. Then he looked at the old eyes regarding him. There was no harm in them.

So he told him.

One morning early, years ago, before going to school, there was commotion in the street. Remember that. Running out eating a slice of bread to see what it was all about. You heard that the woman over had killed herself. She gave up the fight. She used her husband's razor, they said. This interested Sullivan. So what did he do? He went around the back way and he climbed the wall of the house and looked into the backyard.

There was nobody beside him. He did it of his own accord. And he leaned on the back wall and looked into the yard. And in the yard there was nobody at all but this woman lying on a mattress where they had carried her out the back. She had red hair and her throat was gaping and her eyes were open. Sullivan dropped from the wall as if he was shot and he didn't eat any more of the bread. He threw it away. He went to school. He boasted a bit in school about his courage and the thing he had seen. That was fine, but when he went to bed that night he started to shake and tremble and he couldn't sleep. He called his mother. His father was out. He told her that he couldn't sleep, that he was afraid. Afraid of what? Of rivers of blood, he was afraid every time he closed his eyes. She said not to be stupid and go to sleep. Did he think that she had nothing else to do but coming up the stairs every five minutes? Go to sleep. Now. He couldn't and the terror and trembling was so overpowering that he had to call her again. She was furious. He told her again. She said: 'If it's that poor woman across the street, she is in Heaven, and what harm can she do to you, and go to sleep now, Terence Anthony, or I swear I will lather you.'

He didn't call her any more. He wound his arms around his trembling knees and he hid himself under the clothes and he shook and shook. His teeth rattled.

'So you had shock,' said Morgan, 'and your mother didn't know you were shocked. And you should have had the doctor. You didn't have the doctor?'

No, he didn't have the doctor, and it lasted for fifteen nights and after that it was all right, but the shaking remained in his voice so that he stuttered. But he fought that. He found out that if you kind of sang a little with the words high in your head you could cut it out. They went away that time but they would come back. Now he was really bad, he knew this, because even if he tried to sing the words, they still stuck.

'So,' said Morgan, 'we have got to the root of the trouble. Now it is out in the open. You see that. You have said it. You know what is at the back of it. That's finished and done with. There is no more call to fear.'

No call to fear, is it, and he like a coil of barbed wire as far as speaking went.

'Physician, cure thyself,' said Morgan. 'If you had money, which you haven't, you could go and be educated at a school in Dublin that in four years would turn you out beautifully articulated. You can't do that. So you cure yourself.'

How, just tell me how?

'Here you are,' said Morgan, reaching behind him for a large leather-bound volume. 'Here are the collected plays of Shakespeare. Start at the first line of the first play: *Boatswain: Here, master, what cheer*, and finish the last line of the last play: *Myself will straight aboard; and to the state This heavy act with heavy heart relate*. You will read all this aloud and you may not proceed until you can say each speech and the letter of each word without stuttering. You hear that. I'll give you three years. Come back after three years and if you are not cured you are hopeless and not worth curing. At the same time listen to the foul way you pronounce elegant words, like most of the people of this neighbourhood. Listen to yourself and cure your enunciation as well as your articulation, and don't be going around feeling sorry for yourself. Let me tell you that at the present moment in this world there are millions of people worse off than you are. And now where is the tea? I have a hunger. Bernie! Bernie! Where are you, girl? Where are you?'

Sullivan ran the pages of the book through his fingers. What he wanted to do was to throw the book in the fire. But he couldn't do that. He wanted to tell the old man he was cracked.

Bernie came in. 'It's all ready. Come on out to it.' She helped the old man to his feet. She looked over at Sullivan. He was frowning, his hands clutching a thick leather-bound book. I don't know what he said, Bernie thought, but at least he took Sullivan's mind off his immediate troubles.

6

Sullivan lowered the window, leaned his elbows on it, rested his chin on his arms and surveyed the January morning. There was a wintry sun shining and the church bells were warning the recalcitrant that last Mass was about to begin. Sullivan's window looked down at the Back. Each terrace of houses had its own Back, where the ponderous garbage carts came to empty the refuse of the dustbins. His Back was a rectangular place formed by the back walls of their houses and the backs of the houses opposite. Sullivan could look into the backyards of those houses and see nearly everything in them. Some of them were clean, some of them not so clean, one of them having a sow and a litter of six bonhams. Sullivan could smell them. The same pigs caused many outbreaks. He had often seen angry ladies leaning from a window on this side telling the woman who owned the pigs what they thought about her and the way herself and her pigs were smelling up the whole neighbourhood. The woman of the pigs would stand with her hands on her hips and her angry face up, and it was generally a good job that these differences of opinion took place when the kids were at school or their vocabularies would have been full of purple patches. Sullivan grinned.

He could look over the town from here and distinguish the high points – the tall tower of the Protestant church which had a clock that regulated their lives, and the spires of other churches, and away far off the dusted black block of the artificial manure place, which when the wind was right blew phosphate dust in your direction, and people said that it was great stuff to suck into your lungs to cure a cold. He thought that the Back was a part of the lives of the people if you thought about it. It was a playground for children, or a battleground where they hunted cabbage stalks and things from the bins for battles. Sometimes at night if you went out in the dark and listened at your back doors, you could hear the whispers of lovers outside who were sheltering in the recess. This listening wasn't encouraged by parents, who sometimes if they couldn't stop the kids from listening would open the back door suddenly and chase the lovers with a sweeping brush, and as the lovers fled they would knock over a few dustbins, and they would be cursing, and cats screeching and lights going on and doors opening all over the place; so just to encourage this extra-curricular activity, certain kids would go into their mothers and innocently ask what something awful meant, and the poor mother would be outraged and say, 'Where did you hear that? Tell me at once where you heard that?' And the little innocent would say, 'Ooh, Mummie, I just heard a man saying that just now to a girl outside our back door.' That would set off the rooteach. They never incited the fathers, who had probably courted their wives that way anyhow and who would as soon hit you for listening as chase the lovers. But the tired mothers were always ready to spring into action and it was regarded as being great fun by all except the lovers, who would have to depart.

Sullivan sighed and lifted up the window and went back to the book. He hadn't got far in the same bloody book. It seemed to him to be so full of T's and S's and F's that it would daunt a man with the tongue of an angel. But he buckled down to it, making sure the door was closed so that his mother below would not hear, and that the window was shut so that the neighbours wouldn't hear. *'You do look, my son, in a moved sort As if you were dismayed: be cheerful, sir: Our revels now are ended: these our actors As I foretold you were all spirits and Are melted into air, into thin air: And like the baseless fabric of this vision The cloud-capped towers, the gorgeous palaces, The solemn temple, the great globe itself, Yea, all which it inherit, shall dissolve, And, like this insubstantial pageant faded, Leave not a rack behind: We are such stuff As dreams are made on, and our little life Is rounded with a sleep.'*

The old man had the right idea, there was no doubt about that. When he started he would have to say every line at least forty times before he could scream it aloud without a stutter. He was cutting down the number of times now, averaging between five and six. That was fine, but he was still afraid to go among people; even though he was almost sure now that he might get by without stuttering. Then he lay back on the bed and he wondered: Where is my father? What has happened to my father? The question no longer brought the pain to his heart, the sinking feeling in his stomach. But he didn't like to think about it. He said the speech again and again and again. Then he threw it from him in disgust and got up and went to the window.

They were there. The school was forming as the men came from the last Mass. Young men and older men, in blue suits and caps and white shirts, with the little fellow in the ring tossing up the two halfpennies. There was the sound of argument and the clink of copper and silver on the ground. There they were, formed in a ring. A lot of the younger fellows were pressed around watching them. Sullivan's heart started pounding. Now was the time if he wanted to go down and try to become one of the people again. He couldn't choose a better time. They would all be there. He could walk down and make his way in among them, and if they had good manners, as most of them had, they would pretend to ignore him; but if some of them hadn't good manners, what then? He would have to face that. You could keep running away and running away, but it was a lonely business, and to tell the truth you became sick of it, sick of it. Tired of your own thoughts when they were still uncoloured by your fancies.

I will go down, determined Sullivan, and let it come as it will.

He opened the door and went down the stairs. He thought he mightn't meet with his mother. She was not in the kitchen. He heard her in the bedroom. But she emerged as he was at the bottom of the stairs.

'Where are you going?' she asked him.

'Out,' he said. 'I'm going out.' Wondering despairingly, Why can't I get close to my mother? Isn't there something wrong with me that I can't feel sorrow for her sorrow? He tried to be like his father with her, patient, kind, never answering back, trying to do everything that was required of him. But those things too should come from the heart. They should be done spontaneously or they were acts in themselves.

'Bring me back some aspirin from the shop below, if you remember it,' she said. 'My head is killing me, killing me.'

She went to get her purse.

'I have m-money,' he said. If she got to the purse she would say about how she didn't know how they were going to live and what a way she had been left and she wished that he would finish school so that she could get him a job and have a little more money coming in every week. He was to go in as an apprentice to a grocery shop. She had that all fixed with one of her father's friends, who remembered her from the good days. The good days. Not me, thought Sullivan. I'd even go down the Docks, down the Docks with my Latin and French and calculus. What's the difference heaving coal with them or selling bloody sausages with them? What did it matter?

'Won't be long,' he said as he went out at the back. He was wearing a new blue suit himself with the tailor's crease still sharp in the long trousers. He hesitated at the back door of the yard, his hand on the latch. Then he took a deep breath and walked out, closed the door behind him and with his hands in his pockets walked nonchalantly to the school. You could become mad with this dodging people, he thought. You could become so used to it that you would run a mile if you saw a person you knew.

He joined the ring.

For a few seconds there was a pause. They all seemed to be looking at him. The elder men took pipes from their mouths. None of them had seen him since his father's death, not sufficiently close to say 'I'm sorry for your trouble, son.' He hoped none of them would say anything now. He kept his eyes on the ground. They didn't say anything. They suddenly started throwing money at the feet of the tosser. The tosser said: 'How yeh, Sullivan?' and Sullivan looked at him and it was Pi, and for a moment Sullivan was afraid that Pi was going to throw down the tosser and come and throw his arms around him. Pi was impulsive, so he hastily put his hand in his pocket and pulled out a shilling and threw it on the ground and said 'A b-bob to beat you, Pi' and the gambling fever was restored as Pi covered his bet and spat on the two halfpennies and threw them high in the air and they came down two harps so that Sullivan had won a shilling from Pi and he felt it was a good omen.

Things would have remained nice and quiet and peaceful apart from a few red-faced men shouting that it was a head and a harp, no, it wasn't, it was two heads, didn't I see them with my own two so-and-so eyes, and if you did see them you must be crosseyed, and others would hush them so that the gambling would continue – all this would have been fine if Badger hadn't arrived at the school.

Badger was peculiar. He was intelligent enough. He was endowed with great strength which he had since he was a boy. People gifted with strength can do one of two things with it. They can be modest about it as most physically strong people are, or they can assert it. Badger always asserted it. Sullivan and he never got on. Sullivan often had nightmares about being beaten by Badger and thought up many ways of winning victory, like having twelve pennies in his fist to hit him with. When he thought back now over the years of their childhood, it seemed to him that they had always been darkened a little by fear of the bigger boy.

So you can imagine what it was like now, on his first appearance into company, to hear Badger come along and throw down his pennies and say: 'I-I-I-I'll h-h-h-have a p-p-p-penny on h-h-harps.' Not looking at all at Sullivan. Sullivan felt Pi stirring beside him, and he reached a hand to grab at his coat. But he couldn't stop Pi's tongue. 'You shut your big mouth, sow-face,' said Pi. Badger went red, because his face with the big jowls was not unlike the dewlaps of a sow, and he came over towards Pi and asked, 'What did you say?' But the older men intervened and said, 'Lay off, let ye, or we'll put the run on the lot of ye.' Badger subsided, because none of them were of men's estate, and to be barred from the tossing school, and regulated to the boys' pontoon school, would have been a blow to morale. So Badger grunted and went back, and Sullivan said to Pi that he was to keep quiet, and not be getting him into trouble, that he didn't want trouble, and Pi said, 'But listen to him': and there was Badger stuttering away, and suddenly Sullivan himself could stand it no longer and he shouted 'B-B-Badger, if you don't s-s-stop it I'll gut you, hear?' and went over to him, but was taken on the wrong foot when Badger stretched a big hand and pushed him, and he fell on his backside in the mud and could feel the cold of it through the stuff of his trousers. He was mortified sitting there in his new suit in the mud, and a gleam was in his eyes and his face was pale, and some of the men had grabbed Badger and said: 'Lay off that now, let ye! Lay off that now.' And Sullivan rose and walked towards his own back door, and of course Badger thought he was retreating, and Pi thought so too, and the men were glad to see the back of him so that there wouldn't be any trouble.

Badger followed him up to his own back door calling in a feminine voice, 'T-T-T-Terence Anthony', as boys will, and Sullivan went in the back door and closed it, and Badger was calling through it for a while until it opened again and Sullivan appeared there and he had a wood-axe in his hand and Badger's widened eyes saw that there was a speck of froth on his lips. So he backed away from the figure with the axe.

'I'm going to fix you, Badger,' said Sullivan. 'I'm going to fix you, Badger. All the years, Badger, I'm going to fix you!'

'Here, here,' said some of the men.

'Now look here,' said Badger, but he didn't say any more because Sullivan ran for him with the axe raised, and Badger turned and ran. He ran through the school but the school scattered when Sullivan came into the middle of it with the axe swinging. There was a great scattering of the school when they saw the red eyes of Sullivan and the increased froth of his mouth. 'Stop him,' some of them shouted, 'the boy is gone mad.' 'Here, here, here,' Badger was calling appealingly, but Sullivan was after him with the axe, aiming swift blows at him around the back of the tall men hiding him. 'Grab him,' somebody shouted, but the look at his face was enough to daunt any man. They circled away from him, and Badger had no hiding-place and fled down the Back calling, and Sullivan fled after him, with Pi, very worried now, running after Sullivan, calling, and a lot of the men joined in the procession too, some of them saying 'My God, get the police, young Sullivan is off his head.' And Pi was terrible worried, and as the school vanished one or two opportunists paused to pick up all the coppers and silver from the ground and pocket it before joining in the chase.

Out of the Back, Badger ran, with terrified eyes looking over his shoulder, and he ran into the front street, with Sullivan after him, and many doors opened at the sound of the shouting and the running feet. It was all most unusual for a Sunday morning, and many asserted that Badger had it coming to him and they hoped the axe would bite deep, and many said it was a pity about young Sullivan. Anybody could see he would shortly go off his head the way he was dodging the people, and the kids joined in with the dogs, and there was a tremendous audience for the scene, and many spoke afterwards of the blazing eyes of Sullivan, but the most horror was raised by the sight of the frothing mouth.

Badger cleared that street like a greyhound and went into the next street. He made a tentative dart at his own front door, but it was closed, so he ran the length of the street, with the fleeter Sullivan closing on him, and around into the other back, and Sullivan's face was hot on his neck as, calling 'Mammie! Mammie!' in a throwback to the pleas of his childhood, he took a leap at his own back wall, got up there, flung a leg over, dropped inside, and bolted the door.

Sullivan swung the axe.

The wood of the door splintered under the blade.

He swung at it again and again, muttering and mumbling. Badger's mother appeared at a window above screaming blue murder, while inside Badger, with his heart in his mouth, held against the door, watching in horror as the axe bit through it.

Pi reached Sullivan.

He pleaded, catching him by the shoulder. 'Sullivan! Sullivan! Please, Sullivan, come home. For the love of God, Sullivan, come home.'

The axe stopped flailing, Sullivan looked at Pi. His eyes were blank. The froth was dribbling down his chin. Oh, my God, Pi thought, if I could only get Bernie. 'Come home, Sullivan,' he urged. 'Please come home.'

Sullivan turned and walked with him, like a robot, his legs spread, his hands held out from his sides. There was a big crowd there now. All around. Sullivan growled at them and raised the axe in his hand. Some of them retreated screaming. He walked another bit like an ape, Pi's hand still on his arm.

Then Sullivan did a strange thing.

He straightened himself up and he handed the axe to Pi, and he started bowing left and bowing right at the people.

'Thank you. Thank you. Thank you,' said Sullivan to them. 'We thank you, and there will be another performance of the same thrilling scene tomorrow night at eight o'clock, tickets ninepence, one and six and two shillings.' And he then spat the bit of red soap out of his mouth. Pi was looking at him in amazement. Some of the people started to laugh. 'He's all right again, the young demon,' somebody else said. 'He's back at the old tricks.' Then Sullivan waved his hand at the shattered back door of Badger's. 'Goodbye, Mammie,' he called, and turned on his heel and walked away, with Pi trotting after him.

'Do you mean to say it was only all an act?' Pi was asking him, nearly more horrified now if possible.

'Certainly,' said Sullivan. 'Sullivan is back at the old stand. Wasn't I good, Pi? Did you see the staring eye, the frothing mouth, the apelike stance? Man, I'm glad I couldn't see me, I would have been frightened to death. You hear me talking, Pi. Not a stammer, not a stutter in a dozen words. See how the years have paid off, Pi. I know more lockjaw words than any man in Ireland. And I can say them without a stumble. You hear! No more complexes for Sullivan, you hear that. Boy, it's good to be alive, Pi. The sky and the people and the birds in the air.'

He strode along. Pi was beginning to work up a grind. He had been so terribly fooled.

'You shouldn't have done it, Sullivan,' he said aggrievedly. 'You frightened the puddens out of the lot of us.'

Sullivan laughed.

7

It was a long narrow hall. It was thick with the smoke of cigarettes, and the noisy rumbling of the people. Also the seats were wooden kitchen chairs so that everybody was moving uncomfortably. They had to move like that or their behinds would have become atrophied. They had been sitting on them now for about two hours and even the most doting parent was beginning to pray that the final thing would occur and the curtain fall for the last time, and they could get out of there and stretch their legs. They had heard boys singing singly and in fours, and they had seen boys dancing singly and in fours and eights, and they had heard the chief man tell them all about progress last year, assuring them that their fees were not being wasted. So many scholarships, so many prizes; they had been lectured about what they should do at home to put their sons on the straight and narrow path of virtue. All the usual business, and now their programmes told them that the last item would be the performance by the senior boys of the immortal *Death of Fionn*, and most of them were wishing that he would hurry up and die, for God's sake.

The curtain on the stage was very thin and was bulging and blowing so that small boys had to stand behind it and hold it shut. Bernie was sitting a bit straighter in her seat because this was the only thing she was interested in seeing. There it was on the programme, the names of the cast, and number two was *The Shade of Diarmad* .... *T. A. Sullivan*. Sullivan hadn't told her what it was about. Ah, just a thing, he said, and he didn't encourage her or invite her to go so that she had to wangle an invitation, and here she was. She had enjoyed the evening. She liked to see boys dancing, particularly the little fellow in the yellow kilt with all the medals hopping on him, and she liked to hear boys singing, particularly the soaring voice of the boy soprano. But she had really come to see Sullivan.

There was a man sitting beside her. He smoked incessantly. His long fingers were stained badly with nicotine. He wasn't enjoying the business very much. He groaned occasionally, and rustled his programme and crossed his knees, and muttered curses when he hit his knees on the protruding ledges of the chair in front of him. She heard him saying, 'Oh, never again, never again!' And he told her he had come since he was one of the old boys, and the Brothers would have been hurt if he hadn't come and he would have to say how grand it was and how wonderful everything was, and that was hard since he was in the small theatre business himself and he felt like rising every few minutes and shouting, 'No, no, take that light off, and don't let your man stand there, get him back on the incline.'

Then the lights went out and the curtain was pulled back. At least it wasn't pulled back all the way, a long arm had to come out from each side and tug solidly at it and then it was back. The stage was hung in light purple drapes. There were arched doorways at each side painted starkly white, and two shields hanging over them painted in furious colours with Celtic design. At the back was a throne with crossed spears over it trailing vivid ribbons. 'Not bad, not bad at all,' the man muttered to Bernie. He wondered who she was. He had seen her a few times knocking about the town. A student, he supposed. She had very regular features and her hair was cut across the forehead in a fringe and waved closely to the rest of her head. She had a good-shaped head. He always looked at people as suitable or unsuitable for parts. She would have been, say, the tragic mother; the suffering one; bearing pain or sorrow with concealed heartache. She could be Kathleen in *Countess Kathleen*, never Lady Macbeth; she could be Rosalind – och, sort of good girls, he supposed, the type that would make wonderful wives and could be loved or murdered. He laughed. What nonsense! There was a great trumpet call. Actually it was a bugle call, and the bugler broke down in the third bar and brayed like an ass. The audience tittered. Well, the man thought, that starts off the tragedy on a good note. Nothing like a good laugh to establish an honest tragedy.

Two helmeted figures appeared in one of the openings carrying a litter. They could see the black hairy legs of the man on the litter wrapped in the tapes of a warrior. The first two men had a bit of trouble getting the litter through the archway. Space on the stage was sparse, so that they had to turn kind of sideways to get it on. They were dressed in short tunics and cloaks and helmets, and wore long swords. They had to hold the litter with one hand and manœuvre the swords with the other. The litter came in practically by *force majeure*, so that the white pillars were knocked a bit askew. The audience could see the anxious face of the warrior Fionn on the litter, and see one of the juggled swords rise up and hit him a smack in the puss. A hairy arm went up to feel his mouth and he rose a bit and said in an angry voice: 'Here, take it easy, Mulligan!' 'Not in the script, not in the script!' the man beside Bernie said to her, and chortled. So did everybody else. It didn't help either when the man on the litter realised that he was out in the open and people might have heard what he said. He put his hand up to his mouth in anguish this time. He was wearing a grey wig, and there were sort of death-agony lines painted on his face with lake liner, but all the same he was a very black boy, he was shaving twice a day already, so that actually, far from looking as if he was dying, he looked good for about a hundred and twenty years. The sight of all this amused the people.

'Oh, my God,' the man beside Bernie said, holding his stomach.

The dying Fionn had to do something about all the laughing that was going on, so he rose on an elbow and shouted at the top of his lungs. It was a good effort for a dying man. If there was anybody listening to him they could have heard him out on the Aran Islands.

'*Lay me near the window,*' he roared, '*that my dying eyes may see the sun sinking into the western sea, or that my dying gaze may rest upon the shade of my beloved rising from the Land of Youth.*' The litter-bearers brought him over towards the other arch. They intended to let him down easy but the hands of one of them slipped, and the others let go so that the dying Fionn landed with a tremendous wallop on the boards. His body hopped on the hard litter. He said 'Oh' loudly and aggrievedly, and felt for the place he was hurt with his hand.

Even the four litter-bearers thought this was funny and started to giggle behind their hands.

'By the shades of the Fenians,' said the man beside Bernie, 'this tragedy should never be performed any other way.' Bernie was sorry for the boys on the stage, but she couldn't help laughing either.

Fionn recovered his equilibrium and started shouting again, but it was some time before anybody at all heard a word he had to say. Gradually words filtered through to them, like the Crosshaven foghorn through a mist. '... *that so much of my young life was spent in pursuing the faithless body of my spouse. Ah, but she was beautiful; her noble form as graceful as a gazelle moving over the plains of Magh Dara; her long hair like the shivering mists of a golden dawn; her skin as soft to the touch of my fingers as the skin of an Eastern peach. Oh, how my soul longs for you, Grainne, my beloved. Out of the mists of time I call to you, the trembling voice of an old man dying in his loneliness surrounded by his foes, his dappled life behind him forever, tortured by his unforgiveness of the only one who had set the veins of his heart throbbing with eternal love. Grainne, I am calling you, my beloved, come to me!*'

Apparently at this stage somebody should have come to him, but nobody did, so Fionn raised himself again, muttering, settled his wig more firmly on his head and shouted: '*with eternal love. Grainne, I am calling you, my beloved, come to me!*'

Grainne appeared. She seemed to have been pushed, and took a little time to recover her equilibrium. Fionn was glaring at her with anything but love in his dying eyes. Grainne was a nice boy, but a bit small, not like a gazelle, tripping over a long golden gown. The long fair hair was that all right, but sort of badly dyed so that it looked like old sheep's wool which had been dipped in a vat of yellow distemper. That wouldn't have been too bad, but before she appeared Grainne had been obviously taking a few surreptitious pulls at a forbidden cigarette, and when the hurried call came had nipped the butt of the cigarette, pushed back the wig and popped the butt behind her ear. This was unfortunately the ear that was presented to the audience. The audience howled.

Nobody for the next five minutes heard anything at all that was said up there on the stage. Fionn was talking and one of the litter-bearers was talking and Grainne was holding out her arms awkwardly to Fionn as if she was presenting him with twins, and when she walked towards him she had to trip over the gown so that they all saw that she was wearing heavy hobnailed boots, but she remained unperturbed, and caught the gown up in her hands, showing an indecent amount of grey stocking above the boot-tops, and finished her walk and her talk in a great rush, and dropped the gown as if to say: Well, thank God, I got that lot over.

Fionn's voice emerged from the upheaval ... *'my dying eyes have rested once more on your beauty, but to save my shade from the dark beyond you must call to me the one I pursued with such bitter and unrelenting hatred, the young warrior Diarmad, in his youth the noblest warrior of them all, strong of arm, fearless in battle, the tyrant of iniquity, the beloved darling of the women of Ireland. Grainne, from the depths of Hades call to me the young one. Oh, Diarmad, how I have wronged you; with what bitter tears have I endeavoured to push back the aeons of time, that you might forgive the unrelenting persecution with which I favoured you, my bright one. Grainne, call to him, call!'*

Grainne obviously had to move. But she looked at the gown and remembered what had happened to her before, and maybe she got a bit boggled in the script, because she stayed where she was, stretched her arm and shouted: 'Hey, Diarmad!' She said it four times. Nobody heard her the last three. Diarmad was down under the stage. He was strutting for the benefit of his admirers. He was dressed in his Celtic costume and he was wearing a bowler hat and walking up and down using the sword as a walking-stick. He nearly missed his cue. He threw away the bowler and ran for the stairs and hesitated and then walked on with the carriage of a prince.

He wondered why the audience were roaring. He looked at Fionn and he looked at Grainne. They didn't look particularly funny to him. And then as he was looking out of the side of his eye he noted that he was still wearing the horn-rimmed spectacles that he had donned below. Now what are you going to do, Sullivan? He took off the glasses with his right hand (his left was holding a spear), raised the edge of his tunic and shoved the glasses up under the short drawers he was wearing. There was elastic on the ends of them, so that fixed that. He allowed for the laughter, and then he walked forward. But the laughter had increased, not diminished, and he saw both Fionn and Grainne looking down at his legs. The four litter-bearers weren't looking. They were turned away from the audience and were laughing. Sullivan looked down at his own legs. Oh-oh. He was wearing socks and suspenders. He had forgotten to take them off and tape his legs. No wonder everybody was breaking their hearts. What do you do now, Sullivan? Sullivan shrugged and went on with his speech. He said the first line and he kept saying it over and over again, pulling it up from his stomach so that it got greater and greater volume. I am a dead Diarmad and there is a dying Fionn and I have come back from the grave to comfort his dying hours.

Bernie had her hands over her eyes and her head bent, as the waves and waves of embarrassment went through her. For Sullivan's sake. She wanted to shut out the sound of the laughter from her ears, and then she listened and to her amazement noted that the laughter was dying out, and that the man beside her was sitting up as straight as herself. She opened her eyes and she looked up at the stage.

He was standing up there, tall and straight, his copper hair throwing glints from the arc-lamps, and he looked good standing there, even with socks and suspenders and plain black shoes, you could forget them somehow. His legs were well shaped. Sullivan looked like a young warrior. His voice was musical and the words flowed out of his mouth with ease. The man beside Bernie couldn't believe his eyes. Here was carriage. Here was the mysterious something that could silence one of the most upset audiences that the man had ever been among, could silence them and make them listen to him, even after all this, and even after the way he looked.

'... *time cannot heal the pursuit of evil; the decadence of a man's sins will follow him far beyond the grave. I have learned that in the hallways of Hell, Fionn. To a man beyond the grave is given all knowledge, but to none beyond the grave is given the talent of return. But for you, brave Fionn, this the gods say ...*'

It went on. They listened to him. Even Fionn was mesmerised into replying in a tone that implied credibility. Even Grainne, now that her disturbed hair had fallen about and concealed the butt in her ear, even she became so that you could believe her, right up to the end when one on each side of what was now a bier they spoke across the body of the dead warrior, separated for eternity by their sins. Nothing could spoil it. Not even the trumpet call that wavered and brayed at the end, and when the curtain fell and rose again the audience got to their feet and clapped and laughed like mad. And Bernie was on her feet too, and her eyes were glittering because she knew that they were clapping Sullivan, even if they didn't know it, and she knew that Sullivan knew it, standing there, bowing right and bowing left, jeering she could see, sardonically she could see, but oh, enjoying himself to the full, right up to the brim.

'Who is he? Who is he?' the man beside her was asking Bernie.

'Who is he? Oh, that's Sullivan,' she said.

'You know him?' he asked.

Do I know him? Do I know Sullivan? Yes, I know him, she thought. He is seventeen and I am twenty. He is a schoolboy (but this is his last year as a schoolboy). It's all terrible and it's all awful and ridiculous, but I'm afraid of my life that I'm in love with Sullivan, and maybe it will go away. He is older than his years. It's just like getting a sudden sickness. You can recover from that, or can you?

'Yes,' she said, 'I know him.'

'I want to meet him,' the man said. 'Will we go up there and meet him?'

'All right,' said Bernie.

They pushed their way through the crowd to the stage and

the man paused on the way to comfort the Brother who turned his face to the wall when he saw him. The man patted his shoulder. 'It's a tough racket, Brother,' he said. 'But we won't see a good show like that again in the history of the world.' This was the Brother who had to produce the show. He wouldn't turn around. He kept his face to the wall.

Bernie, up the steps and inside, was calling: 'Sullivan! Sullivan!'

He came to her laughing. His face lighted a bit when he saw her. She noted that. She was flushed.

'Hello, Sullivan,' she said. 'Here's a man who wants to meet you. I don't even know his name.'

'Mahon,' the man said, 'Tony Mahon.'

'I know you,' said Sullivan. 'You're the fellow that has the Little Theatre. You want a good actor.'

'How did you know?' Mahon asked, a little squashed.

'Let's face facts,' said Sullivan. 'I'm your man.'

'I can see you have the makings of an actor all right,' said Mahon. 'You start right off with the ego.'

Sullivan laughed.

8

Tony Mahon sat shading in the lines on his face, and in the long mirror watched the behaviour of Sullivan.

Sullivan was a puzzle to him. Mahon himself was a dedicated man. He worked an average of twelve to fourteen hours a day holding the small theatre together. He designed and painted the scenery, he made flats and stretched the canvas on them, he kept the accounts, drew up the advertising, learned off long parts, trained raw actors to become presentable, making as he thought silk purses out of sows' ears. He did all this for a feverish love and enough money to keep his belly half full and fairly respectable clothes on his back. He knew that he was not an oddity. There were people like himself in every country doing exactly the same thing. For love. He wondered how long it could continue, this unrequited love; how long you could go on before you became tired and had to enter into the relaxing jungle of complete professionalism.

Now this Sullivan. Sullivan was a born actor. There are born actors and there are competent actors who can be trained to say a speech as if they meant it, put the emphasis on the right words and carry a part as if it was not a burden. Sullivan was born for that. He had presence. He instinctively used the right emphasis. It didn't have to be pointed out to him. He could hold your attention. He could make you listen to a whisper. He could hold you petrified by an upraised hand. It all came instinctively to him. He didn't have to be taught. He used his voice like a bagpipe. He squeezed the bag of his solar plexus and the sound came clearly from an open throat. All these things. They would normally take years of working before they could be even half mastered. Mahon always said to them: 'It takes ten years, my friends, it takes ten years before you can say that you are anything more than an apprentice. After that you can start to learn the profession, and if you live to act until you are ninety you will be still learning, because no new part is the same as one you have done before, and will inevitably present a new problem.' Mahon was a good actor himself. He knew the tricks of the trade from long association, but he would never fire people. He could make them listen to him and be affected by him, but he could never make them sit up in their seats as he knew Sullivan could.

So all during rehearsals he had watched Sullivan. He was implicitly obedient, which was unusual in the first place. The competents and the half-competents usually gave you a long argument as to why they would be better moving here than moving there, and you would have to explain the whole pattern of your thought to them, how it fitted into the whole and why it was necessary to move here now, so that later you would be in a position for such a movement. Sullivan never argued. He went where he was told and acted. You could feel the joy emanating from him. Sullivan loved to act, and his sincerity was striking. You had to listen to him because he was not listening to himself. So he was a silk purse. All Mahon had to say to him was: Listen, Sullivan, bottle the exuberance. Think of yourself as a can of condensed milk. I don't know how many pints of milk go to make up a pint can of condensed milk, but say it is half a gallon. Well, you have half a gallon squeezed into a pint can. That's what you want to do. That was all he could tell Sullivan, and for the rest sit back and watch in awe an actor who had been fashioned to act from birth.

But there was this. In order to guide an actor's steps you must know something about him; his background; how he lives and moves and feels. But he didn't know a thing about Sullivan. Sullivan was a book closed. He was gay, he was insouciant, sometimes he was inordinately gloomy, tight-lipped and untalking. Why? Mahon couldn't know however much he probed. So he was afraid of Sullivan. Like, say, you would be walking on a beach and you would pick up a narrow canister with no label on it. What was in the canister? You didn't know. It could be tomato soup or it could be dynamite. He knew how Sullivan's father had died. He wondered if that made him shut up in himself. He knew he was well read. Some old eccentric up where Sullivan lived gave him reams of books to read. He could quote Shakespeare for an hour without stopping, but he was not ostentatious about it. It was just something he knew. How had he learned so much of Shakespeare or why? Mahon didn't know that. Nobody learned so much Shakespeare for their Leaving Certificate, which Sullivan had passed with honours. He was always well dressed, not quite conservatively, not quite artistically, but somewhere in between. He didn't appear to have many vices. In a small theatre where young men and women are thrown into each other's company intimately, under rather encouraging conditions for freedom of emotions, of hate or love or intrigue, Sullivan remained controlled and unmoved. There was a luscious girl in the company who liked Sullivan and did all she could to attract his attention. (Would you mind putting this safety-pin in my bra? Be an angel and rub this horrible liquid on my thigh. Ooh, you shouldn't come into the ladies' dressing-room without knocking, see how you saw me with hardly anything on.)

Mahon knew all this went on. The clasping of hands in the wings, the touch of thighs, the movements at rehearsals when a hand caught a soft breast instead of an arm. He was surprised that Sullivan remained nice and polite and jocose and easy about all things. Was there somebody else? That Bernie girl? Was Sullivan in love with her? Was that why he remained pure under pressure?

Mahon sighed. Sometimes he thought it might be preferable to be working only with sows' ears.

There was Sullivan now, standing up cool and collected. (He even had the correct instinct and hand for applying make-up so that it looked right.) He was talking. This was the first time he was ever appearing before an audience for money. Very little money, but money. He should be sensitive. He should be very nervous. Mahon himself was nervous. No matter how many first nights he got over, the next one was always worse than the last. He thought Sullivan would suffer, whether he knew it or not. He called him.

Sullivan came over to him.

'What's up, Tony?' he asked.

'How do you feel, Sullivan?' Tony asked.

'I feel fine,' said Sullivan, his eyebrows raised.

'No nervous feeling in the pit of the stomach?' Tony asked.

'No,' said Sullivan, feeling his stomach with his hand. 'I had a good tea.' He is genuinely puzzled, Mahon thought, God help him.

Upstairs the warning gong sounded.

Sullivan stood back and watched the frantic rushing of the others; the last-minute application of talcum; the last-minute visit to the toilet; and as they went past him mounting the stairs towards the stage, he saw each one muttering a line, pulling down their foreheads or smiling a false smile, donning clothes that changed their personalities. Mahon, changed into the padded suit that made his lithe body look heavy and his face lowering; his daughter, the pretty dark girl with the mole high on her cheek, his wife, the luscious girl with the overflowing figure who brushed past him and kissed him on the cheek as she passed, saying 'Good luck'; the young lead with the coal-black hair and the long nose who nodded as he passed him. He didn't like Sullivan. He was an actor of limited ability. Sullivan's performances during rehearsals made him dislike Sullivan, because he felt that he would be doing all the hard work and this complete newcomer from God knows where was likely to walk off with a lot of kudos. That's what he was afraid of and he didn't like it; he didn't like it at all. Sullivan just sensed that this lad didn't like him. He shrugged his shoulders.

Sullivan followed them up the stairs and stood in the wings waiting. He had his hands in the pockets of the dungarees he was wearing. He was only in the first act. He wished he was in all three. Out front an orchestra of three was sawing away, quite good, quite lively. Mahon was on the stage having a last look up at the position of the lights as they were switched on, nodding at the electrician on the platform. The setting was flooded with an amber glow. It was the office, crudely boarded, with the good office furniture an incongruity, and outside the window, at the back, the streaming factory chimneys could be seen in the blue glaze of the cyclorama. (*This office was good enough for my grandfather, it was good enough for my father, and it's good enough for me. Moving with the times is fine, but money is better invested in a machine than rigid cement that produces nothing.*) Mahon was at the desk. He signalled with his hand. The gong sounded again and the orchestra outside the curtain brought their piece to a conclusion.

It was only then that Sullivan was aware of the audience. He hadn't thought of them at all. They buzzed. It had a depressing effect on him suddenly. He could hear the seats being raised and lowered with a bang. He heard somebody laughing. He knew that it was a small place out there, which full would hold three hundred people, but up to this he had never been behind and heard the empty place come alive with people and it made him feel nervous. He moved his feet. Real people who paid actual money to come and watch and listen, and criticise. That was their privilege if they felt that they weren't getting value for their money.

He heard the sounds of them dying away as the man up

above pulled down on the dimmers of the house lights. He saw Mahon, sitting in the swivel chair, reaching for the pen and wetting his lips with his tongue, first the lower lip, and then the upper lip, and Sullivan suddenly found himself doing the same thing.

Then the runners on the curtain started to click and it swung back and Sullivan had his first look at a paying audience. He could see them through a crack in the window flat behind which he was standing. He could only see three of them in the reflected light from the stage: a fair-haired young man and his girl eating sweets, daintily, and an old woman with a fur coat, glasses, and an austere countenance. He watched them fascinated as the play got under way. He noticed with amazement that you could gradually see the reaction on their faces to the sense of the voices coming from the stage. How they first held themselves in, their faces masks, until Marty, the small man doing the secretary (he had sandy hair and a mouth turning up at the corners), started to warm them up. They were sympathetic to him. They smiled for him. (*Here's a letter from the opposition. He says that he has more men hidden under the sawdust than you have working for you altogether.*) They frowned at the way Mahon gruffly addressed this nice funny little man. They greeted the entrance of Mahon's 'wife' with interest. He noticed the young man's face lighting a little, an eyebrow raised, his lips pursed in a silent wolf whistle at the red hair, the curves in the tight-fitting dress worn under the fox-fur cape. The girl beside him stopped eating sweets and frowned a little, immediately, went over to the side of *The Tycoon.*

Then out of the blue it suddenly struck Sullivan that he himself would have to step on the stage in about ten minutes. He pulled back from his audience-gazing and found that his left leg was trembling. Even when he pressed his foot tightly to the boards, it kept trembling and his mouth was as dry as sand on a sunny shore. He tried frantically to think of his lines. The first one couldn't pass his mind at all. What in the name of God was it? He tightened the muscles of his stomach with his thinking. Then he got it. *You sent for me?* Dots, dots, dots,

dots. *Sir, when you stand in this office . . . You only purchase my labour, my body belongs to myself, and I reserve my respect for people who merit it* – on it would go, building up for ten solid minutes to a climax where *The Tycoon* stood over him waving a heavy paperweight in his hand ready to crash it down on a defiant head. Then he would have the last carefully planted word and he would go, and that was the end of Sullivan in the play. But the part left behind a bomb that would explode into action as the play went on. They will remember Sullivan, he said to himself with tight lips as he rehearsed the lines. He didn't think: They'll remember *Corrigan*, which was his name in the play, but: They'll remember Sullivan. This didn't strike him as being incongruous.

He listened again and from the cues knew that his time was near, but his limbs had not stopped trembling and his mouth was just as dry, and when the electrician shoved the bottle into his hand he put it to his mouth and swirled the stuff around. It was a warm sticky lemonade and it only seemed to make it worse, but he swallowed it and handed it back remembering to say thanks. The electrician watched him and shook his head and thought: He has a bad case of them and no mistake, and then went back up to his perch. Bet his face would be white under the make-up if only you could see it. The electrician had seen a lot of them come and a lot of them go. 'Good luck now,' he whispered down to the lad below. A funny customer, the electrician thought. Pleasant enough but not very forthcoming, but the makings of a smashing actor. He hoped Tony could hold on to this fellow for a while. He might improve receipts and then they might all get a rise.

Sullivan's mind suddenly became a blank. He tried to reason with himself. What does it matter? It's only a play in a small town. Out there are only people you see walking around the town every day. What does it matter? Even if you can't remember a word and stand up there with your mouth open you can be safe because Tony will cover over the period until you can get going. Why didn't I know this was going to happen to me? Why didn't somebody warn me? I would have been prepared. I would have taken myself in hand an hour ago.

He watched the upraised hand of the prompter with petrified attention and as it fell he walked to the door, opened it and stepped on to the stage. It seemed a long half-mile over to the desk where Tony sat. His head was down. He was paying no attention to the entrance of the young radical in the dungarees. That was in the script. (*Corrigan is supposed to be intimidated by the sight of the Tycoon, writing and ignoring the opening of the door. Corrigan looks around the room disdainfully, saunters over to the desk and sinking into the chair in front of it crosses a leg over a knee and says casually 'You sent for me?'*)

Sullivan crossed the room, but he didn't go as it was in the script or as he had been directed or as he had done so compellingly at rehearsals. He thought as he went over of the time the film had gone on fire outside in the yard, when they were all young, and of the years he had devoted to reading and reading out loud, in his room, in the darkness of the night out in the Back, on the lonely beaches far from the town, all those places, so he went over and sat down and forgot to cross his leg over his knee and he said his words and when they came out they weren't right. They came out: 'Y-y-you s-s-sent f-f-for me?' He saw Mahon looking at him with his mouth open, and Sullivan's heart was filled with despair and terror.

The scene went on, but it wasn't Sullivan's. Tony got up from the desk and walked back and forth and shouted, things he wasn't meant to do at all. But there was no covering it up. Sullivan tried. He tried all the tricks he had learned before. He shoved the sentences high in his head and half sang them. But he stuttered at all the important places. And what happened? Some of the audience started to titter (tittering when they should have been stuck to their seats with tension!), and the scene was dead and Tony rushed it and Sullivan came off the stage.

The other actors were in the wings, watching him as he passed below. The electrician was looking down at him, thinking: Oh my God, that's that! Nobody spoke to him. He spoke to nobody. He went below feeling completely numb and he sat in front of the glass and he rubbed cold cream on his face and cleaned it off with a towel, and took off his dungarees and the khaki shirt and got into his own clothes, and by that time he heard the click of the curtain runners and the over-loud clapping of the audience and he turned as Tony came down the stairs.

What did he expect Tony to say?

Tony came close to him and said, quietly, calmly, 'What happened, Sullivan?'

Sullivan told him he had a defect. This defect. He thought it was beaten. It always came back at periods of great excitement. He thought it was beaten. But it wasn't beaten. It was back. So there.

'To-morrow?' asked Tony.

No, no to-morrow for Sullivan. You see. I won't say I'm sorry for all the trouble, Tony. You know. I go now. It's a short part. You shove in a substitute. I'll go out the back door here. So goodbye, Tony.

'Listen, Sullivan, don't go, I can help you. Wait. Come back. Come down in the morning. I can help you.'

Sullivan shook his head and went out of the back door and closed it softly after him. His face was set.

Suddenly he thought, Why, Bernie is out there in front. Bernie! Then he thought, She might come looking for me. That would be just what Bernie would do, so he went quickly and hurriedly out at the side, and as he emerged from the alleyway he peered around it like a criminal on the run, scanned the few people who were outside smoking, and then went off the other way, keeping closely to the walls of the houses.

What am I going to do now? he wondered. Where am I going to go? He thought of Pi. How long ago it seemed that he had spoken to Pi. Just because he had been moving with different people, Pi was avoiding him. Sometimes he saw him long enough to wave a hand. That was all. He wanted to see Pi. That's what he wanted. It would be good to see Pi. Pi was the only one really who was not upset while he stuttered away at him.

He went around the back ways, avoiding the lights of the street lamps, and headed for Pi's home.

9

He lifted the latch and walked into the kitchen saying without looking, 'Is P-P-Pi within, Mrs. Clancy?' Only Mrs. Clancy was not there. A girl was sitting on a stool in front of the open turf fire, her legs spread, and she was reading a cheap paper magazine. She looked up at him. She had fair hair cut long with a strip of purple velvet secured under it and tied in a bow on top of her head.

'Will I do?' she asked him. 'Pi isn't here?'

He looked closely at her. Pi's little sister, if you don't mind, all grown up. All he could remember of her, casting his mind back, was a little child crawling on the floor with a dirty face and a bare bottom. He came in. ' 'lo, Lucy,' he said, glad that he had remembered her name.

'Are you slumming?' she asked him.

He didn't know what she was talking about.

'We don't see much of you lately,' she said.

They didn't see him at all. He didn't like Pi's house, because Pi himself was so different from his house. Pi was a flower growing out of a pail of garbage. So what would Pi's sister be? An orchid growing out of the same pail? She had good eyes and very clear skin and a shapely nose. Her lips were thick and red and held slightly open so that you could always see her teeth. She had a full figure, and if Sullivan knew anything she was wearing nothing at all under the dress. She wore coloured stuff on her legs instead of stockings, and high-heeled shoes that had widened a bit on her feet. She was very well put together, all except her hands, which were ugly and their ugliness was emphasised by a very dark-coloured nail polish. She was smart, she saw him looking at her hands. She didn't hide them.

'If you had to work for a living too,' she said, 'your hands might be hard to keep well, Mister Sullivan.'

She embarrassed him.

He didn't mean to be looking at her that closely, he told her, but she surprised him.

'Why?' she asked. 'There was a time when we saw more of you. Not now that you're movin' in high society.'

Sullivan laughed. He was glad to hear that, he said, and was surprised that he could laugh, when he had a load of lead in his belly.

'Why do you want Pi?' she asked him.

Just for company, he told her.

'Amn't I good company?' she asked him.

She would be what? Eighteen. She was very self-possessed. She would have to be, he thought. Her father was a chronic drinker – but worse, a chronic idler. All his life he got charity from the same story, about how he had pains here and there, he wasn't well, the doctors told him that his back was bad, and he had two childer and wife to support and how was he going to do it? The people called him Kruschen from the advertisement of the fellow with the furrowed forehead holding his back. The mother was lazy, a very indifferent housewife and a whiner. People gave for the sake of charity, but they resented it. They were so different to the hard-working, mostly uncomplaining people of Duke Street, who bore their cares when they came with tight lips or a laugh and said 'Tomorrow is another day'. It only struck him now, how well Pi had come out of the set-up, what effort it must have cost, and he suddenly felt sorry for this girl with her factory-stained hands.

She wasn't sorry for herself.

He told her she was good company. She had very long dark lashes. There were raindrop stains on her instep.

'What would Pi do for you that I couldn't do?' she asked him.

He asked her if he had to answer that. She straightened up and threw the book on the dresser. She had very full breasts for such a young girl. She knew it.

'What would you do with Pi?' she asked. 'Talk? Walk? Or what? What do you see in Pi? Pi is a proper noodagh-nawdha?'

He asked her how she liked the book she was reading.

'Oh, a lot of trash,' she said. 'The skivs always marry the son of the house if they don't let them tickle them in a corner.

Or else they are not skivs at all, but the illegitimate daughters of peers in disguise. So what? It takes you away from this lousy place and you can be dreaming, like the pictures. A way out, it is. You see?'

He saw, he told her.

'I'll walk with you,' she said, standing up. 'I'll talk to you. What do you want to talk about? What a lousy life it is or what?'

He laughed. Right, he told her, they would walk, and they could pick the subject of conversation later.

She went to the back door and took down a cloth coat that was hanging on it. It was a cheap brown coat but it fitted her well.

There was no electricity. The place was lighted by a paraffin lamp.

Who would mind the house?

'The bloody house can mind itself,' she said. 'The whole dump isn't worth a sixpenny bit.'

She closed the door after them and they stood there in the lane. It was quite dark, except for the stars in the rectangle of sky.

'You lead,' she said, 'I follow.'

They started to walk.

'What happened to you tonight?' she asked him. 'You came in looking like the wrath of God.'

They would forget that, he told her.

'How is Bernie Taylor?' she asked him.

He didn't know how Bernie Taylor was, he told her.

'She's hoighty-toighty,' she told him. 'That one is too good to be alive. That one's ambition is to be a sort of Lady Bountiful, the way she goes around dishing out sweets to the kids, so sweet and wholesome she'd give you a pain in the face. Is she a good coort?'

This took Sullivan's breath away. This angle on Bernie.

He didn't know, he said to her.

'Bet she's a cold dish,' Lucy said. 'She's like the Blessed Virgin in Pi's eyes. You never hear anything else from him. Why can't I be like her? If I was brought up that way and had her oul cracked fellow's money to live like a lady, I could be that way too. You put that lady in a factory for a week and you'd see her wilt.'

Sullivan said Bernie wasn't like this picture of her at all. He said Bernie was all right. What had she ever done to Lucy?

'She never did anything at all to me,' Lucy said. 'Just to be alive. That's all.'

Imagine that! He had never thought that people might dislike Bernie.

'Sure, people do, and you too,' she told him. 'Because you set yourself up. You have a way of looking at the people as if they were a lot of muck.'

That's not true, he told her.

'Maybe it's not,' she said, 'but that's the way it feels to them. Because your mother was somebody before she came down in the world and can't forget it and it's like Calvary to her to be living in Duke Street.'

Why are you attacking me like this?

'Only joking,' she said. 'To get you out of the glooms. You are shook out of the glooms, aren't you? I'd hate going walking with anybody that's full of the glooms.'

He agreed that he was pleasantly surprised that he hadn't the glooms now.

'That's good,' she said, holding his arm and pressing it against her left breast. Sullivan got tingles up his arm, and as they walked on the lighted street, he had this feeling and also a slight feeling of shame in case anybody he knew would see him walking so intimately with Lucy. He chided himself about the last one. He wasn't worth the dust on the road if it went to that, and how little will-power he had to let what happened to him tonight happen. He thought of the dreadful panic and he felt comforted by the touch of Lucy.

'I like you stuttering like this,' Lucy told him. 'You should always do it. It gives me a kind of breathless feeling listening to you. Sort of a come-on feeling.'

This was such a startling theory that all Sullivan could do was to stand and laugh loudly.

'See,' she said, watching him. 'I'm funny too. Making you

77

laugh. You haven't seen enough of me, Sullivan. You've had too much of the Purity League.'

He stopped laughing and told her he didn't even know she was there.

'What I say,' she said. 'You are always looking into the blue beyond whenever I've tried to bring you to notice. You know. At dances, out near the sea. Walking on the street. What do you be doing walking with your eyes fixed somewhere else? Why don't you come down to our house now and again like you used long ago?'

Because, well, Pi and he had drifted away. Different jobs and things. Pi working and I stewing for examinations. All that over now of course. But people's lives move at different levels. Sometimes they don't touch at all.

'Well, I'm real,' said Lucy. 'You can touch me any time at all now that we are acquainted.'

He skirted that. He said he didn't know he walked with his eyes in the blue beyond. If he did it was because of dreams.

'What kind of dreams?' she asked.

He said, that was far enough to go on that dialogue. What about her dreams? She had them. What were they like?

'They are very coloured,' she told him. 'I dream I am married to a man with lots of money and country houses and cars and furs left, right, and centre, and no work. No work at all. I'd have a million skivs. I wouldn't do a damn thing. Nothing. That's dreams and you know what the reality will be? I'm smart, see? I have my feet on the ground. I can dream but I know well what's going to happen.'

What's going to happen?

'I go on for another few years and I marry somebody like Badger. You know Badger. He's good-looking in a hairy sort of masculine way. A tough. He's a mechanic. He'll work and he'll get a few pounds a week for the rest of his life and we'll live in a small council house and we'll have kids and he'll try to beat me up and I'll crack him across the skull with the tongs and he won't do it again. And I'll get old and slatternly like my mother and I won't give tuppence about my appearance. And we'll live from hand to mouth and we will be content with our lot because there is no other lot for us. That's it all. I'm a realist, see? That's a word you pick up from reading books.'

Don't be that bitter, he said. She was young. Keep your dreams. Life doesn't have to be like that.

'Not half,' she said. 'All right, I won't stay here. I'll go away, to England maybe, but the same thing will happen there. You'll see. You have to be part of what you were brought up to be. That's what happens to girls from homes like mine. No higher education. You know that. Factory, marriage, kids, death and eternity. So what? So let's have a piece of fun while it's going, Sullivan. Let's go into this nice saloon bar coming up and drink something. Will we?'

They were quite a way out from the town, out by the long concrete walk where the sea lashed the shore and country people came in summer to dunk themselves in the sea, wearing wide-blooming flour-bag nightdresses.

Sullivan paused. He was about to say: Surely you are too young to be permitted to drink in saloon bars, but one look at her and the words died on his lips.

If that was what she wanted, they would do it, he told her. There were glass-topped tables, basketwork chairs, shaded lights and a grey-haired attendant who looked sourly at Lucy.

'I'll have gin and tonic,' Lucy said, looking the old man straight between the eyes.

'Are you sure, miss?' He asked this emphasising the miss.

'What the hell have you here?' Lucy asked him. 'Do you or do you not serve drinks without tracts? Are you my father? Are you in this business for your health or for your wealth? Are you going to give me what I want?'

'I know what I'd like to give you,' he said, his lips tight. 'What'll you have?' he asked Sullivan ungraciously.

'Whiskey,' said Sullivan belligerently.

'My God,' the man asked the ceiling, 'what'll the fry be drinkin' next?'

He went away.

Did Lucy know him, Sullivan wanted to know.

'Yes,' said Lucy, 'I've been here before. Always the same old argument. That's why I come. It hurts him.'

Why is he in the business so? Why doesn't he sell groceries or fish or something?

'He's a yoke beginning with an m, a, s,' said Lucy, 'with an o in the middle and a chist at the end.'

Sullivan said the word for her, stutters and all.

'That's right,' said Lucy. 'He likes suffering. He hates to see young people going to perdition. But he's a nice old boy. I like him. He goes on frightful batthers himself every six months or so. It takes every kind to make a world.'

The man came back and flopped the drinks before them and went away. They drank them. Sullivan didn't ever drink much. An odd bottle of stout. He would never have asked for whiskey only for the old fellow. There was a middle-aged woman with a pot hat at the far end of the place. Two men with her, with heavy coats, and belts trailing in the sawdust. One was pounding the table. He was saying: 'Truth is axiomatic.' And then he would put a finger up beside his nose, and say 'You hear? You say: No truth. That assertion establishes truth.' He pounded the table and roared: 'Hey, John, three more!'

Do you feel better now? Lucy wanted to know.

Why, yes, better, much better, fine, in fact.

Three in all they had. It wasn't a lot, but Sullivan was swirling. They went home linked, along by the road of the sea. It was a bright starry night, and the stars were dancing. They sang songs. Lucy had a hoarse voice. Sullivan had a musical voice but he always went flat on top notes. Their singing wasn't melodious, but they felt good. Sullivan felt marvellous.

The effects had worn off by the time they turned down the lane to Pi's house. The streets were empty. All the children were in bed and their parents were shut up or at the pictures, or at the play that should have been Sullivan's. That jagged him for a minute but he put it away.

'Nobody in,' said Lucy. 'Come on in.'

He didn't want to go into Pi's house. It depressed him. It smelled of paraffin fumes and burning turf. But he went in. Lucy hung up her coat and came over to him and stood so close to him that he could feel the gentle round of her belly against his own. What could he do? His blood was pounding.

His mouth was dry like it was earlier in the evening at an unhappier time. Lucy was nice, a lovely soft seductive anchor to hold on to. He held on to her. The skin of her cheek was so very soft under the tip of his nose and her lips were enveloping. Sullivan lost himself in her embrace until the voice came through to his submerged consciousness.

'Good night,' the voice was saying and it was the voice of Pi.

'Oh, my God,' said Lucy, turning away from Sullivan. 'He would have to turn up at a time like this.'

Sullivan took a long time to turn around.

The eyes of Pi were stormy in the lamplight. Pi would never be very tall, but he was impressive. He had grown wide shoulders. His face was lean, made even leaner-looking by the spiky fair hair standing up on his head.

He looked over at Lucy. She was standing there with her hands on her hips, watching him with a smile, breathing deeply. His own breath was fast. I'm glad Pi came when he did, thought Sullivan, very glad. Haven't I enough complications in my life?

'Good night,' said Lucy, raising a hand. 'Good night, Sullivan.' She meant goodbye by that. He knew it. But it was a near thing.

'Good night, Lucy,' he said. 'See you again.'

Pi stood aside as he passed him, Sullivan waited outside for him.

Pi had his hands in his pockets. They were clenched.

'I was at that play,' said Pi.

Depression flooded over Sullivan.

'Never expected after that exhibition,' said Pi, 'to come home and find you trying to seduce my sister.'

Sullivan laughed inside himself. Seduce Lucy, is it? He couldn't hold in the laugh.

'Oh, brother,' he told Pi, 'you don't know your own sister.'

That maddened Pi more.

'You,' he told Sullivan. 'You never look around you. You are all tied up in yourself. You don't care about other people. If you stopped thinking about yourself for a while and thought about other people, you couldn't have done what you did to-night. You hear that? Bernie was weeping for you, but you know what I was weeping about. All the people you let down. That Tony Mahon and all the other people. Like they say, The show must go on, that's what they say. But you, you make a holy show of it. No guts. You are wrong. No fight in you. You let down everybody and then you end up taking a young girl out and making her drink. I know. I smelled it off her and you. You know what it's like at home. The time I have at home, what it has done to us, and you do a thing like that!'

Sullivan got angry then. You silly bastard, he told Pi, you don't know what you're talking about. You have a good sister. She has a sense of humour and a sense of life you'll never have. You'd be better employed minding your own business instead of defending somebody who has no need of it. He didn't ask Pi to go to the play. What happened there was none of Pi's business and he could tell that to Bernie the next time he saw her, tell her too to keep her nose out of his business. A wonder Pi and she didn't go into a monastery.

'You're maddening me, Sullivan,' Pi shouted at him. 'You're maddening me!' grinding the heel of his shoe into the road.

Sullivan didn't care. All his life he had the two of them hovering around him, until he was sick of the sight of them. He wished they'd go and drown themselves, the pair of them. He wanted to be let alone, let alone. Lucy was good cheer. Lucy lifted him up to the skies, when he needed to be lifted. Pi and the other one would bury a man in a morass of depression. They would depress a bishop. They would depress a saint.

'Not any more! Not any more!' shouted Pi, running away. He said the last one over his shoulder as he ran away. He didn't want to hit Sullivan.

Sullivan turned and shouted other things after him, but what was the use? He went up the Back and sneaked in his own way, climbed on to the galvanised roof of the shed and in through his bedroom window. He threw himself on the bed and he didn't take off his clothes and for the rest of the night he had a really bad time.

10

He ran up the street, almost singing. He was laughing. Inside he was bubbling over. There was a cold north-east March wind blowing down the cavern of the street, but he barely noticed it.

He ran over the scene in the office again in his mind. That damn cursed office. He had been there for two months. Take a whole lot of names in last year's books and transfer them into this year's books. Thousands of names and details. That's all there was in it. Just that. He wondered how he had stuck it so long. He thought he was being very patient and conscientious, until to-day when the Big Fellow called. The Big Fellow was up at the top table surveying his room full of clerks from under black, beetling eyebrows that gave him a ferocious appearance. He wasn't really ferocious, but he didn't mince words either.

Sullivan had been writing in the hundredth name of the morning when he felt the Big Fellow standing beside him. The Big Fellow was really big. He was over six foot. One time long ago he used to live in Duke Street, but as he worked his way up in his job he moved. Sullivan remembered him then. He was so tall that Sullivan got the idea he must be a Protestant. He never knew why he felt this way about him, but he could never get it out of his head that he was a Protestant, which he wasn't, of course. Protestants didn't live in Duke Street.

He nudged Sullivan.

'Come out here,' he said. 'I want to talk to you.'

Surprised, Sullivan followed him out of the room into the corridor. The Big Fellow was leaning on the windowsill. They were on the fourth floor. The window provided a nice view of the river being squeezed out of the lake above, a sheet of water which was blinding now in the cold light of the sun. He could see the gaunt power-lines crossing the river and the gulls wheeling above it. He thought it looked nice.

'What are you doing here?' the Big Fellow asked.

'Working,' said Sullivan, not impolitely.

'No, no, let's call that off,' the Big Fellow said. 'You're only here; any work you are doing is a coincidence.'

Sullivan was surprised.

'Jay, and I thought I was good,' he said.

'You might have thought you were good for yourself,' said the Big Fellow, 'but you're no bloody good for anybody else. Now listen. I know your mother. I like your mother. I think she had a hard time and she did a great job of living. I knew your father and I liked your father. So when your mother asked me to take you in here, I took you in. Right?'

'That's it,' said Sullivan.

'Fine,' said the Big Fellow. 'Now, the only thing you want here in your particular job is to be able to write, but whenever you take a pen in your hand, anybody would think that there were two spiders tied to the tail of it and you were dipping them in ink and letting them walk all over. You understand that?'

'Maybe my writing is a bit screwy,' said Sullivan.

'It should be in an institution,' said the Big Fellow. 'Now we can get over that, even though it's hard on the unfortunates who come after you and who will have to try and interpret your hieroglyphics. But there's something else. This is a bit subtle. You are not cut out for this job. You are like a bird in a cage, boy, except that a caged bird doesn't be whistling all the time. You do.'

'Whistle?' Sullivan asked.

'That's right,' said the Big Fellow. 'Since you came in here you have whistled your way through four operas, nine musical comedies and about three books of ballads. The fact that you don't know you are softly whistling is worse than if you did know, because it really proves that your mind is not on your work.'

'Mind you,' said Sullivan, 'I never knew I whistled.'

'*I* know it,' said the Big Fellow. 'I even dream about it at night now, and everybody else in the room knows it. It is a great distraction. The output of work has gone down in this department considerably since you came into it. There are too many visits being paid by everybody to the washroom. There is too much of an air of gaiety. There is too much surreptitious chuckling. It all emanates from you, Sullivan.'

'But all this should help people at their work,' said Sullivan, '– being lighthearted, I mean. In these places where they play music, it's supposed to increase production.'

'Look,' said the Big Fellow, 'I'm only a poor human being trying to do a job. All I know is that the work is not being turned out. Last night after being awake for a long time I finally boiled it down to you. Now I'm telling you. This job is not for you. You can reform, but it will mean trying to change your whole nature. So make up your mind. Will you reform or will you go? What's it to be?'

'I think you better sack me,' said Sullivan.

'Right,' said the Big Fellow. 'You're sacked. They'll send you a week's wages from the office. I wouldn't be doing this only I know it's what you want. Is that right?'

He was looking at Sullivan's beaming face, at his shining eyes.

'Oh yes, yes, yes,' said Sullivan.

'Well, goodbye,' said the Big Fellow, holding out his hand. Sullivan shook it warmly. 'If you want a reference from me for whatever job you decide to do, I'll give one. You're not lazy. You're not incompetent. You're just not cut out for this.'

'You can't know how happy you've made me,' said Sullivan.

'Good luck,' said the Big Fellow, 'and what a job I'm going to have avoiding your mother!'

He watched Sullivan going down the corridor towards the stairs. He watched him doing a little step of a dance, hopping down three steps and dancing back again, and then three more down and back again, and finally leaping down to the next flight. He shook his head and went back into the room and sat at his table. He raised his head. There were many faces looking up at him. He cleared his throat.

'Mister Sullivan won't be with us any more,' he said. 'He has removed himself to a more suitable position.' Then he lowered his head. They buzzed a bit. We'll miss him in a way, he thought. He was cheerful. Then he chided himself. No more of that damn whistling, thank God. Anyhow, he thought, he was a luxury we couldn't afford.

Sullivan's gaiety stopped right inside the door when his mother looked at him and then looked at the clock on the mantelpiece.

'You are home very early,' she said, puzzled.

Sullivan had never thought of what it might mean to his mother.

'I was sacked,' he said.

Her eyes widened. She sat down on the chair behind her and suddenly started to cry. The tears poured out of her eyes. Sullivan was transfixed. He had never thought it would be like this. He went over to her and put his hand awkwardly on her shoulder. 'Don't, mother,' he said. 'It's not that important.'

'Not important,' she said. 'You don't know. How are we going to live? Where are we going to get the money and pay the rent and eat and clothe ourselves?'

'We'll get it,' he said. 'It was just that job. I didn't like that job.'

'It was respectable,' she said. 'The things I had to do to get that job for you. And it had a future. If you worked hard there you would have become sombody.'

That wretched thing! Become somebody – a tuppenny-half-penny clerk, growing grey and bowed and drinking more than was good for you from frustration. That wasn't for him. But how could he explain?

'I'll get something else,' he said. 'Don't worry. I promise. I'll get all you need.'

'It's so wrong,' she said. 'What will people think? To hear that you were sacked! What will they think? Your father was never that way. It never happened to him, that. How will you live that down? It will be always brought up against you. Always. And I know what it is. It's all that filthy theatre. Why do you have to have anything to do with it? It's not right.'

'I don't have anything to do with it now,' he said.

'No, but it's in your head all the time,' she said. 'Do you know where it will lead you? All that make-belief and late hours. You were never yourself any night you came home from it. Gone far away. I was so pleased when you got this work. It would have been the making of you. And now look what you have done. You are a poor son to me, so you are, a poor son.'

She didn't wait for him to reply. Maybe she didn't want a reply. She went into the bedroom and banged the door after her. Maybe she wanted a good cry. He looked at the closed door and wondered how can a fellow get near to his mother, so that you can tell her what you think, and what you would like to do, and just talk, sort of. He wondered if anybody could get really close like that to their mothers. He wasn't much good anyhow. Here he was coming up to twenty and what was he? Just a nonentity stuffed with multi-coloured dreams. About what? About nothing if you looked at it.

He went into the empty street, his hands sunk deep in his trousers pockets, and walked over and leaned against a gable-end.

His joy was gone. He felt very depressed. He thought it was a pity that you had to grow up at all. Look at all the fun you had when you were young and free of care. Then he reflected, thinking of his father, that being young wasn't fun all the time either. He tried to remember back to the number of times he had been really happy and they were few.

He walked out of the street and round the corner to the canal, which was shut off by iron railings. He leant here for a time and watched the weeds in the calm water. He could see a long black eel weaving his way in and out in the reed roots, as if he was playing. There were empty tins shining on the bottom of the water, and two rusty chamber-pots with holes in their bottoms. There was a small perch playing in and out through the bluebells with them. It wouldn't be much fun being a fish either. Some other fish was bound to eat you. He walked on, thinking of what canals meant in the lives of the young people; of kids falling in and being rescued; of the little fellow who wasn't rescued. Of the sight of his mother walking down the side of the canal with his dripping small body in her arms and her face raised to the cruel sky. Of the sight of the body of the vagrant below in the locks, as if he was standing on the bottom, his body upright in the water, waving like the weeds. It meant rowing boats coming down from the river, the varnish

87

shining on them and a girl idly sitting at the back playing with the ropes of the tiller while the young man rowed and admired her. It meant lots of things, but he left it and walked up by the walls of the College. He had passed the gate and gone some yards when Bernie came out. She was talking to a friend and she turned off the other way, and then remembered the figure she had seen from the corner of her eye, so she looked back and saw him walking away and said, 'Excuse me, I'll see you again,' and started to follow Sullivan.

Then she hesitated. She didn't call him. Why should I call him? – maybe I'll be snubbed again for my pains. But she was curious. What on earth was he doing out alone at this hour of the day, and what had happened to him that he was walking along like a bent bow?

She didn't call. She walked behind him. Let him turn round and see me, she thought, and then we'll see.

After about three miles she was beginning to be sorry that she had followed him. He went clear of the town and circled on the dust road that went up into the hills. The slate houses gave way to thatched cottages, whose walls needed a coat of whitewash after the battering of the winter. Chickens pecked outside the doors, cattle wandered on the road and sheep stared at them from the rocky fields. The men driving by in the horse-carts, either loaded with manure for the top dressing of the soil, or coming back from the fields empty, looked curiously at them, first at the fellow who walked with his head bent and then at the good-looking girl a few hundred yards behind him who carried books under her arm. They said, 'Hello, a fine day, thank God', to each and wondered if they were together or if it was just by chance that they were both taking a walk the same place on the same day. Bernie spotted this curiosity in their faces and blushed each time.

Sullivan ahead of her paused once at the highest point to look. She stopped too. The town was down in a dip near the sea. He could see the cluster of it and the arms of the rocks embracing a piece of the water. The sun was shining from a cold steel-blue sky, and from here you could not see the effect the steady wind had on the waves. Out to the right he could see the long silver beach. He thought, That is where I will go. I will walk on the deserted shore. It was a long way and he increased the speed of his walking. Bernie was breathless trying to keep pace with him. He came down from the hills and onto a winding tarred road through the woods where birds, finches, he thought, were singing tentatively as if they were doubtful that spring was really here, the wind that was shaking the branches was so cold. He never once looked behind him. He paused at the bridge to throw a pebble into the shallow water of a stream that gurgled and wound on its last run to the sea. Then he went on and turned down the sanded road to the beach.

The deserted shore was littered with rocks that had been torn from the hundred-foot cliffs behind. Some of the stones were washed grey, but some of the unresisting granite ones were brown and coated with weed. The sand was as silver as good coins, and the wind was driving the waves in big resounding breaking rollers almost at his feet.

His body was warm from the walking. The shoes were tight on his feet. If I had any courage now, he thought, I would take off my clothes and swim in the cold sea. But then you have no courage, Sullivan. You know what you want and you don't know what you want. If you know what you want you can go and do it and no man can prevent you. So you would like to swim in the cold sea. Well, go to hell and swim in the cold sea and he started to loosen his collar and tie.

Bernie had cut in behind Sullivan to avoid the gaping shore; she had crossed the fields and climbed the rich green grass that covered the cliff. She was alone up there except for a few sheep and some wheeling gulls. The decaying edge of the cliff was cut off by some rusty barbed wire stretched on peeling posts. She crossed the wire and lay on her belly and looked down at the shore. She was glad to lie down. The glint from the sea was blinding. Then her eyes sought Sullivan. He made a small dark figure down there on the sand. She gaped as she saw his coat being discarded, and his shirt and his vest and his shoes and his socks. Her heart was thumping. She rose to her knees. What is he doing? Is he going to commit suicide? Is this the end of Sullivan? When Sullivan's trousers came off, she sank back and dropped her head in her arms, because she reasoned that if Sullivan was going to commit suicide he would surely have done it in his clothes. She peered over one arm and was in time to see him splashing his way into the sea, his long body unnaturally white against the crab-apple green and steel-blue colour of the waves.

Holy God, thought Sullivan, as the water caught his warmed body. He shouted out loud when his head came out of the water, a shout of utter distress, but he dived again and swam, and even the feathered birds above must have felt sorry for the plight of him.

Bernie watched him in the water, but she dropped her eyes when he started to wade to the shore. Now, she thought, I can never confront him, not to-day. How would I explain?

Sullivan ran up and down the shore. He was still roaring, but his body was tingling. He paused to try and dry himself with his handkerchief, but it was too small. The wind was cutting. He raced along the sand up and down, up and down, until near the opening of the lane a man with a horse and cart came down to collect seaweed. Bernie got a flash of this and she laughed.

Sullivan dived for a handful of seaweed, and held it in front of his shivering body.

He would never forget the face of the man. He wore a battered hat and he needed a shave, and the sight of Sullivan opened his eyes so that Sullivan saw the whites of them. Then he laughed and said, 'Gup our that!' to the horse and turned away, and Sullivan backed back along the shore until he reached his clothes and started to get into them, having trouble with all of them because his body was wet.

Well, I did it anyhow, he thought, trying to stop his teeth from chattering, and just because I did that I can bloody well do anything. He shook the sand off himself and rose and Bernie watched him. It's as well he's setting off again, she thought. She was cold. She wondered if she was not as big a fool as Sullivan. All this tracking when she should be at her two-o'clock lectures. Now, she thought, he will go back up the lane and I will follow him. But Sullivan did not go back up the lane. He leaped the stone wall cutting off the cliff field from the shore and started to walk up. Bernie dug her face into her arms and lay perfectly still. Let him go from here, Lord, she prayed. Let him not come to the top of the cliff.

But Sullivan wanted to come to the top of the cliff. He never came here without going there to look down below and feel mighty. So he came up and got over the wire and was about to look all around the horizon, when he saw the body of the girl stretched almost at his feet with her head sunk in her arms. He was startled for a minute. The body wasn't dead; it was breathing. Then he thought, I better go and leave the poor daft creature, because any girl must be daft who would be lying on top of this cliff on a day in March in a cutting north-east wind. Then he wondered, Where have I seen that coat before? And looking closer, he said, Where have I seen those legs before? and all up until he saw the waved brown hair and the books on the ground, and the coat pulled back from her right wrist. She always wore a gold bangle that belonged to her mother, she said, with a small gold and blue enamel medal of Our Lady of Lourdes dangling from it.

He put a shoe under her and applied gentle pressure until Bernie had perforce to turn on her back, but she kept her hands over her eyes, and Sullivan looked down at her and grinned and said: 'Well, hello, Miss Taylor, fancy meeting you here!'

11

She didn't remove her hands from her eyes. Her face was flushed. He got on his knees beside her and put the palms of his hands on the palms of her upturned hands, and wound his fingers around her fingers and forced her hands away from her eyes and held them on the grass each side of her face. Her eyes were closed. She turned her face sideways away from him. He was bending closely over her.

'Hello, Bernie,' he said, 'I haven't seen you for a long time.'

'Whose fault is that?' Bernie asked, opening her eyes to look at him. His hair was disarrayed and tangled. The muscles at the sides of his jaws were white from the cold. His hands pinning her own to the earth were cold, but they could have been red-hot from the way they were sending tingles of something all through her. She found difficulty in getting her words out. Sullivan was laughing. There were crinkles of laughter all around his eyes, and then the laughter went out of them and they opened widely as he looked at her. She couldn't keep her eyes clear of her thoughts.

And suddenly then she ceased for Sullivan to be Bernie Taylor and became part of his life. Like that, as quickly as you could turn the page of a book. Like as if the earth had stopped revolving, the silence that came on the world, like as if his ears were suddenly filled with cotton wool so that every earthly sound was shut away from his hearing. Like as if he had been pounded in the belly by a heavy mallet.

He freed one of his hands and moved it and placed his fingers on her neck where the vein was throbbing. Softly, and she trembled, and he saw that his own fingers were trembling. He was amazed at all this. His mouth was dry. He found it hard to swallow. You will see that Sullivan was noting all these things like a doctor in a clinic working on a patient. But that didn't last long. He bent and placed his mouth on hers. . . .

But from moments like these you have to awaken; you must get back to keeping up with the run of the world.

And they came back.

But looking down at her, seeing the pink in her cheeks, the look in her eyes, the barely opened teeth under the red lips, Sullivan knew that life would never be the same as it had been until a few moments ago. And so did she. It was not so shocking to Bernie, because to her this was the fulfilment of a dream. Of all the dreams Sullivan had had, this had never been one of them. Kiss girls at the back door in the moonlight, or playing forfeits at a party, or falling in love with the form of a picture woman in the coloured pages of a magazine: for her the quick kiss during a lull in a hop in the quadrangle outside the Aula Maxima, under the pale rectangle of stars.

She put up a hand and wiped back the wet hair from Sullivan's forehead. He was amazed at the wonder of the soft palm of her hand on the side of his face.

'Where did you come from?' he asked her. 'Did one of the gulls drop you here?'

'No,' she said, 'I followed you. All the way. When you were passing by the College.'

'I never saw you,' he said. 'Why didn't you call?'

'I'm glad I didn't,' she said.

'I've wasted an awful lot of time,' said Sullivan. 'That last time after the flop business, I was rude to you. Do you know that?'

'I do,' she said.

'Holy God!' said Sullivan. 'What was wrong with me?'

'I don't know,' she said.

'Bernie,' he said then, tasting her name.

'I'm cold,' she said.

Sullivan laughed.

'So am I, perished,' he said. 'I don't know why, unless it's because we are up here on top of a cliff with a heavy north-east wind blowing.'

He pulled her to her feet, and then close into him. It was wonderful. Her hair was very soft against his chin. They clung to one another for a time, but it's no use, time has stopped still, and your moments have passed. But it's wonderful, all the same.

'We'll go down into shelter,' he said, gripping her hand tightly.

'I don't want to go home,' she said. 'Don't let's go home, Sullivan, not yet. Let's not go home for a few hundred years.'

'We won't go home yet,' he said. He ran off down the hill, holding her. She had a job to keep with him. The sheep looked in wonder at those awkward forms running. The sheep didn't think their heavy shod feet and thick legs were good for running down cliff-side hills. The sheep admired their own beautifully slender shanks and delicate hooves, and then went back to their grazing.

They stopped at the end of the hill. Here it was sheltered from the wind. A gigantic stretch of strand was in front of them. The incoming tide had surrounded gentle hillocks of it and had submerged other parts, so that it was a blue-grey and green scene with the other cliffs away from them braving the tide; hoary, brown, weed-covered rocks the sentinels at their feet. Farther away on a headland jutting into the sea they could see a white building glinting in the sun. That was the outpost of the faraway town.

Sullivan stopped near the walls of the fallen house. It had been destroyed for some time, this house. It was perhaps a relic of the day when the land supported more million people than it could provide for, when men scratched the soil in bleak and barren places until the earth could give them no more and killed them off, two million of them, dispassionately, with a potato blight. Around here the land had been tilled and now soft grass grew on the site and the sheep kept it cropped like a well-cared-for lawn. It was the same inside the four walls where at one time men had loved and lived and died. There was a carpet of grass and the shelter of the still-stout walls. And in here they sat.

Said Sullivan suddenly: 'How long were you up there, Bernie?' He found it difficult to stop saying her name: Bernie, Bernie, Bernie, as if he had never said it before.

Bernie turned her head away from him.

'I kept my head down,' she said, 'I didn't look at critical times.' Sullivan laughed uproariously.

'Did you see when your man came around the corner in the cart?' he asked.

'I did,' said Bernie, 'I saw that bit.'

'Jay,' said Sullivan, 'suppose I knew that you were up there looking down at me!'

'Sullivan,' Bernie said, 'did you never think of me at all before this?'

'No,' said Sullivan. 'I just knew that you were there and that the world was still turning. That's all I knew, but I know now, Bernie, I know now. I have so many things to tell you. You don't know. What is it? A person can talk to so few, so few, about things, about everything. What a thing it is to have a person who belongs to yourself! Oh, Bernie, am I going to unload such a lot of things on you? You know something, I'm hungry.'

'Real hungry?'

'Yes,' he said, 'real hungry.'

'Then we'll have to go home,' she said.

'No, no,' he said. 'You don't know Sullivan. Come with me and you'll eat like a queen.'

He was pulling her to her feet again. His eyes were lighting. She had to laugh.

'Life with you won't be easy, Sullivan,' she said. 'Everything will always be on the move.'

'Wait'll you see,' he said, taking her outside. 'I have been here before. Look for a can, Bernie, a common tin can. Somewhere about here there is a common tin can.'

They found it near the shore. Sullivan greeted its presence with a shout of joy. He pointed out the sea wrack to her. 'You test that,' he said, 'and every piece, however small, of dry wood you find, gather it into a bundle to burn. You see, I'm going raiding.'

He ran away from her. She watched him. Up by the house he went and the hill beyond. He stood on a grass-covered dike there and waved to her. Then he was gone. Bernie sought for the bits of wood automatically but she didn't do very well with the search. She would stand up on the shore with a few bits of wood in her hand and look over the sea. The hills on the other side of the bay were barely visible in a blue mist. Bernie just sighed and smiled and wondered.

Sullivan was raiding a potato pit. It was in a field up behind, a long earth-clamped pit. The front of it was free of earth, just covered in with straw to keep the frost away. Sullivan burrowed here. He picked six choice potatoes and he returned. He ran back to Bernie, dropped the potatoes, took her in his arms, 'Hello, Bernie,' he said, 'I'm back again. I was a long time away from you,' kissed her, looked at her, put her away from him and started to wash the earth off the potatoes in the sea. Then he put the potatoes in the tin can and poured sea water in on top of them. 'Wait'll you taste these,' he told her. 'You haven't lived until you have tasted these.' Bernie was laughing, clapping her hands.

Then he collected sticks, many more than she had acquired, added to them from clippings of a stark hawthorn bush that grew behind the old house, and soon with withered bracken and a match had a fire burning in the old chimney of the house and the tin balanced precariously on the fire.

All the time they were coming together and separating, touching, hands and bodies, touching one another with their eyes, incredulous, not talking much, just to say, Do you remember? And Why? and Sullivan burned his fingers taking the tin off the fire and the potatoes were bursting their jackets off, and Sullivan scraped the salt from the side of the burned tin, and they ate three potatoes, hot ones, juggling them from hand to hand, and Bernie said that she never ate anything like them since the day she was born, and after that they sat close and tried to hold back time again, but it wouldn't go, and they stayed there until the sky in front of them seemed to be burning to death and the distant white house on the headland was rosy, and then they got up and walked back the long way they had come, and the many miles seemed to be very short until he stood outside the orchard door and parted from her, but this was different. He was taking some of her with him.

Going to his own door he thought: I set out with what thought in my mind? That I was a new man; that I was going to conquer the world. Now amn't I able to do it twice over? So he didn't go in. He went out of the street and into the quiet tree-lined avenue where he knew Tony Mahon lived.

It was two o'clock in the morning.

You cannot knock up a respectable house at two o'clock in the morning. He knew Tony's room. It was one in front. There was a concrete jut-out over the front door to keep the rain off. He leaped for this and grabbed it and drew himself up, scraping his body on the cement. He could smell Bernie with him, her perfume on his hands, all about him. The window was open. He opened it farther and whispered into the room,

'Hey, Tony! Tony!' He could feel the warm air of the room.

He heard the voice say, 'Here, what the hell!' and the creaking of the bed, and he said 'Hey, Tony, it's me, Sullivan!' 'Sullivan? To the fair hell with Sullivan!' said the sleepy slightly alarmed voice.

'You want a good actor, Tony,' said Sullivan. 'I'm your good actor. I'm back at the old stand. You hear?'

'I hear,' said Tony's voice, 'you cracked character. Now go home to hell and give me some peace.'

'Benedictus,' said Sullivan, full of joy, and he jumped and landed in a flower-bed and danced his way home, his heart singing, and his mouth singing despite himself, and some of the neighbours afterwards said what a poor show it was that Sullivan fellow coming home blind drunk at that hour of the morning waking everybody up, and what harm, but he has a voice like a scalded crow, so he has.

12

Whitefaced, the old man, sturdy, with a strong jaw and a mane of pure white hair, faced them across the mahogany table. He was shouting. There was foam on his lower lip. He was pounding the table with a clenched fist.

'*Not now, nor ever!*' he shouted. '*Not now, nor ever!*'

The youth facing him was not shouting but his low-pitched voice seemed to vibrate with pent-up passion.

'*Then that is the end of you,*' he told him. '*But it is not the end of us.*' He indicated the people around him with his hand: *George*, his elder brother, the tall bulky one, looking so strong, yet so weak under the eye of the old man; young *Gervina*, her eyes wide, looking at her young brother as if she had never seen him before; and *Margaret*, his mother, standing to one side of him, her only sign of nervousness the way she pulled at the lace handkerchief with her long thin hands. '*Because you are no longer faced with frightened people, like we have been*

*all our lives, leaping to your whims, wide-eyed at night; con-
scious of your sleeping. But you slept on, didn't you, yes, you
slept on. You had no cause to fear. You had no cause to
shiver. Well, you can shiver now. Because this is the end. You
have a last chance. You can agree right now, and everything
changes, or you can pound the table and shout "Not now, nor
ever", and we will walk out of the open window into the
storm, and we will never come back. You hear that. We will
never come back!'*

Bernie hoped they wouldn't have to go out of the open
french window. Outside it was thundering. The low rumble of
thunder was a background to the people. Now and again lightning flashes lit up the lowering sky and you could hear the
sibilant hiss of the wind-driven rain. She was biting her
knuckles. Please, let him agree; she demanded, please let him
agree!

But he didn't agree. He was too sure of himself.

'Not now, nor ever!' he repeated, his lips tight. *'You under-
developed snake. That's what you are. You hear that? What
human being would ever believe that I fathered you? To my
sorrow, boy, to my sorrow. You go out now, and you never
come back. Your brother will not go and your sister will not
go. Will you, George? Will you, Gervina? Will you leave me?
Will you leave the soft beds behind? What are you going to
take with you? You are taking nothing with you! Who will
provide for you? Who will wake you in the morning? Who
will keep your hands soft and your heads on a feather pillow?
Tell me that. You won't go, George?'*

George looked undecided. He shifted his feet. O Lord,
Bernie prayed, don't let him let Sullivan down now.

He didn't. He straightened himself. He looked his father in
the eyes.

'I'm going, father,' he said. *'I'm not used to hardness, I
know. That's not my fault. We won't have an easy time. But
I'm going with Leo.' 'You fat fool!'* his father said to him.
*'Wait till your heavy rump is nestling on boards. Wait until
your blood is being sucked with lice.'*

Oh, he's horrible, horrible, Bernie thought.

Gervina didn't say anything. She walked close to Sullivan and she put her hand confidently into his. He looked down and smiled at her.

This gesture infuriated the old man.

'*Then go, go now, the lot of you,*' he said. '*I can stand alone. I have stood alone before. God will keep me!*'

'*God will not keep you,*' said *Leo*. '*God will stir your conscience when you walk the empty rooms. You will have your mansion then and it will be all yours, all yours, every empty inch of it will belong to you.*'

'*Margaret! Margaret!*' the old man shouted almost in despair. '*You cannot leave me!*'

They were all looking at her. Her head was bent. Then she raised it. She clasped her hands. The lace handkerchief, almost tattered, fluttered gently to the floor. She turned and picked up her coat where it was lying on the back of the chair. Then she faced him.

'*Yes,*' she said. '*I can leave you. I am going with my children. You alone can count the reasons. You alone. Because I won't. Freedom is too precious a thing to be denied to the utterly oppressed.*'

She left him speechless. His jaw dropped. He thought she would have been the lever, the last lever. Now she too had failed him. He sat down. He didn't look defeated, but he looked older. There was a sag to his shoulders.

'*Oh, for so many years, so many years,*' said *Leo* to him, '*you had us where you wanted us. Trained to fear. Fear of what? Fear of nothing! Fear of what we would eat or what we would put on, all the time forgetting that God had given us two hands and two feet and bodies and brains; that we didn't have to be slaves. You even had us that we forgot we had souls, you hear that? That was the way you had us, and that is going to be your greatest punishment. We'll get by. Don't imagine for a moment we won't. You just think of it, four people are eight hands and eight feet and four brains and four souls. For the first time, we are free. There is no rain out there for us or dark clouds. There is a blue sky and the sweet caress of the sun on our uplifted faces. You can command the silence of empty rooms. They will obey you. You can lash the furniture with your fist. It will cave in under your blows. And you can call our names and let them rise to the emptiness of the cobwebbed attics. But we shall be gone. We shall be free. We shall be singing.'*

And on that they walked through the window into the rain; into the thunder of the lowering clouds. He looked after them. He rose. He walked to the window. He called: *'Come back! Come back!'* but the crash of thunder drowned his words. You could see him shouting but you could not hear him. Three times he did that and then he came in. He stood in the centre of the room, bewildered but still obstinate. You could see the hardness in his eyes; in the cut of his jaw. And then he saw the lace handkerchief. It was dark in the room now. Whatever light came from outside seemed to be focused on the lace handkerchief on the floor. He came down to it. He went on one knee. He put down his hand and he took it up, infinitely carefully, infinitely gently, and carried it to his lips. *'Oh, Margaret! Margaret!'* he said, but he wasn't broken; he wasn't repentant. He proved it. He rose to his feet and stood there and brayed defiance to the ceiling, as if he was braying it to the sky, as if he was braying it to God.

'Not now, nor ever!' the old man roared. *'Not now, nor ever!'*

And as the lightning flashed and the thunder rolled, slowly and almost inexorably the curtain came across and closed. There was silence in the theatre for a count of five seconds and then applause broke out. It was honest, it was sincere, and Bernie clapped as hard as ever she could, sitting on the edge of her seat.

Back the curtain went and they stood in a line and bowed, now themselves, their faces cleared of other men's minds. Sullivan was the tallest of them, she saw. His eyes were gleaming. Sullivan is happy, she thought, I can see that Sullivan is happy.

And well might Sullivan be happy. He was tremendously exhilarated. Not a single stutter in a thousand-line part – a part that pleased him, a part in which his playing pleased Tony very much. He knew he was good. Tony knew that Sullivan's exuberance had overflowed to the rest of them, so that they were carried away with him, and the onlookers were lifted however much they didn't want to be.

So they went below, afterwards, some of them, to express to Tony how they felt. They had recovered by this of course. They only imagined that they had been moved. So it was a good play. That was a damn fine play, Tony. You gave us a damn fine play there, and who's your man Sullivan? He's good. That fella could go far. Where does he come from? From where? From Duke Street? Holy God, I didn't think anything like that could come out of Duke Street. Oh, I see, I remember now. His father was the docker that was destroyed. Yes, I remember that. Ah, yes, of course. And that's who he is. Pity, you know, with a bit of background that fella could be really something. Well, what's your next one, Tony? That thing! Well, it's always good for a laugh. But this is a powerful play. He is a great writer, that fellow. Ah, a great writer. It must be great for ye to get a good writer that ye can get yeer teeth into like that. Learn a lot from him.

There were other simpler types, of course, who said: Oh, Mister Mahon, I quaked, honest to God, I quaked, so I did. It was so real. I was crying. Would you believe that? Honestly. It was so moving, so moving. You were so good. You put the heart crossways in me, honest to goodness you did, and that young man Sullivan. Could I meet him? Thanks. Oh, Mister Sullivan, you were so masterful. You compelled me. I was with you all the way. It was so good. I hope we will get more like that. So grand.

Sullivan thanked her, trying to smile at her, trying to stop his eyes from going towards the door, where Bernie was. She had come in and was practically hiding herself in a corner. Afraid of her life she would be noticed. Afraid that she was getting in anybody's way. She raised her eyes and her eyes met his and all the shyness and backwardness went from them and Sullivan felt his stomach quailing at the look in her eyes, and the love flowing in him and the exhilaration all mixed up made him want to shout and jump around – the smell of make-up and cold cream and sweat – and he thought, This is the life, oh, dear God, this is the life, as long as Bernie is around somewhere even if she is dodging into corners.

So he smiled and said Thanks, and laid on the charm and said That's nice of you, and Thank you, and when they wanted to know Where did you learn to speak so beautifully, so clearly? he thought back over the agony of the years, and said, 'Oh, Tony, that's the good Tony, Tony is very good. Tony is exceptionally good', and he meant that too, looking where Tony was talking and calmly accepting, and even from the cut of his back Sullivan knew that he was thinking and summing up and assessing and finding fault with and analysing. Tony couldn't be taken in.

They had a small celebration afterwards, business had been so good: bags of fried chips and lumps of fish cooked inside thick flour paste from the place of the Italian next door, and one of the pleased clients came up with a magnum of champagne and that mixed with brandy gave nearly everybody something to drink, an added kick in the stomach and an added gleam to the eye. Sullivan was in his element, like going into the hot sun after the cold winds of winter, feeling it was warm on your body, going into the marrow of your bones. He wasn't obviously with Bernie, but he was conscious of her. She was never out of his sight. He was amazed at himself, feeling the slow rise of angry jealousy when one of the company was talking to her, a glass in his hand, one foot up on a seat and the other hand resting familiarly on her shoulder. Besides, she was smiling at him. He knew that she was being polite, because she was being polite to everybody, but all the same she ought to know that Sullivan was the only one in her life now. He felt proud of being possessive. I have something I can really call my own.

When he did get near her, he managed to get her to the back and then into the night air, and then home. It took them a long time to go home. They paused at the bridge over the river, and watched the moonlight on the tumbling waters where they broke over the stones beneath. Then they walked out the long road by the sea, and sat on a bench in front of the white strand. Not talking much, you see. Just filled with the silence of nearness. Until Bernie said:

'That is really the life you want, Sullivan, isn't it?'

He thought about that.

'I suppose so,' he said, 'but not that below. That's only learning. I want all that comes after that.'

'Will you be happy?'

'You bet,' he said. 'I'm happy now. There is nothing that I couldn't do now.'

'I hope it will give you all you want,' she said.

'You're doubtful about it?' he asked.

'I'm commonplace,' Bernie said. 'I just want to sit in an orchard after coming from work and let the world go by outside. I don't want to be on a stage with lights shining on me, putting on other men's habits and conversation.'

'One of us is enough in the spotlight,' Sullivan said. 'I'm good up there. Am I?'

'You are,' she said.

'Right,' he said. 'It's a living. It can be a very good living. What am I fitted for? You tell me.'

'I think you are fitted for anything at all that you care to put your mind to,' she said.

'And my heart, don't forget that,' he said. 'So you're my business. Listen, there are stars now. I can close my eyes and I see stars all the time. And what do the stars bring? I'll tell you. Decent living. Is it wrong for a man to want decent living?'

'What is decent living?' she asked him.

'That's easy,' he said. 'No darns on your underwear; no holes in your socks; no shine on the backside of your suit; no rolling your shirt-sleeves because the cuffs are frayed; no mending your own shoes on a borrowed last; no stripping in front of a fire at night and bathing yourself from a tin basin; no eating of crubeens and tripe and the offal of beasts because you are poor and can't get a decent cut more than once a year. I want good things. I want sunken baths with scalding-hot water; I want clean new shirts every day. I want to buy so many pairs of shoes that I can throw them away without ever mending them. I want to open my mother's hand and put a thousand pounds in it and say: "Spend that! Go on a spree and spend that. Spend all of it. Don't count it. There's more when that is gone." I want to see you in a fur coat and diamonds. I want to dine in big places with tables gleaming with polished cutlery and sparkling white cloths. I want all of that. I want to get out of Duke Street. I want to get Duke Street out of my bones and my blood, with all its nagging making-do, all its bloody borderline poverty. I want to get away from the humble patient poor. You hear that? Some day I want to come back and roll down the main street of this town with a big long limousine that will be so big and so long that it will find it hard to turn corners, and every time I press the button of the horn it will play the first few bars of "Clear the way for the Bould Fenian Men".'

She laughed.

'Oh, Sullivan,' she said, 'but that's all material.'

'I mean it,' he said. 'Listen, Bernie, don't tell me. I know it. I have seen it. You can't be spiritual unless you are comfortable. First comfort and then you can afford to moralise. You hear?'

'Has Duke Street done that to you, Sullivan?'

'It has,' he said. 'I hate it. I have the smell of it in the hairs of my nostrils. All the time. I can smell Pi's house. All the time I see long faded skirts and black stockings, shawls and snuff snuffed out of Colman's Mustard tins. I can smell the blood of the suicides; the bursting bags of the drowned dogs in the canals; the constantly washed red tiles in the kitchens; the home-made wagons with the rickety wheels bringing home a stone of coal or two stone of coal, or the bits and pieces scavenged from the city dumps in the Swamp. All that. You don't know. You have had your orchard with the high walls. You don't know what it is to see a frustrated man on a Friday night, half tight, hitting his wife with his fist, and never being able to say I'm sorry, sorry, or why he did it. You've never seen a man working for one firm for thirty years and then being fired for no reason that anybody can understand, or seen and noted the shame the same decent man covers up with a sort of boastful braggadocio when he goes down to the line of the damned to sign up every morning for his few lousy shillings a week. All this is inarticulate. It has no expression. But I can see and I can learn and I can get away from it. I can bury it so deep that it will never again disturb me. Wait'll you see. You bet. I have ambition. I have talent and I'm going to make use of it, and where I go, you go.'

'Sullivan,' she said, 'someday you won't think like you do now.'

'Talk to me then,' he said. 'Talk to me then. Now, we'll go. Let us go and talk to old Morgan. Where will he be? Will he be in bed or abroad?'

'He'll be sitting up in bed,' she said. 'He nearly always waits for me. He will be reading a big book, and he will have his glasses on, but when I go in with you he will take his glasses off because he takes great pride out of his eyes. He is nearly eighty years of age, you know, and his eyes are as good as the day they were created, he will say, and also he says that when he is interviewed on his hundredth birthday he will say about how he still has all his faculties, and the reason he has lived so long is because he has ignored the living and lived with the dead.'

He was in bed and he did have his glasses on and he was reading a book and he dropped the book on the counterpane and he put his glasses under his pillow. Sullivan looked at his face, trying to remember what he was like when he had first seen him. He didn't seem to be much changed. The hair was a bit whiter and the beard a bit whiter. The window was wide open. It was a calm night. You could smell the fading apple blossoms on the trees. Most of them had formed into hard round little bullets with whiskers. They would grow and grow.

'Well, well, well,' said he when they came in. With the big bed and the books there didn't seem to be much room left once the two of them stood in it as well.

'Mister Taylor,' said Sullivan, 'Bernie and I wish to get married.'

He was full of glee at that. Bernie didn't know he was going to say it. She turned around to him startled, her hand up to her mouth. That was a bombshell. Well, it was the answer. Sullivan wanted her. She was Sullivan's. What was the use of fiddling around about it?

'No,' said the old man. 'No, nor never,' and he threw the leather-bound book he was reading from him so that it fell with a clump on the floor. Sullivan was startled. He was bemused. As if he was back again on the stage facing Tony, and Tony pounding the table and shouting: Not now nor ever! Not now nor ever!

'What's wrong with me?' he asked. His face was slowly flushing.

'Everything in the world. Everything in the world.' The old man was waving a thin hand in the air. 'Why didn't I know? Maybe I should have known. I didn't know it was going on. I should have known.'

'Father,' said Bernie, 'please be calm.'

'No, no,' he said. 'I refuse the pattern. You hear that? I refuse the pattern.' He was sitting up in the bed, supporting his body with a fist on the mattress. The mattress was trembling from the tremble of his limbs.

'What pattern are you talking about?' Sullivan asked. He was growing angry. He was only doing the old bird a favour. He wouldn't have said it at all but for his apeing of good manners. Like long ago: May I beseech the hand of your daughter in marriage, kind sir? Dead at the dodo, and he walks into it like this. That was what infuriated him.

'Her mother is the pattern.' The old man was red-faced trying to get out the words. 'A brain, knowledge, character, strength, and what does she do! Meets like you. Somebody like you. An inferior mind. Yes, yes, an inferior mind. Can a hyena lie down with a lion? Can a cabbage talk to a king? You cannot have Bernie. I forbid it.'

'Father, father,' said Bernie.

'No good. He was no good. He didn't have the brain of a louse. He was a flea on a pedigree dog. He was a virus in the throat of a giant. He was the offscouring of a Dublin slum. And he killed her! You hear that? He killed my daughter. Because he was like a disease, a loathsome disease that grew on her and destroyed her. My girl. I found her when he had

106

done with her. You hear that? I found her. I reared her, when my son died. She was light and sun to me. She was a treasure of heaven. And she threw herself away on a scab, a festering scab, who wasn't fit to lick her shoes or the sores of a dog. Swinging she was from the chandelier in the big panelled room. By her own hand, they said, but it was a lie. It was a god-damned lie. I know. I know so well.'

There were frustrated tears in his eyes.

'So I had Bernie. All behind me I leave my life. Good company. Talented minds. Conversation of peers over a good wine in the evenings. All that I abandoned for this. No, not for this. You won't do this to her. You are he all over again and I refuse the pattern. You hear me? I would shoot her first. I could cut her throat. Bernie! Bernie! What have you done to me?'

'Nothing,' said Bernie. She was white-faced.

'But you will, you will,' he said. 'You wish to be the death of me. Why? Up in the College there are boys. There are men with educated minds. Not him. Not this! Out of Duke Street. He will be the same. He is as feckless as a bird. What does he know? What is he? Where is he going? Well, where are you going? What do you do for a living? What will you do for a living in the future? What have you to offer Bernie? Tell me that? After all I did for you.'

Sullivan didn't answer him.

Sullivan turned on his heel and went out of the room and into the hall and out of the house and down the stairs into the moon-soaked orchard.

She was behind him. She caught his arm.

'Sullivan,' she said. 'He is very old. He was very hurt.'

'I'm hurt too,' said Sullivan. 'For an old withered man he can hand out a lot of hurt.'

'Sullivan,' she said, 'whatever you want me to do, I will do. If you want me to come with you now I will go with you and I will never come back.'

Her earnestness pierced into the welter of his wounded ego. He smiled and turned to her and curled his hands around her arms.

'You would, Bernie?' he asked.

'Yes,' she said.

'But you won't,' he said. 'He's right in one way. What am I? Where am I going? What am I going to do?'

'I don't care,' she said. 'I don't care.'

'Well, we'll win,' he said. 'In time. You wait and see. Did you know all this story about your mother?'

'Yes,' she said. 'He doesn't know. But he kept clippings. They are in a box. That was the way my mother died. So you see, Sullivan, you are not getting such a bargain after all, are you?'

Sullivan kissed her.

'You mind the orchard and the old man and yourself,' he said. 'I'm going out after the long limousine.'

13

You could hear the click of billiard balls. That was in the big room off the hall where there were three billiard tables. It was afternoon but somehow there always seemed to be men who could click billiard balls, no matter what time of the day it was, and whether they were working or not. Sullivan examined the room now, saw the big tall windows (the place had at one time been a workhouse) with daylight barely able to get through the dirt of years on the glass, and the rectangle of pale yellow light shining on the ironed greens, and men in shirt-sleeves with hats or caps on the backs of their heads, and cigarettes angled in their gobs, sighting or resting on the cues, lazily intent on their game, completely uninterested in the rehearsal that was going on in the stuffy hall inside.

You could hardly call it a theatre. It was probably the dining-room of the workhouse where the unfortunates long ago came to have their buckets of slops thrown to them. When it wasn't occupied by Gregory's Dramatic Players, the owner showed films in it. You could see the fireproof box at the back with the four squares gazing blankly at you. At the front there were plush seats. They looked decrepit in the daytime. At night, when the shaded lights were lit, they probably looked lush. They smelled of people and dampness and stale cigarette smoke, and he was certain that there were fleas, large families of fleas, being reared inside the red plush. The air-purifier that was swooshed at the place seemed to have become absorbed in the heavy atmosphere and become part of the general decay. On the other side of the hall there was a sign that said MEN. You could hear it from here, the pipes weren't working very well. It was just an annexe with no roof, open to the sky, with lead-lined walls; so what with the sound of water constantly on the move from the defective plumbing and the click of balls from the other side and the smell and sight of it all, Sullivan thought if he owned the place and he was offered sixpence for it he would think he was cheating if he sold it at that sum.

'Mr. Sullivan! Mr. Sullivan! If it is not too much trouble could you ever manage, dear boy, to come in on your cue?'

Sullivan came to with a start as the fruity voice reached his ears. He was standing on the stage. They were limited for space and you had to scrape some of the skin off your body to get in through the doors of the Regency drawing-room. The set looked battered. With no coloured lights on it you could see all the places where the holes in the canvas had been patched. No matter how often they were distempered they continued to show. The boarded door-recesses were black from the hands that erected them. The borrowed furniture looked moth-eaten, rickety and anything but Regency.

The only fresh thing on the stage at all was Gregory himself. He prided himself on his appearance, the still-black hair (was it dyed?) carefully waved and one lock falling over the high forehead. A black shirt and a silver tie and a grey-flannel suit with a gentle stripe in it. The chest swelled, the stomach went in, the back was as straight as a board (was he wearing corsets?), the shoes shone, the well-shaved face was smooth with applied talc.

Right, you could look at Gregory, at his immaculate commanding presence with just a hint of the artist in it all, and then look at his company, all mostly around Sullivan's age, with two old hams to do the character parts, the male to help load the lorries and travel with the scenery, and the old lady to collect the tickets, sell programmes and do the day booking, if any. For the rest they were young, four male and three female. Sullivan could look at himself to see what the others looked like, crumpled shirts, unpressed pants, no time to shave after being up nearly all the night before, getting the lorries unloaded; nails broken and dirtied from grease paint which you could never properly wash off because there was rarely hot water in any of these places. (But there was always a bucket of hot water brought in for the Great Gregory, who didn't need it, anyhow, because he always stayed at the best hotel.)

A fine sight they made, a bunch of dirty artistic-looking bums. See them rushing for last Mass on a Sunday morning, with their clothes crumpled and some No. 4 still at the backs of their ears. One look at them and you knew for a certainty that Gregory's Dramatic Players were in town, as scruffy-looking a bunch as you would meet only once a year when the tour came around. Sullivan felt sad about it sometimes, to see the girls, think of the pleasant things they had at home, cleanliness and decency, and then they are out on the road looking like tramps and in a way revelling in it because their carelessness set them apart from the many, and on Sunday, as sure as shooting, from the long red nails and the careless hair and the hurriedly thrown-on coats, still retaining a look of a good city cut about them, all this put the sign on them so that people would say: These must be the actors, not analysing why they picked them out, but just that they were different, and perhaps that was a compensation for poor pay, dreadful conditions of living, damp beds, foetid bedrooms, with three sleeping in a room because they couldn't afford any better, greasy meals, carelessly cooked ...

'Mr. Sullivan! If your lordship pleases. We can't afford two great actors around here, dear boy.'

Sullivan waited for the sniggers to come from the front row where the rest of the cast were. He wasn't disappointed. They sniggered. It was dutifully done. Gregory had to have his audience even if it was only a rehearsal. But what spineless people they were!

'How do I open this door?' he asked. 'We either knock the wall of the theatre or we move in the door. Otherwise I can't appear.'

'What a tragedy!' said Gregory, then shouted, 'Martin! Martin!'

Now I made a mistake, Sullivan thought; I have turned the torrent on to poor Martin.

'Yes, Mr. Gregory; yes, Mr. Gregory,' said Martin, coming from the other side. He wore his white hair long. His body was very thin. His nose was very red.

'Haven't you learned yet to put in a door so that it can be opened?' Gregory asked him. 'See what you can do for Love locked Out.' More sniggers from below. Martin was at the door shifting the flats a little, not looking at Sullivan. 'I'm sorry, Martin,' Sullivan whispered, but it was no good. Sullivan knew that Martin would blame him, not the Great Gregory who made his life a misery. You get an old actor like that who was never very good anyhow. He is getting old. He is terrified of age and life and death, and you can do what you like with him.

'You must do things better, Martin,' Gregory was telling him. 'I'm afraid you are getting old, you know.'

'No, no, Mr. Gregory. It's just that there's not much room, you know. We are a bit cramped, you know.'

'Well, we must see about getting the place expanded.' He waited for it. He got it. 'You'll have to have to see to these things, Martin, you know. Delay costs money. You know that. And you haven't got the lights ready yet. In fact nothing seems to be ready yet.'

'It's not my fault, Mr. Gregory,' Martin said. 'There was nobody here when we got in last night. It was nearly three o'clock in the morning before we got the keys and started unloading. I wasn't in bed at all.'

'I don't want to hear excuses,' said Gregory. 'All I know is that I hire people to do work; I pay them for it, and I expect results.'

Sullivan was fuming.

He saw him, coming from the last place in his car. Sitting in the lounge of the hotel after a good meal, local notabilities chatting and listening to him as if they were listening to an oracle. Sipping away at his brandy. It would be free, from other people – he was most abstemious if he had to pay for his own – and all the others out working like beavers, dirty and searching the town for digs; being accepted at one place, refused at another place, because the lady remembered how the last crowd had vomited all over her best carpet.

'But, Mr. Gregory,' said Martin.

'For God's sake don't talk back to him,' Sullivan whispered. 'Don't make excuses to him.' If Martin only kept his mouth shut, he would be better off. If Gregory had no target, of necessity he would have to be still.

'You go and — yourself!' Martin hissed in at him. Right, he could take it out on Sullivan. Sullivan didn't care.

'And now, if we may proceed with the rehearsal,' Gregory said.

'Try it now,' said Martin loudly.

Sullivan tried it. He could get in now all right.

'Leave the world to darkness and to me, Martin. How about it?' This because the light on the stage had suddenly gone out.

'I'll fix it, Mr. Gregory, I'll fix it. Won't be a jiff. I was just connecting the floods when you called me.'

'Well, hurry up and do so,' said Gregory. There was effeminate annoyance in his voice. He was in darkness. He could barely be seen. He stamped his foot on the boards. The big bulb lighted again.

'Ah,' he said, 'Abracadabra.' The silly fools even giggled at this, thought Sullivan. 'Well, Mr. Sullivan, if you are quite ready, I will give you your cue.'

Sullivan said nothing.

'Well, are you or are you not ready?' he asked.

'Are you ready?' Sullivan asked. There was silence on the stage at this bit of *lèse-majesté*. Careful, Sullivan, or you'll lose your job, that kind of silence.

'Right,' said Gregory, 'I am about to commence.' He cleared his throat, walked a little to the left wing, then came back, pounded a fist into a palm. All his gestures were stagy: the widened eyes, each gesture of the foot or the hand, the thrown-back head, the rolling fruity voice from the puffed-up chest. He's as phony as hell is real, thought Sullivan, and he gets away with it. Is it because people have a big drum beaten in their faces that they are overcome by sound and can't see the lump of lard under it? He's a great actor, they would say, as he roared and shouted and fought his way in the grand manner, strangling and shooting and fighting. It was all just showmanship, so that the spotlight was ever on him. Where he was, there was his spotlight also. Let somebody like Sullivan come on the stage with him and get a laugh or draw a tear and next day there would be a freshing-up rehearsal and the lines that drew the laugh or the tear would be carefully excised because they weren't quite necessary to the action of the drama. A stinking vainglorious nonentity, that was Gregory, but unfortunately he paid the salaries, miserable ones, but salaries.

'Fawcett! Fawcett!' he called. 'I want you. Come when I call, damme. Must I strut and sweat on the waiting time of a fool? Fawcett!'

Sullivan appeared; bowed.

'You called, my lord?' he asked.

'Called?' my lord said. 'I have no lung left whole with roaring. Are you deaf, man, or are you free of senses? How about Lady Grace? What news of her?'

'She will not come, my lord. She says that when she came last night, she thought she came for tea.'

That stopped the conversation.

'The last time we did that, Mr. Sullivan, for some unaccountable reason the audience laughed heartily. Will you tell me why?'

'I really don't know,' said Sullivan. 'It doesn't seem a very funny line to me.'

'If,' said Gregory, 'if by any chance you were even a fairly competent actor, Mr. Sullivan, I personally would believe that

113

you put a certain obscene emphasis on the last line, that induced the audience to laugh and spoiled my following lines.'

'What you mean to say,' said Sullivan, 'is that if you were anything except a colossal ham you would have been able to make your following lines go across. But you can't. Because you lack subtlety, Gregory. You are about as subtle as an unringed bull.'

He could see him going pale.

'What did you say?' he asked.

'I don't like repeating myself,' said Sullivan, 'but the gist of it is that you are such a lousy actor that you can't put across a line requiring subtlety. Not one line.'

He saw the face swelling, the chest puffing, the slow menacing walk as Gregory came over to him, the clenched fists raised. It was a scene from any number of plays that Sullivan could remember.

'Don't come any closer, Gregory, dear boy,' said Sullivan, 'because if you do it will give me great pleasure to break the classical nose, to blacken the eye-shadowed eyes, and to test my fist on the two-way stretch.'

Gregory didn't come any closer. The wide brown eyes became piggy, and Sullivan saw the glint in them.

'That's what you wanted, Gregory,' he said then, realising it. 'You wanted something like this to happen. I have a good mind to beat you up, Gregory. You have me annoyed with you.'

'Martin! Martin!' Gregory called. He was frightened. It gave Sullivan pleasure to see the fright in him.

'Why I should have left it to now, I don't know,' Sullivan said. 'I've taken nearly seven months of you. Watching you prancing and mincing and terrorising. Why did I do it? Because I thought you were a fount and I would learn something. I learned a lot, dear Gregory. By watching you I have learned all the bad habits that it is essential to avoid. You hear that? You can't act for a row of potato skins. You have no more sincerity in you than a whore on a beat. You have sold whatever genuine talent you possessed for a lot of padded-up tricks. And you'll go on until you end up where you are going. Where will it be? You are on your way now. From the big

114

halls to the small halls to the little halls, until you're a small-time fit-up man selling crocodile oil at country fairs. Remember that I told you that, Gregory. Don't ever forget it!'

He jumped off the stage and set out for the door at the back.

Gregory awoke from his terror as soon as Sullivan had left the stage. He thought Sullivan had looked horribly menacing, standing there, a long lean figure with his legs spread and his body taut, and sparks coming out of green eyes.

He shouted after Sullivan.

'You will never be any good,' he shouted. 'You will never be an actor. You will never get another job. I'll have you black-balled from every place in the country. You hear. You won't put a foot into any theatre in the British Isles.'

Sullivan was gone. It was useless shouting after him.

Gregory looked down at his cast. They were not looking at him. They were looking at scripts or looking at their nails.

It won't be the same again, he thought. I can never get on top of those again. Next time, none of them. They will all have to go. All new people. If he could have had Sullivan tied with ropes in front of him he would have gutted him with a knife. He stamped his foot.

'Well, what are we doing?' he asked. His voice was high-pitched now. 'Who is understudy for that monster? Come, then, and let us get on with it. He, that thing, he is buried. I'll bury him. I'll bury him so deep that nobody will ever dig him up again. Come on. Let us have action. What are you all doing sitting there on your arses? What am I supposed to be paying you for? Am I a charity?'

He said a lot more insulting things, but none of them protested. None of them hit him. None of them got up and walked away from him.

This made him feel a bit better. Maybe, he thought, I might keep one or two of them.

14

Sullivan stood on the steps outside the hall and filled his lungs with air. He felt as free as a bird. All the same, he thought, it's a good job the birds of the air have nests, and I'll have to go and look for one. He paused a few moments longer. The sun was shining from a blue sky and the town looked very nice. He saw this suddenly. He tried to think of how many towns he had been in. He couldn't count them. He couldn't even sort them out in his mind. Certainly, he thought, he had never seen them. Each town to him had been either good or bad according to the box-office; the people of the town had been good or bad according to the reception they had given the plays. But now he realised he had never even seen the towns; never even stood back to look at them.

The old workhouse had been built on a hill overlooking the town. So below it looked well. It was all grey and green, grey stones and green trees. It was a southern town in the middle of the fabulous Golden Vale. The town was neat and compact. From here he could contain it all in the spread of his arms. Two church towers rose from it, and it petered out on the left to great stretches of fat farmland and on the right it was cut off from the towering mountains by a broad easy-going river, deep and winding. The mountains looked steep but they were all clothed.

I will not go home, he said, without the long limousine. He made that promise there on the steps of the strange town. Not because my pride would be hurt, going home a sort of beaten dog, but just because if a person sets out to do a thing they will just have to complete it. So it might be that I would never see home again. Or Bernie? Ho, that's different.

He ran down the steps and dug his heels into the stones to negotiate the steep walk down into the town. Here he sauntered, looking at the shops, watching the faces of the passing people, who glanced curiously at him. They would know everyone, so he would be a stranger. Not a very prepossessing one either. The shop windows were well kept and well stocked.

He wondered if he should have worked in a shop, meeting the glance of a grocery assistant dressed in a white coat and apron, his sleeves rolled. He was putting fat gammons of Limerick smoked ham in the window. Sullivan knew it was Limerick ham because it was stamped on each gammon in a kind of star. The hams made him feel hungry, so he winked at the assistant through the glass and walked on.

To the digs. Near the tail-end of the town. Small two-storey stone houses, that had been built for troops when the place was a garrison town way back. He had to knock on the door. Mrs. A. didn't give out keys. If you were late home, she said, she would be waiting up for you, so she hoped that you wouldn't keep her up too late.

He knocked now and she came to the door. She had been talking to a visitor in the kitchen, and she had come to the door smiling. Now when she saw him the smile faded, and caution overcame it. It was always the same, he thought, whatever digs you stayed at. An air of apprehension on the faces of landladies. Actors were not to be trusted. You had to watch your spoons and watch your linen and watch your daughter if you had one, because she might be young enough and ignorant enough not to be able to see beyond the rose spots.

'You're early,' she said. 'I haven't the meal ready yet.'

'That's all right, ma'am,' he said. 'I just wanted to pick up my stuff. I'm leaving.'

'You mean you've got another place,' she said. 'I told you I couldn't do anything else than put the three of you in one room.'

'No,' he said. 'I'm leaving town altogether.'

'You mean you're not in the plays any more?' she asked.

'No,' he said. 'Mr. Gregory and I don't agree, so I'm on my way.'

'Do you mean you had a row with him or what?' she asked.

He was going up the narrow stairs to the room now. He turned and looked at her. She was curious.

'You could say that,' he said.

'How could you?' she asked. 'He's such a lovely man. He's

been coming to this town for years and years.'

'Sic transit gloria mundi,' said Sullivan. 'I'll pay you on the way down.'

He heard her going back to the kitchen. There would be a black range in there gleaming with range polish, and scrubbed white kitchen chairs and the table scrubbed white. Sullivan felt he would like to go in there for an hour and put his feet up and listen to her talking about the town and her neighbours and the price of groceries and her operation, but you never got into the kitchen. That was the place where the family went into quarantine.

It was easy to pack his stuff. He had only one bag and it was locked. He looked at the bundles of letters in there. They were in Bernie's handwriting, neat, precise, intelligent, educated, and no passion. All the love was in meiosis. You know that one. I'm a citizen of no mean city. That was Bernie, but each time she wrote to him her letter lasted for a whole day in his mind and all around him. He touched them now, and then threw in his few clothes and gear on top of them. He left out the scripts, dirty, dog-eared, doodled. There was barely space to move in the room with the three single beds. The other two cases were also locked. How can people lead such enclosed, distrustful lives? Always on guard. He supposed it was a kind of defence mechanism.

He counted his money. It was pitifully small. He always sent what he had over after paying his digs and incidentals to his mother. He supposed the rest of them thought he was as mean as a skate. But he never took something for nothing, anyhow. He made up his mind how much one-seventh of his digs would be, and put it in one pocket. What was left belonged to himself and his future. About ten shillings. Brother, he thought, it wouldn't even pay to wash the dust off the long limousine. He went down then. He didn't want to be there when the others came to their lunch. He might be inclined to tell them a few home truths, which would do nobody any good. They would rejoice in a way that he was gone, because it would mean somebody else would step into his shoes and they would have a chance to read in the local paper that ... *last night, Mr.*

Gregory in his own fashion and artistry stole the whole play. He was well supported by John Brown and a talented company.

'Here's what I owe you, ma'am,' he said at the kitchen door.

'You mustn't go like that,' she said. 'Here, come in and have a sup of tea and a bit to eat.'

He hesitated, but he couldn't resist. He smelled frying bacon. So he finally got into the kitchen, sitting on one of the white scrubbed chairs. He had to get his diploma. He had to cease to be an actor. The bacon was good and the white home-baked cake and country butter. The friend was by the range; a middle-aged skinny lady, with her grey hair in a bun, smoking Woodbines like mad, her fingers badly stained with nicotine. Like one of the ladies from Duke Street.

They asked him questions. Where he was from originally? He told them. They exclaimed. Mrs. A. had been there one time on an excursion train. It left awful early, five o'clock in the morning. They went bathing on the shore and they had rock buns and tea in a little place there. Did he know her? No, he didn't. This was twenty years ago. He was just born then so it would be hard for him to remember. Mrs. A. remembered every moment of that day as if it had been yesterday. There were horse trams then. Were they still there? Oh no. Buses now. A pity the way they scrap useful things. It was very pleasant to be in a horse tram and smell the horses as well as the salt of the sea. Up high on the second deck they were. It had no top on it, so you had a wonderful view. Her husband, Lord have mercy on him, was with her. It was a sort of honeymoon. The sea was lovely, but it was very cold and there were a lot of jellyfish. It was August. That brought up a memory to him of himself on the lonely shore of silver sand, running up and down naked and not knowing that up behind him Bernie was on the cliff. It almost made him choke, but he stuffed the choke down with bread.

Then he was away.

He parted from Mrs. A. kindly. If ever he was back again he was to come and see her, and if he ever ran into Mrs. the

Rock Bun woman he was to tell her that Mrs. A. was asking for her.

Then he was out and on his own, the bag banging against his leg. Where do I go from here? he wondered as he walked through the town again. He reached the river and followed it. The road ran beside it. His shoes were soon white with dust. He came to a crossroads where the road went on into the valley and another narrower one crossed a bridge and went winding away towards the mountains. He sat on the low wall of the bridge and looked into the water. The river ran over a gravel bed here. It was pleasant. He watched closely and saw the small trout come out from the shelter of the rushes and gyrate on the gravel. He wondered if he would emulate Raftery the Poet and start wandering over the length and breadth of the land, working a day here and a day there. Where would that get him? Well, he would let it go. Soon he would toss a coin in the air and follow its direction.

He was so sunken in thought that he didn't hear the rattle of the gaily coloured van that turned from the main road behind him and came over the bridge. He didn't notice the driver looking casually and then gawking and then bringing the van to a stop with rattling and screaming of brakes.

It was only when the man got out of the driver's seat and started to run towards him shouting in wonder 'Sullivan! Sullivan!' that he turned from his contemplation and saw that it was Pi. Pi!

He threw down his bag in the dust and he spread his arms.

'Pi!' he said in wonder. 'Pi Clancy!'

And he ran to meet him. Pi didn't seem to have grown much, but if he was a giant Sullivan would have raised him in his arms as he did Pi, and kissed him soundly on the cheek. They were laughing there for ages, with their eyes shining, laughing and their eyes glinting, and clapping one another big thumps on the back as if they hadn't met for fifty years. It was a miracle. Sullivan couldn't believe his eyes.

Pi was dressed in dungarees and a khaki shirt with rolled sleeves and his arms and face were nut-brown from the sun. His face was pleasant, and for the rest of him he had grown

120

into a low-sized man, lithe and well proportioned.

'I couldn't believe,' he was saying. 'Jay, I couldn't believe when I saw you there on the bridge,' and he laughed again. 'You look like a fella could do with a bit of feeding up,' he said then, standing back to look at him. Sullivan did too. The lack of air and sunlight made his skin look sallow. There were lines under his eyes, and lines beginning to form at the sides of his lean jaws. 'And what are you doing here on the bridge with a bag and where are you going and where did you come from? Long ago, Tony Mahon told me that you had gone off with a travelling company. You never said goodbye,' he finished up sadly, shaking his head.

'I didn't get a chance, you sinner,' said Sullivan. 'It all happened quick. They sent looking for an actor time they were in town for a small part, like they do, and I went and Gregory asked me to tour, and I went and back there in the town to-day I got sick of him, and I went again, but God sent you, you fair-haired bastard. See how it was arranged that we should meet at this particular spot at this particular time? Just when I needed you, Pi. How did it happen? Listen, do you realise all the movements of millions of molecules and billions of people and time and the stars and eternity, so that all should come to a point on this bridge?'

'You looked bad,' said Pi. 'Were you going to drown yourself?'

'Not in there,' said Sullivan, 'unless you could burrow under the gravel.' Then he took time to look at the van. It was violently painted in yellow, red, and blue; BOHAN'S CARNIVAL CREATIONS BOHAN'S, with twists and curlicues. You couldn't miss it. 'What is it?' Sullivan asked.

'Oh,' said Pi, stopping from looking closely at Sullivan, 'that's me. I'm in the theatre business too, sort of.'

'You are?' Sullivan asked.

'Different from you,' said Pi. 'You know the carnival? Games and bumpers and shooting galleries and things. I got into that after you went. I like it. They are nice people. Good money too. You see lots of places and people. Listen, I didn't think there were so many places in the world, Sullivan. And so many people. Where are you going? What are you doing?'

'I don't know,' said Sullivan. 'It was going to depend on the spin of a coin. I didn't have to spin. You came, Pi!'

'Come on with me,' said Pi. 'Come until you make up your mind what you want to do. Bo will fix you up. For a time. They are always short of people. Come on. You come with me, Sullivan.'

Sullivan noticed with a smile that Pi hadn't lost his habit of sort of dancing when he was excited.

'Sure,' said Sullivan, 'I'll go with you, Pi, old Pi; this thing was meant, I tell you. I can't tell you how glad I am to see you. How were they all when you left home?'

They moved towards the van.

'Jay, fine, I suppose. I didn't say goodbye to anybody either, see? I know my mother. She'd start crying like. You know. And what would I do then? I wouldn't have gone. I wouldn't have the heart to go.'

They got into the van. Sullivan threw his bag into the back. It was filled with the oddest sort of things.

Pi started it up. The engine seemed quite sound. 'We are over in a village in the mountains,' he went on. 'You know, one of these parish carnivals fifty-fifty between Bo and the parish committee, with one week free for all. It's a small place. It doesn't have everything like nuts and bolts, so Bo sent me into the town here to get them to-day. Imagine, Sullivan, right at the right time. How we should want bolts at the right time and Bo should send me instead of somebody else! Jay, I'm glad to see you, Sullivan, honest, I'm glad to see you.'

They went along the dirt road on the far side of the river and then turned in and started to screw their way up the side of the mountain. It was steep. The engine laboured at it in low gear. It made terrible noises. You couldn't hear yourself talking. So Sullivan could look down below. The whole vale was unfolding under his eyes. It seemed, the lot of it, to be covered in a light-blue haze. The oats were ripening and the wheat stretches were yellow, and the great tracts of dairy land were as green as the imagination of an exile, and then the broad river glinting bluely. Sullivan sighed. He felt happy. He had a warm feeling in the pit of his stomach. He felt that the taste of Gregory had been wiped out of his mouth. He got rid of the last of it, spitting through the window.

When they reached the last wind and the top of the hill, Pi stopped the van and they got out. There was a grass-covered dike protecting the edge of the road from a hundred-foot drop to the next bend below. They sat on this.

'Isn't that something?' Pi asked. 'Every time I'm sent in I stop here on the way back and have a look at it. You know, Sullivan, we have a great country. Listen, there's no two parts of it the same, wherever you go.'

'I've been all over it too, Pi,' said Sullivan, 'and I don't think I ever saw it. Imagine that.'

'Laugh,' said Pi. 'Ever since I came away I send back money. You know Lucy? I send it to Lucy. My, she has the two parents hopping. You should read her letters. It's terrific. It's the best thing I did. You see, she has all the money now, with what she earns in the factory and what I send her and what does she do, Sullivan? Listen, she doles it out to them at a bob a time.'

Sullivan could picture that. Lucy and the lazy father. He laughed. 'Lucy has great stuff in her,' he said.

'Oh, she has them hopping. My mother had to stop wearing the black shawl and take to a coat and hat. Lucy said she had to near beat her to get her into them. And they have a small wireless set in the kitchen, and guess this – this is the big laugh – a new lavatory in the yard, two new beds with Lucy having a room of her own. And the old man has to whitewash the front and the yard every three months or no price of a drink. Oh, it's a revolution. Lucy is terrific. Who'd think Lucy would turn out like that? So you see, Sullivan, it was the best thing that I left home. Now it'll be worth going back to.'

Sullivan thought of Pi's house and how he had shunned it. He thought of Pi's mother and father and what they were, and here was Pi loving them. You could feel that from his voice. His own house was as clean as a pin, and he thought of his mother and the few stilted letters he wrote her. Is it because Pi has the capacity to love, and I haven't, or what?

He saw that when they drove into the village among the hills. It was a small enough place, neat, with houses on each side and the new school with wide windows and the church and a banner across the street crying CARNIVAL. The place was a few fields on. It was filled with Bohan's: gaily coloured caravans, and tents and stalls and outmoded lorries that still managed to give off power, shooting range, roulette stall, ring the ring, lines of washing hanging between the caravans, appealing hobby-horses painted in white and gold. It was all there.

Every one of them, taking their ease or washing, shouted at Pi. Pi was welcome. They wondered with their eyes at the tall fellow with the crumpled shirt and disordered hair. The lady that told fortunes crossed herself when she saw his green eyes. Somehow over all this you would think of the owner as a gigantic man with amazing muscles, tough and coarse, but Bohan himself, whom everybody called Bo, was a small man with bandy legs dressed very conservatively in a blue suit and a white shirt and tie, with black, black hair, barely flecked with grey, falling in curls over his forehead.

He looked Sullivan up and down after Pi had talked to him. He shook hands with him. His hand was as hard as marble but warmer.

'We always need extra,' he said. 'You're welcome. Pi will show you somewhere. Listen, Pi, bad news, you'll have to do the barrel again to-night.'

'Oh, God, no, Bo!' said Pi.

'You'll have to,' said Bo. 'You come and see Johnjo.' They followed him. He led them to a caravan, and behind the caravan there was a small old man lying in the sun. Every time he breathed you could smell the strong drink off him. He was wearing a grey suit that was too big for him. Even lying down you could see this. The turn-ups of the trousers were crumpled where they could not accommodate themselves to his shortness.

'He's plastered,' said Bo, almost proudly. 'Listen, we were watching him like hawks. I don't know how he did it. Look at the old bastard,' nudging the flaccid body gently with the toe of his shoe. He had a grey moustache that was brown in the middle as if it was scorched from the fumes of drink. 'He's as drunk as a Lord, by the holy,' said Bo, 'and none of us spotted him at it. Isn't that remarkable?'

Sullivan thought of Martin and Gregory, and he thought of Johnjo and Bo.

'Ah, but the oul barrel, Bo,' said Pi. 'Janey!'

'Look, it'll only be for the one night, Pi, I swear,' said Bo, catching Pi earnestly by the arm, and talking intimately into his face. Putting on the charm. 'Look, who are the three smallest men in the place? Johnjo, you, or me. Listen, Pi, I can't go into the barrel. I have too much to do. You know that. Or I'd go into the barrel. Don't think I never went into the barrel. I spent half of my life in that bloody barrel.'

'All right,' said Pi, 'I'll go in, but it's the last time, remember, Bo.'

'On me oath,' said Bo solemnly.

'Yes, until the next time,' said Pi bitterly. 'I know you, Bo. You think you can talk me into anything. And you're right.'

'I knew you'd do it, Pi,' said Bo, clapping him on the back. 'To-morrow we'll watch Johnjo like double-eyed hawks. Some night he'll go into that barrel carrying a load and somebody will decapitate him.' This thought amused Bo. He walked away hurriedly, covering a lot of ground with his quick bandy-legged walk.

'Come on,' said Pi. Sullivan followed him.

'Bo is all right,' said Sullivan. 'He seems to have a heart.'

'Oh, indeed he is,' said Pi. 'Bo is a gentleman.'

They found the tent that Pi shared with the donkey-engine man. There was plenty of room for a third in it. Just groundsheets on the grass, worn away and withered now. Pi showed Sullivan how to round out a hole where you could fit your hipbone. They laughed about this. Then they sat outside the tent in the sun. It was afternoon. The sun was still warm. You could smell the harvest all around you, from the sun and the fields outside, cattle and clover, and flies buzzing about, mixed up with the smell of petrol fumes and cooking stoves and oil, and they passed a solid two hours like this, talking their way back into one another's acquaintance. And it was easy.

Then they got a plate of food from a sort of communal pot. Sullivan didn't know what was in it – he could taste rabbit and mutton and vegetables – but he cleaned his plate.

After that the night began to close in and the place started to come alive. The engine of the big lorry chugged power into the dynamo and the lights of the bulbs sprang up all over the place. Sullivan was on the hobbyhorses. The man that worked the engine and the mechanical music had enough to do looking after that, which was a bit defective, so Sullivan was a help to him. Nothing much happened until about nine o'clock when the work in the farms was finished and then the kids started to come and the young people and the old people, and the mechanical music blared and brayed when it missed a few notes. Sullivan was really enjoying himself. Out in the air all the time, not baked under lights, sweating in heavy costumes.

He nearly died laughing seeing Pi in the barrel.

This was just an ordinary barrel. It was roped off by stakes and men could stand outside the rope and try and hit Pi every time he popped up out of the barrel. They were throwing wooden balls at his fair head with the hair standing up on it. It wasn't dangerous, Pi said. He showed Sullivan the eye-holes where you could watch the thrower. Some of them too cute, said Pi, they pretend to throw, you duck, and then when you come up they hope you get a crack in the snot. It doesn't work, see; you can tempt them to throw and you can watch them. Sullivan watched, convulsed for a time. All you could hear was the clunk of the balls hitting the heavy canvas screen behind. He thought that Pi rather enjoyed it. Sometimes if he didn't like a thrower he would stick out a red tongue at him.

Sullivan helped children on to the horses and watched their faces. You could get joy out of that. The way they held tightly to the twisted, highly polished brass poles, their eyes gleaming; their parents below watching them, waving hands at them. Sullivan thought that in the theatre you never got among the paying customers like this to watch their reactions. You had to wait for their spokesman, the critic, to tell you how badly or how well they had enjoyed what they had seen. It took him a time to get used to the platform going around and around, and if you looked up at the sky the galaxy of stars seemed to be dancing. He thought that he was content and he hummed with the braying music, wondering where Bernie was and what she was doing. The music was saying: I'm forever blowing bubbles, pretty bubbles in the air. There were a few of the bubbles missing and it sounded most incongruous, but Sullivan was happy.

The trouble is that you can't keep blowing bubbles forever.

15

'Tony also says,' she wrote, 'that it's completely up to yourself. He wrote to me, because he didn't know where you were. He heard that you were with that horrible Gregory man (I can smell him just from the words of your letter) and that you had broken away from him and he didn't know what happened to you after that. I didn't tell him you ended up with a Carnival. Should I? or are you too proud? They seem awful nice people to me from what you say, and Pi, isn't it wonderful that you have Pi? Tony likes this theatre in Dublin, although reading between the lines he seems to be a bit heart-scalded to have left his beloved small theatre below. But, he says belligerently, a man has to live. If you have no money you can nearly live on appreciation. If you haven't even that, what have you? You see! Anyhow the directors of this place had already heard about you and are interested, and if you go there (have you the fare to Dublin?) you are almost sure (if you are any good, are you?) of getting the job. It will at least keep you in the one spot for a while so that we can all know where you are. And it's what you want, isn't it, or do you want to drift around with Bohan's for the rest of your life? Honest, whatever you wish, I wish, but it seems a waste of talent to me.

'Sometimes I miss you a lot. At the moment I don't miss you. I make myself not, because the final is looming up, and I'm terrified, and if I let myself drift off into dreaming none of the tomes make sense. All the same it is a long time. Couldn't you even think of dropping the long limousine in the interim and just borrow Bohan's van and let Pi and you make an official descent on the town? I would be out with a flag anyhow, so the welcome wouldn't be too cold.'

He was lying on the big flat boulder near the shore. He tried to see Pi and himself driving down the main street in BOHAN'S CARNIVAL CREATIONS BOHAN'S, waving right and left to the empty streets, empty save for the brave figure of Bernie standing with her legs spread waving a big flag. He had to laugh.

Her information came at the right time. He turned on his belly and looked at the town. It was depressing. It was on a flat plain. The houses, two-storey barracky-looking places, were built one each side of the broad main road that cut a swath to the south. Few cars stopped in the place. They dawdled a bit, looked at its flatness, the soggy sloblands behind, the rugged uncompromising shore by an eternally angry-seeming and weed-loaded sea, and they headed screaming to the mounting cliff roads far ahead. Sullivan didn't blame them. It was worse when the sea was out. The littoral was rocks and rocks and no sand at all, and green-weeded and smelly places where the river oozed instead of running joyfully to meet the sea.

He thought how places affected people. The people of the Carnival could be joyful or expectant or bored or drunk. The place always set their mood. This place had everybody surly. It was a good stand. There was money in it, but the people seemed very reluctant to be separated from it. They were cautious. They were closed up in themselves. They partook of the pleasures of the Carnival with a sort of dogmatic puritanism that knocked all the good out of it. They were a rugged hard-working people, who minded their own business and regarded anybody from over the hill as a foreigner and a perverter of morals and society. They seemed to dress in an old-fashioned way. The children were wrapped up in too many clothes. They loved the merry-go-round, but the sight of their unsmiling parents watching them from below seemed to dampen them.

Am I thinking all this, he thought then, because the time has come for Bohan's and myself to part? And I want to paint it all in very black colours so that my ambition will be brisked up sufficiently to have the excuse for parting from them. Because he didn't want to part. This was the sort of colourful working community, almost pagan in its sense of freedom, which attracted you and brought you on and on. Quite a percentage of the Carnival people had gypsy blood in them, almost thinly overlaid with Christianity. They were good but they were unpredictable. They were different from other people. They knew it and you knew it, so anything they might do could be written off to that difference, and that gave them a sort of licence of world citizenry; that the only law that applied to them was the law of the universe.

Cod, he said then to himself, rising and jumping his way from stone to stone towards the shore. What's really biting you is that you don't want to part from Pi.

That was his real trouble, parting from Pi. He thought that there were only two people in his life for whom his selfish affections were really engaged. These were Bernie and Pi. They seemed to be part of him. Nearly as far back as he could remember they were part of him. Finding Pi seemed like a miracle. He didn't want to part from Pi. But if you parted from Bohan's you parted from Pi, because it seemed to Sullivan that by this time Bohan's was Pi. Perhaps, he thought, thinking of Pi's parents, that there was definitely a bit of the tinker in both of them. They weren't long out of rounded canvas, as the saying went. Was that why Pi was so successful with the Carnival people, because of that, that he had some of their blood in him too?

Everybody liked him. Nobody ever saw Pi frowning. He minded babies and he bedded drunks and he came between drunken husbands and their wives with great harmony and no injury to himself. Pi didn't seem to have any vices. His main vice was that he was so palpably enjoying life, and that was the feeling you always got from him.

So, he thought with a sigh, the best thing to do is not to tell him that I'm going at all, just to go, and it will save the both of us from all sorts of feelings. Also, he decided, I will go to-morrow morning.

He went back to the somnolent place. It reminded him of the first time he had come to it. The day was almost the same. The sun was shining from a sort of harvest sky. You could hear mowing machines humming in the distance like mechanised bees, and in the few fertile meadows on each side of the morass of a river you could see men rearing the hay into tramp cocks. Some of the ladies were sitting at the doors of their caravans, sleeping with their mouths open, or knitting or embroidering. The men were in the village drinking or doing a bit of business. The dogs were lying with their tongues lolling. He was greeted with a nod or a wave. They never took to him like they took to Pi, now. His going would not even leave a ripple in the pool of their lives. Just the donkey-engine man might be sorry to see him go because he would have to collect money as well as looking after the so-and-so asteriskical benighted music machine.

Inside in the tent he gathered his few bits and pieces and put them into his bag. The minute he had done this he felt completely alienated from the Carnival. He lay down and looked out at it through the open flap and wondered what had come over him and his ambition that he had let so much time pass over his head. He must have been sunk in a colourful inertia. Well, that was over now. His vision was clearer. He seemed to be looking at the place with a clearer eye. It was tawdry if you looked at it that way. The caravans wanted painting and the booths wanted cleaning and some of the people could do with a cleaning too. Some of them.

Then he saw Pi coming through with a staggering and wildly singing Johnjo hanging on to him and laughing and singing. The sleepers came awake to regard the spectacle. 'Love you, Pi,' he would say and bend over and kiss Pi avidly on the cheek. You could see Pi pulling away his head from the fumes and closing his nostrils. 'All right, Johnjo,' he would say. 'All right, Johnjo.' Johnjo flings his free arm wide then and sings: *'From the shores of Salamanca came the wild Arabian tide'*, a few lines and he would kiss Pi avidly again.

Pi called: 'Hey, Sullivan, give 's a hand with him, will you, for the love of God.'

Sullivan went towards him, laughing.

Johnjo tried to change his affections, but Sullivan wouldn't take any of them. He turned him around and hoisted him and carried him over to the usual place behind Bo's caravan where he placed him in the shade. He lay there placidly now, breathing deeply and soon sleeping.

Pi was looking down at him bitterly.

'You know what that means,' Pi said. 'Everybody knows what that means. Well, I'm not going to do it, you hear. I'm just not going into that barrel and I don't care who knows it.'

He shouted this up at the open window of Bo's caravan. Sullivan knew that Bo was in there listening. But there wasn't a peep out of him. Later on, Sullivan thought, he will emerge, his old-looking creased face twisted into an ingratiating and heart-breaking look of complete helplessness, and Pi will end up in the barrel.

'Certainly,' said Sullivan. 'Nobody will get you into that barrel, Pi.'

It was a pity they did.

Sullivan saw Bo working on Pi. He didn't have to hear a word of it, he just saw him working, the spread hands, the shrugging shoulders, the dark eyebrows raised, the hands brought to the chest in a gesture of infinite appeal. He saw Pi's face, adamant, unflinching, unmoving, stony, and then he saw it breaking down, to indecision, and hope and defence and retreat and attack and retreat and sympathy and eventual reluctant agreement. I should have told Pi, Sullivan thought, to save himself a lot of emotions and just agree.

Pi went into the barrel, and was up and down like a jack-in-the-box and the balls were clumping on the canvas wall behind, and Sullivan knew when the night was half-way through that he couldn't walk out like that without letting Pi know that he was going. It was the least he owed to Pi. What was he trying to do anyhow? – save himself a bit of heartache, not Pi. Pi wouldn't mind as long as he knew.

When the merry-go-round was filled and winding he jumped off the platform and went over towards the jack-jumping Pi. I will call him out of the barrel, he thought, and tell him now. That was Sullivan, impulsive. Couldn't it have waited until the evening was over and they were in their tent and the night had folded? Not Sullivan.

Over he goes and stands there. There were two men throwing balls at Pi. They were big fellows. They had obviously come from the hayfields. One of them was leaning on a two-pronged pitchfork. He wore no coat. His shirt-sleeves were rolled. His muscles were rippling in the forearms. There was still some hayseed in his dark hair. His teeth were big and white and he was laughing so much that Sullivan thought they must have had a porter jug in the hayfields. Because none of these people were given to laughing much. His companion was a bit older than himself, a black man needing a shave. He threw his last ball and it was then that Sullivan caught Pi's eye and beckoned to him.

It was a mistake. Pi came up and said 'What?' and the fellow firing still had a ball in his hand and flung it gleefully. Pi sensed it. He had a good instinct. Sullivan saw consternation on his face and then he was gone and the ball fluffed his hair as he went down. This seemed to incense the black man. He hopped over the rope and he went up and bent into the barrel and he fished for Pi and held him up in front of him and then bent down behind him and roared: 'Now, Jack.' He was strong. He was holding Pi half out of the barrel, helpless in the grip of his hands. The man with the fork grabbed one of the wooden balls from the tray and flung it at the wriggling Pi. Pi saw it coming straight for his face and just managed to turn his head. It hit off the side of his head in a glancing blow and bounced away. Sullivan heard it. The laughing Jack reached for another ball and at the same time Sullivan and Bo and the still half drunken Johnjo jumped the rope and went for the fellow who was holding Pi. Sullivan got to him first, caught him blindly by the shoulder and struck out with his fist as he half rose. He hit him again and again and his knuckles hurt him, but he was blind with rage. Bo swarmed on him then and

Johnjo fell on him and Sullivan turned at a shout and saw the other fellow coming for him with the two-pronged fork raised. He heard women screaming. Your man flung the fork from him like you would fling a spear and he was very close to Sullivan. It was Pi who shouted and it was Pi who half leaped out of the barrel in the fork's path, and they all saw the prong of the fork hitting him on the cheekbone and penetrating, and the barrel overturned with his weight, and himself and the fork sticking in his cheek went down on the grass.

There was nothing Sullivan could have done. He was half turned when the shout came. He hadn't time to turn on his feet. He was looking at that fork coming towards him like a bullet and there was nothing he could do about it.

The night seemed to stand still. The fellow who flung the fork stood still. The fracas behind Sullivan ended. He bent over Pi. One side of his face was streaming with blood. Sullivan caught the smooth handle of the fork and pulled. He could feel it leaving the skin.

'Pi, Pi!' said Sullivan.

'I'm sorry, listen, I'm sorry,' the fork man was crying. 'I didn't mean it, it was only a joke, only a joke.'

Nobody paid any attention to him. They were gathered around Pi. Sullivan had his head on his knees, trying to staunch the blood with his handkerchief. It had pierced his cheek, the prong of the fork, like a needle in a piece of cloth.

'All right, all right,' Pi was saying, 'all right.'

Bo was on his feet. He was practically crying with rage. Two of the men were holding him. The black man had joined Jack. He was rubbing a bloody nose. They were very confused. They didn't want to be in the limelight at all. They were very sober men. They edged away into the crowd that was now running up to surround the barrel. Bo finally stopped fuming and swearing.

'You are all right, Pi, aren't you? Sure, you are all right. Tell me you are all right.'

'One thing, Bo,' said Pi, holding the handkerchief to his face, the blood seeping through it and staining the fingers of his hand. 'No more barrel. You hear. No more bloody barrel.'

They got a doctor. He fixed it up. You'll have a scar like a German officer, he told Pi.

The whole of the male Carnival chorus was scouring the place for the two men. They didn't find them. It was fortunate they didn't find them. Nobody thought of calling in the police. This was private business. But who started it, who started it?

Sullivan knew well who started it. Oughtn't he to have learned long ago what his impulsiveness led to? But had he learned? No, he hadn't learned.

He told this to Pi, accusing himself about what he wanted to tell him and how it could have waited until much later, what he was telling him now about the letter from Bernie. Wasn't I always getting you into trouble, Pi?

Pi laughing and wincing. No, no. Tell you something, Sullivan. I'm tired of the Carnival anyhow. You are, but I thought you loved it. Yes, I do, I suppose I do in a way. It's a way of life that appeals to me. But I want to be settled too. You know that. You get tired of going from place to place. So I tell you what, you go to Dublin, I go too. I'll get some sort of a job there.

Sullivan couldn't believe it. Happening like this. (But did it have to take a few pints of Pi's blood to make it happen?) It didn't really. It was because Pi had a letter from Bernie too. Pi often had letters from Bernie that Sullivan knew nothing about. It was none of his business. They were friends. Like Bernie, never said anything out, just sort of that now they had met again it would be good for them to be together? Sullivan was odd. Sullivan was fond of Pi. Sullivan wouldn't believe this but Pi gave him stability. All that sort of thing. And Pi knew damn well that Sullivan would be leaving and he was making up his own mind if he, Pi, really wanted to leave too, or if he was just going where he could be with Sullivan. They talked it out. Sullivan was hopping with ambition. Sullivan was full of dreams again. Maybe I mightn't have gone only for the barrel all the same, Pi told himself.

There was wailing in Bohan's. Nobody wanted to see Pi going. They didn't know whether to blame Sullivan or the pitchfork or Bohan and the barrel or Johnjo, a repentant, streamy-eyed, humble, penitent Johnjo, or what to blame. But Pi was going. He was kissed and cried over so much that Sullivan was afraid that from sorrow Pi would change his mind. He didn't.

Bo himself drove them to the station in the van. He never let up on Pi. He had Pi wriggling. If it was the barrel, oh, great God, how sorry he was, and how he wasn't going to leave that miserable poxed town until he laid his hands on the two bastards if he had to search for them night and day. Never again, he swore his oath, would Pi have to go into the barrel. No, no, it wasn't that, Bo, just that a fella liked a change, honest. Was it more money? Didn't he want more money? No, no, Bo, I swear it was just that a fella couldn't be an old stick-in-the mud.

He only gave in finally when he stood on the station platform and watched the train away. He walked beside the carriage as the train pulled out and said, 'Any time at all, Pi, that you want to come back to us, come back. Any time at all. We will all be waiting for you. Come back.'

Pi was leaning out of the window waving back at him. Bo looked small and the gaily coloured van looked incongruous against the grey building of the small station.

'Nobody can stay in one spot all the time anyhow,' said Pi. He looked odd with his face swathed in cotton wool and sticking plaster. He sat down on the hard seat. Dust rose from it. He rubbed his nose with the palm of his hand, gently because his face hurt him.

'They were nice people,' he said. 'I hope other people we meet will be as nice as them. But nobody can stay in the one place all the time.'

16

Tony said: 'Now you see how it all adds up, Sullivan. All the suffering and even Gregory. Can you even include Gregory in it?'

They could see one another in the mirror. Like old times, thought Sullivan, with an instant warm nostalgic glow.

'Yes,' he said. 'I will even count in Gregory. I learned a lot from him, mostly trickery.'

'The time will come,' Tony said, 'when you will be glad of the trickery you learned from him. How many different parts have you played since I saw you doing the Shade of Diarmad? Can you remember?'

'It's hard to remember,' said Sullivan. 'Say twelve different ones with you and about fifty with Gregory. Everything under the sun, lord and peasant, tinker, tailor, soldier, sailor, all of them, priest and poet, but you cannot say that I distinguished myself since I came here. Look back at it; the biggest thing I did was an old farmer drinking a bottle of stout through the whole of an act.'

'It's all waiting. You waited, somewhat impatiently,' said Tony, 'but here is your chance now in a good part in a good play. To-night's the night. After to-night, Brother Sullivan, there will be no more of "the carriage awaits without", and may I say that I thought you took it all well. You were more impatient long ago, weren't you? You wanted to be a comet, but you didn't have the fuel. Where did you learn the patience, Sullivan?'

'You don't know me, Tony,' said Sullivan. 'I'm not patient. I'm burning up.'

'You see,' said Tony, carefully shading the hard lines under his cheekbones, 'the good days are gone, Sullivan. That's why I say you need the trickery. Those lovely days long ago, when you could go on the stage with your heart on fire and you could act with your heart. You have to have that burned out of you with boredom. The parties of the long ago, the amateur intrigue, all that you must lose. The happy hobby. You remember that's what it was, Sullivan? You remember?'

'Yes,' said Sullivan, 'I remember, Tony. I remembered you often, and the others, when I was with Gregory. Those were gentle days. But you don't want to go back to them. If you are a man how can you be a child?'

'We might be better to be children,' said Tony.

'You're not happy,' said Sullivan.

'I'm happy as they go,' said Tony. 'All I did was to change from being my own boss, from being a moulder, into a mouldee. And in the process I'm moulding myself. Maybe I can't cope with all that goes with professionalism, the vanity leading to hatred and burning bile, a knife in the back, frustrations, false smiles, with sometimes rare flashes of love and companionship. Am I drinking too much, Sullivan?'

Sullivan didn't answer.

Tony *was* drinking too much. Maybe Tony should never have left what he was. He had more money now and no responsibility, but his eyes were clouded.

'Maybe you think too much, Tony,' he said.

'Think, drink, don't they go hand in hand?' Tony asked. 'I am often tortured with the idea that we as actors are not necessary. We are the clothes to dress another man's dreams; cavorters to other men's laughter and tears. Suppose that all the actors in the world were to be killed overnight, what would the world miss? Nothing much. Just entertainment.'

'Tony,' said Sullivan, 'this is a first night. It's the first night of a good play and I have a good part in it and you have a good part in it, and to-morrow maybe we'll get good write-ups, and even with the help of God and the critics we might get a raise in salary. Let us think of that and not be gloomy before we have cause to be.'

'You have a glow about you, Sullivan,' said Tony, meeting his eyes in the mirror, 'that I envy. A special glow. It's the first-night glow, and the glow of a fellow who knows he can be successful. Maybe I am gloomy, Sullivan, because I know that you are about to be very successful. That hurts me, that it is possible I might be jealous of your success; that this gruesome professionalism has reduced me to that, even about you. If

137

such is true, Sullivan, I ask your forgiveness, and I know I should not have taken that last drink. But lately I get so nervous. I say: I simply cannot put a foot on the stage unless I am bolstered. I usedn't to be like that, Sullivan?'

'No, Tony,' said Sullivan, and his heart was heavy. 'The Tony of long ago was a martinet about drinking in the theatre. No man on the stage is his own master if his speech is a split second behind his mind, and that's what happens when you drink. You think you never acted as well as then, but you are not acting well. You were never like that.'

'See,' said Tony, 'my corruption has begun and I don't know why. Why should I be sad? Listen, Sullivan, you have another glow. I can spot that. Nobody can fool me on that. There is a glow all over the other glows. Is it so?'

'Don't know what you mean, Tony,' said Sullivan, the bright flame burning inside him, and wondering at the perspicacity of Tony. It was just like him to get two things on top of him at the same time: a sinking in his stomach at the thought of his part, and a burning of his heart at the thought of Bernie; to see her, touch her, feel her eyes on his own, big eyes, so clear and so collected, with a flame of incipient desire at the back of them. He couldn't tell Tony about it: that to-night he would see her, that even now the wheels of the train were clacking out the rhythm of her name and his own, depending on the ears there were listening to them.

They heard the first gong booming, and Sullivan's burning heart went down into his stomach, and as he applied the powder to his make-up he hurriedly scanned the dog-eared script resting on the bench in front of him.

Outside the chap banged on the door and shouted, 'On the stage, Tony, on the stage!'

'All right,' said Tony, and drew his face into the hard mask that it had to assume. Satisfied with it he pulled on the heavy dark coat.

'Good luck, Tony,' said Sullivan.

'Thanks,' said Tony, 'and good luck to you, Sullivan. This is your chance and you'll make the most of it. I will be thankful that I taught you a little of what you know. Is that so?'

'More than that, Tony,' said Sullivan. 'Listen, if it wasn't for you I would still be a stutter-bum holding up a gable-end in Duke Street.'

'Oh no, you would not,' said Tony.

'Many people and things go to the making of an actor,' said Sullivan. 'There's a whole cloth, but it has been woven by different hands. You wove well for me.'

Tony was smiling.

'I can at least see things clearly, Sullivan,' he said. 'You spoke from a big heart. Listen. They may get you. I know. I have seen it happen. And you know how they get you? They wrap you around in flattery. You can be like a fly in a cocoon when they are done with you. Keep your feet on the ground, Sullivan. Don't let them excite your pride.'

'I'll try, Tony,' he said.

'Tony! Tony! Tony!' the voice was calling impatiently.

Tony went. Sullivan thought how there always seemed to be voices calling, calling. You never seemed to get away from them. Like the Last Trump. Why should he feel sorry for Tony? Tony was a good actor. He was an unfailingly good workman. A solid technician, but he could never set people on fire. Just: You were fine, Tony; fine, Tony. Sullivan wondered if he had been sincere when he had told Tony that he had woven well for him. Did he in his heart believe that a lot of hands had gone into the weaving of himself, or was he assured that he had grown himself from the seed of his own talent? Sullivan didn't know, but he hoped sincerely that he had meant it.

He took the snap of Bernie from his pocket and looked at it once more. Prim-seeming, smiling, with the kind eyes, a load of books in her arms, her tight hair ruffled by the wind. What affinity was there between that day on the cliff-side and the sea breezes, and here now with the smell of sweat and melting grease-paint and hot bulbs ranged around a mirror? I don't know, Sullivan thought, but my heart is hot with the thought of her and nothing must ever get in the way, nothing – and the time since he had last seen her seemed to be centuries ago, and then he firmly put the thought of her out of his head with the

139

snap back in his pocket and he looked in the mirror and changed himself from Sullivan to *The Stranger*, clear-eyed, cool, tall, burning with the simple words of compassion and hope and the calm acceptance of mutilation. He was the kernel of *The Hazel Shell*. He heard the third gong booming, listened to hear the rising curtain as the strains of the orchestra ceased, and then he blessed himself and went down the stairs, noting with resignation that his legs were shaking and that his hands were shaking, and that he would have to visit the toilet before he made his first appearance.

'Good luck, Sullivan.' 'Good luck to you, too.' All the others who weren't on, as nervous as himself, more likeable in their nervousness. Think back over coming into the middle of them: their original resentment; the time it had taken to find out about them, to become as much part of them as a member of a company ever can, since all actors are mainly self-contained units revolving, revolving, and only touching at times, in unity against harshness or unfairness or bad pay, like members of a family who have lived together for too long. Like that. It is the only way you can protect yourself, to be wrapped around in a shell, superficial, charming, joking. 'Good luck, Sullivan.' That was the producer, looking at him, thinking he will be good all right, but he wouldn't have been half as good if I hadn't humiliated him a little, reduced his ego.

'Good luck, Sullivan, not that you need it, you lucky bastard.' This was Mona. 'Good luck, Mona, and I'll need all I can get of it with you mauling me. Right?' Her small hand was comforting. It was sweating like his own. He could see that her mouth was as dry as his own, she swallowed and swallowed. Why are we afraid? Aren't we like trained athletes? All you have to do is run. They were drawn together in this moment of fear. Normally they didn't get on. Mona was a small, very good-looking girl with plenty of charm and appeal. She thought Sullivan should have become one of her admirers. He didn't and didn't explain why not, so she thought at one time he might have gone Greek, but no, it wasn't that either, and he puzzled her and she said things about him and they came back to him as all good things do, and so – on the stage they were terrific. They were filled with love. If Bernie was an actress could Sullivan make love to her on the stage? Not he, because on the stage true love would be too real and would embarrass the people who had come to savour unreality.

Sullivan got away to a good start by blotting out the people. They didn't exist. Just Pi was out there and Pi was always a sucker for a good play. You could work on Pi's emotions as you could shape a lump of dough in your hands. Make Pi cry. Make Pi laugh. Make Pi feel romantic.

That got him on and after that it was easy.

With Mona: *Your hands are scarred. These are burns you collect when you gather stars. I see the start of life in your eyes – already. Where you come from there must be no beginning and no end; where girls are born from God and never tread on the leaves of the fruit trees. We will go into the night and stumble on the furrows of the ploughed field. If your soul is free, then what does it matter if your feet are bound in the mud of the earth?*

That was Mona, and then Tony and the blow on the face; the staggering blow on the face. *You provincial dung-pit! You jester's get from the end of nowhere! You craw-thumping monstrosity!* His body tied to the chair with heavy cart-ropes; the people around avid or savage; sorrowful or scornful or doubtful. His calm acceptance of fate; his quiet words thrown back into the teeth of bleak savagery: and theirs: *What we do with the animals, because you are lower than the animals. No animal will eat at our table, consume our salt and then betray. Not even an animal!* Lustrous eyes and the complete faith that brings the miracle of confession. His freedom from the biting ropes; his battered face, the beautifully created exit, all so well known now, so new then, that people will remember for a long time how it succeeded.

It was all in the air. A new situation for Sullivan; the feeling of excitement in everybody like a drug that keys men up to excel themselves. Holding on to this moment, because there cannot be a lot of them and if there are many then their effect will pall. What is it? It is more than a successful gamble, more than the result of an eagerly awaited football game, but in essence it carries the same tense excitement, the same exhilaration, except that the gamble once made is over, and so is the game; but the play must go on night after night.

And Sullivan was like a football captain carrying the Cup high over their heads. You could have lighted candles from the gleam of his eyes. To be enveloped in congratulation is heady wine. Perfumed women and girls, and men, and even Gregory, towards whom he could feel no resentment now, booming over the mob: 'I made him. You see him! He is a Gregory production. Eh, my boy. Did I teach you?' Laughing, Sullivan expected him to hand around small cards advertising the Gregory Academy of Dramatic Art, wondering how one time in the long ago he could have allowed this preening, pirouetting little man to affect him so deeply.

But with it all he didn't neglect his main purpose in life. He kept his eye on the clock, and he saw the train rushing through the darkness of the night. That's why he kept his head that time. He managed to get to the dressing-room.

'What did I say, Sullivan?' said Tony. 'Didn't I tell you?'

'That's right, Tony. You told me.'

'We'll have to drink to it.'

'Not to-night.'

'Not to-night! Where are you going? Are you going to a wedding?'

Sullivan laughed. Nearly told him. If only. But he couldn't. He didn't want anyone to know. He wanted Bernie to be a thing apart from all this. This was instinctive. He couldn't explain it.

'Maybe I *am* going to a wedding,' he said. 'I have an important date.'

'You can't rush away like that,' said Tony.

'Oh yes, I can,' said Sullivan.

'My God!' said Tony.

'My God!' said the producer.

'My God!' said the author. 'I want to talk to you. Giving a little do to-night.'

'Not to-night,' said Sullivan.

'To-morrow night then, to-morrow night then,' said the author. 'You must be there.'

'To-morrow night,' said Sullivan, and got out of the crush, pulling on his coat, shoving up his tie.

'My God!' said Sullivan's new-found fans. 'Not to-night.'

Many surmises were made about his destination. None of them could hit the mark. He got out into the air. So cool, so fresh. The tide was full in the river.

Pi was waiting outside. Part of the fresh air, was Pi. Of reality. That was Pi.

'What time is it? What time is it? Will we ever make it? Call a taxi!' This was Sullivan fussing. Running across the street towards the bridge. Pi running beside him laughing, excited. 'You were great, Sullivan. Man, you were great. Like long ago. Just like long ago. See, I told you they couldn't hold you down. Like trying to boil a bullock in a three-legged pot. Good man, Sullivan!' hitting him on the back.

'Suppose we were late,' said Sullivan. 'Wouldn't it be bloody awful if we were late? What in the name of God would she think of me?'

'Man, Sullivan, it was powerful, powerful,' said Pi.

They weren't late.

Sullivan paced the platform. He would have fallen off many times if Pi hadn't held on to his arm. He was urging the train on with his heart. Suppose the thing crashed somewhere? Suppose she wasn't on the train at all?

But the train came and she was on it.

Sullivan's heart stopped racing when he saw her coming out of the carriage door. She was looking around. Her eyes were searching frantically for him. She was as full of fears as himself. Her eyes found his. They lighted up. Her face flushed. Those eyes and the smooth skin. Something like the school-girl who had come to comfort him on a raft in the Quarry. A light frock and a coat swinging open, the small tidy feet, and a bag in her hand. Sullivan's legs were trembling. He thought he could never get under way, to move to her, to envelop her with his love. But he did and she was in his arms, and she was saying, 'Sullivan, oh, Sullivan' into his ear with a wealth of longing at last satisfied, and he thought: Of all else this is the best of all. This is really the best of all.

17

He held her away from him to look at her. He was holding her body close to his own, feeling the warmth of her under his fingers, savouring the scent of her; herself and light lavender, cleanliness, order, decency; he couldn't get enough of looking at her. She lit up the big, grimy, smoke-blackened station. He couldn't hear the shunting engines, the whistling, the calling of porters.

'Oh, it is good to see you, Bernie!' he said. 'It is good to see you!'

No change much in him. Smartly dressed. A brown suit and a white shirt. His jaw was grooved but it made him look handsome, responsible.

'I thought you would never come,' he said.

'I nearly got out and pushed the train,' she said. 'Oh, Sullivan.'

'Remember me, miss?' said Pi at her elbow.

'Oh, Pi!' she said, stretching an arm and wrapping it around his neck. Pi hadn't grown. He was of a height with her. She noticed the scar under his jawbone. It wasn't ugly. It pulled up one side of his mouth so that he had an appearance of constantly smiling. She knew how he got that scar. She pressed her own soft cheek to his face.

'Pi,' she said then, laughing, 'It seems so strange to see you the fine gentleman.' Pi was well dressed.

Pi looked down at himself.

'This is probably the first suit I ever had that fitted me,' he said.

They laughed. Sullivan took her case. He kept his arm about her, pulling her close to him, and they walked down the long ramp to the street.

'How did you manage it?' Sullivan was asking her. 'I never thought you would manage it. I never thought that you would agree. What did he say? Did you tell him?'

'No,' said Bernie. 'I couldn't tell him, Sullivan. Please forgive me, but I couldn't tell him. Not now. But I will later, I promise, when he gets a bit better.'

'It might be as well that he doesn't know. He would feel so sorry for you. He might even shoot me to know. What will you do? Hang your wedding ring around your neck on a cord?'

'On a golden cord,' she said.

'And what did my mother say? Did she abuse you, tell me?'

'She is pleased, I think,' said Bernie. 'At least she started to treat me like a daughter-in-law. She is in the house now for a few days. She will look after him.'

Sullivan had a picture of his mother in the house in the orchard. A house something like what she had been used to so long ago. She would like that. A little bit of class. Out of Duke Street. Old Morgan would be a gentleman to her. Somebody to be looked after, like her own father.

'I'll bet she will like that,' said Sullivan.

'Yes,' said Bernie. But the old man didn't like it. Why are you bringing that woman in here? Keep her away from me. I don't care if she *is* Tim Sullivan's wife. Tim is dead. He doesn't have to put up with her fussing about him. Don't be long away. Come back to me, Bernie. Soon. Or I might strangle the woman. 'She likes it,' said Bernie. Then under the light of the street lamp as they waited for the taxi she saw the slick of grease-paint behind his ear.

She rubbed it off on a finger.

'Oh,' she said, 'I should have asked first thing, first thing. How did it go, Sullivan? What happened? Was it good? You were so keen on it.'

'Oh, Bernie,' said Pi, 'you should have seen. It was like before. He was good. You should have heard what they said.'

'No, Pi, not now,' said Sullivan. 'Look, that's a bargain. We forget all that until to-morrow night. Soon enough to-morrow night will be on top of us. Is that a bargain? Right?'

'Right,' said Pi.

'Right,' said Bernie.

They got into the taxi.

'We're going home to the digs. Mrs. Feathers. Wait'll you

see. She has everything laid on. She thinks it's romantic.'

'So it is,' said Pi. 'It is romantic.'

'Are you sure you can afford the taxi, Sullivan?' asked Bernie.

Sullivan and Pi looked at each other and laughed.

'That's a bit of Duke Street,' said Sullivan, holding her hand. 'Remember the time we hadn't two ha'pence to rattle in our pockets, eh, Pi?'

'Had to go raiding orchards,' said Pi.

'And getting hung up on barbed wire,' said Bernie. 'Oh, I will never forget you hanging on the barbed wire, Pi, like washing left out to dry.'

'And he holding his hand on the hole in his modesty,' laughed Sullivan.

'Ah, lay off,' said Pi.

'Remember what a half-crown meant long ago?' Sullivan asked. 'The half-crown that I am going to tip the driver now. What would we do with it long ago?'

'Sherbets with a stick of liquorice to suck,' said Bernie.

'Bull's eyes and Peggy's leg,' said Pi.

'Whipped cream walnuts,' said Sullivan.

'Monkey nuts and Woodbines,' said Pi.

'Love lozenges,' said Bernie.

'You remember the cooked crubeens?' said Sullivan. 'Tuppence each, and they would be lying in the big willow-patterned dish, and the cold jelly succulent under them, in the window of that restaurant near the bridge.'

'Oh, boy,' said Pi, licking his lips. 'I hope Mrs. Feathers has a nice supper waiting for us.'

They laughed.

They swung from the main street into a maze of avenues and terraces.

'This is it,' said Sullivan. 'The middle-class man's Duke Street.'

Long long streets, crossing and criss-crossing, houses on top of houses, full-bricked and half-bricked and quarter-bricked. All very neat gardens front and back.

'Go out in the back garden in your pelt,' said Sullivan, 'and

146

you have two hundred windows looking at you, with four hundred eyes behind them. But classier than Duke Street. Remember the sow and the bonhams, Pi, at the back of our place?'

Pi held his nose.

Mrs. Feathers was waiting at the door for them. At least she was waiting well inside the door with a dressing-gown on her and her hair all tied up in curlers. She was a fat woman with a round jolly face, beaming red cheeks. Not waiting for an introduction, she enveloped Bernie, kissed her soundly. 'Aren't you a gorgeous little girl!' she commented. 'My God, isn't Sullivan lucky to get you, and all the sloozies that's going around? Here's Maisie.'

'Maisie is the bridesmaid,' said Pi. 'She's the only one we could dig up.'

'Hello,' said Maisie. 'Isn't it gorgeous? It'll be lovely. It's the first time I was ever a bridesmaid. Know what too? Only one that can get the bouquet, so I'll be fixed.'

Bernie laughed, happy at feeling their friendliness. Maisie was about seventeen, tall, flat-chested and slightly adenoidal. She had lovely eyes.

'Maybe you'll get Pi,' said Bernie.

'Wouldn't have him on a plate,' said Maisie. 'He's a kind of a monk.'

'That fixed you, Pi,' said Mrs. Feathers. 'Here, what are we doing hanging around in the hall at midnight with all the neighbours listening to our words? Go in and stir up the fire, Pi. Maisie, make the tea. You come upstairs with me, love, until I show you your room. There's a lock on it so that Sullivan won't trespass.'

She laughed at this. She mounted the stairs laughing, holding on to the banisters, wheezing her way up.

Bernie met Sullivan's eyes. They were suffused with mirth.

'Go on up,' he said.

She went.

Mrs. Feathers threw open the door of the bedroom. It was very neat, very clean, bright wall-paper, gleaming mahogany furniture, but the room was made smaller than it was by the enormous, wide, comfortable-looking bed that occupied it. Mrs. Feathers sat on the bed. It didn't even creak under her.

'It's a good broad bed,' said Mrs. Feathers. 'It was Ignatius'.' She nodded her head at the picture hanging on the wall. He was looking down at the bed. He had a bald head and black moustache and a high starched collar. 'Poor Ignatius,' sighed Mrs. Feathers. 'He liked his comfort. The bathroom and the bed. Them was Ignatius' special care. He often said it. Between the two places, Sybil, he'd say to me, we spend nearly half our lives and they got to be good. Wasn't he right? He died in this very bed, Bernie, and he had no pain. Three months he was in it and he went gently. You'll find it comfortable.' She rose to her feet puffing. 'Now I'll leave you. I'm sure ye want a talk. But don't be too long. The kettle will be on the boil.'

She went and Sullivan looked at Bernie. Bernie was looking at Ignatius.

Sullivan sat down on the bed, laughing.

'Never mind, Bernie,' he said. 'You'll only have to put up with Ignatius for one night. Then I'll take over for him.' He reached for her hand, pulled her sitting on the bed beside him.

'Somehow,' said Bernie, 'I wouldn't trust Ignatius. He has a gamy look in his eye. He was too fond of beds.'

They both laughed, then suppressed it, in case Mrs. Feathers would hear.

'But I like it,' said Bernie. 'I like it all.'

'I knew you would,' said Sullivan.

Then the reality hit them, and they sobered. Sullivan kissed her. A long kiss.

'I've been wanting that,' he said. 'Oh, for a long time. You are no longer a shade. You're real and that's wonderful. Listen, Bernie, you're sure, aren't you? You're sure?'

'It's a bit late in the day now for me to draw back,' said Bernie.

'But to do it like that,' said Sullivan. 'To call you out of the blue like that. Let's get married, and you have to do it all; all the planning and letters of freedom and the millions of things. And you did it. You didn't mind?'

'Well, since I have known you, Sullivan,' she said, the palm of her hand on his face, 'I have learned to expect the unexpected. That's why I'm practised in it.'

'You'll never regret it,' said Sullivan. 'I swear my solemn oath on that.'

'It will be worth it,' said Bernie, thinking that it's here now, all the time that it was longed for, sometimes the swift flash of regret that you could be so bound to a human being; that your own life would be confined by a longing, of a person not even in your reach, who could have been only a dream. 'We mustn't be parted too long, Sullivan,' she said, burying her face on his shoulder. 'Not too long. Sometimes it becomes unbearable.'

'Me too,' said Sullivan. 'And we won't, I swear we won't. To-morrow will settle that, you'll see. To-morrow.'

'We better go down to Mrs. Feathers' supper,' said Bernie. 'It would be a pity to spoil it.'

It was a good supper. There was a lot of laughter served up with the cold chicken. Bernie was to remember that supper for a long time.

Her fingers were cold in his hand when he put on the ring. The gold of the ring was warm. Her fingers were long. They were trembling. He looked at her, her head bent watching, the small nose, the regular lips, the firmly rounded chin, and the sheen of health on her skin, and Sullivan felt his heart over-flowing with helplessness. That he couldn't do enough for her; that he would like to take her away to a castle in the clouds and the two of them just live there forever alone. No world at all for him outside the high peaceful dome of the church; the massive pillars reaching towards the coloured glass-filtered light of early morning; themselves, Mr. and Mrs. Sullivan, kneeling on the *prie-dieu* inside the altar, while the young priest intoned the Mass for their very especial benefit.

Pi was very soft-hearted. He was nearly crying. He watched the bowed backs of his friends and thought over the years. And this was the fulfilment of the years, but Pi thought how good it would have been back in Duke Street. Man, all of Duke Street would have been at the wedding. All the little presents they would have got, pots and pans and pillow-covers and Infant of Prague statues, lots of little things all wrapped around with the expansive hearts of the lowly. Pi sighed.

Just Pi and Maisie and themselves at their wedding breakfast in the hotel. Mrs. Feathers couldn't come. She had to look after the other lodgers.

So there you are. None of them had anything much to say, except Maisie. And then Pi took Maisie away and Sullivan and Bernie went on their honeymoon to that public garden where strange blooms and shrubs grew in careful profusion. The sun favoured them. It shone from a clear sky like a good omen. They walked slowly, Sullivan was holding her hand. She wore new high-heeled shoes that looked good on her slim feet. Sometimes she would look up at him and sigh with satisfaction. In this place there was a clear stream that flowed shallowly, caressed by the trailing vines of the weeping willows, and right down there you could see the plump protected trout waving lazily to the flow of the water, and here under the ragged trunk of a faintly smelling eucalyptus tree they lay side by side on the dry grass, their faces to the warm sun, Sullivan's fingers still holding Bernie's and twisting the gold ring on her finger. All mine. He sighed.

'Bernie,' he said, 'we have so little time. Just until the sun goes behind those trees and then we have to part. Isn't it like me to be like this: that I must leave you and go to work? Isn't that a horrible thing?'

'As long as you come back to me,' said Bernie.

'I often wish I wasn't,' he said.

'What?' she asked.

'What I am now,' he said. 'It's not normal. Why should you have to work when most other people have stopped working and dressed themselves so that they can enjoy? That's not fair.'

'You're an entertainer,' she said.

'That's what Tony said, too,' said Sullivan. 'You remember Tony?'

'Aye,' she said.

'He's changed,' said Sullivan. 'You remember his decision?

The confidence he could inspire; his determination and accomplishment of a fixed end. You haven't seen him. He's suffering. He drinks. Imagine that! Even going on the stage.'

'Don't let's be unhappy, Sullivan,' she said. 'Let's worry about Tony to-morrow. See the tracery that the sunbeams are making shining through the trees.'

'It's all unfair this,' said Sullivan. 'You shouldn't have been married like this in a corner. You should have been married at home, in white, with confetti and a great do. We would have had a hooley in the orchard and as the night fell we would have hung Japanese lanterns from the branches of every fruit tree. Boy, that would be something. And all the neighbours sitting around under the lights sipping porter from mugs and snuffing from their tins.'

'I wish we were at home now,' sighed Bernie, 'lying on the grass under the fruit trees and there forever and ever, inside the walls. With the world passing by.'

'You like it there, Bernie, don't you?'

'Oh yes,' she said. 'Even with Morgan. Hard to manage him at times. But he seems part of it too. It is the shelter that he built.'

'Can you stay in a shelter forever?' Sullivan asked.

'No,' she said. 'Because if you weren't there it wouldn't be one.'

'Tell me about your day,' he said. 'What do you do all day, so that I will know?'

'I rise,' she said, 'every day, as they say in the compositions, and I put on my clothes and I come down and I light the fires and then I go to Mass and when I come back the kettle is boiling and I bring Morgan up his tea. Then he comes down, taps the barometer glass, sniffs the air and tells me whether I should wear a coat or no, if it will be fine or wet; and then I cycle to the school and I leave Bernie in the cloakroom and put on horn-rimmed glasses and become Miss Taylor, teaching little girls *amo, amas, amat*. I like that word. I think of you. I wish you were with me.'

'Teaching little girls *amo, amas, amat*?'

'No, just within reaching distance of me, so that any time I wanted I would know where to lay my hand on you, just to say Hello.'

'Right,' said Sullivan. 'I go back with you. What will I do? Prune fruit trees? Plant potatoes in surburban gardens? Unload coal boats at the Docks? Is that what you want of me?'

'I wouldn't care,' said Bernie. 'I could scrub the coal off you.'

He laughed. 'I can see Sullivan at that all right. Not me. Listen, Bernie, I'm going to burn up the world.'

'What will you do then when you have burned up the world?' Bernie asked. 'You will have no place to go.'

He rose on his elbows, and bent over her. The long lashes uncovered her eyes. She blinked. He shaded her eyes from the glare of the sun with his hand.

'Oh yes, I will,' he said. 'Because when I have burned up the world I will sell the ashes so that I will be loaded with gold. Then I will come back and I will dally with you forever in the place of the fruit trees. Forever. Never let you out of my sight. And I will watch my sons playing with the apple blossoms.'

'Sullivan,' she said. 'Do you write any more?'

'I do,' he said. 'A lot of love poems to an independent character. Other things too. That's the hard way. You don't know. The other way is so different. You don't know what it means to get on top of people. To experience them. To play on them, sensing them out, all your nerves open to receive their reactions, so that they are in your hand and you can play on them like an orchestra. That's power. Sense of power. The other way only with unseen minds. Can't get at them, as real people. No sense of moving them.'

'I think you are wrong,' she said. 'I think the other way is the more powerful way. You will still be in it. Why do you live to me when you write to me of all the people you have met and what they do? I know them all, even better than on the stage, because on the stage there's only one person, but the others, your letters to me, they are alive with persons.'

'We won't fight, so soon,' said Sullivan. 'One day there will be a lot of time and I will tell you what you mean to me. When you are not with me I make wonderful declarations. When you are this close to me, I am practically inarticulate. All I can do is look in your eyes and see soft sandy beaches and wheeling gulls and stretches of heather, and Pi playing piggy-back with the kids in Duke Street, and you in your white dress competently dousing the flames of Sullivan's first flop.'

She said: 'Oh, Sullivan.'

Sullivan kissed her.

Then he raised his head and looked at her closed eyes. Her breast was heaving. He tipped at her lashes with his finger.

'You are as beautiful as a dream,' said Sullivan, 'and our time is running out. Why can't we hold on to even a second of life? And now I can't kiss you any more, because I see a loathsome fellow in a bureaucrat's uniform strolling casually towards us. His days of love are dead. Not even a dream. Each grey hair of his head has pushed those good days farther and farther into his minute brain. See how he whistles, his pug face up to the sky as if he loved the sun and the clouds. No love in beautiful gardens. You must only look. Rise up, beloved, and we will walk before his wretched reproof. We will seek another tree, another stretch of lawn, and try and hold the sun high in the heavens.'

'Oh, Sullivan,' said Bernie as he pulled her to her feet, 'I love you, I love you, I love you.'

Their time was really running out. The sun was already, dear God, shading part of the river.

18

Sullivan came to work with his mind filled with soft lips and cloudless skies and a gentle breath on his face; the scent of flowers and the smell of grass, and the wonderful reality of the most important day in his life.

He had to adjust very fast. The adjustment was forced on him. It had to knock away at him like a battering-ram knocking at a wall to force itself on his attention. It took him a long time to awaken to the knocking, but when he did he gave himself to it.

Even outside the theatre, the young man he scarcely knew grabbing his arm, shouting: 'Great show, Sullivan! Great show! This is Sullivan,' to his companion, a wide-eyed girl with a soft hand. 'You were wonderful,' she said, breathing the words almost. Sullivan was pleased. 'Is that so?' he said. 'Thanks.' Inside himself wondering at what could have happened. Then he ran in.

It was the notices, of course. He had almost completely forgotten them. My God, I *am* in love, his mind said as they jeered him about them. Imagine having forgotten the notices to that extent. Some people claim, and of course they are wrong, that actors can't read anything unless they are favourable words written by drama critics.

'Hey, Sullivan, did you see your notices, you lucky bastard?'

'No, I didn't see them.'

'Laugh, you hear that? Sullivan didn't read his notices. G'wan, where were you all day? Look at his fingers full of printer's ink. That boy is modest. Look at him, bleary-eyed, waiting up half the night to read them.'

'On me solemn, I swear I didn't. I was away. I wasn't here.'

'Fine, pretend to believe him. Get the notices for him. Put them in his hand.'

'Read them upstairs. I'm late.'

'Take them away, and purr, pussy.'

Running up the stairs and there was Tony.

'Thought you would never make it, Sullivan. Where the hell were you?'

'On a binge,' said Sullivan, tearing off his clothes.

'You don't look like that to me,' said Tony. 'What do you think of the notices?'

'Didn't read them, Tony. Believe me. Just going to read them now.'

'My God,' said Tony, 'wherever you were you must have been unconscious.'

154

'Oh, I was,' said Sullivan. 'Indeed I was unconscious.'

As he struggled into his stage clothes he bent over the notices on the bench. They began to excite him now. It's wonderful the habit an actor acquires of skipping through a column of fine print until he lights on his own name and reads from there on. He always says he will get around to the rest of it again. Sometimes he does.

Sullivan felt a flush rising in him as he read what was said about him. He couldn't help it. Can you help growing if somebody gives you food? There was a pleasant warm glow in his stomach that emerged as a glitter in his eyes. 'Boy!' Sullivan said now and again.

Tony was watching him, amused, puzzled by him, now certain that this was the first time he had read them.

Sullivan was basking in praise. He let it flow over him. Submerged. Flattered. Caressed. Like being intoxicated. Saying in his mind: I will enjoy this for a short time. It is good to be praised.

'Don't let it get you, Sullivan,' said Tony. 'Don't let them capture you. They raise you up to-day and to-morrow they kick you soundly in the arse.'

Sullivan barely heard him. He was humming. He was filled with his part. He was on the stage acting his part, particularly the parts of his part which had been praised and commented upon. True for them, he told himself, I was red-hot there, and there. It was a wonderful thing to have unstinting admirers. You cannot hold two worlds in your mind at the same time in a situation like this. One is bound to eclipse the other. Sullivan for a time was swept away on this current. His new wife could have been a tiny figure waving on a distant grassy shore.

It lasted. It built up. It grew to a climax. You know the way a lot of people are reluctant to admire until they have received imprimaturs. They were all out on this one.

Another time Sullivan would have been more than conscious that Bernie was below watching him. He would have performed for her, but to-night he performed for 'his' audience. And they liked him. He knew they did. They knew they did.

It was a long time since Bernie had watched Sullivan on the

155

stage. She watched him now with breathless attention. But she didn't lose her critical faculties, even listening to the words of praise that rose from all around her. Sullivan was good. You could see that. It was no change. He had always been good. But now he glittered. He was controlled. He had learned tricks. He was using them. Sigh for the heart-moving uncontrolled sincerity of long ago. Like Tony. Tony hadn't changed. Tony now was still the expert workman, but Sullivan in the third act sweated and he was good. He moved Bernie, not just because she loved him and was his wife of a few hours. Just because she believed in him as *The Stranger* and rejoiced at his victory of faith over brutality. Deserved applause, but leaving Bernie disturbed was Sullivan's reception of it. Those glittering eyes, the light reflecting off the copper hair. A phrase from the past came back to her, the piping of Pi: 'Sullivan is acting again,' and that was just what the tall smiling bright-eyed figure on the stage was doing.

She went around back stage for him. By then he would have returned to normal and the fever would have gone.

Sad, it wasn't gone. Sullivan was still acting.

He was surrounded by people, young and old and middle-aged, and the compliments were flying like the confetti they didn't have at their wedding this morning. Was it only this morning? She stood outside the ring and tried to catch his eye. She caught his eye. If he had been back to normal, he would have winked broadly at her and she would have been assured. They would have shared Sullivan's cynical enjoyment of what was bound to be passing praise. But he didn't wink. He nodded gravely as if he was going to grant her an interview so that she could put in her sixpennyworth too. Sullivan was liking what they were saying to him. He was lapping it all up like a cat licking cream. Sullivan! Am I jealous of all this attention? she wondered. She examined her thoughts. She didn't think it was that. She pulled back into a corner, as stage hands passed by with gruff 'Excuse me's' and actors ready for home came down the stairs taking off her coat with their eyes; uncovering her breasts, stripping her down to her toes, casually.

She expected Sullivan to take her to his room, even if he

shared it with Tony, and the three of them would have chatted about long ago and how things have changed. Tony needn't know they were married, just that she was Sullivan's girl as she had always been.

No. Sullivan levered himself from his fans and said (to them as well as to her): 'Back in a few minutes' and flew up the stairs. Nobody tried to talk to her. She stayed in her corner feeling like a kitten caught in the rain looking in through a lighted window. Well, at least he will come down and we will go away and we will be alone.

Indeed they weren't alone. Sullivan was like somebody with a high temperature. He gathered his fans and then he gathered her by the arm. 'Sure you won't mind, Bernie. Promised last night I would go to this party. The author. Don't want to hurt the chap. Can't get out of it. Everybody would be hurt.' No time for her to agree or to disagree. Just swept along feeling forlorn, as if she was dreaming a slightly unpleasant dream.

This party was held in a cellar, just a common or garden cellar, painted starkly white, the floors covered in scarlet tintawn, the walls decorated with huge paintings startling in colour and meaningless, like nightmares. Mainly sherry, and sausages on sticks and a record player, sleezy sort of music; oddly dressed girls and boys dancing, holding trailing glasses in their hands, smooching. My God, Bernie thought, where am I, what am I doing here? Thought of her class of little girls chiming *amo, amas, amat*. Saw Sullivan like a god on a pedestal, people practically lining up to talk to him. He was drinking sherry. He shouldn't do that. She shook her head. Drinking only made Sullivan morose, never joyful. The small man beside him with the balding hair and the gentle eyes behind horn-rimmed glasses was the author. Amazing that such brutal thoughts could come from one so mild.

Bernie stood back and watched all this and she would say to herself again and again: But this is my wedding night. My wedding night. It must be me that is wrong (ungrammatically, she chided herself, instinctively).

Then Tony came to her and she thought that would be a relief. But Tony had been drinking too. There was a strong

157

smell of it off his breath. And she thought that his eyes were slightly haunted and his strong dark hair was tinged with grey streaks and they were real.

'Bernie,' he said, 'Bernie Taylor! What in the name of God are you doing here, out of place, like a primrose in a manure heap?'

'Oh, Tony,' said Bernie. His clouded eyes were trying to focus on her. He looked from her and looked towards Sullivan. He blinked his eyes, shook his head.

'What's wrong?' he asked, but before he could go any further, this other fellow, a thin fellow with a red polo-necked jersey and black lanky hair hanging over one side of his face, swept Tony aside, saying, 'Tony, where have you been hiding this lovely, lovely girl?' and before she could protest had swept her out where the other couples were dancing. This fellow was half tight. He wanted a shave. There was dandruff on the neck of his jersey. 'Darling,' he said, 'where have you been all my life?' And he bent to kiss her neck while one hand caught at and pressed her right breast.

That was the finish for Bernie.

She stamped on his foot and pushed him away from her. His eyes were widened with pain and amazement. Bernie pressed her way through the people surrounding Sullivan. She stood in front of him with her legs spread and her face very flushed and she said: 'I'm going now, Sullivan. You can come if you want to.'

She just turned on her heel then and made for the low archway and she ran up the stone steps, dodging polo-jersey who was still reaching for her and closing her ears to the call of Tony, 'Hey, Bernie! Bernie!' Near enough to tears but her anger fighting them back, because she remembered a flush spreading over Sullivan's face, a flush of embarrassment.

She stood outside and gulped in the air, breathing it deeply, even if it was tainted with petrol fumes.

And then Sullivan was beside her. And Sullivan was angry. His jaw was tight.

'What did you do that for?' he asked. 'Why did you do a terrible thing like that?'

*   *   *

What a different homecoming it was to what it should have been! You have often been walking on a street and on the opposite side you have seen a man and a woman walking, their bodies rigid with anger, not wanting to draw attention to their arguing; not looking at one another, their eyes sparking, biting out words over their shoulders. You have shaken your head, sorry for whatever has come between them, imagining how long it will take for their angers to cool; for them to get back into one another's graces.

Sullivan and Bernie walked the almost empty streets now in the same way, hardly seeing; hardly knowing where they were going. Sullivan's eyebrows were pulled down.

'Why did you do it?' he was asking. 'Just tell me why did you do it. Did you know how you shamed me?'

'If you can't even see it, what you did, how can I show you?'

'Show me! Show me!'

'To-night, that you should be like that to-night. Just puffed up. Lost in a dream of adoration at your own shrine. You!'

'Fine, oh, fine. Tell me more!'

'You leave me at the foot of the stairs. A spare appendage. You leave me to be gruesomely pawed with drunken hands. Your wife. All alone, and you, where are you? A tin god, surrounded by candles lighted to the shrine of your pride; a blind god to leave me there and let things like that happen to me, and you didn't care, didn't care!'

'Oh, sweet God!' This is Sullivan, his hands in fists, his teeth clenched, his face up to the sky. 'To whom belongs the hurt pride? Who are you thinking of? Not me. You are thinking of yourself. What happens to you. Not what happens to me.'

'You are the one I think of. Can't you open your eyes and see what it was doing to you? The terrible change it had wrought in you? With your own consent.'

'My wife,' he said. 'My loving trustful wife. My comforter. The one I waited for.'

He sank his hands in his pockets and walked away ahead of her, nuzzling his collar with his chin.

She looked after him. She had to hurry to keep him in sight. She didn't know where to go. If he turned a corner fast he would be out of her sight and she could be wandering the streets all night.

Sullivan was flaming. He had never been so angry. His suppressed anger was making sweat break out all over him. His whole mind was a white cloud of anger. He couldn't stop thinking about what the people in the cellar must have thought about the scene; about what they were saying now; about how they would be skittering; about how they would invent stories. He was crawling with shame.

He was at the house almost before he knew it. He looked at the door blankly and then felt in his pocket for the key. He opened the door. A slight pang took him then and he turned back. She was rounding the corner, her head down. She was wearing a hobble skirt. She couldn't take big steps. Under the light of the street lamps, he could see the shape of her thighs. She looks so helpless, he thought, so helpless, and she's like a viper. Imagine doing a thing like that to the man you only married that very morning! My God! He walked into the room where a table was laid with a cold supper on it. She didn't follow him. He heard her coming in, closing the door and going up the stairs.

He didn't notice how discreetly everything was done. Not a sinner in sight even though it wasn't very late. All gone to bed. Even though they never went to bed early. Mrs. Feathers would stay up chatting about anything until the small hours of the morning. About Sullivan; about actors; about actresses; about little bits of scandal. But now everything was discreet. The whole house seemed to be holding its breath in preparation for Sullivan's wedding night. Maybe Sullivan was five minutes there fuming, gathering words, before he put out the light and went up the stairs.

He went into the room and closed the door and put his back against it. He had at least enough intelligence to keep his voice low.

'I know what it is,' he said. 'You just don't like the stage. That's it. Now that I come to think back on it, you never liked it. Why? Is it because you want to deprive me of it? Is it because you want me living in Duke Street on four pounds a bloody week just being nothing? What do you want me to be? Tell me that? What do you want me to be?'

She was sitting at the dressing-table. Her coat and blouse were lying on the bed. Her skin was creamy white. Her arms were up. She was brushing her hair. Her eyes met his in the mirror.

'I want you to be what you wish,' she said. 'You know that. It's just what it can do to you. Like now. It's not Sullivan. I just want you to be Sullivan, the real Sullivan, not to become a dream, a pale shadow, a thoughtless one. What has happened to this morning, Sullivan? How far have you left it behind you?'

'I have left nothing behind me,' he said, going over to her. She rose. He followed her. She loosened her skirt, reached for the pale-blue nightdress placed carefully by Mrs. Feathers on the turned-back bedclothes. 'But you have lost something. All that is part of being an actor. You have to listen to people. They pay the money, don't they? What are you to do? Insult them because your wife is a prude?'

'Don't dare call me that!' said Bernie. 'Don't dare call me that.'

'It's what you are,' he said. 'These people are as good as you and better. Why should you insult them?'

'You couldn't possibly insult them,' said Bernie.

'You know so much,' he said. 'You know so much. A girl who has been out of a small town three or four times in her life. Where did you find this wonderful knowledge?'

'In my heart,' she said, 'in my heart,' standing up facing him, practically naked, ready to pull the nightdress over her head, her eyes bright with anger. 'I love you; and what's good for you pleases me, and what's bad for you hurts me. That knowledge is from no book or life, it's just from love, that's all, if you ever heard of it.'

'A lovely love, I must say,' he said. 'A lovely broad-minded love. What's good enough for Bernie is good enough for Sullivan. A lot of give and take in love like that, isn't there? My

161

God, a selfless love like that would transfix a Turk.'

'A Turk wouldn't do to me what you did to me,' she said, throwing back the clothes, getting into bed. Her short hair was tossed. A bit of it was falling over her eye. 'If he had three hundred wives he wouldn't even hurt one of them like you hurt me.'

'A one like you,' he said, 'wouldn't even get to first base in a harem. They'd know what to do with bossy women like you. You know what they'd do to you?' he asked, going over to her side of the bed to say it to her because she had flung herself on the pillow with her back turned to him. 'I'll tell you what they would do to her? They'd drown her. They'd hold her bloody head in a bucket of water as soon as she started to talk, because they would know then what she would be like. What misfortune ever possessed me to meet up with you? Why didn't I meet and marry a girl who would agree with me and love me no matter what I did; who would take part in my profession and rejoice when I rejoiced and weep when I wept? Where could a man have found a girl like that? He would have found her if he wasn't an eejit like me, building up a picture in my heart of a girl, and the first time I really need her I find that she is only a dream; that she doesn't exist.'

He was down on one knee, his hand clutching the pillow beside her head, talking to her ear, because her face was buried in the pillow.

He had to pause for breath anyhow, so he decided to let her have her say. But she didn't say. She was just silent. He stood up. She kept her head buried. Sullivan was abashed. This was Bernie. Mother of God, don't say she's crying. He wanted her to come up from the pillow blazing at him. He had a lot more to say. He wasn't finished yet. So he took off his coat and his tie and his shirt. But she didn't stir. He couldn't tell if she was crying. He hoped she wasn't crying. What was the use of crying? Where did that get anybody? He went back again beside her.

'Bernie,' he said tentatively.

It didn't draw her.

'Listen, Bernie,' he said, realising all that he had seen.

'You're beautiful, Bernie, I love you.' It didn't move her. Now he knew she was crying. So he got on his knee again and caught her bare arm and tried gently to turn her. The arm came, but her head resisted.

'Look, Bernie,' he said. 'I know. I know. I was a monster of vanity. Look, Bernie. I know. I went in head over heels, but it hurts to be told. Listen. You wouldn't have been you if you hadn't told me. I wouldn't have been me if I had taken it without anger. You'll have to forgive me, Bernie. I'm sorry. I made a bags of everything, didn't I? I made a bags of your wedding day and a bags of your wedding night. That's me, isn't it, Bernie? Holy God, I always make a bags of everything, don't I? Look, Bernie, you'll have to look at me. For the love of Ignatius hanging on the wall.'

That brought her head up and her arm around his neck in a mixture of laughter and tears, buried in his neck her head was.

'Oh, I was a prude, Sullivan,' she said. 'I was a prude and you should have married somebody else.'

'Oh God, don't say that,' said Sullivan. 'I wouldn't give a wisp of your hair for the whole lot of them.'

'I'm sorry if I hurt you, Sullivan, please,' she said. 'I'm sorry.'

'You can hurt me like that any time, Bernie,' said Sullivan. 'All I want is that you will always be around to hurt me like that.'

'Oh, Sullivan,' she said.

'Right,' said Sullivan. 'I have so much to say to you. All the things that I should have been saying to you if I wasn't in a fever. But before I turn out the light, you know something I'm going to do, Bernie?'

'What?' she asked.

'I'm going to turn Ignatius with his face to the wall,' he said. 'Whatever Mrs. Feathers thought about him, I don't want that fella looking down at us.'

'I told you that,' said Bernie, laughing. 'I told you Ignatius had a gamy eye.'

And Sullivan really did turn him face to the wall and Bernie knew that Sullivan was back to normal, when in the middle of the night with his arm around her he said: 'Bernie, I just thought of something. You know what one of these flattering lassies actually said to me?'

'What?' Bernie asked.

'She said: "Mister Sullivan, I thought you were the re-incarnation of Finn McCool."'

'No!' said Bernie.

'Yes,' said Sullivan.

And they laughed heartily, and if Mrs. Feathers heard them she must have been pleased.

19

It was a detached house facing the shore, a long sandy shore broken here and there by clumps of black seaweed-ribboned rocks. The sea was calm, the sky was misty blue and the waves broke casually upon the sand. Bernie admired the view and then opened the delicate wrought-iron gate and walked the crazy-paved path to the door. Everything very clean, very neat, garden and flower borders, a good hand watching over it. She rang the bell.

A young woman opened the door. She had a cigarette in her mouth, a cloth in her hand and her hair tied up by a red silk square. Her forehead puckered as she looked Bernie up and down. She shook her head.

'No,' she said. 'I'm afraid you're not. For one wild minute I thought you might be a new maid. That's the way they are now. Swear their oaths they will come, even the day and the minute, and each time you believe and each time you are wrong.'

'I'm sorry I'm not the maid,' said Bernie. 'I'm looking for Mr. Clancy.'

'You mean Pi?' the woman asked, taking the cigarette out of her mouth.

'Yes,' said Bernie.

She waited for an explanation. Bernie said, 'Nice house you have. Nice garden.'

'Come on through,' the woman said, 'he's out back. Will you receive him in the living-room or will you go out to him?'

Bernie laughed. 'He can receive me,' she said.

The woman was unable to stifle her curiosity.

'Why Pi?' she asked.

'He's just my friend,' said Bernie.

'Are you married?' she asked next.

'Very recently,' said Bernie, her heart jumping.

'Pity,' said the woman. 'If you weren't I would have advised you against it. Brother, the golden dreams they spin and what happens to them? You still have to work as hard as when we were all living in caves, progress or no progress.'

They were at the back door.

Pi was squatting on his hunkers beside a motor mower. He was scraping a plug with a penknife. It was a nice garden. Green lawn between the back and the apple trees at the end where vegetables grew in neat rows. There was a small girl standing up beside Pi. She had fair hair tied with a ribbon and her hands were behind her back. Her arms were pudgy, her limbs under the short cotton frock sturdy and brown. She was talking away fourteen to the dozen. Pi was nodding his head, laughing occasionally.

'She's turning out just like her mother,' the woman said. 'She'd talk the leg off a pot. I'm her mother.'

'She's as pretty as her mother too,' said Bernie, laughing.

'Now I know you must come from the same place as Pi,' the woman said. 'You are all full of the old soft soap down there. But I like it. Tell me more.' She called then, 'Hey, Pi, a visitor for you. You, Cliona, come on in.'

Pi looked, saw Bernie, rose; surprised and pleased.

'Please don't bring Cliona in out of the sun,' said Bernie.

'She'll tell me all your secrets in six months' time,' said the mother wisely.

'I don't mind,' said Bernie.

'Nice kind of a visitor to get during working hours, Pi,' she said. 'Wish I could have a bit of glam calling on me in working hours. What a hope! God love ye.' She went in then and shut the door after her.

Bernie went down the steps into the garden.

'There's nothing wrong, is there, Bernie?' said Pi anxiously.

'Not a thing, Pi,' said Bernie. 'I just wanted to talk to you. I haven't seen you to talk to since I came. I'm going home today. You know that?'

'Yes,' said Pi. 'I know that. I thought maybe you would stay forever.'

'Why?' she asked.

'That would be good,' said Pi. They walked over, sat on the wooden garden seat. 'Oh, this is Cliona. Say hello to Bernie, I mean Mrs. Sullivan.'

'Hello, Bernie, I mean Mrs. Sullivan,' said Cliona. She had been sucking her thumb for a minute. Bernie shook her fat hand gravely.

'Hello, Cliona,' she said. Then she shut her eyes to the feel of the sun, allowed her shoes to fall off her feet and wriggled her toes. She was unused to city pavements, bus trips, stopping, starting, stopping.

'It's very nice here, Pi, very peaceful,' she said. Contrasting this with Sullivan's environment. Tried to place Sullivan here, say a jobbing gardener like his father. It would be nice, but not for Sullivan. 'Are you happy, Pi?' she asked.

'Pi Mister Clancy is always happy,' said Cliona. 'Mammy says so.'

'There you are,' said Pi, 'I don't even have to talk.'

'What would you like to do most in the world now, Pi?' Bernie asked.

'Why,' said Pi, 'that's easy. I'd like to go back to Bo. Great fun with Bo. Sullivan told you about Bo?'

'Yes,' she said. 'He wrote to me about Bo. He seems to be nice. It was my writing to you that made you leave Bo, wasn't it?'

'I don't know,' said Pi. 'Ach, who knows? Sullivan is like a magnet too, you know. He picks people up.'

'Like you and me,' said Bernie. 'How many different jobs are you able to do now, Pi?'

'Let's see,' said Pi. 'Apart from the Carnival I have been a messenger boy, an apprentice mechanic, slot-machine attend-

166

ant, public-convenience attendant, road-mender, docker, and here I am a jobbing gardener.'

'What's a public-convenience attendant?' Cliona asked, having trouble getting all the words out.

'You better tell her,' Bernie said laughing, 'or she'll ask her mother.'

'He is a man,' Pi said, 'who attends to the convenience of the public.'

'What's the public?' Cliona asked.

'You and me and Mrs. Sullivan. All the people in the world. They are the public,' said Pi.

'You must have been kept busy,' said Cliona.

Bernie looked at the little girl, her intent face, and thought how nice it would be to be sitting in the orchard at home with a little girl like that; you could hug as much as you liked. But Sullivan would have to be there too, that was the trouble. She sighed.

'Please stay with Sullivan, Pi,' she asked. He was looking closely at her.

'Why?' he asked her.

'He needs somebody like you, Pi,' she said. 'Sometimes I am afraid of what I did; of so impulsively answering his call. Like this. To be Mrs. Sullivan almost before I know it and not to be able to be Mrs. Sullivan.'

'Why is that?' Pi asked.

'Because there are other people in the world besides us,' she said. 'I know you can ignore them. But if everybody did that, we might as well be living in a jungle.' She sighed. 'I know. Maybe I am very selfish. I don't know. How could I leave Morgan now?'

'Don't worry,' said Pi, patting her hand. 'I'll look after Sullivan for you, until you come.'

'You know what that means?' she asked. 'It's not just Morgan either. There's Sullivan's mother too. Somebody has to look after her. Sullivan thinks you just send money home and that's that.'

'Me too,' said Pi.

'Oh no,' said Bernie. 'You have Lucy. Lucy is very nice. I

see her sometimes and your mother and father. She has effected a great change in their way of living. Lucy is very determined. She is training Badger too. You won't know him when you see him. She will marry him. Will you come home for their wedding? Sullivan won't come home. I know that.'

'Why won't he?' Pi asked.

'He is waiting,' she said, 'until he has a long limousine that plays a tune on the horn.'

Pi laughed. 'I'll have to be there for that,' he said.

She rose. 'I'll have to go,' she said. 'Would you walk to the bus stop with me?'

'I will if I'm not fired,' said Pi. He called in the back door. 'Back soon, ma'am, just going down the road.'

The woman appeared drying her hands.

'All right, Pi,' she said.

'Thanks for the loan of his time,' said Bernie, 'and the loan of your daughter.' Cliona was holding her hand.

'That's all right,' she said. 'Try and make him stay with us. He's like a pixie. One day, pop, and he might be gone.'

'Mammy, what's a public convenience?' Cliona asked.

'We didn't hear that question, Cliona,' her mother said warningly.

'I just wanted to know,' said Cliona.

'Now you do,' said her mother. 'Interesting conversations you have, Pi,' she said then, and all of them laughed.

They said goodbye and they walked down the road to the bus stop. Bernie thought it had been a very peaceful interlude. The child walked between them holding a hand of each.

'Pity you are going,' said Pi.

'Pity you are not coming,' said Bernie. 'You and Sullivan. I wish Sullivan had been born a baker.'

Pi laughed.

She stooped and kissed Cliona as the bus came. So soft and silky the touch of the child's skin.

'You have to kiss Pi Mister Clancy too,' said Cliona.

'I'll do that,' said Bernie, and kissed him on the cheek. Pi flushed a little under the sardonic glance of the bus-driver.

Bernie climbed aboard.

'Some people have all the luck, Jack,' shouted the driver to Pi as he pulled away.

The two of them stayed there waving until the bus had turned the corner.

'Why is Bernie Mrs. Sullivan sad?' Cliona asked.

'Because she has to go home,' said Pi.

'But if she is going home why is she sad?' Cliona asked. 'I'm going home and I'm not sad.'

'You have somebody to look after you,' said Pi. 'She has to look after other people.'

'Is that wrong?' Cliona asked.

'It's not wrong,' said Pi, 'but it's not right either.'

'It's very mixed up,' said Cliona.

'Now you said it, babe and infant,' sighed Pi. 'Now you said it.'

'Have you got everything?' he asked.

'Yes,' she said.

'Pity you can't wait even a few more days,' he said.

'I know,' she said.

They were standing side by side right down at the end of the platform.

'You tell old Morgan he was wrong about Sullivan,' said Sullivan. 'Brother, one day I'm going to surprise that old man. I'll stuff a double Corona in his mouth and light it with a five-pound note.'

'He would love you,' she said, 'if he got time to really know you. If you were to come home and spend a week or two with him.'

'Oh no,' he said, 'not that. You know how I will go home.'

'I'm afraid so,' she sighed. 'But please get rich quick, Sullivan, if that's what you want.'

'I will,' he said. 'Pity about Mrs. Feathers' bed. All empty it will be again. Come and fill it soon.'

'It will have to be next summer,' she said. 'When the school holidays come again.'

'But that's nearly a year,' he said. 'This is autumn.'

'What can I do, Sullivan?' she asked.

'You could leave everything and cling to me,' said Sullivan.

'Please, Sullivan,' she said.

'All right,' he said. 'Anyhow it was myself forced the issue and I am glad. You're mine now. That I can be sure of. I have the contract. Don't let any of those charming boys down there talk you into anything. Remember you have Sullivan's brand on you.' He was only joking. 'Oh my God, Bernie,' he said, reaching for her and pulling her close to him, 'here's the bloody train. Look, you're not sorry I made you do it, are you? You wanted to do it, didn't you? I didn't force you into it. All the upset, the hole in the corner. That's all right, isn't it, just the main thing?'

'It's fine, Sullivan, fine, only worse, much worse, much harder to bear.'

'If only I had the money to take you and old Morgan out of there. It wouldn't work anyhow. I'll make it! I'll do it, you'll see. I'll be home in that town faster than any man would believe.'

'Do, do,' she said.

It was there. The doors of the thing were yawning, inexorably. She had to go in. There was a fellow with a red flag, a whistle in his mouth.

'I love you,' he said. 'Now you are my anchor, holding me down to the ground, in case I take to the air. Always know that. A strong chain forged in heaven between you and me, and nobody on God's earth can break it. You feel that, don't you, Bernie? You know that, don't you?'

'Oh yes,' she said.

He was moving with the train.

'I didn't touch you enough, talk to you enough. I haven't said anything at all that I wanted to say. I'll write it to you.'

'Oh do, do,' she said.

He was running. He kept talking up to her, holding her hand. He didn't know that the people on the platform were laughing at him, pointing him out.

Where the ramp sloped he had to let go her hand as she went higher and he went lower. Then he had to stop and watch her until very abruptly the train went around a bend and he was left on his own.

Now, he thought, she is gone and about ninety per cent of Sullivan is gone with her. But I was right, he told himself, I was right. It was the right thing to do. And now watch my smoke.

20

'Can you make smoke without motion, Tony?' Sullivan asked.

'I don't know,' said Tony. 'Maybe Sil would know. Hey, Sil!' he called. 'Come here, we want you.'

The place was redolent with the gentle fumes of porter and spirits. It was an old-fashioned place, all heavy mahogany, and mirrors with advertisements written in red on them, and oak barrels with brass taps on them, and the brass hoops binding them polished and gleaming. They were in one of the four private compartments; these just partitions of mahogany and opaque glass. One marble-topped table, round, with cast-iron legs on it. The benches were narrow. You kept slipping off them. You had to brace your body with your feet on the floor, or against the edge of the table whose massive weight could easily resist your pressure.

Sil appeared at the counter part. You could just see him from the waist up. Sullivan often wondered what he was like from that down. Shirt-sleeves rolled so that you could see the edges of his woollen vest. Pale muscular arms, the strings of the black apron around his neck. He had thin hair, bulging eyes, a pursed mouth that gave him an air of astonishment. This was because he was never without a cigarette in his mouth. He rarely removed it. The ashes grew on the tip of it and he would blow them off by expelling his breath. If he didn't blow them off, they fell off on to the top part of the black apron. It was well grey now.

'What is it?' he asked ungraciously. 'Your credit is nearly

spun out, Tony. You'll get a pain in your belly if you drink any more of that swill, Sullivan.'

Sullivan laughed. He was drinking a mineral. It fascinated him to see how well Sil could always articulate with the cigarette in his mouth. Sil looked very tough, very hard, but he wasn't. He was the actors' banker, father, mother and bailsman, all in one. 'Yiz have me head grey,' he would say. The walls of the place were full of signed photographs of Sil's former clients, all famous or dead. That's what Sullivan said to him once: 'One day I'll be dead too, and I'll be hung on the wall, Sil.' Sil snorted. It was the nearest he ever came to laughing. If he laughed he would have to swallow the cigarette.

'Sil is doing it,' said Tony.

'Doing what?' Sil asked.

'Making smoke without motion,' said Tony. 'Look at the cigarette.'

'He is making motions,' said Sullivan. 'He's breathing.'

'Would you mind not breathing, Sil?' said Tony.

'If you think I have nothing else to do,' said Sil.

'It's a problem,' said Sullivan. 'How can you make smoke without motion? Can you think of a way, Sil?'

'I can,' said Sil, and told him how, pungently, and went away.

'I'm fed up,' said Sullivan. He was walking almost around the table, blocked each time by Tony's feet so that he would have to turn and go back. 'You know that eagle up in the zoo. He is in a cage. That's what I feel like, an eagle in a cage.'

'Take is easy,' said Tony. 'You're doing all right.'

'I am like hell,' said Sullivan. 'This week sees the end of *The Hazel Shell*. Good success. Fine. Sullivan was wonderful. Fine. Where does that get Sullivan? Next week we'll be back again to "Ah, Mrs. Murphy, me dear woman, and how is yer oul ass?" Where then? The same old piddle on and on forever.'

'That's the best of this racket,' said Tony. 'You never know. Maybe at this minute there's a big producer scouring the town for Sullivan, with the part of a lifetime and a hundred pounds a week to boot. It can happen.'

'It can like hell,' said Sullivan. 'You have to make things

happen in this life. People don't make them happen for you.'

He was getting sick of a routine. Three hours' rehearsal in the morning, lazing all the afternoons, or reading, or slowly, slowly learning how to use a battered typewriter that he had picked up in the Quays for two pounds. Pi put it together for him. It was so much easier than getting cramp in your fingers clutching a pen. But how long would he have to be writing the little red fox jumped over the fecking grey wall or something? And even after that, what then?

'Here, Sil,' he shouted, 'give me another mineral.'

'Don't get reckless,' said Tony, sipping his pint.

Sil didn't come. He was polishing a glass and watching with astonishment the behaviour of two people who had come into his establishment. One was the most beautiful woman Sil had ever seen. She was tall and very fair and wore a tight-fitting blue suit. Her features were regular. Her fair hair was very long and was wound in a bun at the back of her head. It became her, to be able to see the line of her jaw. She half sat on one of the high stools with a leg swinging and she smiled at Sil. Perfect teeth, Sil thought. He bulged at her, and then he had to watch the other person. This was a small squat man with powerful shoulders, dressed all in black with a white shirt and a black cravat, flowing free, and a big black wide-brimmed hat.

He ran the rounds of the snugs impatiently, whipped open the door of one; tsk-tsked when he saw it was empty; opened the door of another to disclose two ladies with shawls and hats on their heads, clutching their pints. The man swept off the black hat, bowed low, said 'Pardon, pardon, dear ladies', astonishing them although one of them nodded her head in a regal fashion before the door closed on her; whipped open the other to encounter the cold gaze of two well-dressed men who abashed him. He closed the door on them and then went over to the place where Sullivan and Tony were, took one look and called, 'Greta! Greta! Come here, darling, and look, just look!'

Sullivan and Tony regarded him with astonishment. He had a round face, with red cheeks and small glinting eyes. Small feet and hands, natty, but giving them the impression that they were standing close to a fair-sized dynamo. Sil saw Greta leaving her stool and walking over to the open door of the snug. Whether he had the impression because he had been talking about zoos a minute ago or not, Sullivan felt for a weird moment as if he was in a zoo and was being inspected through the bars.

'Look at them,' the man said to her as she stood beside him. Tony took his feet off the table, gulped his mouthful of porter and sat up straight at the sight of her. 'Paul and Nitro. Paul and Nitro to the very life. Aren't they? Aren't they?'

'Um-um,' said Greta. She has even got a nice voice, thought Sil, who had appeared behind them at the counter, even if it's only a sort of grunt.

The man walked over in front of Sullivan. 'That burnished copper hair,' he said. 'Those green eyes! That haughty imperial look. The slim body betokening latent strength and energy.' He left Sullivan and stood in front of the gaping Tony.

'My God, the contrast,' he said. 'Look at it! Dark wiry hair turning grey; the sharp nose, the cynically grooved twist to the mouth; down the sides of the jaw. Wouldn't you swear it? See him and the slow burning in the eyes. Built up over so many years. Imprisonment; torture borne with resolution. Some day it will end and I will be the one. Isn't it, Greta? Isn't the contrast perfect? What did I say to you last night?'

'Yes,' said Greta.

'Pardon me,' said Sullivan tentatively.

The man awoke from his inspection. He swept off the hat. He threw it on the table. His hair was almost pure white, prematurely so, one would say from the youngish face. It curled up at the ends where the hat had shaped it.

'I am Oswald Gurnett, gentlemen,' he said. 'No need to express astonishment. You do not know me. You should, but you don't. I find your city provincial in many senses; at least provincial in its ignorance of contemporary English letters. Right. I saw you acting last night, in the play *The Hazel Shell*, a play with an idea, good tense situations, but a little too brutally spiritual for the ordinary run of theatregoers. I liked it. But I liked you more.' He was holding Sullivan's arm. 'You have talent. If I may say so, you have talent to spare. I sat transfixed at your performance. I was in terror when you and our friend here clashed. I was petrified, and only when the great relief of tension came I knew that I had found the answer to a dreadful equation. You, Sullivan, and you, Mahon. You have saved my life, my reason. I want you both.'

Sullivan had no words.

Neither had Tony.

Greta coughed.

'Forgive me,' said Oswald. 'This is Greta. What can you think of her but admire her? Turn around, Greta.' Greta turned. 'Walk away and come back,' he said. She did so. As she returned they saw the twinkle in her deep-sunken blue eyes. Sullivan laughed.

'You see,' said Oswald, spreading his arms as if now they knew all. 'Katherina.'

'Oh,' said Sullivan.

'This is Sil,' said Tony, indicating Sil who was leaning on his elbows on the counter just as bewildered as they were.

'Hello, miss,' said Sil.

'You have champagne?' Oswald asked. 'Good champagne?' Sil was indignant.

'Certainly I have good champagne,' he said.

'A magnum,' said Oswald, clicking his fingers. 'Bring a magnum. Come in, Greta, and close the door.' Greta did so. Tony rose hurriedly to see her seated. She thanked him with a luminous smile. Sil departed, shaking his head as if he had a hangover, although it would be very difficult to surprise Sil.

'I will explain,' said Oswald. 'It is very simple. I am talking about a play.'

'Oh,' said Sullivan.

'Not just another play,' said Oswald, sitting on the one chair the place possessed and practically embracing the table with his arms. 'I have been engaged on this play for, I might say, the whole of my life. It is about kings. It is called *I The King*. It is a dramatic assessment of kingship in our time. There are sixteen scenes in this play. It will be one of the greatest plays ever

written. I say this. I wrote it. Don't be surprised at the assertion. I am not boasting. I am speaking from a position of
strength; knowledge, assessment of the theatre-going public of
England over a period of forty years. I could afford to wait
until now. Why?'

'Why?' Tony asked.

He smacked the table with the flat of his hand. 'Because I
would not perform it until I had found perfection,' he said.
'There are three main characters in the play. There is Katherina the Queen. How long did it take me to find Katherina?
Five years. But I found her. Look at her!'

But can she act? Sullivan was going to say, but didn't.
Brother, if she can act too, she has everything.

'There is Paul the King,' said Oswald. 'I saw you last night,
Mr. Sullivan. I knew. I had a feeling in here, the minute I saw
you put a foot on the stage.' He thumped his heart with a
closed fist.

Sullivan mumbled.

'And when you and Mr. Mahon clashed in that scene, my
heart, my whole heart, turned over, because then I saw you
and him in *I The King*. Nitro and Paul; Paul and Nitro. I
shouted it out loud. Didn't I, Greta?'

'You did,' said Greta.

'People may have thought I was mad,' said Oswald.

'The champagne,' said Sil, putting it down carefully.

'Thank you,' said Oswald, rising and taking it and loosening
the foil with a practised hand.

'The glasses,' said Sil.

'Thank you,' said Greta, taking them from him.

'The money,' said Oswald, taking a white five-pound note
from his pocket and throwing it on the counter, and then he
popped the cork.

Sullivan and Tony were looking at one another. Sullivan
was beginning to feel a bubble of laughter rising in him. As if
all this was something you were hearing about from somebody
else and not believing.

'Drink,' said Oswald, who had half filled the glasses. He held
his own up. 'To the assured success of *I The King*, to me

myself for the genius of persistent searching. To the three of you and your future fortune; success; money; undying acclaim.'

He drank and then he sat at the table again.

'Have you any questions?' he asked as if they knew anything.

'Tell us more about the play,' said Sullivan.

'The play,' said Oswald. 'I have lived in it so long that I am astonished that everybody else in the world doesn't know all about it. How can I describe it? The thought that kingship can be saved; that kingship is from God; how it has been distorted, abused, negatived, and how it can be revived to a surging triumph. You have the King, moulded in an old mould. He must be patched. He must be torn apart. He must be built anew from a fresh cloth. He must be new wine in a new bottle. How can I make you see it? The glory, the empty trappings; the luxurious empty trappings. The wedding. The glittering pageant, empty as the gold and trappings of dead kings in a museum or an Egyptian tomb. And then the resurrection. By Nitro. By the people. All good things can only come from the bones of the people. I'll show you scenes. Burning pyres. Flaming cannons, tattered banners, palls of smoke; the calm and beauty of a peaceful state before the onslaught; the onslaught itself; the forces of freedom converging on the state, and the tragic and glorious, the pent-up, releasing death of the Queen. Can't you see it? The begrimed King, his glorious uniform in tatters, coming down the steps into the advancing spears with the body of the Queen in his arms; her long fair hair sweeping the ground; her pitiful sword-pierced breast exposed to the gaze of the ravening wolves; in her death, in his learning, the fall of an oligarchic kingship; the rise of a new king of the people, purged by death, suffering and destruction; a new seed rising from the purging of the old. How does it sound?'

'It sounds good,' said Sullivan.

'It is good,' said Oswald. 'When I show you the lines they will inflame your heart. When you read what you have to say. Things that you will have to search your soul for. I will drag every emotion in the frame of man from the depths of your

177

heart. And Nitro too. What he has to say. This play is very good. I'm saying this. I know. Not, I may say, since Shakespeare will there be such beautiful things said; will there be such dramatic emotions unloosed. Are you free to come?'

'It sounds good,' said Sullivan. 'What do you think, Tony? Doesn't it sound good?'

'What?' said Tony, who had been exchanging looks with Greta.

'Doesn't it sound good?' Sullivan asked.

'Terrific,' said Tony.

'What did I say?' said Oswald. 'Will you be free in a week?' he asked.

'My God!' said Sullivan. 'Hey, Tony, will we be free in a week?'

'Certainly you'll be free in a week,' said Sil, who was still there. 'Man, it sounds powerful. I can see you in that, Sullivan. Janey, you'll be smashing in that.'

'Out of the mouths of men,' said Oswald. 'How much money are you getting per week now?'

Sullivan told him.

'Street sweeper's salary,' said Oswald. 'Listen, from once you come with me I will give you double that and six times it when we start on the road. Is that good?'

'Is that good!' said Sullivan.

'Is that colossal!' said Sil.

'The end of the week, is it?' Sullivan asked.

'The end of the week,' said Oswald.

'What about it, Tony?' Sullivan asked. Tony was still looking at Greta, trying to find flaws in her. He couldn't do it. Unless her character is all wrong, he was thinking, she is the most perfect person I have ever seen.

'What about it, Greta?' Tony asked, sipping his champagne.

'You'll enjoy it,' Greta said. 'It's really a tremendous piece.'

'What's the answer, Sullivan?' Tony said. 'Didn't I prophesy half an hour ago? What did I tell you half an hour ago? About the man looking for you. Man, was that sharp? About smoke from motion. Here's the motion. I'm in. I'll sign anything. This is ordained.'

178

Sullivan was hesitating. This was unlike Sullivan. Sullivan wasn't a one for hesitating.

'You have my word,' said Oswald, holding his arm, almost piercing him with his eyes. 'You have my word, boy. This play will make you great.'

Sullivan hesitated no more.

'I'm your man,' he said. 'You were sent from the sky. In the name of God let us make smoke.'

21

There were questions. In the dress-circle bar.

'How long have you been acting?'

'All my life.'

'This is your first major part in London?'

'Yes.'

Oswald says: 'All due to me, men. I was the one who found him. Don't forget that, Sullivan. Always remember that.'

'Yes,' said Sullivan.

'Any film experience?'

'Just one,' said Sullivan, thinking of that one. 'Disastrous.'

'Are you married?' His heart was contracting. He was very despondent. He must be tired. All that rehearsing. All that work. Five weeks, and then four travelling a different place each week. Different digs. A hard part. Five costume changes. All that was why he was weary. He would give an awful lot just to have Bernie there in front of him. Saying, 'Hello, Sullivan.'

'Fancy free,' he said. That's what he always said. Apart from the fact that if it percolated through the papers, it would reach home and what would Morgan say to Bernie then? Besides, she was his. He could have at least some secret thing to treasure. A treasure so far away, though.

Oswald said: 'Not for long. Not for long. They will soon be drooling over him.'

Oswald answered questions. Yes, this was his first theatrical venture. Yes, he was the author of *The Isles of Greece* and the well-known *Appreciation of Homer*. How long did it take him to write *I The King*? How long indeed! A lifetime. A lifetime of scholarship and hard work. Would he lose money? Yes, the settings were expensive. It was a big cast. It was costing a lot of money to put on. Yes, perhaps even five thousand pounds. But worth it. He considered it worth while. It would be an unusual theatrical experience for most people. Assuredly. He could make a fortune on it but that wasn't his sole aim. He felt he could put a lot of honour back into the popular theatre. Humbly. He would try. Yes, he was producing it himself. He knew it so well. Every nuance. He could have had a professional producer, but after all he knew a lot about the theatre. He had been criticising the theatre all his life, as they knew, in that good journal. He had learned a lot. Yes, he was pleased with the reception the play got in the provinces: spectacle, blinding colour, magnificent scenery, Shakespearean dialogue, the tensions, the tremendous drama. One or two dissenting notices? Yes, these pleased me. Why, a full paean of praise means nothing. Objections, dissenters, these mean controversy. I am very pleased. I am confident of what I am presenting tonight.

Sullivan again.

'What profession was your father?' Sullivan wanted to double up, as if he had a sudden pain in his heart. Why should all these intimacies be brought into it? What had they to do with it?

'My father was a nurseryman. He loved flowers.' That's for you, Tim. Why should they know how you died?

'Miss Porteous.' That was Greta.

'Yes, I always loved the theatre.'

Greta came the certificate way; Academy of Dramatic Art. More academies, and repertory and back and forward. Nothing spectacular. Oswald told how he discovered her. The casual calling in to the small theatre. An Arts Theatre, holding about thirty people. Because it was a Greek play, he went. Couldn't believe his eyes. That classic beauty; the long flowing white gown. No, Miss Porteous wasn't married.

'Won't be long,' said the reporters and went after drinks.

'Back to work,' said Oswald. 'Back to work, my children. Just that one scene. So little time left.' He bustled out. Sullivan rose wearily.

'Are you tired?' Greta asked.

'Yes,' he said.

'I wish Oswald wouldn't keep going over and over the same speech,' she said.

'That's his way,' said Sullivan. 'Come on.'

She followed him docilely.

The stage was as if it was hit by a hurricane. The great theatre looked small with all the confusion, wrapped in wires, men crawling all over it.

They had to feel their way onto the stage, past lamps on heavy stands and criss-crossing wires, and men hammering and cursing. Mr. Gurnett, do we have to have a rehearsal now? How will we get the stage done? How will we ever be ready? All the old shouts. Sullivan was thinking how confused he was. It was hard work moving in with a lot of new people. Trying to get to know them. Never getting to know them apart from the surface that each presented to the other; wondering what they were like at home, when they got home; what were their dreams (apart from being very famous and wealthy actors and actresses). All that was work too, trying not to hurt anyone's sensitivities. Like Martin long ago with the Great Gregory. He wondered what had happened to Martin. Thought of the way he had dramatically exited from that company; about meeting Pi. Grinned now when he thought of Pi as his dresser. A new job for Pi. Comforting to know that Pi was in the flat getting the dinner ready. Thought of Bernie's orchard. Imagined lying on the grass and having a good long sleep, knowing she was there; that when you opened your eyes you would see her.

'Right, now! Right now!' Oswald shouting. Up at the back. 'You know the lines I want from you both. Greta, please concentrate. You must sense what I desire from them.'

Fifteen times Sullivan said his lines so that she could say hers.

'The first time I saw you, I thought you were a statue stolen from a Greek shrine, classical, beautiful, but as cold as marble.'

She had to answer: 'I was marble, Paul, until your touch awakened me.' And later he had to say: 'The diadem which you wore, Katherina, grubbed from the bowels of the earth by the labours of men, is no longer a crown of gold, but a crown of thorns.'

She had to say: 'To have known you, Paul, was the beginning of life for me; to have loved you was the living of life for me: to die for you would not be suffering but immeasurable glory.'

Oswald wasn't satisfied with the way she spoke them.

Tony leaned his arms on the plush upper circle and watched her. Even under the naked lights she was beautiful. Even with the frown on her forehead. He thought Oswald was trying her too hard. Tony thought that Oswald himself was trying too hard. He looked at the magnificent bits of scenery jumbled on the stage. You could have held a real court in the palace rooms, you could have lived and slept and died in Oswald's bedrooms. You could have fought a real battle on his platforms with real soldiers and real weapons, and cannon alone would have destroyed them. 'I am sick of make-do,' cried Oswald. 'I want magnificence. I want reality. I want solidity.' Oswald could afford these things. He got them.

Yet, Tony reflected, the real art of the theatre is simulating, making a thing appear to be what it is not. But maybe Oswald was right. Maybe people could be blinded with magnificence.

She has a nice voice, he was thinking. Certainly she ought to be a big success with that appearance and a good melodious voice. Tony felt himself bereft of critical faculties when he looked at her. He had never been interested in women apart from typing them to parts in plays and imagining how they would perform in the parts. With her it was different. He envied Sullivan, not because he had the principal part, but because he could be with her so much, touch her, talk to her. My God, I must be mad, Tony thought, after all this time. She was pleasant. She spoke to everybody. She had no side. Wait until she was successful, his mind told him, and you will see then. No, not Greta.

Greta was saying the lines over and over again, with Oswald shouting: 'No, darling, not quite that. You know when you stretch out your hand in the darkness to lay it on a stone and you find a live frog under your fingers – try it that way.'

She tried it that way.

She is not a good actress, Sullivan was saying in his mind. She says it all right. She puts emphasis on the right word. She looks beautiful and maybe that will save her. Beautiful women are rare, and men's critical faculties can be dulled by their appearance. Maybe it's because I'm tired that I am so critical. Oswald was like a gadfly buzzing up the stairs and down the stairs from this balcony to the next. There were people moving scenery, fixing lights, subdued voices off stage. How can we get on with it and an effing rehearsal going on up to the last minute? Voices coming from the walls. Greta suddenly tore at the string of pearls on her neck and scattered them; pulled her hair out of its bun so that it fell in fair cascades around her; raised her head and bit out a filthy word four times, screaming up at Oswald. 'Stop them! Stop them! Stop them!' she screamed. 'How the — hell can I talk or speak or hear? Stop them! You hear!'

Dead silence then. Stage hands appearing from corners like rabbits out of burrows to look at the lips that uttered such a word. Shaking their heads. Greta knelt on the stage, her hair sweeping the floor. Sullivan tried to collect some of the pearls, laughing, thinking, Now she is human.

'Don't mind them,' says Greta. 'They are only Woolworth's, anyhow.'

'But, darling,' said Oswald from way up above, 'that is exactly the way I want you to say the lines.'

Silly, thought Tony. That's not the way to handle her. Wished he could have the handling of her. How he would have gently brought these things out of her, coaxing, squeezing, gently, gently. She was just a big beautiful girl who had to be handled carefully, with caution, to appear as something she was not.

'To-night,' shouted Oswald. 'Until to-night. Go home and rest and pray. That is all.'

Sullivan helped Greta to her feet, feeling close to her for the first time, liking the feel of her silky hair brushing his face as he helped her up; hoping that everything would be good, that Greta would succeed.

They lived in a room in one of the tall houses off a square. A quiet placid backwater, built off a great main road eternally rumbling with traffic. Back here you didn't notice the traffic. There were beech trees planted in the grass of the square. No railings; the railings had gone to war one time, and had never come home. It was filled with fat, fat, London cats stretching in the spring sunshine. All the tall houses were noble and symmetrical. Long ago it would have been a plush place. Sullivan would close his eyes and imagine it, when these houses were homes of the wealthy, with carriages and gaslight and tween-ies. Now all the houses were divided into flats, or used as boarding-houses. Hardly any of the windows were painted the same colour. Outside the doors prams were parked, and go-carts and bicycles, and auto-cycles and small motor-cars that had seen better days. Sullivan often thought of the look that would come upon the faces of the original owners if they were permitted for a time to come back and view their square. He could see that look on their faces.

But it was a friendly place. You got to say hello to people; to the coloured students, and the office workers, and the friendly prostitutes who patrolled at the top of the square where it went out on to the main road.

He climbed three flights of stairs to their room. It was a very big room with two beds in it and room for four more, a beautiful, wasteful Georgian fireplace, settee, chairs and a table. It was a beautiful ceiling, but spoiled at the far end where the room was partitioned for a bathroom and a linen closet.

Pi was bending over the small gas-ring. He was stirring things in a pot. He was looking over his shoulder, grinning, as Sullivan came in. Sullivan thought how good it was that Pi was there. Pi didn't give a tuppenny damn about the theatre. Pi didn't care if Chekhov had never lived, or Shaw or Ibsen. He could sit and listen to all the usual claptrap of the outsiders, the hangers-on, who would talk theatre until the cows came home. They didn't have to work at it for a living.

'Smells good, Pi,' he said. He threw off his overcoat and went over and lay on the bed. He sighed.

'How did it go?' Pi asked.

'Oh, fine, fine,' said Sullivan.

'Are you very depressed?' Pi asked.

'Yes,' said Sullivan.

'It will probably be a great success so,' said Pi.

'It should be,' said Sullivan. 'They are certainly getting everything in it. If this succeeds, Pi, we'll be rolling in money. You know that?'

'What will you do with it?' Pi asked.

'Don't know,' said Sullivan, 'but, boy, we will be rolling in it. No more need to make do. No worry about the rent. No cold breath of the wolf on the back of your neck. Heaven!'

'Hum,' said Pi.

'Thinking of Duke Street,' said Sullivan. 'Nice to be home for a while in Duke Street. Just for a while. Going up to Morgan Taylor's for a pennyworth of apples. Batting at the door. Door opens. Who's there? Bernie is there, in a white dress, looking at you with clear eyes. Saying: Come in, Sullivan. Welcome home, Pi. How would you like that, Pi? Eh?'

'I would like that fine,' said Pi. 'That would be good. Let's do it, Sullivan. Let's pack up now and go home and do it.'

'Nearly would, Pi,' said Sullivan. 'Very nearly would. But not now. First we have to raise the knocker on the door of fame and fortune and let it fall. After that. After that maybe.' He sighed again.

'You know, Sullivan,' said Pi, stirring away at the appetising stew. It was all out of a tin, mushroom soup, beef, kidney, carrots and potatoes. 'There's a woman down in the street below and she has triplets. Saw them over in the Park a couple of times. Janey, you should see the pram. It's a big wide pram. You should see the three kids side by side in this pram. Three fat bouncing babies all dressed in blue. Wonderful to see people's eyes brightening up when they see this sight. Nice people too. Her husband is very proud of the three. I do all things well, he says, laughing.'

There was no sound from Sullivan. Pi looked up at him. He went over to him. Sullivan was asleep. Pi looked down at him. His face was pale. There were blue circles under his eyes. You poor old bastard, Pi said silently to him, wasn't it a pity you ever had to start reading Shakespeare in order to cure your stutters? That fixed you. But then he would have gone that road anyhow, he supposed. He thought of the pace; theatres, rehearsals, touring, different digs, clashings of temperaments; the fabulous striving; living on nervous tension and worry, and all for what. To get to the top of the tree. Well, you got to the top of the tree and where did you go from there? Suppose you put the same amount of sweat and talent and energy into some other profession, where would you end up? Maybe in jail, Pi thought, chuckling, and went back to his stew shaking his head.

When he woke him for the meal Sullivan had beads of sweat on his forehead. He was shivering.

'Oh God,' he said, sitting on the edge of the bed, shaking his head, 'now for another first night.'

He remembered very little of it afterwards. He remembered Oswald resplendent in dress clothes, looking a different person; being introduced to some of Oswald's colleagues, vague, untidy men who spoke Johnsonese and seemed completely out of place amongst theatrical people. Oswald saying: 'You will take them by storm, and after this a series of more great plays stretching away into infinity.'

The horror of his first words; the fear that haunted him, even now, after all his experience, that his words would turn into stutters, that he would leave the people in the theatre molten with embarrassment for him; but his words came out clean: *So you are Katherina. You surprise me. I expected a child and I see a beautiful woman. We will walk in the garden where the sunlight will be your rival. No other.*

After that, so many costume changes, he didn't have time to

think about how is it going, or what do they say. No time for the relayed rumours.

After that, a horrible moment. When he was with Tony. It seemed to him that Tony had a sardonic gleam in his eye. Why should he notice that? *What can you give us beyond assurance? Why should we choose life at your hands when we can embrace death to our own advantage? You are so wrong. In the end of kings you see the beginning of new life. When I think of the end of kings, I see rivers of blood flowing over the plains that are filled with the bones of the people; the poor grinning skulls of democracy crying to the sky.*

Normally he would build a picture in front of his mind's eye. He would see each picture as he described it with his mouth; and know that out of his unselfconsciousness would come sincerity: that by convincing himself first he had the power to convince the people who were listening to him. Now suddenly pictures refused to come, and he found himself listening to his own words in cold blood; a desperate moment of blind panic; his brain shouting: clichés, clichés, clichés, after each sentence. He didn't know what held him from running from the stage, with what desperate endeavour he forced his mind to look at the meaning and not the words; and then he was flooded with calm again and could finish the scene: *I may die, Nitro, but when I am dead, you will be only half alive. You are not fighting for a cause; you are merely fighting me, and when I am gone you will have no cause and you will be left alone, and then they will destroy you and reap the benefit of your years in prison and city sewers. If blood is all that will resolve it, then blood let there be, but remember when you shed the blood of a king you are sending tears rolling forever down the corridor of time. You have two minutes to get back to your rabble.*

After that when he changed again he said to Pi: 'This play is a failure, Pi. I know it.'

Pi said: 'Relax, Sullivan. Every play you say the same thing after the second act. I know you.'

'This time I know,' said Sullivan. 'I really know.'

He didn't know of course. How measure applause? There

was prolonged applause. How know in the middle of beautiful gowned ladies, elegant gentlemen, drinking champagne?

You don't know, until you get the papers, Sullivan, and they walked the silent streets, the three of them, Sullivan, Tony and Pi, until the delivery vans rattled and their fate was clunked at their feet.

22

Sullivan had never been beaten badly, physically. One time he remembered watching a fight between two men at the Docks. One of them was very big and drunk. The other was butty and very angry. He got the big man down and before he could be restrained he kicked him three or four times under the ribs with his heavy hob-nailed boot. Watching this, Sullivan had winced each time the heavy boot went home.

He felt himself now as if he was being kicked by a heavy boot in the stomach. It was almost physical. He would bend forward and groan and then straighten up and run his hand tightly over his head, grinding his teeth.

Pi was sitting on the window stool watching him, saying nothing.

Tony was half lying, half sitting on the settee, watching him.

'No,' said Sullivan, 'I won't believe it. It couldn't have been that bad.'

'It wasn't good,' said Tony. 'You know that. You must have known that deep down in you all the time. I knew it the first day I read the script.'

'Then why did you go on with it, tell me that?' Sullivan asked.

'Committed,' said Tony. 'You can't go back on your word. What does it matter anyhow? We had fun. It was a change. I wanted a change.' Also he wanted to be near Greta. He wouldn't tell Sullivan that. But that was part of it too.

'Why didn't you tell me?' Sullivan asked. 'Why in the name

of God didn't you tell me? How could I have been so blind!'

'I tried to tell you,' said Tony. 'You wouldn't listen. You read the script too.'

'Only my own part,' said Sullivan. 'It seemed good. It seemed full of meat; full of drama. But was I that bad?'

'You were as good as you could be,' said Tony. 'You tried too hard. You try too hard with something mediocre and you are only showing it up, to make it fall. And you fall with it.'

'Oh, my God,' said Sullivan groaning, sitting on the bed, covering his face with his hands.

'You think you are bad,' said Tony. 'Look what they did to Oswald. Mediocrity; pretentiousness, stick to your last; ponderous rumbling settings; boredom; messages; vague philosophy; and the fellow who said: Gurnett, go back to sea. Think of the collapse of his dream and what it means to him. You only got panned as an actor. You can rise again. Oswald was just blotted out.'

'Damn it,' said Sullivan, 'he deserves to be blotted out, writing tripe like that.' He saw the protest on Tony's face. 'No, no, I'm sorry. I didn't mean that. I'm sorry for Oswald. It was a tough break. But I was relying too much on this. All right, I confess it. I didn't think it was so wonderful but I thought that I, Sullivan, the great Sullivan, could pull it through, by my own power. What an ego! Well, it's bust now, anyhow, and be damned to it.'

'We're going to have a visitor now,' said Pi, looking out of the window. He saw the figure of Oswald coming out of the taxi. He looked very round and squat from this height. He paid off the taxi, looked at the number on the door, was baulked by one of the fat cats stretched across his path. He put out a polished shoe and he kicked the cat in the belly; not a hard kick, one of impulsion. Pi had to laugh at the outrage of the cat, who spat and raised its fur and walked away on tight legs.

'He kicked a cat,' Pi reported. None of them moved. They traced Oswald's coming. Only the bottom flight was carpeted. The other two were covered in linoleum, so they could listen to the tap-tap of his feet on the stairs. Then he flung open the

189

door. His eyes were gleaming. He spread his arms.

'Louts; morons; imcompetents; nincompoops; gutter merchants; boors and blatherskites, that's what they are!' he said. He closed the door behind him and leaned against it. 'You read what they have done to me?' he asked. 'You read what they have done to the drama? A death-blow! Let them go back to their farces and drawing-room comedies and inanities and disguised leg shows. Look what I gave them; something they have been crying out for for many years, and what do they do to me? They crucify me! They drag me into the market-place and pelt me with ordure. Who could imagine that the London of Shakespeare would sink so low?' He sat on a chair. He looked at Sullivan. Sullivan was looking at him apathetically.

'For what they did to you, my boy,' Oswald said, 'I am sorry. I gave them talent and they threw it back in my teeth. You will rise again, never fear, and I will rise again too, have no fear of that.'

'Tell me something, Oswald,' said Tony, 'just one thing. Before you came over and discovered Sullivan and myself had you shown the scripts to any actors over here?'

'Certainly,' said Oswald. 'I am not altogether a simpleton. I know that in order to put over a good work you must have an established name. But most of them were busy. They were engaged on films or rehearsing for other plays. They couldn't accept and I was glad. Then I saw Sullivan. Believe me, Sullivan, no other actor on the face of the earth could have done Paul as you have performed him. No matter what they say, to me you will always be Paul. You put flesh on my dream.'

Sullivan smiled wanly.

'But what they did to Greta was unforgivable, unforgivable!' said Oswald. 'I am strong, you are strong, we can fight back. But that girl. Their sneers were unforgivable. How could they? That wonderful scene! Sullivan walking down the steps with her bloodstained body in his arms; her breast bared to the vulgar gaze, she in death. I tell you every single time I saw that scene the tears came to my eyes. What happened? What kind of prosaic minds have they? Who will ever explain it to me?'

Tony's heart contracted, thinking of Greta and what they

had said. She was inexperienced all right, but it would have taken great genius to have carried off some of the scenes she was saddled with.

'So what are you going to do, Oswald?' he asked.

'Fight,' said Oswald. 'I'm going to fight them to the last penny I have, and I'll tell you something, the people will be on my side. You'll see. No matter what they say, the simple plain common people are going to besiege that box-office.' He sat down again. His hands drooped, upturned on his knees. 'It's a blow. I have to admit that. A dream of a lifetime. A man fashions a dream, piece by piece, bit by bit, like a mosaic, each separate piece nothing of itself until the whole is revealed. I think of all that, how I did it, and it should have been acclaimed. I swear if there was any justice at all in the world it would have been acclaimed. Ah, what they did to me! I must say, I am sad.'

Pi felt very sorry for him anyhow. His face looked old, almost haggard. The red cheeks were fine-drawn with purple lines; the great shoulders were slumped.

'Cheer up, Mr. Gurnett,' said Pi, 'the buses are still running.'

Gurnett straightened himself up. He laughed. He got to his feet.

'How true, Pi, how true!' he said. 'The buses are still running. And we will run too, ahead of those literary murderers. You'll see. You have to put your faith in the people. Watch the people. Well, I'll go. One must face them. One mustn't hide one's head as if one were ashamed. One must be seen wherever it is customary for one to be seen. No skulking behind the arras. Let our light shine in the open for all to see, and let no man say that we are dismayed. Thank you for the comfort you have given me. The support. All will be well. You'll see. I will be vindicated by the people. Until to-night.'

Then he was gone.

The three of them kept looking at the closed door.

'The poor little bastard,' said Tony. 'He's like a child who had built a cardboard castle and somebody knocked it down on him.'

'And me with it,' said Sullivan. 'I was up on the loftiest pinnacle holding the flag.'

'I'm going out to get a little drink,' said Tony. 'I will see you to-night.'

'And you came well out of it, Tony,' said Sullivan. 'How is it that you came well out of it?'

'Ah, the old dog for the hard road,' said Tony. 'That's something you have yet to learn, Sullivan. You have to learn how to duck. Trickery. Dodging missiles. Throwing away. You could have thrown away half your part instead of dishing it out fully and your heart with it. Where there's no blood the heart runs dry.'

'Goodbye,' said Sullivan sourly. And Tony went.

Sullivan wished with all his heart that he could hold back the night. That was impossible. The thing you don't want to face always rushes on you like an avalanche. You think of it. All pretence of success is snatched away. A thing is exposed as a failure. That should be the end of it. But actors have to conquer their feelings of helplessness and hopelessness and present their show as if it was the most successful thing that ever happened; raise their hearts from their boots, and play.

Oddly enough, it wasn't nearly as bad as he had expected it to be. Written on the notice-board were three chalked words, FIGHT! FIGHT! FIGHT! That was Oswald. Oswald appeared. He went to each one of them. He encouraged them. He pleaded with them. He soothed them. He spoke about the all-conquering people until they had visions of millions of the little people from all over the country marching on their theatre to book the place out for five years.

In the event there were only about forty people in the house, all told, and half of these were deadheads, complimentary tickets. Once it got under way, a feeling of light-headedness seemed to take hold of all of them. It seemed as if the ends to which they had been reduced caused them to cast off their masks and be themselves. You know how people will behave in success, all slightly drunk with the heady wine of flattery; eyes shining; feelings bubbling; glittering eyes mostly downcast; the quippery; the knowledge that for a certain foreseeable time they had security. But now the struggle to make the best of a bad job made them feel for each other for the first time; to help each other; to commiserate with each other; even between scenes to be able to quote the bad things which had been said and to talk without malice. To-morrow the blame would be apportioned, to everybody but yourself. But to-night it seemed as if they were all spiritually, companionably and unexplainably uplifted in the midst of disaster. It was a good feeling. And Sullivan unaccountably enjoyed it, even if he knew that it was a temporary thing, that tomorrow or even late to-night might see the end of it.

Of them all, Sullivan felt most sorry for Greta. She had been badly handled. From none had she got praise; from all blame and barbed jeers. Had she been in any other part, her beauty might have been the saving of her, but in this particular part she had been an outstanding target. And her final appearance, bare-breasted, blood-spattered; this to Oswald should have been the petrifying climax of his play, and somehow it turned out as something to jeer at, a sort of hopelessly futile and insulting gesture to a bored and bedevilled audience.

So Sullivan nurtured her. He smiled at her, and when he touched her on the stage felt genuine love for her, because behind her eyes you could see the hurt and bewilderment, and when in the end he had to carry her down the steps, and felt the way her body was shrinking from that indignity, he walked down the steps defiantly, daringly, demanding respect from the people gazing unfeelingly on her beautifully modelled breast; and in a nebulous sort of way he felt that he had won respect for her.

It's odd how deserted the back of a theatre can be when the play is not a success. Nobody wants to be in at a death like this, Sullivan thought as he dressed himself for the street. Corridors empty; no loud voices coming from the dressing-rooms; more like a lonely house after the corpse is buried.

He was walking by Greta's room. The door was open. She was dressed to go out. Just putting on earrings. Her face was wiped clean of grease-paint. She hadn't bothered to put on ordinary war-paint. All her defences were down, he thought.

He went in to her. She was completely alone. She might have had a contagious disease.

'Are you going home, Greta?' he asked her.

'I am,' she said. 'I am very tired.'

'I will go with you,' he said suddenly. 'Do you mind if I go with you?'

Her eyes widened.

'You don't have to be that sorry for me, Sullivan,' she said. All Sullivan had ever been to her was Hello, Good-night, How are you this morning, Greta?

'I'm sorry for myself,' he said. 'Let's share our sorrows.'

'We can do that,' said Greta.

They walked out. Pi was locking Sullivan's door.

'I'll be home after you, Pi,' said Sullivan. 'Seeing Greta home.'

'Oh,' said Pi. 'All right. Goodnight, Miss Porteous.'

'Goodnight, Pi,' said Greta.

They walked away. Pi looked after them. Greta was nearly as tall as Sullivan. Pi hoped that Sullivan knew what he was doing. Pi was sorry for Greta too, but he wouldn't go home with her. Not that she would have wanted that anyhow.

They walked. She didn't live very far away. It was a fine evening. Most of the heavy traffic was gone.

'It was very bad, Sullivan,' said Greta. 'Why were they so cruel? I didn't write the play. I only tried to do as well as I could. Weren't they very cruel?'

'They have licences,' said Sullivan. 'Wherever people pay money to see something, they are licensed to criticise.'

'But so cruel,' she said. 'I must be so very bad, very bad.'

He held her arm. To console her.

'We were all bad,' he said. 'To the lot of us the blame for it. Not you alone. You mustn't take it so much to heart, Greta. Just think how few people read reviews anyhow. There is no need for us to squirm as if the whole world were watching our failure.'

'I thought I was quite good, too,' she said. 'That was the trouble. Not wonderful. Just quite good; that the next chance I got I would be really good. I never expected to be held up like that, examined, wrung out, jeered at and discarded.'

'It's not that bad, for God's sake,' Sullivan said. 'It's happening all the time, all the time. Things cannot be good forever. Even those who are up get rapped. Wait until the next time.'

'There won't be a next time for me,' said Greta. 'After a roasting like that, there will be nothing left of Greta Porteous.'

'You mustn't say that,' Sullivan said. 'My God, if everybody said that there would be nobody left to act at all. Everybody gets it.'

'Not this way,' said Greta. 'Not the way I got it.'

He thought how wrong it was that some of her friends hadn't called for Greta that night, taken her out somewhere, cheered her up. He didn't know enough about her, how she felt, what she read, to be able to help her.

She lived in a small flat near a church. It had a blue door with a white knocker on it. Inside it was tiny, just two small rooms with a kitchenette. She switched on the electric fire. She sat on the small settee, resting her head in her hand, looking at the reddening bars of the fire. She looked very forlorn. Sullivan felt very sorry for her. He sat beside her, put an arm around her shoulders. 'Don't be so bleak,' said Sullivan. 'I tell you it will work out all right. You'll get by.'

'I will,' she said. 'But in what way? I doubt if it will be the theatre.' She turned and faced him. 'I'll be sorry that it's over with you, Sullivan. I liked acting with you. You were always kind to me. I know I'm not very bright, but I'm not dull, either. I know when people talk over my head as if I wasn't there. Like a decorative piece of furniture. You never did that.'

Sullivan had been closer than this to Greta before. But somehow that was different. That was when she was somebody else. He could talk to her, handle her, kiss her. It wasn't meant. Now he was close to her, her blue eyes regarding him intently. He was holding one of her hands. This wasn't the same. His mouth dried up. What have I let myself in for? Did I seek this of my own accord, because I am hurt myself, or what? He was suddenly conscious of her skin, of the fair almost luminous hair in the light of the shaded lamp, the glow of the fire.

'Oh, Greta,' he said. 'How could I be anything but kind to you? What harm do you do to anybody, just being beautiful?'

'I don't make passes at people, either,' she said. 'I like you, Sullivan. It's always they who makes passes at me. But don't be sorry for me. I don't want you to be sorry for me. And I'm not Katherina. Not any more. I'm just myself. Don't stay if you feel sorry for me.'

'I don't feel sorry for you, Greta,' said Sullivan, amazed at the hoarseness of his voice, and he held her and kissed her. He marvelled now at how many times he had kissed Greta before. It could have been the kisses implanted on a statue. But this was real. This was real flesh and blood, and the bell shrilled.

They came apart with half-closed, clouded eyes.

'That's the door,' said Greta. The bell shrilled again. 'I'll have to go,' she said and she rose. He heard voices and then she came back and Tony was with her. Tony standing so straight and clean that Sullivan knew he was nearly drunk.

'Pi told me you were here with Greta, Sullivan,' said Tony. 'I wanted to see Greta.'

So Pi told you, Sullivan thought, ready to get mad at Pi, but then he saw the way Tony was looking at Greta, and his heart sank. Why, Holy God, his mind said, Tony is in love with Greta. Tony! Why? How? Where? Feeling sorry now for Tony. What hope had Tony? It wouldn't do. How could a thing like that work? Tony was not that way.

He rose.

'I was going, Tony,' he said. 'I was trying to cheer Greta up.'

'Greta doesn't need to be cheered up,' said Tony. 'She's all right. I'll tell her what's wrong with her. I'll cure her.'

'Goodnight, Greta,' said Sullivan.

She saw him to the door.

'Will I see you again?' she asked.

Sullivan held her hand, looked closely at her.

'No, Greta,' he said. Couldn't tell her that a shadow was standing beside him. Greta couldn't see this shadow. The name of the shadow was Bernie. Sullivan felt sorrier about her than he did about Greta or Tony or himself or anybody.

He walked home with her, explaining it to her. I didn't know. Dangerous? I know. But my morale so low, so kicked about. You have to have somebody soft to comfort you. You should be here. I should have been able to go home with you, and tell you everything, the way I feel; the mad anger boiling in me. They can't do this to Sullivan. And cringing the next minute because they have. How can I fight back? Where am I going to get the courage to fight back, and if you had been here, where you should be, where it is your duty to be, it wouldn't have happened. Greta, I mean. That was just temptation, and I was inclined to fall, for comfort, so it is really your fault. And that's the principal function of a wife, to take blame, so Bernie took it.

Tony Mahon's heart was a large ache as he sat and looked at Greta. She no more felt for him than she would feel for a cat or a dog or a street beggar to whom she might throw a copper. He was just somebody to her. This he knew. And if he was to get on his knees and declare his love for her, he would just cause her mild surprise.

So he said: 'Don't mind what they say about you. You can be good. You are beautiful. All you want is somebody to present you in the right way.'

'Who?' she asked.

'Damn it, I would do it,' he said. 'I could work on you and make you something big, not great, but big.'

'And who are you?' she asked.

That's right, who am I? Nothing. To make you something, you have to have more than nothing.

'I'm just a fellow who loves you,' he said. 'No money, no job after to-morrow. Just a fellow. Celtic, don't know where I am going, but I could build you.' He is inarticulate. Not always that way. But the moment of his life most important to him and he is inarticulate. 'Never said that to a woman before. Never will again. Hope you understand.'

'I think you have had too much to drink, Tony,' was all she said. 'I think you should go home.' She said it softly, kindly.

Tony laughed.

'There it is,' he said. 'I said it. And that's the end. Never thought I would say it in this life. Because too perceptive; see too closely under the skin of people. You are perfect to me. You are without flaw. Not bright. But kindly. And no love for Tony in those bright eyes. Ever, hah?'

'You must go home,' she said.

Tony left her. No more words. Weeping outside on the pavement although no tears. Can any man explain that? A thing like that happening to him. Why after all the years? And why should he have been such a fool? She was alien to him. Different background. Different way of thought, of life. Never was it possible that they should get on common ground. Why?

'Tony Mahon is in love with Greta,' said Sullivan to Pi. 'Oh, the poor devil. The poor unfortunate devil.'

'Why?' said Pi.

'Can't you see?' Sullivan asked. 'Even if she loved him, which she never could, there would be nothing ahead for him but misery.'

'Maybe he would be happy being miserable,' said Pi.

Sullivan was disgusted with him and went to bed.

23

Sullivan cursed, pulled the sheet of paper from the typewriter and threw it away. That was small satisfaction. He would have to pick it up again and get rid of it. The room was very small. A curtained recess hiding a wash-basin and a gas stove; a shaft of sunlight blinding on the once white lace curtain. It was a room with a view: of the backs of tall higgledy-piggledy houses, some fire-escapes, window-pots, and washing on lines or hung from windows, and begrimed brick walls festooned with big pipes and small pipes and middling-sized pipes.

Sullivan laughed and paced the room. It should be good atmosphere for the play he was trying to write. About the people of Duke Street. The *Street of Anger*, he called it in his play. His father was there, big and broad and kind, and his mother and Mrs. K. and Mrs. B. Trying to show the colour and action and drama and movement of the people of the street who worked for a living and sought for distraction after work in the drama of their own lives. He would too; he would get it yet. Time, it took, time. And you would want to be a little free from care. In three months he had worked two and a half weeks. Two weeks at two plays; just suburban rep, and three times on the radio. Fine. Not even enough to keep the wolf from the door. Actors were tuppence a dozen. Very many unemployed. Agents' books filled. What was he? Just another Irish actor. What could he boast about? Oswald Gurnett's play. They were willing to stand up and chat to him about that with reminiscent smiles, but he didn't get a job out of it.

Which set him thinking about Oswald. Thinking of Oswald's great promises to them. Before they came. And all he did was to reduce them to a metropolitan Duke Street. Sullivan put on his coat. He looked fairly well in the grey suit. It was well pressed by the mattress of the bed. His white shirt and red tie made him look as if he was only living down here in King Street to soak up atmosphere. King Street, Duke Street; well, at least we are going up in the world. Why shouldn't he go and see Oswald? Oswald still had influence. Maybe a word from him to somebody. He had always been in the know. He still had power. Not that Sullivan liked asking anybody for anything, but he was so low now; what had he to lose? He didn't like living on the few pounds Pi was making. Pi was back in the gardening business. He actually liked it. He looked well on it. You could always get work as a gardener. Sullivan thought it was a pity that he had no love for gardening. How much better off he would be! He locked the door after him and went into the street. It was a very narrow street, with tall houses. If you half closed your eyes and peered at it you might be in Pepys' London. One or two Italian restaurants in cellars. Shops with small cluttered dusty windows. The sun managed to shine on one side of it. It smelled of roast chestnuts and olive oil and garbage.

He walked out of it briskly. It was just a few minutes to one of the thronged circuses. He was greeted by one or two people standing at their doors. You couldn't but know one another in

King Street. Fine. Nice decent people, some living on the borderline of the laws. You knew them. They were warmhearted. They could joke, laugh. They were the same in Duke Street and that's what he was trying to get away from, damn it to hell!

Oswald's place was more to his taste. Oh, very quiet backwater, large detached houses. Peaceful, smug with prosperity; large cars lounging outside the railings; window-panes bluely clean. In the days of Oswald's optimism they had been to a few parties in his house. Everything laid on. Big rooms. Carpets, library, lovely furniture, that invited you to feel its ancient polished wood. Discreet. All the things that Sullivan wanted and was determined to have for himself and his family; all there under his nose as if to present him with the way he should be. Not the fish and chips of King Street, dear God!

He was looking forward to being in Oswald's house for a while; sitting in the soft chairs, smoking a cigarette, drinking a glass of wine, looking through the french windows at the sun-drenched garden. He shivered as he rang the bell. He had pawned his overcoat with a lot of other things.

The small manservant in the white coat remembered him, took him through the hall past the modernised kitchen that looked surgical, as if you could have your appendix whipped out while they were beating up the eggs in the electric mixer.

The library was in confusion. There were opened cases on the floor. Oswald was on his knees packing books and little things into them. The floor was littered with the things and the tissue paper he was packing them with. He was in shirt sleeves. He looked up. His face beamed.

'Ah, Sullivan,' he said, 'how nice of you to call! You heard I was leaving?'

'That's right,' said Sullivan, who hadn't. 'Wanted to say goodbye.'

'I appreciate it,' said Oswald. 'Please sit down. Don't mind if I don't get up. We have only two hours to catch our train.'

'Hello, Sullivan,' said Greta then. She had been sitting on one of the high-backed chairs. He hadn't noticed her. He walked over to her, held out his hand, took hers.

200

'I'm very pleased to see you, Greta,' he said. 'You look well.'
She did. She was very elegantly dressed.

'I am going to show Greta the Isles of Greece,' said Oswald.
'Isn't it wonderful? What joy I will have watching them again
through her eyes! It will be just the same as if I were seeing
them myself for the first time.'

'That will be grand,' said Sullivan, looking at Greta.

She looked steadily back at him. Sullivan looked down at
Oswald. He thought he had become thinner. His stomach
wobbled. He could see the pink of his scalp shining through the
thinning hair. Sullivan's eyes said to Greta: No, you are not
going to do this! Her eyes said back: You bet your bloody life
I am going to do it! Sullivan's heart sank.

'How about a glass of wine, my boy?' Oswald asked.

'No, no, thanks,' said Sullivan. 'I really haven't time.'

'How are things going, Sullivan?' Greta asked him.

'Very well, thank God,' said Sullivan. 'Everything is fine.'
He looked at her again. She knew that everything wasn't fine.
Her eyes told him that she had seen through the one good suit.
She had probably pressed things under a mattress herself.

'Will you be coming back to the theatre again, Greta?' he
asked.

'Please don't mention that word,' said Oswald.

'You are not defeated, are you?' Sullivan asked.

Oswald sat on his hunkers and looked up at him.

'Frankly, yes,' he said. 'Every time I think of it, I get a sick
stomach. You have no idea, Sullivan. You are an actor. Whom
do you know in this great city? Who can point you out and
laugh about you? Very few. Not so me. You understand this?
Everywhere I go, I see lurking smiles in the corners of eyes.
Colleagues, friends, acquaintances.'

'To hell with them,' said Sullivan.

'Easy said,' sighed Oswald. 'What possessed me? I had a
good life. People appreciated the little books I wrote. What
came over me, to destroy it all? Flying too near the sun, so
that the wax on my wings melted and I fell to the earth. I don't
like earth, Sullivan. Nasty thing.'

It wasn't pleasant to see the defeat in his eyes. Cushioned

defeat it would be. He had a lot of things to fall back on. He didn't have to earn his daily bread at it. All the same, it wasn't pleasant to see the defeat in his face. Sullivan thought of him as he had first known him, bursting like a bomb into Sil's place to sell them a dream. He sold it to them all right.

'Ah well,' said Sullivan. 'I better go. If you ever write another one, Oswald, don't forget to call on me.'

Oswald looked at him, surprised.

'Do you really mean that?' he asked.

'I do,' said Sullivan. 'I really meant it.' And he did.

'That's the nicest thing anybody has said to me for three months,' said Oswald. He held out his hand. Sullivan hoped sincerely that he would get back his bounce in the Grecian Isles, that he would leave his defeat behind him. Greta would leave a lot more than that behind her, he thought, as he shook hands with her. This time she avoided his eyes.

Oswald saw him to the front door, and waved him good-bye from the steps.

All right, said Bernie, if that is what you want, that nice house and the good living in it, would you exchange what you are, even low as you are now, and be Oswald? Would you be poor Greta? he asked, to tease her. Look, kid, he said, you don't understand. It's the use of the things that counts. If I had the use of them, they would be properly used. See what I mean? You wouldn't be unhappy? she asked. Don't be silly, he said. But he went back to King Street a little more content with his lot and determined to plough on with the *Street of Anger*, and go searching again for jobs in the morning even if he had to put cigarette packets inside his shoes where the holes were wearing in them.

He bought hot chips when the time for supper came. Pi would be home. He cooked a dozen sausages in the pan. He cut the bread and buttered it. There was a lot of shouting in the street. He went to look. There was a game of football going on. Sullivan grinned as he leaned against the frame of the outer door.

Pi was on one side and the bandy-legged chap from the fruit stall was on the other. The teams were made up of nearly all the races under the sun. London boys and West Indian boys, and Italian boys and Greek boys and Chinese boys. The conglomeration was incredible. They were all dressed in the oddest clothes. They could all laugh or frown in the same way, or curse in the same way. The veins in their necks could stand out the same way. It was a very fast and furious game and the ball was a bundle of tied-up rags.

Sullivan pursed his lips and whistled loudly at Pi. Pi looked up and waved his arm, and then got back into the game as the ball came to him. It was more like a battle than a game. It surged up and down the street. Passers-by had a job keeping out of the way. They looked indignant. It literally enveloped one man who came around the corner straight into the mêleé. He was an American; blue suit of light cloth, trousers held up by a leather belt, a conservative tie and a white shirt with a buttoned-down collar.

Sullivan laughed when he was swamped. That's democracy wiped out for you. But then the man emerged from the scrabble like a professional centre forward with the rag ball at his toes. He could run too. The combatants watched his performance in amazement and then with a howl of glee they ran after him and submerged him and passed over him, leaving him sitting on the cobble-stones. He was laughing. He had a wide mouth. Pi paused to help him to his feet to brush him down. The man asked Pi a question. Sullivan saw the surprise on Pi's face, and him nodding towards Sullivan. Then the man saw Sullivan and came towards him settling his tie.

'Not a patch on American football,' he was saying to Pi. 'If that was one of our ball games I'd have a broken clavicle by now or a bust nose.'

Then he was facing Sullivan.

'Sure, I remember you,' he said. 'You're the one. *The Hazel Shell*. Right?'

'Hello,' said Sullivan, his heart starting a slow heavy pound. He was saying: This is good, Sullivan. Always the way. When you are down there is always something around the corner. That's the beauty of it. It is so unpredictable. Only good is going to come from this. I know it.

'I'm Jay Stormer,' he said, holding out his hand.

'Glad to meet you,' said Sullivan. Jay had a hearty handclasp.

'This is Pi,' said Sullivan.

'Hello,' said Jay, shaking hands with him. 'I believe we have met.' He laughed. Pi laughed. 'Let's go in,' he said then. 'What's cooking?'

'Sausages,' said Sullivan.

'My dish,' said Jay as they went into the room. The room was littered with the *Street of Anger*. Sullivan gathered the bits and pieces and threw them on the bed. Jay went over to the pan and took a hot sausage in his fingers and started eating it. Keeping his lips away from the heat of it. 'That's good,' he said. 'I like your sausages. I had a tough job finding you, Sullivan.'

'You succeeded,' said Sullivan in awe.

'Sure,' he said. 'But it was tough. Tracked you from Dublin. Then some play you were in that flopped. No address there. Got it through the Labour Exchange. Nice work, hah?'

'Persistent,' said Sullivan. 'Why?'

'I bought that *Hazel Shell*,' Jay said. 'Going to do it. Wonder if you would come and play the part in it.'

'Where?' Sullivan asked.

'New York, of course,' Jay said.

'But why me?' Sullivan asked.

'Because I saw you doing it,' he said. 'Meant to go around and see you afterwards. But no time. Flying to Moscow the next morning. Back now though. Had a tough job finding you. Will you come? Are you booked?'

'You're not a phoney American, by any chance?' Sullivan asked. 'This is not a gag, is it, thought up by a couple of bright boys somewhere?'

Stormer laughed.

'Look,' he said. 'Don't give yourself away. Bargain, man. Say that you have forty-seven different contracts, and it would cost a fortune to break them.'

'You only have to look around here,' said Sullivan, 'to know what's what.'

204

'You might be a genius,' said Jay, taking another sausage. 'You might be living here because you like it. Some people do.'

'Do I have to say yes now?' Sullivan asked. 'Or do I have to think it over for half a minute before I say yes?'

Jay laughed.

'Look, Sullivan,' he said. 'I'm not a mug. I know you're good. I doubt if anybody could do the part better than you can. I like the play. I want to do it. It may be successful. It may not be successful. I don't know the hell. But it has quality. I like the quality. That's all that's to it. Just to make an agreement, fair to you, fair to me.'

Sullivan's excitement was just steaming up. Caution said to him: This happened before. You were sold a bill of goods before. But he knew *The Hazel Shell*, didn't he? And all right? What was the difference poking around here looking for a job and poking around New York looking for a job?

'I'm your man,' he said. 'You are my man. This is Pi. Pi must come with me. You bring Pi too, and take it out of what's coming to me. That's the only bargain. Is it all right?'

'That's fine,' said Jay. 'I like Pi. Pi and me will get on together. I'll take Pi and show him some real football.'

Pi was lost in this. It was too fast for Pi. Things, Pi was thinking, shouldn't move so fast.

'Fine,' said Jay, taking another sausage. 'Now let's go and have something to eat somewhere and we will hammer out the details.'

'You'll have to wait,' Pi wailed. 'I'm not washed. I'm not cleaned.'

'All right, don't get excited,' Stormer said. 'We'll wait.' He went over and looked out of the window. 'Nice view,' he said. 'For a plumber.'

'Listen, man,' said Sullivan. 'You know the part of *Bart* in the play. Could you use him? You remember the man who played *Bart*?'

'Sure I do,' said Jay. 'Sardonic-looking fellow. Good actor. What was his name?'

'Mahon,' said Sullivan. 'Tony Mahon. Look, he's in a play

right now outside a bit. Will you come and see him? Can't you take him? He's good. How can you get any better?'

'All right,' said Jay. 'We'll go look at him. I'm open. As long as you say yes, I can go ahead.'

'For the love of God hurry up, Pi,' said Sullivan. Pi had to be shameless.

'You know,' said Sullivan, 'this is all like a dream. Things don't happen like this. They shouldn't happen like this. It's all wrong. You're no pixie.'

'That's true,' said Jay. 'What the hell is wrong with it? I buy a play. I want to put it on. I want you in it. I come for you. I find you. That's it. You don't have to be a pixie to be business-like. What's wrong with it?'

'Not a thing,' said Sullivan, 'not a thing in the world.'

Wasn't that always the way things happened? You go down and down but the principal thing to remember is that you must never lose heart. And if you work hard and do something good, some day it will benefit you, like *The Hazel Shell*. Why, maybe even some day *I The King* work would come into its own. And Tony. He always felt bad about having dragged Tony away from a place where he was fairly happy. Into a place where he had found a well of unhappiness and drunk deeply from it.

Sullivan said: 'Whatever happens, whether you get to hate the sight of me, and you become sorry for having sought me out in King Street, whether the play is a failure or a success, I will always remember how I feel about you this moment. You are blood walking into a man's heart; you are steps under a man's soles; you are plankton for a whale.'

Stormer laughed.

'Boy,' he said, 'you've gone all Celtic.'

Pi was ready, and they left. Pi held Sullivan by the coat-tails to whisper: 'Hey, Sullivan, do you know what you are doing? Are you sure what you are doing is right?'

'Get behind me, Satan,' said Sullivan grandly and followed Jay. Pi came after them shaking his head.

They dined in an expensive place. Sullivan revelled in it: the clean tablecloths; the shining cutlery; the unobtrusive service;

the dishes that you could never afford. Stormer was good company. He had been everywhere. He had met and talked with a lot of famous people. They were just crumbs, bums or good guys. He laughed a lot. His eyes were never done darting, watching, taking everything in. Sullivan sat back and enjoyed him. He became used to the feeling of fear departing from him. He didn't allow himself to think that this was only tentative; that it might fizzle away like white frost in sunshine. This has to be, he told himself. Never again King Street. Please God, let us be done with King Street.

It wasn't a good play that Tony was in, and Sullivan nearly crawled under the seat when he saw that Tony was slightly drunk. Maybe others didn't know. But Sullivan knew. Tony all dressed up in a dinner suit, acting in a sort of polite English drawing-room comedy.

'Is this the same guy?' Jay whispered to Sullivan.

'Yes,' said Sullivan. It is the same guy and it is not the same guy. But he was making a good hand of what he had to do. Whatever laugh was in it he was getting it out with skill. He was doing a slightly drunken character in the play, so that the fact that he was really drunk wasn't visible to the audience. Sullivan prayed that it wasn't.

It wasn't either, until the third act, when Tony dried. He dried at a point where nobody could help him. There was panic in the house. You could hear the voice of the prompter. Sullivan's nails were biting into his palms. Tony said: *The quality of mercy is not strained. It droppeth like the gentle rain from heaven Upon the place beneath.* Then he caught the prompt and he went on with his lines. The house relaxed. There were a few titters. Jay Stormer guffawed.

'Quality of mercy indeed,' he said to Sullivan.

'I hope you have it, buckets of it,' said Sullivan. 'He is the best *Bart* you can get. It will make a great difference to him.'

Tony wanted mercy.

The manager was talking to him when they went back to see him. 'You're finished,' he was saying, 'here and everywhere else. There's not another theatre in the British Isles will make use of you. I'll see to that.'

He walked past them angrily. Every cause to be angry, thought Sullivan. Tony himself of old would have been the first to admit it.

'It's yourself, Sullivan,' he said. 'And the brave Pi. You came at an embarrassing moment for me, but all will be well. How are you, Pi? How are you, Sullivan?' He looked extremely decadent, the tall silk hat on one side of his head. Where are you going, Tony?

'Tony,' Sullivan said. 'This is Jay Stormer.'

'Hello,' said Jay. 'You're loaded, boy.'

'I am,' said Tony. 'I am a disgrace to my own principles. Forgive me. You saw the play?'

'Yes,' said Jay, 'unripe corn. I'm doing *The Hazel Shell* in New York. I've got Sullivan. Sullivan would like me to take you.'

Tony got to his feet.

'You chose a bad time to come and see me,' he said.

'Look,' said Jay. 'Do you really have to be like this? Is there a cure for you?'

'There might be one cure,' said Tony. 'A man's trust.'

'A guy is taking a long chance on that,' said Jay. 'Could you cut the corn?'

Tony put his hand on his breast. He bowed.

'If you trust me,' he said, 'you will never have cause to complain of me.'

'You're in,' said Jay.

'Good God,' said Tony. 'I thank you, Sullivan, I owe you thanks. I would like to think that if the positions were reversed I would do the same for you.'

Sullivan snorted.

'Don't be daft,' he said. 'Whose fault is it that you are where you are now? Mine. Maybe you'll have no cause to thank me. Maybe you will be cursing me later on. Maybe I will have done the wrong thing again. What does it matter?'

'Tell me,' said Tony, 'have you seen anything of that poor Oswald man?'

'I have,' said Sullivan. 'He is gone to Greece. He went to-day.' He didn't say anything else although he knew that Tony really wanted to know about Greta. Greta!

'Tell me, Jay,' said Tony. 'New York is in America, isn't it?'

'I believe so,' said Jay.

'Approximately three thousand miles from our present geographical position.'

'Yes,' said Jay, laughing.

Tony put his hand on his shoulder.

'Dear Jay,' he said, 'you're an angel.'

'That's right too,' said Stormer laughing. 'I really am an angel.'

Here we go again, thought Pi, sighing, as they laughed.

24

There came a time when Sullivan's mind almost gave itself up to a state of incoherency. That was when his letters to Bernie became almost scatter-brained. As he told her, there was too much movement; everything was done in such a fever of excitement and drama that no cool, detached attitude could keep up with it. The mind just had to go along hectically or give up altogether.

Too much to assimilate at the one time, that was the trouble. Not enough time to settle down to a strange new way of life; where everything seemed perforce to have to move at a fast pace; where decisions and engagements were made on the phone so fast that you had to run to keep up with them, and no man can move faster than a message on a wire. None of this leisurely attitude of seeing you on Tuesday, old chap, and we'll hammer the thing out together over lunch.

It was a kind of relief to Sullivan to get home in the small hours of the morning to the unpretentious hotel where Pi and himself and Tony had rooms, which they rarely saw. Just to flop on the bed and sleep if your seething mind would let you. Pi was sane enough. He had the pleasure of working as what they called a hash-slinger, serving meals in a pub with a restaurant. The proprietor's grandfather had been Irish and he loved Pi. He questioned him closely all day. He knew more about Ireland and the Irish than Sullivan who read the papers closely. Jimo could go back to the Firbolgs and tell you what way they were dressed and what they liked for their main dish (mainly long pig, Sullivan gathered).

Tony was no worry. He was very sober. He had turned over a lot of new leaves. You haven't been through it, he told Sullivan. You haven't been caught on a stage without words, just because you had too much to drink. I know you were caught without words but that was not your fault. But it was my fault. Like having the ten commandments smashed on your head. All the things I preached all my life. To see them broken there. That frightened him. Another thing, it was so dishonest. Even if the play wasn't good, people were paying to see it. They were entitled to see it done as well as the actors were paid to do it. And what happened? They were cheated. Never again, Sullivan, never again. Tony took to wandering the straight streets in the little spare time he had, just looking at people, he told Sullivan. And the buildings. What monsters! What wonder! The tremendous brashness of man! How the builders of Babel would have envied! The piers on the river and the docks with the great liners, and the beautiful bridges that would transfix you with the soar of them, when they shouldn't have been beautiful at all, they were so gigantic and so slender at the same time. All right, Tony, all right, Tony. Glad that Tony was that way.

Sullivan himself, who never walked a street without looking at the creases on men's faces; that's what gives faces the character they possess. You could almost guess from a man's grooves what life had done to him. The grooves of bitterness or laughter or worry; or the good grooves carved on the face of a man who took fate as it came, weathered it, and pressed on. All these that he would notice, and store away for future use; how a highlight here or a highlight there could reproduce in your own face the remembered lines from the face of a man in a throng. Early on he was like that, walking and pointing them out to Bernie. See him! Or see that! My, there's a beautiful girl! Can you tell her status from her clothes in this strange land where servant girls can look like duchesses on account of the mass producing of the dreams of a cutting artist? You will have to come over somehow, sometime, he would write to Bernie. You will just have to see it, just once, and then go back to your bloody apple trees.

None of that did he have time for in the long run. In the evening too tired; in the morning in too much of a rush.

He remembered just the one time in Jay's office where they had picked the girl.

You go seventeen floors up in the lift to the corner office where a wide window looks down on what could be eternally scuttling beetles. At night it is a blinding fairyland of flashing lights of all the colours in the spectrum captured and contained in glass bottles. It is garish or exciting, or disturbing, or vulgar, or wonderful, as your fancy takes you. Wondering, apart from the practical reasons, if man built so high because like a mountain he could look down way below and feel like a god. Trouble was you had to go down and become small again. You couldn't be a god up there all the time.

Jay is in his office, behind the barricade of good-looking typing girls. He has his feet on the desk sitting back in a swivel chair. You can see a good expanse of hairy leg above a short blue sock. He is talking into a telephone which he holds in one hand and he is shaving himself with an electric razor which he holds in the other. All interspersed with talk, talk, talk, putting down one phone, taking up another as it rings. Sort of legerdemain. 'Lo, Sullivan. Big deal on to-day. Wait'll you see. Charlie, what the hell's the idea? That setting. Don't want to live in the joint. What's it made of, gold leaf? But thirty-three thousand dollars, for that? Sure, I want it good, but not that good. Come over. I have the plans here. Got to knock three thousand dollars off that baby. Hey, Lance, you explain to Sullivan.

Lance, tall, elegant, very long-lashed eyes, almost too handsome to be a man. But charming. He was the director. A calm exterior hiding a well of nervous energy. He has to be good in this one, Jay said. This is probably his last chance. Last three were flops. He wants to redeem himself.

I'll tell you, Lance says. Jay has a girl. I have a girl. Mine is an actress. Jay thinks his is an actress. He could force in his girl but he won't. He's honest. Pity she's not an actress. She looks good. You go over the script with both of them and you decide. Not me. Who am I? What do I know about them? Why should I have to do it? You'll know it, boy. In here, in the actor's heart. It's easy; who do you want opposite you? Jay's girl is not known. Mine is known. She is a name. She comes expensive. Jay will ruin the ship for the ha'porth of tar. Unless we're careful. I won't influence you. Not half, said Sullivan. I won't give any advice. Trot out the girls. Let them do their pieces. It should be obvious which of the two is the best.

Jay is wheedling: Hey, Princess, you read the script. Hasn't it class? What you think of the quality? Yes, that's right. Tough but tender. Certainly it will go. I know it. Look at all the money I'm putting into it. Just want to cut you in for a slice. Say five thousand. Look, don't decide now. I'll be over. To-night. Sure. Tell you all about it. You must meet Sullivan. Yeh, that's right. Wait'll you see. Fine.

Then he is finished shaving and comes soft-footed behind Sullivan, puts his arms around his hips and raises him in the air. Sullivan shouting: Hey! Jay is strong. Jay is full of action. If he is not doing something he is at a loss. He always has a limb twitching.

Don't mind Lance. Wait'll you see Frances. Like a nun out of uniform. That is what we want for this girl. Cool clear eyes of a virgin. Right? If she can act, Sullivan says, thinking of Greta, with the poor part too big for her. She will, Jay says. Voice like water flowing over round stones. Boy, what a girl! She's a bit too big, Jay, Lance says. Fit Sullivan like a glove, Jay asserts. Then he laughs. Hee-hee, wait'll you see Lance's one. Like an unemployed call-girl. Eh, Lance, old boy, old boy? punching Lance in the ribs, Lance riding with the punch casually, as if he has by now become accustomed to them.

212

You're wrong, Jay, all wrong. You want a nun in a play, hire a whore, if you like. If she can act. She will be better. You know that. Canons of the theatre.

The girls are here now, Mr. Stormer, the girl says from the door. Send them in, send them in, Jay says, and goes over to meet them. He puts an arm around the shoulder of each. Welcome, girls. This is Lance. You know Lance and you'll have to fit this other fellow for size. He's Sullivan. Babies, he's your fate. Hello, Mr. Sullivan, so pleased to meet you. Frances and Stella. Frances as tall as himself. Elegant. Fair hair, smelling sweetly. Soft talcumed hands. Stella, not tall, legs spread, bitten fingernails, hair cut across the forehead. Slightly untidy, but good eyes, widened, active. If I had my choice, Sullivan thought, I would take Frances. She looks untouched. Her appearance is so right.

All right, Jay says, rubbing his hands, let the contest commence. Sullivan is embarrassed. Should it be openly done like this? That is Jay's way. Who goes first? All right, we'll take Frances first. You wait outside, Stella. Great chance for you; extra look at the part. Slaps her, keeps his arm around her, closes the door on her, then comes back and sits at the desk, his feet up again, chewing on a pencil

Don't be nervous, Lance says to her. She smiles at him. Thank you. Are you ready, Mr. Sullivan? Yes. Sullivan so embarrassed, wondering why all this can't be done without his being there. Hating to have any hand, act or part in deciding a girl's future.

They do the confession scene, where she tells Sullivan why and how it happened. It is a very tender scene this, almost as delicate as the tendril of a vine, the pollen of a flower. It requires art to say the uncouth things she has to say with an air of supreme innocence, non-knowledge. Frances couldn't do it. She had only said four sentences when Sullivan knew she could never do it. His heart sank. But then he looked at her eyes and he found relief in the knowledge that she didn't know it. She thought she was doing fine. Jay, one pencil bitten through, had started on another one. She played the scene to its end.

Jay jumping over to her, giving her a kiss on the cheek. Grand! Grand! Boy, what sweetness! What purity! Good! Wait outside now, until we have seen the other one. Frances is flushed. She is pleased. She is clutching her script to her breast.

And Stella comes in and walks through it. Practised. Experienced. She knows how to do innocent girls. It's as near perfection as doesn't matter. Sullivan feels she is one with him. All the same, slightly disappointed that this girl, with talent, can appear to be what she is not; can be all things that she is supposed to be to the eyes of the beholder; and that the other girl who appears to be perfect, and looks perfect, can be awkward and unconvincing.

All right, all right, dammit, Jay shouting. That's it. All right, Lance. Get in touch with her agent. She's in. Thanks, Stella says. Not particularly overjoyed. Just knowing that she had no opposition really. Think it will go, Jay? Think this one will go? Why not? Why wouldn't it go? With you and Sullivan. You'll have them sizzling in their seats. Just a wee bit highbrow though, ain't it? Stella asks. I mean, does it get right down in their pants pocket? Angel, Lance says, you leave that to us. You don't worry your pretty tossed head about that. I got to know for how long I eat without doing the rounds again, she says.

Be optimistic, optimistic, girl, Jay says to her. You clear off now, the lot of you. Send that girl Frances in to me. I want to soothe her. She is a nice girl. She will be hurt. I'll take her to lunch.

They left.

I cannot sort out impressions, he told Bernie, because they follow one another too fast. How to sit down and be lucid, I don't know. I like boiled knuckle of Virginia ham. It must be smoked over some kind of scented wood or something. The janitor's wife is going to have her sixth baby and I'm not even a father of one yet. Maybe I ought to chuck all this and work on the other. I think Pi is happy. He seems to have got to know a lot of people in a short time. You know the way. Everybody calling him Pi after a few minutes. You have known Pi all your life. Pi is a giver, that's why. He doesn't

214

want to take anything from you, just to give. No wonder Bo loved him and said that the heart was gone out of Bohan's. Tony is becoming the Tony of yore, slightly grizzled, but the same. That girl did something to him. Falling in love with the impossible. Imagine Tony. Now I think she is really a dream for him. He measures everybody beside her, principally her beauty, and none of them measure up, so he goes around as if he was a child hugging I Know A Secret. He doesn't know what I know. I don't know what he would do if he knew.

Buzz-buzz, like Jay's razor, which always seemed to be buzzing at odd moments and in the strangest places. Big empty theatre to-day, the naked flies looking pitiful in the cold glare of a big bulb. Shrouded seats. Make-belief, a door here and a staircase here and a window here. Avoiding the invisible chalk lines. The charming Lance, still charming but like steel, with his coat off and his shirt-front open. Is it really that time? Well, let's just have that scene over again before we quit. We want this to be good, don't we?

From that to a room, looking out on a crowded street, dust rising off the boards. New coloured chalks on the floor. Imagine this and imagine that. Back again to a gaunt theatre, hateful to look at in the light of day; impossible to imagine it dressed and bedizened embracing a public. Or to a theatre where a success is running; has been running for years. A smug place, sure of itself, knowing its number of booked seats. Dressed the stage is for success, bored; mind this bit of furniture and mind that bit of furniture. Hateful smug doorman. No dust on this setting. Watch for interlopers. This is big time. You ought to be happy to tread the boards. Rub your elbow on the furniture, it might bring the same success to you.

All that and then the trains. Away here. Big barn of a place. Small town. Prissy town. Three-storey building in it looking gigantic after all the others. But homely. You have to throw your voice back to the back of this one. Hotel. Moving in the unfamiliar surroundings of a real setting behind you, real staircase in front of you, lights, effects, properties, hardly recognising the real thing after the using of the make-do. Not so good. Have to change lines here, lines there. They didn't laugh there. They should have laughed. What's wrong? Cut it or point it or throw it or polish it. No rest. Day after day. Matinee, or if no matinee then a rehearsal. Not happy. Had this one from New York last night or the other one. He says this; he says that. Pack up your traps, you are on your way again. To a bigger place. Can't remember it. Lost in the dream. More trouble. Somebody doesn't like the little fellow who is doing the young brother. He is a charming little chap. Always smiling. Good too. But somebody doesn't like him. Not like a dour seducer. Do seducers have to be dour? Anyhow they don't like him. The fellow who came. A mysterious image nobody sees, but who pronounces. The patient is sick; call in the doctor. The play is sick; call in the doctor. So he doesn't like the little fellow. So the little fellow is fired, the last night in this town. Sullivan is sad. What does it matter? He's good enough to do. He has personality. His smile is wiped away when he is cut off. Sullivan is sad. I'm sorry they did this to you. I know they are wrong. But what can I do?

Jay is adamant. He has to go. Wait until you see the improvement. The improvement is good all right. But it means everybody has to work all over again working-in the improvement. Minds dizzy.

One good thing here, he told Bernie. You know Fenimore Cooper. This is it. Stripped trees with black trunks in the snow. Dutch churches with tall wooden spires. All snow. Crisp, crunching under your feet. Air as clear in your lungs as a burst of spring water, but no time.

Another town. Here the pace is intense. The small author is there. He is bewildered. He has three men around him, four men around him, waving arms convincing him; explaining to him; cajoling him. But that wasn't what I meant exactly. You see, I thought... Don't we know what you thought and isn't that what we want too? But you've got to see it through Their eyes. They look at it just a little differently. They wouldn't understand that it is quite what you are aiming at. Do you see? I suppose so. You want this to be a success? Why, certainly, what else? Does any man like to be a failure? Well, that's the way to go. You don't know Them. They are exact-

216

ing; down to earth. It has to be laid on a plate in front of their noses. Not suggested; acted; presented. You see? Yes, I suppose so, well, all right, if that's the way you think it should be.

Grinding, eliding, knitting, bearing down. But that's the way I did it at rehearsals. I know, darling, but the situation is changed. Now it is this way. Can you see? Well, it's difficult. Naturally it is, but to one of your talents, where is the obstacle?

Every last drop of blood, Jay shouts. Squeeze yourself like a lemon. There is so much tied up in this. Not money, which is immaterial, but effort, sweat, talent, team. You see, boy. You see, girl. Soon, soon all this will be over. And you can sleep then every day, imagine, from midnight until eight o'clock the next evening. Life will be sweet. The bank managers will be greeting you with smiles. Give, kid, and to-morrow you will possess.

Last round. Another one fired. The mother. So hard to see her go, when she was so near the magic lights. Blotted out. A replacement in before she knows it. The replacement rehearsed in a hotel room so that the woman won't know and her playing won't be affected. Sullivan's heart being wrung again. Why do they do that? She is old too. Parts aren't coming her way with the fervour and frequency that they used to come at one time. She will have it tough enough now finding another job. When she was so near to those lights.

You learn, Sullivan told Bernie. That lesson. What happens to me in this when I am old? Like Martin long ago. And Gregory. Told you about him. Haunting me now. Will I be like that? No! No! Get it while you are hot and hold on to it. So that you will never be that dependent on them. I walked by a river to be alone. It is a small river in this land of gigantic rivers. It flows through grasslands. The snow is off the grass. It wears a surprised look, the grass, but it is cautious. The snow might be back again. I sit on a seat. A plain wooden seat. The river is muddied up, on account of the melting snow. It carries odds and ends wherever it is going; into another river. That's me too, an odd end, being carried to a great river where I could disappear forever. Might too, if not you to hold on to. Always the feel of your hand stretching out to me, so that I can scratch your palm.

The big place. Swallowing your heart each time you think about it. And it is on top of you before you know where you are. Once seeming so unattainable, now here. An overwhelming challenge. All those lights. All those white lights that come awake in the evening. And Stella's name in big lights and the young film actor who is doing the young brother. Sullivan's name too. Small. Sullivan couldn't care. Just to be done with it; to have it over. Not all full of optimism like that time long ago. Now caution itself. It could be, and you never know and wait until you read the papers. Yes, I know it should, but will it? Afraid to play a poker hand in case you would be toppled.

And yet the basic enjoyment of it. Enjoying the gamble. More like a gamble than any other thing. Almost no sure thing. Making the nerves tingle. Not like put on a play and run it for two weeks and take it off and run another for two weeks. Oh, no. This is the gambler's paradise. The turn of a wrist; two men's enjoyment; the fire of endeavour, one man gambling a lot of money; another man gambling his writing brain; others gambling their reputations; their jobs; their pasts; and their futures.

I did it as well as I could, he would tell her. I forgot where I was, as best as I could. I thought: they are the same as people all over the world. Men have the same hearts and emotions. They are stirred over the same basic things. Their hearts are elevated or amused. They should be lost in that rectangular pageant, moved, stirred, set to thinking. I remember feeling that they were held, at times, that is all I remember. The rest is a haze. Just a haze. I sit here in the dressing-room. The bulbs are hot. I am sweating. I am cold. I am very tired. I feel as if I had walked many miles more than the walk to the hill long ago where I found you covering your face on the green grass. I would like to rub my face in that grass or rub it in the hollow of your neck, but I really am tired now. I feel drained.

And soon, soon, they will be knocking on the door.

25

The knock came.

This was Pi, to put his arms around Sullivan's shoulders and say: 'It was terrific, Sullivan. Honest. It'll be goin' on for years, we'll never get home again, so we won't.'

'Do you really think so, Pi?' very hopefully, longing for the bark to be at rest for a while.

'Janey, why wouldn't I?' said Pi. 'There was Jimo, you should have seen Jimo. The tears were pouring down his face.'

'But dammit,' said Sullivan, 'all you have to do to get Jimo crying is to show him a shamrock.'

'Ah, but he meant it, honest, Sullivan,' said Pi. 'He'll tell you. He says it's the best play he ever saw in his life.'

'How many plays did he see in his life?' Sullivan asked. 'Probably two and this is the second.'

'Ah, don't be like that, Sullivan,' said Pi. 'You'll see. A fella like Jimo is a sort of opinion of the people.'

'All right, Pi,' said Sullivan laughing. 'God bless Jimo.'

Then it was Lance, to clap him on the back.

'That was really good, Sullivan. You were never better than to-night. Never better.' Then he moved back to disclose the man who came in behind him. His voice changed a little. 'This is Philmill, Sullivan. He wanted to see you.'

'Hello,' said Sullivan, holding out his hand. Philmill was tall and lithe. He had blue-black curly hair, brown intelligent eyes which he seemed to keep hooded, except rarely. His complexion was shallow and one side of his mouth was pulled up in a sort of permanent grin. Sullivan noticed him particularly because there was a sort of electricity coming from him, and because the touch of his hand made him look at him more closely.

'You've heard of Philmill,' said Lance.

'No, sorry,' said Sullivan. 'I don't think I had time to hear of anybody. Your fault, Lance.'

'Well, you will,' said Lance. 'Philmill is the one who doesn't miss. When Philmill decides to do a thing it is almost a mathematical certainty that it will succeed.'

'That and a lot of brainwork,' said Philmill, 'and a lot of talent. Lance. Know what that is?'

'He doesn't hire directors,' said Lance. 'You still haven't said what you think of the show.'

'Nice performance, Sullivan,' said Philmill.

'Anything further?' Lance asked.

'Look, Lance,' said Philmill. 'I don't give advice or information free. You know that? What you want me to do, scratch your back? Why, hello, Pi. Glad to see you out of the jacket.' He shook hands with Pi.

'He knows Pi, anyhow,' said Sullivan to Lance.

'Hello, Philmill,' said Pi. 'Wasn't it smashing? The play. You should have seen Jimo. The tears were pouring down his face.'

'I'm sorry I missed that,' said Philmill. 'I really am, Pi.'

'You should have seen him,' said Pi.

'Well, see you at the party, Sullivan,' said Lance.

'Right,' said Sullivan.

'Goodbye, Philmill,' said Lance. 'Don't give anything away for free.'

Philmill didn't answer him. He left.

'Lance doesn't seem to like you,' said Sullivan. Philmill was leaning against the bench, his arms folded.

'I'll sleep,' said Philmill.

'I must go and see Tony,' said Pi. 'Wasn't Tony good too, Philmill? Didn't you like Tony? Janey, when he opened that knife!'

'I liked Tony,' said Philmill. 'That boy is a good workman.'

'I'll be back,' said Pi, and left.

Sullivan and Philmill regarded one another.

'I remember now,' said Sullivan. 'It's up on at least two shows. Directed by Philip Millar. You the one?'

'That's right,' said Philmill. 'I liked your performance. You work well. It's nice to see a good worker.'

'What about it?' Sullivan asked. 'You ought to know. What do they think?'

'It's a turkey,' said Philmill. Sullivan felt as if he had been kicked in the belly. 'What?' he gasped.

'Hadn't you guessed?' Philmill asked. 'If you hadn't, I'm sorry. Maybe I'm wrong.'

'How is it a turkey?' Sullivan asked.

'Ach, hard to say,' said Philmill. 'You just know. It's long-haired stuff. It doesn't go down and tickle the heart. For the campus. This boy will be done on the campus. It doesn't get in among the people and make them hop.'

'You are sure of this?' Sullivan asked.

'What's sure?' Philmill asked, shrugging. 'Listen, don't believe me. I'm sorry. I have been wrong many times before. You never can tell.'

'Don't put in the clichés anyhow,' said Sullivan.

'Boy, why should I come in here like this, and talk my head off? You see the trouble. Could I say: It's fine, it's a success, when it isn't? Thing to do, keep away altogether. But you excited me, Sullivan. You're good.'

'That's a lot of good,' said Sullivan, turning back to the mirror and slapping on cold cream. Then he was determined. 'You might be wrong,' he said. 'With the help of God you are wrong. Damn it to hell, I don't want to start all over again, all over again.'

'Listen, Sullivan,' said Philmill. 'Pi told me all about your adventures. Your trouble. I'll tell you. That London business and now here. It's almost amateur stuff. You don't know. This is a very very hard profession. You have to be in with the professionals. Men who have spent their lives studying it. They know what the people want. And even they go down. You mustn't be downhearted if this thing fails. You'll be all right. People will like you. The same as if it was good. You'll see.'

Jay irrupted upon them then. He was resplendent in evening dress. He was widely grinning. He had a few gorgeous girls with him. They smelled beautiful. They looked into Sullivan's eyes and clasped his hand and breathed at him. He had to smile. Like of yore. Back before. 'You were wonderful, Sullivan.' He thought they were sincere.

'Of course he was,' shouted Jay. Then he saw Philmill.

'Well, you old bastard, Philmill,' he said, going over to him and aiming a punch at him. Philmill dodged. 'Hello, Jay. Big night! Big times!'

'You can say,' said Jay. 'This is good, Sullivan. All the people that talked to me said it was good. We're in, kid. You can start filling the old stocking. A few years of *The Hazel Shell* and you'll be paying corporation tax. Eh, Philmill? You mad? What was the betting Jay Stormer would never get there? Bet you all had your shirt on that. Jay will never make it. I can tell. And there it is out in nice bright lights: Jay Stormer Presents. How do you like that, Philmill?'

'How much an inch did it cost, Jay?' Philmill asked.

'Hug yourself,' said Jay. 'How you wince, you boys, to see a client like me making it. Just on his dough, you say. A lot more than that too, Philmill. It's only a trade. I can buy my way in and after that I can hold it, you'll see. And provide quality.'

'Boast away, man,' said Philmill. 'I wish you luck.'

'You can come to the party,' said Jay. 'How is that, Philmill? You come and we'll celebrate together. Will you?'

'Fine,' said Philmill.

'Come on, girls,' said Jay. 'I have other men for you to meet. Sullivan is only a perch in comparison. Eh, Sullivan? Good man. You did a good job. I knew I was right to follow you to that place. That was good. Remember that? The football. Took Pi to see football. Gee, Pi gets so excited. He nearly beat in two of my ribs.'

'Goodbye, Mr. Sullivan,' the girls said, their eyes wide. 'See you again, Mr. Sullivan.'

They were gone. Sullivan sighed. 'It's nice to get a bit of that lovely water flowing over you,' he said. 'Just a little. Restores the morale. Like oil on a wound. Not like you, Philmill.'

'Lap it up, Sullivan,' said Philmill, laughing. 'Make the most of it. Rub it on.'

More came. Mostly girls, Sullivan noticed. If their menfolk were with them, they didn't gush at all. They were non-committal. Just shook hands. Didn't talk about the play.

It was the same way over in the hotel room. There was a

table well laden with food and drink. But the tension was hardly bearable. Nobody at all would commit themselves. The gamble was being played out to its bitter end. Nobody would commit themselves except Philmill. Because Philmill liked Sullivan. He had got a nice impression from him. He had wanted to save him a drop. A situation like this is hardly bearable. People's nerves are stretching to breaking point. It is always the last stretch of any endeavour which is the worst. Here is a situation, with actors sweating on their jobs; envisaging what is before them if it fails; the trudging up to offices, day after day, maybe two visits or three visits in a row. Almost without notice having to plunge again into the maelstrom, counting the money in your wallet; watching it fading away; or the blessed relief of knowing, Oh, how lovely, we are right for maybe six months or more; don't have to worry for six months or more. You can sleep. People who are afraid of committing themselves in case they are proved wrong in the event. So you talk about anything under the sun except what you want to talk about.

Jay was the gayest. The author was the glummest. Almost anonymous; sitting in a corner with a glass in his hand, occasionally rubbing his hand over his face.

Philmill watched all this. He rarely went to parties. He didn't have to. He knew what he was doing and where he was going. Knew the hard way. He had one or two of these tension parties, long ago, and he didn't want any more of them. He told this to Tony. Tony was watching Sullivan. Sullivan was drinking. He was getting tight very fast. Pi was watching Sullivan. His forehead was creased. Well, to hell with it, Sullivan thought, I know. I know that Philmill is right, wishing Philmill had kept away from him, had left him a few hours' extra of hope. He came over to him. 'You should have left me alone, Philmill,' he said. 'Why did you come near me?' 'I'm sorry,' Philmill said. 'I may be wrong.' 'No, you're not wrong,' said Sullivan. 'You are too sure. I wish you were wrong.' Then Sullivan went over to the corner and sat beside the author and put his arms about him and said, 'Cheer up, everything is fine, fine. We're all in.'

223

It was very crowded. It was very hot. It was very sweaty and the atmosphere got thicker and thicker. Sullivan felt that he couldn't breath. He had to loosen his tie, open his shirt, wondering if it was all worth it; deciding that it was not worth it. Went back to Philmill. Was a little belligerent with Philmill. I know the secret of it, he told him. To be like you. Have slaves working for you. Go home and sleep, you can. What about the poor slaves? They love it, Philmill told him. You go home and put your feet on the mantelpiece. You don't have to worry. Not your money. Not your soul. Where are we going? Look at Tony, drinking water. You talk to Tony. Tony will tell you. What has it done to Tony, tell me?

The papers came. Jay played it very dramatically. He was the first one to get the papers. He stood on a chair. They stood around him in a circle. There were three papers. The ink was scarcely dry on them. He stood on the chair and he read one. Then he said: 'Hee-hee!' and he threw it over his shoulder. Then he read another one, giggled even longer, and threw it over his shoulder. The others crowding around him reached for them, started to read them avidly. Jay finished the third one. He read it very quickly.

'Well, my friends,' he said. 'We lost. The show is over.'

There was silence in the place, a deadly silence, broken by a sigh.

'We tried,' said Jay, 'and we failed. All right! All right! That's it. Let's go home and go to bed. Anybody who wants to make a speech is welcome.'

'I do,' said Philmill surprisingly. 'I want to make a speech.'

'Woo-woo, stand back from the great man,' said Lance. There was dislike in his voice.

'Talk away,' said Jay. 'Stand on the chair, Philmill. It cost about a hundred thousand dollars.'

'No chair,' said Philmill. 'Just this, Jay. I will even shake your hand. You are a first-class loser.'

A lot of good that is, Sullivan thought, as he searched for his coat. He found it. A lot of good to a bloody first-class loser. He wandered a lot before he found the lift and was shot down. Tony came after him, shouting: 'Hey, Sullivan, wait!' Sullivan waited for him. They stood outside on the pavement. The streets were deserted, except for an occasional cab. They walked.

'Sorry, Tony,' Sullivan said. 'Shouldn't have walked you into it. I thought it would be sure-fire, that it couldn't miss.'

'I'm grateful to you,' said Tony. 'I really am.'

'Hey, Sullivan!' This was Philmill running after them. 'Don't go away like that. I didn't call to see you just to be a Cassandra. I wanted to see you. I have plans for you.'

Sullivan stood on the pavement.

'Philmill,' he said. 'Please leave me alone. I don't want anyone to have plans for me any more. From now on I make my own plans. You hear that?'

'Look, Sullivan,' said Philmill patiently. 'I want you. You will do me good. I'm not taking you just because I like you. I'm in the market to buy ability. You have ability. You sell, I buy. What's wrong with that?'

'Just this,' said Sullivan, 'I want to be left alone. Leave me along. That's all. I'm tired of strange men finding me, and getting the bounce. I've had enough of it. Leave me alone now, Philmill.' He walked away from them.

'Wrong approach,' said Philmill. 'He's touchy. Dammit, what am I worrying about? I can find hundreds of Sullivans.'

'No you can't,' said Tony. 'Odd as he is, there is only one Sullivan. Leave him alone. Just like he said.'

'Let him stew,' said Philmill, angrily. 'Let him stew.'

'Irish stew is good,' said Tony, laughing. 'You never know what will come out of it.'

'I don't care,' said Philmill. 'I could have given him all the things he seems to want, and he throws them back in my teeth. Let him stew. Goodnight, Tony,' and he whistled for a cab and went the other way.

Tony caught up with Sullivan. It wasn't hard.

'It was good of you to speak up for me, Sullivan, that time. You remember that night you called with Jay?'

'Yes,' said Sullivan.

'I had a letter from Greta that day. That was why I was so drunk. You'll never guess what, Sullivan. She was going away

225

with that little old man, Oswald. Bet you could never guess that. You knew he was going. I'll bet you never knew that she was going with him.'

Sullivan blinked his eyes, shook his head to rid it of the unaccustomed fumes of drink.

'No, Tony,' he said. 'I never knew that. That was a terrible thing.'

'Yes,' said Tony. 'It was. You see the tragedy. Greta is really only a big slob. She hasn't a lot of intelligence. She is just a big girl with beauty. I take her and she would have been fine. You know what? She would have turned into a cheerful contented wife, if I got her. That was it, Sullivan. She hadn't the makings at all of a great courtesan, just a big happy suburban wife she could have been. Only for the notions. I told her. I would even have made an actress out of her. If that was what she wanted. But I knew what she really wanted. I would even have gone home. Worked at home. Small house. Five children. I tell you, she would have been happy at that. You know something? Now she will never know happiness. Such a pity, such a waste.'

'Yes,' said Sullivan.

'What I'm saying, Sullivan, is that you came like an angel to me at that time. Anything I ever did for you doesn't bear comparison with your thought for me at that time. God knows where I would have ended up. Now I feel fine. What I'm saying: all these things – plays failing, plays succeeding, they don't matter. It's people. After all it's only getting a job. It's only like a carpenter making a bad table and having to turn around again and make a new table. We did all right. You did all right. We don't suffer as much. Think of the groaning of the poor author. And Jay. He may be a cheerful loser, but nobody likes defeat. But don't you be despondent. Not badly. Just a little. You have talent. You will get by. But don't take to drinking in disappointment.'

Sullivan laughed.

'Good man, Tony,' he said, turning to look at him. Tony had the grooves on his face all right. Now Sullivan could look at him. His thick hair was quite grey. But his eyes were calm.

Sullivan knew that his own eyes were not calm. That they were resentful. They can't do this to me. Like before.

'And besides,' said Tony, 'you have a good wife and a great happiness stretching ahead of you.'

'Who told you that?' Sullivan asked. 'Was it Pi told you that?'

'You ought to know Pi better,' said Tony. 'It is obvious. I remember that night of *The Hazel Shell*. When I saw Bernie at that party. Saw her looking at you. I'm not blind. What happened that night? You tell me. I want to know.'

'Obvious? Obvious?' Sullivan asked.

'Yes,' said Tony. 'The lovely way you have of avoiding female admirers. The calm detachment. To me obvious. I knew you both, don't forget.'

'Glad you know,' said Sullivan. 'I don't know why I try to hide it. It's like having something precious that you don't want to be destroyed by the breath of the world.'

'Seems to me,' said Tony, 'it would take a lot to destroy her.'

'Yes,' said Sullivan,' yes, it would. But still.'

Pi and the author were sitting on an old couch on the street near the hotel. Sometimes like this, Sullivan noticed people left old couches out hopefully with their dustbins, as if expecting angels from heaven to get rid of them. Sometimes they remained for many weeks before they disappeared piecemeal.

Pi was saying to the author: Look, cheer up, the buses are still running.'

The author was sad.

'I wasn't trying to preach sermons to anybody,' he said as they came up. They sat on an arm each of the couch, avoiding the protruding springs. 'All I did was to try and write a play. It was a good play. At least I thought it was a good play. Know what it was? A rough-hewn gem, and then when they turn around and polish it you see all the flaws. It should never have been polished. You hear that, Sullivan. It should never have been polished.'

'That's right,' said Sullivan.

'Come on up and go to bed,' said Pi, hefting at him.

'I'll never understand,' he said. 'You know something? An artist should never show his work. Right? Where is your pleasure? An artist creates. It should be all in his own hands. Suppose you paint a picture and some other fellows come along and use their brushes on it too, correcting. How can it be the work of the artist? You see what I mean? Different brush strokes. Different colours. How can it be the same as the original creation? Solution? Create and then don't sell. Leave it. Lock it away. Don't let anybody get their hands on it.'

'What do you use for bread?' Sullivan asked.

'You are fed from secret knowledge,' the author said. 'The manna of creation. Not the applause of the mob. Secret satisfaction. Jewels turned over in the mind. Taken into the air, they are handled, polluted by handling. You get the idea?'

'I do,' said Sullivan. 'You ought to write a play about it.'

This left the author startled. He looked up at Sullivan, peering through his glasses.

'My God, Sullivan,' he said. 'What a brilliant suggestion! You are right. What a theme for a play!'

'There you are,' said Pi. 'Can't you go to bed now and dream about it?'

'I will, Pi,' said the author. 'That's just what I will do.' He allowed Pi to raise him to his feet. 'Food for the mind. Feeding on the dreams of creation. Something like *Faust*. A great theme. You never know.'

Before they reached the steps Pi called back : 'Hey, Sullivan, are you all right? You're not moping, are you?'

'No, Pi,' said Sullivan, laughing. 'I'm not moping.'

'Good,' said Pi, helping the author up the steps. 'One at a time is enough.'

'What would we do without Pi?' Tony asked.

'Life would be very bleak without Pi,' said Sullivan.

'I'm going,' said Tony. 'We'll have to get out looking for jobs in the morning. Can't go into the theatre for six months. That means radio; television. What a life!'

'I'll follow you in, Tony,' said Sullivan.

'All right,' said Tony.

So Sullivan sat there on the old spring-sprung couch in the

empty street. The street looked odd in the night lights. Away at the far end he could see a policeman slowly approaching, ambling, his hands behind his back; the street light reflecting occasionally from the peak of his hat. Here we go again, Bernie, he said. Each time we seem to be nearer and nearer to being permanently nearer and then something like this happens. And each time we are farther and farther away. If only he could reach out and feel the touch of her hand in his own. And so near, he thought. Only a matter of three men liking what they saw, and all the dreams would come from remote recesses into the light of day.

The policeman was coming closer. He would naturally wonder what a man was doing sitting out on an old couch at that hour of the morning. Odd.

So Sullivan rose, sighing, and went into the glass passage fronting the double doors.

26

Sullivan came walking from the subway and turned into the street where they lived. It was a street with a name, not a number. It seemed to be a sort of square set on its own, bounded for its full length on the far side by the five-storey hospital. They lived this side almost in the middle of the block. All of them brownstone houses which had one time been very tony, placid and supercilious. Not now. They were swarming with life. Humming at all times. Even at night when everybody was asleep there seemed to be a distant hum going on somewhere.

Not much humming now. The sun was very hot, seeming to be beating you into the hot pavements. A few dogs were stretched supine in doorways, panting. Only the children were out in the sun. Wearing hats, straw hats and hardly anything else. They should have been dead from the heat of the sun. But they weren't. They were active. Nice clean kids in the main. Curly black hair, or fair curly hair. Charlie the policeman leaning against a lamp-post, hat off, rubbing at the sweat with a handkerchief. He carried a lot of weight. That was why he sweated so much.

'It'll break,' he said to Sullivan as he passed.

'I hope so,' said Sullivan. Sullivan carried no weight and his shirt was wet. He was carrying his coat on his arm. His sleeves were rolled. His arm was sweating where the coat rested on it.

'Boy, won't I be glad when I get my pension!' said Charlie.

'Me too,' said Sullivan.

'You'll wait,' said Charlie. 'You'll put them in. Not me. Three years now and I will be down on a beach all day with my dogs in the brine.'

'You will like hell,' said Sullivan.

'A man can dream,' said Charlie.

Sullivan went on. He went up the steps. A blast of hot air hit him as he got into the hall. He paused there to adjust himself. You think it is hot outside. Wait'll you see what we have for you. He blew out his cheeks and went up the stairs. Only two flights. That wasn't as bad as it could have been, but it was bad enough. Like being in a hot-house. Hardly able to raise your feet to put them down.

He paused at the first landing. He went in the door there.

'Hey, Joe,' he called.

'Out here,' Joe answered. Sullivan walked through the living-room and the kitchen and out onto the balcony. Joe was here. He was in his wheel chair. He had no legs. He lost them in machinery in a factory. The stumps were too short to fit tin legs for him. He never would have tin legs. He was young too, only just over thirty. A fine body. Just wearing a vest. He had a thick column of a neck, fair hair curling down the back of it. His arms were powerful, glistening with sweat on the bronzed skin.

'Brought you a magazine, Joe,' said Sullivan. He threw it on the table beside the wheel chair.

'Gee, thanks, Sullivan,' Joe said. 'Saw you on that show Friday. You carved that dame some. Boy, that was some carving. Hey, Bonnie, see who's here. Sullivan is here. How about a nice cool drink?'

'All right,' said Bonnie. She rose from the canvas lounge pulling up straps over her shoulders. Sullivan averted his eyes. She had very little on. She was well built. But Sullivan knew how it was with Joe. Joe loved his Bonnie. Why? Just because, and imagine all that thing, losing his legs and all, imagine she stuck with him. Imagine that. She could have hoofed off with some guy with two legs. Bonnie worked. Joe was happy. He could manage to do a lot of things around the place. Sad case. Found by Pi. Pi loved Joe. Spent all his spare time with him. Made you think no matter what happened to yourself at least you could walk. But Sullivan always kept his eyes away from Bonnie. Joe was always watching the eyes of men who might be with them. She was blonde and very good-looking. Her own colour too. Her colour was her own, she would say, raising her arms. Sullivan was always conscious of her desire to please, not him specifically; her desire to be admired. She meant nothing by it; just second nature. But he felt that you could hurt Joe by looking at Bonnie. Just because you had two legs and Joe hadn't. He always preferred to call and see Joe when Bonnie wasn't there.

'Bonnie got a half day,' said Joe. 'Stinking hot. Listen, all that blood, Sullivan. How they manage all that blood when you carved the dame?'

Sullivan laughed.

'You bloodthirsty, Joe? Honest, I don't know. Coloured water or something maybe. I don't know.'

'Gee, it was real,' said Joe. 'When you on again? We like you. All around everybody likes you. Should be on the movies, that's what everybody says. Honest.'

Sullivan sighed.

'I don't know, Joe,' he said. 'That series is finished now. Haven't got anything else for the moment.'

'Out,' said Joe. 'That's tough, Sullivan. Makes you mad. Me, this chair I could break it to pieces sometimes with my hands. Just to be out working. Give a lot for it. Boy, you get hot pants not working, I tell you. Hear that, Bonnie? Sullivan is out of a job again. Ain't that tough?'

'Sure is,' said Bonnie, coming back with a tray. 'Don't know

231

how they can not use you. You're good.'

'That's what I say,' said Joe.

'That's the way,' said Sullivan. He drank. It was ice cold but he knew it would be only a slight relief, in fact any liquid that went in would have to come out of the pores again.

He looked out. They were ringed by the backs of apartments. The balconies and flat roofs and the waste ground in the middle were all festooned with naked or semi-naked bodies. Remember the back at home? He grinned. The pigs and the bonhams. But never as hot as this. Good job with those pigs.

'I'll go up,' he said. 'Try and cool off.'

'Thanks for the magazine, Sullivan,' Joe said. 'Come and see us again. Pi was here all the morning. He's a character. Pi meets some odd people down at Jimo's. Laugh. Ain't he funny on that, Bonnie?'

'Sure is,' said Bonnie. 'Don't rush away, Sullivan.' She was lying down again, her straps loosened.

'Thanks,' said Sullivan. 'I have things to do. Goodbye.'

'Call again,' said Joe.

Sullivan went. He wasn't sure he wanted to leave them. Nice to talk to people, not in his profession, sane ordinary people. Glad you're not here now, he told Bernie. You wouldn't like this. Their own apartment on the next landing was very hot too. A blast of hot air came out to him as he opened the door. The sight of it depressed him. Two rooms and a bathroom. At least there is a bath, he thought. That's progress. He threw off his clothes. There was no shower, so he lowered himself into the cold water. That would last for a short time. He went into the living-room when he had dried himself. Wore shorts. He went to the desk and took out the manuscript. He tried to read a bit of it. It seemed awful, stale, and sour to him. He threw it to one side and then lay down on the floor, near the window. It was a linoleum-covered floor, so it was cool to the touch of his body. For a while.

Nice fix now, Sullivan. Where do you go from here? All these months and just enough to get by. Acting in stuff that was pallid, in which you could inject no force at all. What was he doing? Waiting around, just waiting around, hoping. For

232

what? Like he said to Philmill, he would make his own plans. Well, he was making them and they weren't getting him anywhere, anywhere at all. Oh, Bernie, he thought, if only you were here to kick me.

He heard the feet coming up the stairs. He had left the door unlocked. If that's Bonnie now, he thought, I must rise and leave the door open after her so that if Joe comes and looks up he will see the door open and see me in the doorway. I'm not taking chances of hurting Joe. Bonnie doesn't know. It's just casual to her. She would come sometimes for the loan of milk or coffee or something she had run out of. Lifting things, feelings things, laughing at you out of the corner of the blue eyes. Almost daring. She didn't mean that. It was just the way she was.

There was a knock at the door. That couldn't be Bonnie. 'Come in,' said Sullivan, 'if you are good-looking.' The door opened.

'Do I qualify?' Philmill asked.

Sullivan looked at him, his head supported by his arms.

'Hello, Philmill,' he said. He let his head fall back again.

Philmill stood over him and looked down at him. Already he was sweating again.

'You know something?' Sullivan said.

'What's this?' Philmill asked.

'The thing I would like most in the world?' said Sullivan.

'What?' Philmill thought Sullivan looked tired and a bit worn. But he still liked the cut of his jaw.

'Lying on a cliff-top of green grass, or under the shade of apple trees, and feeling the Atlantic breeze on my face. But since I can't have that, you know what I'll settle for?'

'What?' asked Philmill.

'You,' said Sullivan. 'You, Philmill. The sight of your ugly face. Here, man, sit down.' Sullivan was on his feet. 'Why should you stand?' He insisted on him sitting. 'And I go to the kitchen' – he was running as he said it – 'and from the ice-box, I take a long cool drink in an iced bottle and I pour it into a glass and I put it into your hand.'

'I'm welcome, huh?' Philmill asked.

'As the flowers in May,' said Sullivan. 'As a thaw in February, as water in the desert; good grapes on the vine.'

Philmill laughed.

'I'm glad,' he said. 'I nearly wasn't coming. I had to make an effort to come.'

'Look, you have more sense than I have,' said Sullivan. 'What have I? I'll tell you. Only pride, that's all, Philmill. Look, I'll tell you a secret. Pride possesses mostly the people who can't afford it. But they have it, and when all else dwindles you hang on to that. You understand.'

'Sure,' said Philmill. 'I have been there too, Sullivan. That's what you don't realise. Most of us have to go through all that. It's like a formula. Some, but very few, skip it. Circumstances. I've been in places like here for long long periods. Born in worse, but got out of it. You'll get out of it if that's what you want. Let me tell you, something is left behind; but that's something else. Can you come with me now?'

'New? Something new? New proposition?' Sullivan was eager.

'You bet,' said Philmill. 'And hot. Wait'll you see. But come with me. The fellow who is putting up the dough. You will have to meet him. He is the only one. Then we can get to work. Are you eager?'

'Beaver,' said Sullivan, racing for the bathroom heedless of the sweat he was sending pouring through him. 'Two minutes, Philmill.'

Philmill got up, went to the window, looking out at the burning sky and the half-roasted beef on the balconies. Tons of beef. He shook his head. Went back to lay his glass on the desk. Saw the picture of the girl. She made him smile; the sight of her. Cool and clean and no sweat. 'Hey, who's the doll?' he called. Sullivan came out, pulling on his pants.

'What doll?' he asked. Philmill had her photo in his hands looking at her, smiling.

'That doll? She's my wife Bernie,' he said, wondering, surprised that he could tell Philmill. 'Isn't she nice?'

'She is,' said Philmill, 'but how come she is there and you are here? She's not dead, is she?' This with a hint of anxiety.

Sullivan laughed.

'Oh no,' he said. 'Very much alive. Very much.'

'But why?' Philmill asked. 'If I had her I wouldn't let her out of my sight. Not a dish like this.'

'Me neither,' said Sullivan. 'Maybe you can cure that?'

'You mean it only wants that?' Philmill asked. 'Why, that's easy. She's practically in your arms.'

'Oh, I wish she was,' said Sullivan, struggling into his shirt.

'No bother,' said Philmill. 'What's this?' he said then. 'Are you operatic too?' taking up the script. *Street of Anger.*

Sullivan took it out of his hands.

'No, leave that, Philmill,' he said. 'That's only a germ. Maybe some day. I don't know. Just a germ. I'm glad to see you, Philmill. I can't tell you how glad I am that you called.'

'Me too, now,' said Philmill. 'We'll go places. Where's Tony? What's Tony doing?'

'I don't know. I haven't seen him for some time. I think he is still in that small hotel. I don't think he left it.'

'Let's track him down and give him a surprise,' said Philmill. 'How about that?'

'That's it,' said Sullivan. 'Won't he be surprised. Boy, Philmill, you don't look it but you are like a very pleasant dream.'

27

'This is Benny. This is Tommy,' said Philmill.

Sullivan shook hands with them. He was surprised at their appearance. Benny wore heavy horn-rimmed glasses and a healthy head of skin; Tommy was dressed in a brown conservative suit, wore rimless spectacles, a brown moustache and gingery-coloured hair. They were a very successful team. But he wanted them to look different, have poetic eyes or something. With their preciseness and brief-cases they looked like junior bank executives.

Philmill was watching him, smiling.

'Don't judge the books by the covers,' he said. 'What you

235

want? That they should have long hair and heads shaped like eggs? I'm the one who provides the inspiration. They do the work.'

Sullivan knew that. Their names were decorating more than one theatrical poster.

'Hello, Tommy. Hello, Benny,' he said, shaking hands with them.

'Sorry we couldn't get in before this hour, Philmill,' Benny said. 'We barely got the thing finished. You set a keen deadline.'

'You got it finished?' Philmill asked.

'Yes,' said Tommy, throwing scripts on the table.

'You surprise even me,' said Philmill, taking one up.

Benny snorted. 'Praise indeed,' he said. 'I have hardly seen a bed for the last two weeks.'

'You read the book, Sullivan,' said Philmill. 'What did you think of it?'

'It's very dramatic,' said Sullivan, 'but I don't know how you make a play out of it.'

'You'll see,' said Philmill, rustling through the pages. '*The Tide Flows East*. Brother, people are going to get sick looking at that name, they will know it so well.'

'How do you see all that, Philmill?' Sullivan asked.

'It's a natural,' said Philmill. 'Look at it. People love plays about strange places, particularly strange places almost in their own back yard. So here we have the swamp lands with the houses raised on stilts to avoid the swollen waters. There's a chance for strange settings. They can say: Imagine places like that almost on our doorstep! We could take out the car and go down and see that place, right now.' He walked to the window. 'What's keeping Tony? I wanted Tony to be here.' He tried to look into the street. It was futile. All the flashing lights were on. It was impossible to see.

Tony was coming.

But on the way, as he came, one of the most scutty and at the same time the most important incidents of his life occurred. You know those barren-looking streets where there seems to be no life in the daytime. A street of tall storehouses.

236

They wake up after midnight when the great trucks start moving into them. They are not well lighted, for who wants to look at great blank storehouses? The side streets off them are not very fashionable. Occasionally there is a pub on a corner – not very prosperous. Tavern type of the old style.

Well, Tony was walking up this long storehouse street. Away ahead of him he could see the sky lighted up with the multi-coloured glow that always seemed to be a guide-post to Broadway. He was walking because it was chilly. He was wearing an overcoat. The Indian summer was past. So was the sweat and humidity. He had timed himself to arrive at Philmill's office to meet the Great Adapters as Philmill called them, right on time.

He would have too, only for the incident.

He was about two hundred yards from this pub when the man came out of it. He was lighted up for a moment from the brightness within, and then the door closed and he staggered out into the street. He was drunk. Almost at the same time the shadows of two men came from behind him, got one each side of him, and Tony saw a raised arm about to fall.

He shouted: 'Hey!' He did this instinctively. Then he paused. This is the sort of thing you read in a very small obscure column in a newspaper. You don't know it happens. All your life you may never see a thing like this happen. You may even wonder, if you did see a thing like this happen, what you would do. Would you pass by?

Tony stood to make up his mind. He shouldn't have done that. The arm fell. Tony started to run. Felt outraged; suffused with anger. But his hesitation was fatal. The two men were bending over the man.

They were, until they had to look up at the low-sized figure that was running down on them from the other side. A small man in a black suit. Tony hadn't noticed him before. But there was no hesitation about him. The two men knew this. They both rose to meet him. They had things in their hands. The short fellow didn't mind. He was all attack. He dodged a blow. Even running, Tony could hear the swish, and then he struck. The man who had aimed at him fell. The small man's foot swung and the man howled as his wrist was kicked. Then the little fellow went for the second man. It was brief. He caught his falling hand, hit him soundly in the belly. The man grunted and fell.

Tony was near them now. The two men scrambled from the ground and ran into Tony. Tony came the worst out of it. He fell, winded. Then the two rose and ran, like shadows. But they were hurt. He knew that. He got to his feet. He went to run after them, around the corner. The little fellow held him.

'Let them go,' he said. 'Are you all right?'

'I am,' said Tony, feeling sore in his chest where he had met a shoulder. 'I wasn't much help to you,' then he added 'Father,' as he saw the collar.

'Not Father,' the man said, 'Brother. Let's look at this poor man.'

He bent over the man on the ground. He wasn't very hurt. There was a little blood on his forehead.

'I don't think he's too bad,' the Brother said.

'He's well canned anyhow,' said Tony, smelling.

'Remind you of home on a Saturday night,' said the Brother. He placed the man in a sitting position against the wall.

'You're Irish,' Tony said. 'For a holy man you know how to handle yourself.'

The Brother chuckled. 'Used to belong to the Ringsend Boxing Club,' he said. 'All things are useful to the Lord. I think we better get him to hospital. You never know. He might have concussion.'

'Will I call the police, ambulance?' Tony asked.

'No,' the Brother said. 'He looks a respectable man. Let's call a cab and get him there. Maybe it would be worse for him if all this was known.'

'Charity?' Tony asked.

'That's what I am,' he said, 'a Brother of Charity. Clancy is the name. What's yours?'

'Mahon,' said Tony.

'A good name,' said Brother Clancy. 'Have you any money?'

238

'I have,' said Tony laughing.

'Good man,' said Brother Clancy. 'You can pay for the cab.'

Tony went looking for the cab.

'I want you to meet the author,' said Philmill. 'This is Sullivan. He will be doing the part of *Axel*, and this is Charlie and Tommy. Wait until you see what they have done with your book.'

He was a tall young man with wispy red beard and freckles. He had a lot of hair on the backs of his hands; his nails were bitten to the quicks and his blue eyes looked puzzled.

Sullivan felt sorry for him. Why feel sorry for a chap who with the success of the book, and with Philmill handling the play of the book, was on his way to making a million? All the same, he felt sorry for him.

'Hello, hello,' he said, looking around vaguely.

'We are getting on with your book,' Philmill said. 'You are going to be very pleased. We haven't altered a line in it. It will go on the stage just as it flowed from your pen. You'll see. We'll give you a script to read when it's finalised.'

'Good, good,' the young man said. He wore a tweed jacket too big for him, a high-necked jersey and corduroy trousers. 'Don't mistake me. I know very little about the theatre. It's foreign to me, foreign. You just must be careful with the girl, very careful.'

Philmill told him how careful they would be. He looked a bit bewildered. Everything was happening too suddenly for him.

Brother Clancy had very dark hair, with dark eyebrows, and a square chin, and indeed there was black hair on the backs of his hands, but his eyes were brown and very gentle. That's what Tony noticed most about him as they held the snoring man propped between them on the car seat. He was a very respectable man. Good overcoat; good suit. His hair was grey, almost white, and his hands and face well cared for. Tony felt pity for him. A man like that must have a family. Starting to think how they would feel if they knew he was like this.

'Why Charity?' he asked Brother Clancy.

'Just that,' said the Brother. 'Great city like this, there is always more occasion than enough; hospitals; prisons; homes; slums; crowded living conditions. You understand. A great city. Very wealthy. Millions who don't know what's happening under their noses. Why should they? They are never in a position to meet it. Like you. Out of the blue. It came on you. You didn't seek it. Charity seeks it, you understand, in all these places. Just walking the streets at night, like to-night. You helped to-night, like Christ would. You understand this? This is the breath of Charity. Seeking out. Not sitting down waiting for it to come to you.'

'I think I understand,' said Tony.

They stopped outside the great hospital.

'You have an appointment?' Brother Clancy asked.

'Yes,' said Tony, thumbing back at the reflected street of glory.

'Oh, up there?' the Brother asked.

'Yes,' said Tony.

'You better not wait so,' said the Brother. 'You might lose what you are going after. The gentlemen up there move very fast.'

'Hump them,' said Tony with sudden decision and helped the Brother to get the man out of the cab. He was able to walk now, shaking his head, screwing up his eyes. He would have a pain in his head now.

Philmill was inclined to be angry when Tony appeared.

'Look, Tony,' he said, 'honest. This is all timed to a schedule from now. Very tight. Blinding work. It's all to be done inside a certain time. Every minute will count. Don't do that to me again.'

'I'm really sorry, Philmill,' said Tony.

What's wrong with Tony, Sullivan was wondering. His eyes were glistening. My God, has he gone back on the drink again? No, no (looking at him more closely), not that. But something. He looks hoist, elevated. Why?

'What do you think of the book, Tony?' Philmill asked. 'What do you think of the part of *Chobel*?'

240

'Oh, good, good,' said Tony, bringing himself back with an effort. '*Chobel* is a sex-ridden drunkard endeavouring to seduce a fourteen-year-old girl closely related to him. It should suit me fine.' He laughed.

There were howls of protest from the Adaptors.

'No! No!'

'You got it wrong there,' said Charlie. 'That's the play, you see.'

'That's the drama,' said Tommy. 'It will petrify them. That part where he is alone with her. The waters outside are rising, and she in a wet nightie. It's terrific.'

'It's gripping, Tony,' said Philmill. 'It's the part of a lifetime. There won't be a sinner who doesn't hate you and love you at the same time. Man, can't you see it? *Axel*, that's Sullivan, coming in, and you and the fight, and fourteen alligators down below waiting for the result of the fight. We'll have the bull alligators roaring or champing or whatever they do. We'll frighten the lives out of them. And it's good, Tony. Not melodrama. A slice of life that will strike home at the most cynical.'

'I was joking, Philmill,' said Tony. 'I know you will make it good. Have you ever been walking through a great hospital, Philmill?'

Philmill stared at him. Sullivan stared at him.

'What the hell is wrong with you, Tony?' he asked. 'Are you nuts?'

'Maybe I am,' said Tony, rubbing his hand on his forehead. Sullivan felt disturbed about him. I should have seen more of Tony in the past few weeks, but our lives seemed to be so separated from one another. 'All right, Philmill, tell me more about the play.'

'Right,' said Philmill. 'There's Sullivan and you. Then there's *Uncle Hibbert*. Listen, that old boy will be one of the greatest characters in theatrical fiction when we are finished with him. He will cost plenty. We're getting that great character actor from Hollywood' (naming a household name) 'to do him. He'll be worth it.'

'He will be very good in it,' said Tony. 'It might be written for him.'

'After that,' said Philmill, 'we have *Mrs. Treen* and the coloured girl *Josephine*, and the toughest one of all to fill, *Doll*.'

'And who will she be?' Tony asked.

'I wish I knew,' said Philmill, suddenly walking the floor. 'I don't know how many girl actresses there are in this country, but she will have to come from one of them, even if I have to talk to every one of them personally. That will be the secret of this play. That girl. And I'm going to find her, if it takes me months. I'm not going to do a line of this until I find her.'

'You know, Philmill,' said Tony. 'You are going to succeed in this. I can see that. It will be very successful. Everybody in it will get plenty of money out of it. It was decent of you to call me into it.'

'It's not the money either, Tony,' said Philmill. 'To hell with the money. It's the job. Of taking a thing and moulding it; studying the minds of the people who will watch it; playing on them, like the conductor of an orchestra.'

'Fine for you, Philmill,' said Sullivan. 'But money for me. You hear that? You can be taken up with the power and the glory, but I can't afford it. I want money, Philmill.'

'If that's what you want, you'll get it,' said Philmill. 'But listen, even if I hadn't a cent I would be doing this for the thrill of it. How many times have I done it? Why don't I get bored? See?'

'I thank you again, Philmill, for the opportunity,' said Tony, 'but I can't go along with you.'

'What do you mean, Tony?' Philmill asked.

Tony looked at him. He was smiling. How can I tell him about something inside me, that is as nebulous as a mist, just a warm knowledge? I might as well have been hit on the head with a hammer. Only Sullivan. Sullivan might know. Would Sullivan know? Would he be able to show him the eyes of Brother Clancy? Tony rose to his feet.

'I'm finished with the theatre, Philmill,' he said. 'That is the beginning and the end of it. I'm tired of it. I want to rest from it. Maybe I may not succeed. Maybe I may come back again to it, when it stretches out its arms to me like the tentacles of an octopus. But not now. I am leaving.'

242

Sullivan was bewildered, bemused. He couldn't understand.

Oddly enough, Philmill didn't protest. Tony looked at him. Their eyes met. Philmill tried to pull knowledge from Tony's eyes with his own widely opened, almost mesmeric ones. He shook his head.

'You got me, Tony,' he said. 'I don't understand.'

'It would be hard for you,' said Tony. 'Since I barely understand myself. Why it should have to fall on me here, now, at this time, I don't know. But I'm really grateful to you. And now I must go.'

'I'll go with you,' said Sullivan. This would have to be probed. What was wrong with him? Was he light in the head?

'Sure,' said Philmill. 'But don't forget the morning, Sullivan. We start on those dames at nine o'clock in the morning.'

'I won't forget,' said Sullivan, following Tony out.

'What goes?' Tommy asked. 'What's the angle, Philmill?'

'I don't know,' said Philmill. 'I honestly don't know.'

'I know,' said Tommy. 'The guy's nuts. Just nuts.'

Outside.

'What is it, Tony? What happened?'

The lights were still on. Some restaurants and drug-stores were still open. You could smell peanuts. Tony was standing up turning his head, looking all around him.

'I saw a hospital, Sullivan,' said Tony, 'but it wasn't that. All those people lying in beds. It wasn't that. But the way they looked at this Brother. He was like the sun shining into a dark room. What have I done all my life? Who have I helped?'

'You have helped a lot of people,' said Sullivan.

'It's deeper than that,' said Tony. 'No direction, see? I was there at home in that theatre and then in Dublin and after that London and I had to come here to find out that what I was doing wasn't worth a damn. You see?'

'No, Tony,' said Sullivan. 'I don't see.' He felt anguished. He couldn't understand. He couldn't get near to it. 'You would have been good in this. This will succeed. We will all do well out of this. Isn't that a help?'

'No, no, not that at all,' Tony said. 'That would be just more

243

waste. I cannot tell you, Sullivan. I am incoherent. I cannot make you understand.'

He was holding Sullivan's arm. His hand was trembling. His eyes were very bright. Like he had a fever.

'I wish I could understand, Tony,' said Sullivan. 'What about all we went through?'

'All that is a pattern,' said Tony. 'All direction. But you don't see it at the time. Even Greta, see? Love for her. Pity. Sorrow. That was maybe the beginning. I don't know. But now Brother Clancy and his Brothers of Charity. All leading up to him. You haven't seen him. Not him but what is inside him. Like a knock on the door of your heart, saying: Come. All this! This great city. All these blinding lights. What's behind them, Sullivan? Work, see? Real work. Real direction. The knowledge that now you are right. I'm going now, Sullivan. I want to see Brother Clancy. He will be found. Either in the monastery place or out about. All you have to do. Search the hospital or the prisons or the slums, or the side streets where men are mugged.'

He laughed. He was backing away.

'Goodbye, Sullivan. I'll try to tell you again. I'll try to explain to you again.'

'Tony,' said Sullivan, holding out his hand.

'Again,' said Tony, and left him there.

Sullivan looked after him. He didn't understand, and so at that moment he felt afraid.

28

They were tired; they were weary. Sullivan was lying across the desk, his head on his arms. Even Philmill, that seemingly inexhaustible spring of energy and decision, was nearly at the end of his tether.

He pulled down the button on the voice-box.

'Yes?' the girl asked.

'How many more, for God's sake?' Philmill asked her.

'Just three,' she said, 'for to-day. Fifty-two for to-morrow.'

'Oh God,' Philmill groaned. 'All right. Send in the next one.' He shut off the voice. 'Hep it up, Sullivan. There are only three more to go.'

Sullivan groaned.

'If only I knew what Tony was up to or what came over him,' said Sullivan. 'How many girls have you seen now?'

'Forty-eight,' said Philmill.

'You know something?' said Sullivan. 'I'm beginning to hate this play already.'

'When I'm done with you,' said Philmill grimly, 'you'll hate every comma of it. But you will be good.'

The door opened. The girl came in. Sullivan's heart stopped still for a moment and then started to pound dully. She was the image of Bernie. Then she wasn't. She was herself. It was just a fleeting resemblance. Maybe wish-fulfilment. This girl had level eyebrows. She was small. Her hair was cut short to the shape of her small head. It was brown hair. Her skin was slightly sallow, and her black-lashed eyes looked enormous.

'You are Mary Berry?' Philmill asked, looking at the list tiredly.

'Yes,' she said, 'Mary Berry. At least I think I am. I'm so tired. Do you mind if I sit down? You are the fifth to-day.'

Philmill looked up at her, scrutinised her. He grinned.

'No,' he said. 'Go on, sit.'

'Thanks,' she said, sitting back with a sigh into the armchair. She put her head back, closed her eyes. She wasn't putting on an act. She was really tired. It was unusual. They had to put on an act. If they didn't put on an act how were you to know they were actresses?

Philmill came around the desk to look at her.

'Did you have any luck with the others?' he asked her.

She opened her eyes at him.

'They said they would let me know,' she said.

'That's not so good,' said Philmill. He was smiling down at her. She looked like a jaded schoolgirl.

'I think they thought I was too young for all the parts,' she said. 'I'm not really. I'm twenty-three.'

That surprised them.

'You are!' he said. 'I'd put you down for sixteen.'

'You see! That's my trouble,' she said.

She had a soft voice, Sullivan was thinking. Nice voice. And it would carry. He was sitting up, taking notice.

'That's just the quality that we want,' said Philmill.

The girl swallowed.

'Please don't raise any hopes in me,' she said. 'I haven't a hope of the girl's part in this. You have to be somebody big to be in it.'

'Who says so?' Philmill asked. 'I'm the one that is fixing it. If you thought you hadn't a chance of the girl's part, what brought you? You want to do *Mrs. Treen*?'

'Yes,' she said.

He laughed. 'She's over forty,' he said.

The girl startled them. A change came over her face. Her skin appeared to wrinkle and grow old. A husky voice came from her puckered lips. *'It's many years now, dear, since your Uncle Hibbert carried me off. The years were not light on me. I am only forty-five.'*

They laughed at her. Sullivan slapped his hand on the desk in delight.

'I believe you could do *Mrs. Treen* if you were put to it,' Philmill said. 'But I'd like to hear you trying *Doll*. Have you studied it?'

'I'm afraid that I have,' she said.

'You see this fellow?' Philmill asked, pointing at Sullivan. She turned her eyes on him. He felt them warm on his face. She had candid eyes, widely spaced. He rose.

'I see him,' she said, looking up at him.

'This is Sullivan,' said Philmill. 'He is *Axel*.'

'Hello, Mr. Sullivan,' she said. 'I saw you in *The Hazel Shell*. I really liked you. I thought you were super. Not olive oil. Honest.'

'That's nice to hear,' said Sullivan. He shook hands with her. Her hands were very small. Sullivan liked her. She made him feel cheerful. I hope she is very good, he thought. I hope that she is good enough for this.

'Could you do a few lines now?' Philmill asked.

'If you give me a few minutes to look at it again,' she said.

'Take your time,' said Philmill. She rose and went into the corner with the script open. She presented her back to them. Philmill drew Sullivan's attention to her back and grinned. From behind she looked as slim as a fourteen-year-old girl. The back of her head looked young; her neck looked childish.

She turned around after a while and faced them, her lips tight, her eyes closed, holding on to words. Then she opened her eyes.

'Now?' she asked.

'Now,' said Philmill.

Her hands behind her back, she walked slowly until she was standing in front of Sullivan. Her big eyes examined his face; fastened on his eyes.

'You are Axel?'

'Yes. I came over. We are new. In the house above. Two days ago.'

'Will you let me do something?'

'What?'

'This' (raising a finger and rubbing it on his cheek).

'Why do you do that?'

'Just to feel. Your face is soft. Your face is soft as mine.'

'Is that strange?'

'Yes. I did not know that there was a man in the world with soft skin and no wrinkles in his face. But you are not a man. Are you a man?'

'I think so.'

'But why is your face smooth and your skin soft? I have never seen the like.'

'Perhaps because I came in with the tide. Perhaps because I have not always been here. Maybe it is because I am not a skinner.'

'Will you be a skinner now?'

'I might.'

'And will wrinkles grow on you then, and will your face become hard and rough like a board, when you become a skinner?'

247

'I don't know.'

'Will you bend your head and kiss me, Axel?'

(He bends and kisses her, one of her hands presses the back of his neck. They look at one another. She tastes his kiss almost as if she was licking molasses from her lips.)

'It is so different when there are no bristles.'

'That will do. That will do mighty well,' said Philmill. 'That's it now. You are in, Mary Berry. Your search is over. My search is over. Eh, Sullivan?'

'Oh yes,' said Sullivan, who was still holding on to her hand. 'Oh yes, indeed.' She was good. So good. He could feel it from her. Know that she was taken with it. Their search was indeed ended.

'You're not joking, not joking?' she asked. Her hand was trembling.

'I don't joke,' said Philmill. 'I can't afford jokes.' He went to the door, opened it; shouted out: 'That's all! That's all for to-day.'

'Does he mean it?' she asked Sullivan. 'Does he really mean it?'

'Yes, he does,' said Sullivan, 'and I am pleased. I am very pleased.'

Philmill is a business man; Philmill is a slave-driver, but Philmill is human. Philmill doesn't get the best out of everybody by bullying, by cursing. Philmill doesn't have to fire anybody because before he hires them he knows that they are the people he wants and no others. His settings never have to be altered from the original drawings. They are just what he wants. He doesn't work very long hours. He works inside a limit and works intensively; cajoling, repeating, encouraging: working on each person's personality because he has studied them, each one of them. He knows how to get what he wants without hurting them, without humiliating them. Rehearsals are on time, conferences are on time. Philmill is like a very competent contractor who before he starts building a house has everything prepared, so that no labourer has cause to idle, no carpenter is idle through late delivery of material. It is all streamlined, efficient, exacting. And when they move out of town, they don't have to worry. Everything is as efficiently arranged as ever. No play doctors. No advisers. It was art of a kind, Sullivan knew, the way Philmill worked, but it was cold-blooded, assessed, scrutinised, deliberate, almost as efficient as a machine. It wasn't even a gamble. The gamble was reduced to very small proportions. Sullivan might regret the appalling tensions of the first night of *The Hazel Shell*, the twist of the wrist. But everybody expected Philmill's *The Tide Flows East* to be successful. Not that it was easy. It wasn't. Because everybody raised the sights instead of lowering them. They didn't expect it to be good; they expected it to be better than the last. And if it hadn't been better, Philmill would have been torn apart, because even if all of them came out of it with great kudos all round, it was a Philmill show, and Sullivan sensed some of Philmill's anxiety. How was he going to keep this up? He would have to keep it up. You set a standard and you must be always up to it. Other men had risen and fallen: the streets of Broadway were littered with their reputations. All right, let Philmill worry about the future. The rest of them were up. Their heads were in the clouds. The warm waters of unstinted praise were lapping gently at their feet. They could relax and they could enjoy.

Pi closed the last case, clicked the latch on it, and then stood and looked about the room. It smelled like all rooms when you are leaving them and have emptied the cupboards, but Pi had tidied it. Pi was sorry to go. They had had good times in this place. It was the best place they had been in yet. For the first time, Pi felt revolt at the thought of leaving it. He might have revolted too, if he hadn't remembered Bernie and that day in the garden with the little Cliona. He wondered about Cliona. She would be much bigger now. He wondered if a lot of her chatter would have ceased; if she would remember him if he called again. And Bernie too. Pi was getting tired. Now that things were right for Sullivan. Now that Sullivan was on top of the heap, where he had wanted to be; the culmination of all their years of frantic endeavour. Now he could order his life.

Now was the time for Bernie to come back in and let Pi out. He sighed, hefted the case and closed the door after him.

On the next flight, he dropped the case and knocked at Joe's door. He went in when he heard Joe's voice.

The television screen was blank. It wouldn't be, normally. It was a Sunday evening. Bonnie was leaning back in an armchair, a glass of beer in her hand. Pi liked Bonnie. She worked very hard. But Joe was always happy when she was home. He always shaved before she came in. He was always worried if she was late; she might have been knocked down by a car or a bus. He was a good cook. When Bonnie came home and sat down to a meal she would say: 'Darling, you can cook too!' and they would laugh.

Joe was sombre now. He was resting his cheek on his palm. Pi didn't feel comfortable. Like a deserter. But that was silly. Just at night he and Joe could talk for ages. They liked the same things on television; boxing, wrestling, baseball, football and ice hockey. Joe had been born in the city. He knew every bit of it. He would tell Pi to go here and go there, out-of-the-way things to see, people to talk to who had known Joe, and when Pi came back he would question him and they would laugh a lot about Joe's people and places.

They didn't talk to him. They kept looking at him.

'I'm off now,' said Pi, then.

'Look, Pi,' said Joe, 'what you want to leave for? What's wrong with here? It's clean, ain't it, and nice people, and not too cheap. Why can't you stay?'

'It's that Sullivan,' said Bonnie. 'He's a sensation now. Place like here wouldn't do Sullivan. Wonder if he would wave to us in the street.'

'Please, Bonnie,' said Pi. 'Sullivan is not like that. Just that he moves about a lot more now. Has to have an address. People coming in. You know, all that.'

'Why can't he bring them here?' Joe asked. 'What's wrong with here and us, Pi?'

'It ain't high society,' said Bonnie. 'You got to have one of those classy places with black walls and red ceilings.'

'But why do *you* have to go, Pi? You're making good

money. You could afford to stay here. Do you have to go running when Sullivan calls?' Joe was genuinely puzzled.

'It's this way,' said Pi. 'Sullivan and I have been through a lot together, Joe. All over. I like him. Maybe I can be a help to him. Since we were kids I know him. It's that way.'

'Oh, well,' said Joe, 'please yourself. We're sorry to see you go.'

'I'll come back,' said Pi.

'In a dog's collar you will,' said Joe. 'No, Pi, once you go, you go. I know.'

'You don't know me, Joe,' said Pi. Then he laughed. 'It's like a wake so it is. You can't fool me. This is a tricky business. One day you are up and the next day you are down. We might be glad to come back here for good. You'll see. I have to go. Will we shake hands on it or will we leave it?'

'Leave it,' said Joe. 'You'll come back and talk soon, Pi. I'll miss you if you don't come back and talk.'

'I will,' said Pi earnestly. 'I'll come back.'

'Right, you can go now so,' said Joe.

'You are dismissed, man,' said Bonnie. 'So-long, good neighbour.'

Joe turned his head away. He propelled his chair over towards the television. 'Something good on to-night,' he said.

Pi went out and closed the door.

I've always been coming and going anyhow, he thought. Meeting nice people, just getting to know them, and zoom, off again. He lifted the bag, went down the stairs slowly. Places are no good without people. It's people that make places, no matter what they are like. He stood on the pavement outside waiting for a cab to pass. They didn't pass here very often, but they passed. Look at the place. A friendly place. That street outside. Lived in. That was it. Occupied, not by shops and stores, but people. Only great organisation was that big hospital across the street and that was filled to overflowing with people and the birdlike nuns who swished around it. Past the corner you could see the steeple of the red-brick church. The delicatessen there, with Louis, an old friend. The whole thing mightn't look beautiful but Pi thought that real good architecture was in the hearts of people and not in stones.

He got his cab and as they pulled away he looked back at their building. It was ugly-looking all right, mainly on account of the iron fire-escape that completely defaced the front of it. He saw Joe, looking out of the window, the curtain pulled back. He waved, but Joe didn't. Joe let the curtain fall. Damn it, thought Pi, it's a pity the play wasn't a flop. And then he took that back fast, for Sullivan's sake. Well, half a flop, he conceded.

He alighted at a different building in a different street. You'd think somebody had been working with a Hoover on the pavements. It was quiet, discreet, broad. A striped canvas awning led out to the kerb from the doorway. A nicely uniformed man with shining shoes came and opened the door of the cab. The cab driver didn't say anything. Just raised an eloquent eyebrow as Pi paid him off. Pi just shrugged his shoulders. The man took the bag. Pi didn't even have to carry it. 'It's a pleasant day now, sir,' he said. That nearly crippled Pi. He didn't answer. In the lift and up, and walking out, and his feet are in carpets and Pi looks down at his feet and then he comes to the door and presses the bell. It chimes, it doesn't ring, and the door opens and Sullivan is there. His arms are wide. He hauls Pi in.

Sullivan is like a child with a new toy.

'Look at that, Pi,' he says, bringing him over to the long wide windows, showing him the sweeping view of the river. 'And sit on that, you bastard, and feel yourself sink into it.' That was the lounge. 'And come over here and see your room, boy. Where have you ever had a room like that outside your dreams?'

Pi whistled at the room, and at the bathroom off it, and at the bright wallpaper and the fittings, and at Sullivan's room.

'Gee, Sullivan,' he said. 'It has everything, hasn't it? This is what you wanted, isn't it?'

'This is it, Pi,' said Sullivan. 'We have come a long way to get here but we are home and dried.'

'Tell me,' said Pi, 'what are the other people like who live here?'

Sullivan laughed.

'I don't care,' he said. 'I don't give a damn. Don't you see, Pi? This is it. You don't have to give a damn. You don't have to know. You don't even have to know they exist. You don't have to be smelling their chops frying on a Friday.'

'Janey,' said Pi, 'it's awful posh.' And he was uneasy. Sullivan fitted into it. Sullivan had new clothes on him. Pi wouldn't ever ask the price of new clothes or this place. He was just uneasy.

'Relax,' Pi,' said Sullivan. 'I swear I can afford it. Nobody is going to come and put us out of it. It's ours. This is it. This is what we were striving for.'

Sullivan wasn't uneasy.

29

My, but you are looking well, Sullivan, Bernie said to him. He was standing in front of the long mirror looking at himself. It was midday. He was just after getting up. He had got to bed late the night before. I know I look a sight, he said, but you have to do it, kid. You have to go to these parties. You have to keep your face in the news. Look at that! The magazine spread of *The Tide Flows East*. They were all there. I'll send this on to you. It's necessary. If you are not to be seen people will forget you. People have short memories.

He proceeded to shave himself. Well, as long as you are happy, Sullivan, she said. Certainly I'm happy, he said. Haven't I got everything I set out to get? You seem to have, she said. But are you happy? Why wouldn't I be happy? I find it hard to write, but that's because I have so little time. What's time? she said. Haven't you more time and security now than ever you had? You have the whole day free. Don't forget the matinees, he said, two a week. Yes, but all the mornings, she said. It's not easy to write, he told her, out of your own place. You want to be back in the place you are writing about in order to soak in it. You did all right in King Street, she said, and you were out of your own place and you were up against it. The two acts you got through there are very good. It should be easier now. All the time on your hands. All the security on your shoulders. Are you happy?

Why do you keep asking me am I happy? Your letters are odd, Sullivan. I am worried about them. Have I offended you? Why are you going away in your letters? They are not as open. I can't say what's wrong. There's something wrong. Why do you find it hard to write to me? Why are your letters now so stilted? What's wrong, Sullivan?

He knew what was wrong, but he kept putting it out of his mind.

He finished shaving and went into the living-room. Her picture stood on the low walnut table. Yes, you are there all right. But there is a veil drawn over your countenance. I can't see you as clearly as I used to. What do you mean, my letters are not open? I say all the same things. I tell you all the news. People can't keep on writing love letters all the time. You run out of phrases. How can you run out of phrases if your heart is still the same? Oh yes, it is, yes, it is, I swear it is. My mother finds nothing wrong with my letters. Listen to her. *The neighbours all stop and ask about you, Terence Anthony. It was in the papers. I knew that you would turn out well. Even if other people were shaking their heads about it, I knew. I always knew. I have a nice new dress and coat and hat. It is so good again to feel dressed in what I was used to at one time. You are a very good son not to forget your mother.*

There you are. She's happy. She likes it all. What's wrong with you? Why don't you buy a new dress and new clothes and forget all about it too? You bought enough new clothes to suit both of us, she said. That was a joke. Sullivan was looking at his wardrobe. For a moment the fever of spending that had come over him was recalled. The first time he knew he really had money in his pocket, thousands of dollars, and he had said to himself, Why, I can buy nearly anything at all I like.

You remember all these things I said to you long ago, time we walked out the long strand on that moonlight night and sat on a bench in front of the shore? Remember all those things I

254

said? You may not remember them but I meant them. No darns in underwear; no holes in socks; no shine on the backside of your suit. You remember all that? So many pairs of shoes that you throw them away without ever mending them. All the nagging making-do. All the borderline poverty. You remember? Said I wanted to put a thousand pounds in my mother's hand. You remember the way old Morgan turned on me? All that I wanted wiped out. If I wasn't the way I was then, he would never have given me that treatment. Well, I have the shoes and I have the underwear and I have the clothes and my mother will be well away. Haven't I done all those things? I might have indulged in an orgy of spending. But that was natural.

Not all these things, she said. How can you wear them all? All those things are so unimportant, Sullivan.

They are not unimportant, he almost shouted back at her. They are important. You didn't live in Duke Street. You can't know. And soon I will be able to work again. I will be able to apportion my time. And I will not drink any more at these bloody parties. It does take hours in the morning to recover. All right. That's all out of the way.

He was looking down at the magazine spread. Looking at Mary Berry. Thinking about her. About the way when he would turn suddenly and see her eyes on him and then she would turn away as if she was caught peeping. And his heart would go faster. But nobody knew better than himself that he had given her no encouragement. After all, he was married, even if she didn't know that. He was in love with his wife, of whom he had seen so little because she was far far away. But he loved her and he married her so that she would keep him sane. And he wasn't insane about Mary Berry. It was just an odd tenderness grew in you when you saw her watching you surreptitiously; when sometimes as you talked with her, she would drop her eyes from yours and you would see the vein throbbing, throbbing in her neck, and because you knew her mouth was dry your own would start to become so; and you would turn away from her.

Careful, Sullivan, careful, said Bernie.

Isn't that what I am being? Great God, how many times have I left her as if she had a disease? Can I help the puzzled look in her eyes that makes you want to put your hand on her head and say: Easy, easy, it's not that I don't want to be nearer to you, but there lies an obstacle? I am in love with my wife and she is far away. And why are you far away? You should be here. Is it any wonder that my letters are growing colder? Not colder, just how can I tell you all that's in my heart when it is becoming divided? It's just pity, I tell you. All right, if it is just pity, tell her about me, about Bernie, how I love you and how you are my husband. That will cure her, do you think? You are not such a great attraction, Sullivan. Sometimes you can spread light and happiness, but also you can spread gloom and despondency. Isn't it only somebody like myself would ever marry you?

True, true, true, and I will tell her, and that will cure her. That will take that look out of her eyes

'Sullivan! Sullivan!' Pi was calling. 'Where are you? Come here until I show you something.'

Sullivan's heart lightened a little. He sighed, adjusted his tie, slipped on his jacket and went out to the living-room.

He stood there for a moment goggling. A man in a black suit and a half priest's collar was standing beside Pi. It took Sullivan a moment or two to recognise him.

'My God, Tony,' he said, 'it's you. What fancy-dress ball are you going to?'

'Hello, Sullivan,' said Tony, holding out his hand.

'They just let him out, Sullivan,' said Pi. 'Doesn't he look terrific? Brother Mahon. He'll get us all into heaven, half price, eh, Tony?'

'My God, Tony,' said Sullivan, 'I'm staggered. You really meant it? This is what you meant? We didn't know where you were. We couldn't find you and this is the way you end up.'

'This is it, Sullivan,' said Tony.

Sullivan looked closely at his face. He was thinner. His eyes were clear. They looked back steadily into his own, slightly amused.

'Don't be so surprised, Sullivan,' Tony said. 'It's happening all the time.'

'But to you,' said Sullivan. 'To you, Tony! You really mean it? All thrown away for this? I can't credit it.'

'But I told you,' said Tony. 'That evening. I made it all clear to you.'

'Oh no, you didn't,' said Sullivan. 'Oh no, you didn't.'

Tony laughed.

'Well, maybe not,' he said. 'But you shouldn't be surprised. You know how quickly a man can fall in love. Like that!' He clicked his fingers. 'It only takes a second or two and your heart is tied for life. Isn't that so?'

'Yes,' said Sullivan uneasily, 'that's so, Tony.'

'And he has a Brother Clancy, Sullivan,' said Pi, wide-eyed. 'My name. Imagine that! The same name as me.'

'Well, for God's sake, Pi, don't end up like him,' said Sullivan.

'Oh, not me,' said Pi seriously, 'I'm not a bit holy.'

Tony laughed.

'You might be holier than you think, Pi,' he said. Then he looked around for the first time. He whistled. 'You two are certainly doing yourselves proud,' he said.

'Isn't it terrific?' asked Pi. 'All this and come in and see the room I have, Tony.' He practically dragged him in by the arm. 'See that room, Tony, and the pink bathroom in here. Amn't I posh? I hardly know myself. I pinch myself every morning when I wake up. And come on here until you see Sullivan's joint. There,' he said, standing back and indicating Sullivan's sun-flooded room. 'Not bad for the boys from Duke Street, eh, Tony? You remember? Gee!' Pi bent over laughing. 'You think of Duke Street, Tony, and think of this.'

Sullivan's wardrobe with the sliding panels was wide open. Tony went and looked in the wardrobe, at the suits and the shoes and the ties, and he opened the sliding drawers and saw the shirts.

Sullivan, watching him, felt an unaccountable resentment.

'Lord, Sullivan,' said he then, 'but you are well turned out.' He counted, looked back at Sullivan and then said, laughing, 'Sullivan of the Seven Suits.'

257

'What's wrong with seven suits?' Sullivan asked, his jaw tight.

Tony looked at him in surprise. So did Pi.

'Nothing at all,' he said. 'I was only remarking.'

'No,' said Sullivan, 'you were criticising. Well, you went one way, Tony, and I went another way. You could have had seven suits too if you wanted to. There was nothing to stop you.'

'I'm sorry, Sullivan,' Tony said. 'I didn't mean anything.'

'He's only joking, Sullivan,' said Pi.

'Well, let him mind his own business,' said Sullivan, raging at himself for being so unaccountably angry over nothing at all. 'I saw you looking around. Maybe you think I am full of folly. Well, I'm not. That is what I wanted. All my life. I have got it now. And I'm not apologising to anybody about it.'

'But, Sullivan,' said Tony, 'I didn't mean anything by it. I'm glad to see you like this. You have earned it.'

'I know,' said Sullivan. 'I can see it through your eyes. What did you want me to do? Sit on the backside of a shiny britches and dole out money to the poor and the poverty-stricken, the hospitals, the prisons, all the rest of them?'

'Look, Sullivan,' said Tony. 'If you have a chip on your shoulder I didn't put it there. I don't want to knock it off.'

'I have no chips on my shoulder,' said Sullivan.

'Well, you have something funny on it,' said Pi. 'What's wrong with you, Sullivan?'

'There's not a damn thing wrong with me,' said Sullivan, turning away, his hands in his pockets, staring blindly out of the window.

'Come on, Tony,' said Pi. 'We better go. I thought he would be glad to see you.'

'Sure I'm glad to see him,' said Sullivan. 'Why wouldn't I? Just to see him. He to mind his own business and make no remarks.'

'I'm sorry, Sullivan,' said Tony again. 'If I hurt you inadvertently I am very sorry.'

'Ah, sorry, sorry, sorry,' said Sullivan. What's come over me? Why am I acting like this? Give me another second or two and I will turn around and apologise. I will be abject. He might have turned too, maybe, but it was the click of the latch that made him turn. They were gone. They were not there. He ran a few steps to the door. Then he paused. Well, if that's the way they want it, that is the way they want it. I didn't say anything that bad. Tony came at the wrong time, that is all.

He sat on the couch, his head in his hands. It should have gone differently. He should have joked with Tony. About it all. They should have been happy. They should have gone back over all the times; talking about all the things that had happened to them since long ago.

Sullivan groaned. What kind of a bastard am I at all? What in the name of God is wrong with me?

The chimes struck musically.

He was relieved. He jumped up. That would be Tony coming back. Pi might be too angry to come back. Pi could be quick-tempered too. Well, I am glad. I will say how sorry I am.

He opened the door.

Mary Berry stood looking at him. Her eyes were anxious. She had nerved herself up to this. He took one look at her, and he knew what was wrong with him. He groaned inside himself, looking at her. He didn't speak. Just stood looking at her.

'Can I come in?' She asked this almost timidly, her head on one side like a bird.

Sullivan laughed.

'Yes, come in, come in, come in,' he said, almost ungraciously. She moved past him. He closed the door. Stood looking at her. Beautifully dressed. Very well dressed. Big difference to now and the little almost ragged girl who had come for the audience with Philmill. Still looked young, defenceless, made your heart ache. She turned.

'You never asked me here at all, ever,' she said. 'All the others but not me. Is there something wrong with me?'

'You ought to know,' he said.

'What?' she said. 'You don't like me? I'm sorry.'

'You know better than that,' he said.

'Oh, no,' she said. 'I thought you liked me, at first. But you turn away from me. We are not friends. I want to know what I did to you.'

'Don't you know?' he asked. 'Don't you know very well?'

'No,' she said, 'honest, Sullivan, I don't know. I don't know.' She turned away towards the window. Her eyes alighted on the framed picture on the table. She went towards it, took it up in her hands. 'Oh,' she said. 'How nice! She is nice.' She turned back to him. 'Who is she?' she asked.

'She's my wife,' said Sullivan. He didn't say her name. Couldn't say her name.

'Oh,' she said. 'I never knew.'

'You had no cause to know, did you?' he asked her.

'Oh, no,' she said. 'Just I wondered why, that's all. Why. Now I know, don't I?'

'Yes,' said Sullivan. He thought: This is the point of no return. Go to the door now, and say so pleased you called, Mary Berry, and see you to-night at the play. That was all he had to do. He thought: Buy seven suits, don't buy seven suits. Nothing to do with suits really, just the strength of your will. Hear the voice of Bernie in your ears. Like long ago. That party. Where they got him all balled up. Didn't think. Drove her out of his mind. Pride, she said, and vanity, Not that. Just that her voice was fading.

'You know why now,' he said. He was beside her. He was going to escort her to the door and bid her goodbye. But he didn't because his will wasn't with it. Many times he had wanted to talk to her to try and get her to explain how he could love another and be affected by her at the same time. Can a man have two natures?

'You understand now,' he said. 'Why. I didn't want to avoid your eyes. Why should I want to hurt you?'

'Will I go now so?' she asked. 'Is that what you want?'

'No, no,' said Sullivan, 'that is not what I want.'

He reached for her and she went to him and he kissed her, and the door opened. He wouldn't have heard the key in the latch anyhow. He couldn't have done anything about it anyhow. The door was opened and Pi was there, standing up, looking at them, his face slowly paling and the scar under his cheekbone standing out vividly. He closed the door.

Sullivan only heard the closing of the door dimly. It was a consciousness of the change in the atmosphere that brought his head slowly up. Then he saw Pi. Mary looked at Sullivan's face and turned her head. She saw Pi. Pi saw the fading passion in their faces and his heart sickened.

He didn't say anything.

He walked into his room. He pulled the case from the wardrobe. He started to throw his things into it. He hadn't a lot of things. It didn't take him long to fill the case. To close it, to snap the latches on it.

All this time they were watching him through the doorway, still holding tightly to one another. Then Sullivan released her. He took a few paces towards the room door. Pi came out of it.

'Pi,' said Sullivan hoarsely, 'what are you doing?'

'What do you think? What do you think, you bastard?' Pi asked him.

Sullivan said: 'Don't talk like that, Pi. You don't understand. She knows about Bernie.'

Pi laughed shortly.

'That makes it good, Sullivan. That makes it holy. Boy! You Sullivan! This only the thing you were heading for. This was all it wanted. You were going there. You got there.'

'Don't talk like that, Pi,' said Sullivan.

'You ditch Tony. That was lovely,' said Pi. 'All right. Don't know what's wrong with you. I go along. Not this. This has your snout in the trough, Sullivan. No decency. All swallowed up. Now I'm finished. This is the end for me. What I wanted to do! Thought of you! What Bernie said. All gone. You are on your own now, Sullivan. You're lost now, Sullivan.'

He headed for the door.

Sullivan's jaws were tight. He was seeing red. There were red spots in front of his eyes. Following Pi.

'You say things like that. You don't understand. Do you make any effort to understand? Can a man talk to you when he is tortured? Will you listen? All I have to say. Come back, Pi. I want to say things to you.'

261

It was too late. The door closed in his face. He wrenched it open. He ran into the corridor. But the grille was closed, and the lift was going down. He held on to the bars, grasped them with his hands until they hurt him.

'Pi,' he shouted, 'I'll never forgive you for this. I'll never forgive you for this.'

It was no use. Pi was gone. He released the bars. He walked back into the room, closed the door.

She came over to him.

'What have I done? It's all my fault, isn't it, Sullivan?'

She came close to him. He put his arms about her.

'No,' he said, 'not your fault. It's in the cards. Who does he think he is anyhow? All I did for him, for that Pi.' Saying this, knowing it was wrong. All that Pi did for me. But you have to have barricades. Raging and almost crying inside at the same time. So mixed up.

'It's not your fault,' he said, looking into her face, rubbing his hand on her soft hair. 'These things are written. Who can help them? You tell me that, and you will be the wisest woman in the world.'

30

Pi walked home from the subway. It was Saturday night. He always got off fairly early on Saturday night. Spring was in the air. You could notice that. But not the winter of Pi's sadness. It was good being back in the old place. No people in that place with Sullivan. Couldn't go in to one of these people and put up your feet and take off your coat. You could with Joe. It was good to be back with Joe. And Bonnie. They were very kind to him. All the other people too. He was happy with them. Disturbed of course. Oh, very disturbed. About Bernie. Sometimes he saw pictures of Sullivan in the papers. Always stabbed at him. The stars of *The Tide Flows East* at such and such a place. She was nearly always with him. Smiling up at him, or her hand on his arm. Even in the gossip columns. What couple are going to launch a bark on *The Tide*? What must Bernie feel? Pi couldn't write. Not any more. What must she think? It was nearly two months since that night. Don't let anybody for God's sake send her one of those pictures. What was Sullivan doing to them? He seemed to be bent on their destruction. Now, now, all Pi wanted to do was to save enough and go home. He was nearly there. It wouldn't be long now. Then he would be away. If nothing happened before then, he would have to tell Bernie. Straight out. If he had the courage. What had Sullivan done? Wasn't it like Sullivan? Oh my God, all the things he had ruined!

(If he could have seen Bernie. She was in her room, weeping. It was so hard. With the old man on the rampage about Mrs. Sullivan. Keep her away from me! Keep her away from me! He is being testy, she said. Just like my own father. Tantrums, that's what he has. You must make him do this. You must make him do that. Talking about Sullivan. What Sullivan had done. The name of Sullivan would drive the old man to a fury. The gall of him. That young no-good. His aspirations. My girl. Never, madam, over my dying body. Terrified that Sullivan's mother would one day say it straight out. But she didn't. She would tighten her lips and nod her head. Secretly pleased that she knew something he didn't. Oh, Sullivan, Bernie cried into her handkerchief, what's wrong? Please tell me what's wrong. What's happening? Why am I left in a dream of doubt? What has happened? Her nice room, all chintzes. Outside, the smell of spring. All the fruit trees are in blossom. If only you were here. If we could only walk together under the blossoms. It must be something very bad, on account of Pi. No letters from Pi. No mention of Pi in Sullivan's bald epistles. She had to dry her eyes. She couldn't afford the luxury of crying. Too much to do. She went down. Morgan was calm. Another year has gone by, Bernie. I am scenting another spring. How good it is! Tomorrow I will go into the orchard. Nodding his head, the heavy rug about his shoulders. Yes, Morgan, and many more springs, you'll see – hating herself for the fugitive thought that if it wasn't for Morgan she could find out. She could go. She would travel the earth. Hating herself for the thought. What! Would I deprive an old man of another spring? She was herself again.) I'm sorry, Bernie, Pi said to himself, but what in the name of God could I do, short of shooting him or her or something?

There was a car standing under the light. Right under the light outside the apartment house. Pi didn't notice it until he got close, and then looked casually. He couldn't miss seeing Bonnie. She was laughing, bending back her head. There was a dark-haired man beside her, at the wheel. He had his arm along the back seat and was bending over her. Pi was shocked. Then he wasn't shocked. The fact that the car stood under the light, that showed how innocent Bonnie was. If she wasn't innocent about this she wouldn't have to have the car stopped under the light.

Pi sighed. Nothing but trouble. Bonnie liked men around her. When she walked men often walked with her to the corner of the street, when she was coming home from work. But that was all that was in it. It was all as innocent as the day. Pi hoped it was. She didn't realise that she might be hurting Joe. Joe could be hurt. It was hard to be tied to a chair when you were young and so potentially active and strong. She just didn't think of that, he thought, and about how much Joe thought of her; how he resented every minute that she was away from him. But he hid it. Joe's trouble, thought Pi, was that he had no religion. He didn't believe in anything. Pi was shocked at this. He would have been helped a lot to have faith. He could have conquered his affliction easier. Pi knew this. He tried to tell Joe about it. He tried to get Tony to tell Joe about it. Joe really wasn't interested. He wasn't bitter about what had happened to him. He was bewildered. The only thing he could hold on to was Bonnie, and she was God for him and night and day and morning and everything else in life. She shouldn't do things like that, however innocent. Pi kept thinking that. Suppose you said it to her. It was none of your business. But she would see no harm in it. She would tell you that.

Instinctively Pi looked up at the second-floor window. He saw the curtain moving. Or did he see the curtain moving? He wasn't sure. He hoped Joe was in bed, or sitting in the chair looking at the television. Maybe I didn't see the curtain move. I hope I didn't see the curtain move. He went in. He walked up the stairs.

He stood outside Joe's door and listened. He had his hand raised to knock, but he didn't knock. He paused and then he went up to his own place, opened the door and went in.

Gee, thought Pi, can't there be a lot of unhappiness in the world! Why can't it all happen at once and get it over with? He switched on the light, took off his coat and threw it on a chair. Then he went to pull down the blind on the window. He stood there for a second. Bonnie had got out of the car. So had the man. He was standing up, his face close to hers. He was laughing. She was joshing him. You could see that. Then he bent forward and kissed her. She turned away from him, waved and came towards the apartment house. He waved after her, got into the car and drove away.

Pi thought: I hope Joe didn't see that. That wouldn't be good if Joe saw that. Then he sat down in a chair. What business is it of mine anyhow? he thought: just that you get to like people and you don't like to see them being hurt if you can help it. You indeed! What can you do? Except to be nice to people, to go out of your way to talk to them or walk with them. Let them talk to you. That way you learned a lot about life and how people lived. That was a good business. You knew people then and you could look on them. Why, even the worst person in the world would have something to say for himself if you listened to him. About why evil? There had to be a cause. Sure, no man could be entirely evil without a cause. What had happened to Sullivan? Pi couldn't see. Something. A worm or something eating inside of him.

He was conscious of the steps of Bonnie coming up the bare stairs. He knew her step. He had often heard it before. Unconsciously he had tensed in his chair. There could be no reason. But there was an eerie stillness about everything. That could be Saturday night. A lot of people went away Saturday nights once the spring came.

He heard her opening the door.

He listened and then he relaxed. He got up and started

265

loosening his tie and walked towards the bathroom. He would have a bath and he would go to bed and forget people's troubles.

Then he heard the scream.

The hair rose on the back of his neck. But Pi wasn't a one to question, or to hesitate.

He flung open his door and ran down the stairs.

Joe's door was open.

He hadn't anticipated this; hadn't anticipated this at all. Bonnie was screaming. She was screaming 'Joe! Joe! No!' You can take in a lot in a second. She wasn't screaming this at Joe because she was afraid for herself. It was for Joe. Pi knew this from the tone of her voice. Even though one of Joe's hands was gripping her blouse in the front and had practically torn it away from her and she had a long thin cut down one side of her cheek that was slowly starting to well blood. Her hands were held out. Joe was as white as a sheet. His eyes were very small. His teeth were so tightly clenched that the words weren't able to come through them. Just bitten-out expletives, that was all.

Pi shouted: 'Joe! Joe!' and he ran in straight on him, pushing her away, so that she turned and collapsed, her blouse tearing, and at the same time he reached for Joe's hand that was holding the thing in it. But he failed to catch it. He was between them at least, but Joe was still biting things through his teeth and was raising and striking, raising and striking.

Tony was never to know what inspiration brought him down to the hospital in Pi's street on this Saturday night. He could have been anywhere else in the great city, where there were always people on all sides of it, dying and being born, and being neglected and dying with nobody to hold their hand. A city attracts so many of the really lonely. There is always somebody whose hand you can hold.

So it was that he came into the street of the hospital and saw all the commotion around the door of Pi's place. A terrible lot of people and an ambulance and policemen. He ran over in his mind all the people who lived in Pi's apartment house. He couldn't think what was wrong. But he crossed the street, just at that time, and he saw the stretcher coming down the steps and he saw blood-stained bandages and what he thought was fair spiky hair. That looks like Pi's hair, was the thought that came into his head, and then he thought: But that couldn't be! He was madly forcing his way through the crowd to the circle of police who were holding the people back until he could reach Charlie, who looked very pale in the street light, and he said: 'Charlie! Charlie! Who is that? Tell me who is that?'

'It's Pi, Brother,' said Charlie. 'You wouldn't believe it's Pi.'

Tony didn't wait for any more. Just to be shocked. They would have to bring him across the street. He raced across the street, through the swinging doors, into the rubber-paved hall. What could he do there? Just waited, and waited, and waited.

Until he was in this room and Pi was on the bed, and they had bottles raised on high that were pouring things into his veins. It was only one side of his face that was covered. And you could see the skin of the rest of it. And there was a tinge of green on the skin. Pi's mouth was open in a surprised Oh, and he was breathing badly. Reaching for his hand. 'Pi! Pi!' One bandaged hand, the other one free. The skin of his hand as white as a wax candle. The nun very upset. Crying. 'Pi was so friendly. We all knew Pi.' The doctors working on him and then stopping working on him. There is nothing else they can do. They have done all the things that should be done. 'He has lost so much blood, so much blood,' the nun said.

Tony standing there, helpless, praying. Pi so far away from home. So far away from anyone.

Charlie, the policeman, really pale.

'Never mind people. People are like tigers, I say. More dangerous than tigers. What happens now? Pi dies. What do they do to Joe? He didn't mean it. How they going to give the hot seat to a cripple? Why should Joe go like that? Bonnie never meant any harm. You lose your two legs and you don't feel so good. Shut up all day. No wonder you might become savage like a tiger, see? He didn't mean it. How is that going to help? If Pi minded his own business who would have been the worse for it? Pi is gone. Look at him. You seen that colour before. I seen it before.'

Charlie got down on his knees. There was a small crucifix over the bed. Charlie took off his hat and shut his eyes and bowed his head. He looked very defenceless, with his white hair and the white part of his forehead which was sheltered from the weather by his hat.

But I can't just stand here, Tony thought, waiting for him to die.

To the Mother he said: 'Is there no hope for him? Is there no hope for him at all?'

'He lost so much blood,' she said. 'But God is good. Is there no friend?'

'I am a friend,' said Tony, 'but I'm here. What good is that?'

'No closer friend? No relation?' she asked. 'It helps. Sometimes.'

'How long?' he asked. 'How long will it take him to die like this?'

'God knows,' she said. 'He is a strong boy. Maybe now, maybe two days, maybe three. It depends. All the intravenous injections. The blood plasma – you don't know how his body will take it. But he is very low. Very low. The doctors hold out no hope.'

'Hold him,' said Tony. 'For the love of God hold him until I get back. Don't let him go.'

'The sisters are in the chapel praying for him,' she said. 'We can do no more. He was a nice boy.'

Tony left her. Now, Sullivan, he thought as he ran. Now, Sullivan, you can come to Pi. Pi really needs you now, Sullivan.

When he got there, the porter told him, No, Sullivan wasn't there. Gone away for the week-end. Didn't come home after the show at all. Would just clear off from the theatre. Back Monday in time for the show. That was all. Any use trying the theatre now? No, wouldn't think so. Too late now. They always clear out fast.

Tony stood outside there, and first he cursed Sullivan. The one time! The one time he was really needed and where was he? Then he prayed. Lord, give me inspiration. I don't know what to do. But please don't let Pi die. Pi and Bernie. Bernie was as much a mother and sister to Pi as his own. More so. Bernie was something special for Pi. He had always been so. But where was Bernie? Bernie was over three thousand miles away. He remembered that; asking Jay that question. New York is approximately three thousand miles from our present geographical position.

Philmill! Philmill would know where Sullivan was. Surely to God he would know. Didn't know where Philmill lived. He had to look it up. He had to travel in a cab without money.

It was about half an hour's drive. Couldn't see much of it in the dark. But a pleasant-looking place. Lights on. 'Wait here,' to the cabman. Up the long steps. Ring the bell. Hop from foot to foot. Door opens. Philmill, in shirt-sleeves and slippers. Old slippers. Philmill! The tycoon. 'Loan me money, Philmill, to pay the cab.' Philmill peering, turning on the light in the porch. 'Tony! Tony Mahon. What play are you in? Why didn't you take off the costume?' 'Please, Philmill!' Urgency in his voice. Philmill goes down to the cab, pays, comes back. 'Come on in.'

He goes in. In the room. A woman standing there. She has a nice face, very black hair. 'This is Judith, Tony Mahon.' 'Tony Mahon. Oh, I remember, you are the one who dropped a brick on Philmill's foot.' 'How?' 'Oh, he was all set for you and you walked out on him. You'll get a medal. You are the only one ever to walk out on Philmill.'

Tony surprised. 'Didn't know you were married, Philmill. Can't see you married somehow?' Putting off Pi. Poor Pi!

'Oh no,' said Philmill. 'Hey, kids!' Calling up the stairs. 'Yes, Pop.' Down they come. Five of them. Steps of stairs. In pyjamas. Two black-haired girls, three boys. Shy in their night clothes. 'I'm human,' says Philmill. 'What do you think I am, a robot? Back to bed, kids.' They make no move. 'What a mother!' Philmill says. 'What a way to bring up a family!'

'Go to bed, kids,' Judith says, and they go.

'Tony, what's wrong, something bad, heh, something really bad?'

Tony tells him. Philmill has to sit down. Philmill is horrified. He rubs his hand on his face.

'That Pi,' he said. 'Oh, that Pi. Too mixed up with people, that Pi. Soft as a pound of butter in the sun. No Sullivan, Tony. I don't know. I haven't an idea in God's earth where he is gone. Of all times. Haven't seen a lot of him lately. He and Mary Berry. You know that. Unhappy. But doesn't let it interfere in his work. Not yet. But dodging me a little, I think. Great God, you'd want to start at the A's in the phone book and go down them.'

'Oh Lord God,' Tony groaned. 'What will we do now, Philmill? I know. In here in my heart if we could get someone to him. Only that he won't die alone. It's terrible, Philmill.'

'Stop,' said Philmill. 'Great God! We have to do something. This is America. Where's his mother, his father?'

'Bernie would be the one,' said Tony. 'She was the one. He doted on her all his life. Hear him talking about her.'

'Bernie, Bernie,' said Philmill. 'That's Sullivan's dish. You mean her. The washed one in the photograph. She would do him good?'

'She's three thousand miles away, Philmill,' said Tony.

'It's impossible, isn't it?' said Philmill. 'How long do they give Pi? How long before he goes? How long they say?'

'They don't know,' said Tony. 'Now or tomorrow or the day after.'

'Right,' said Philmill. 'Listen, Tony, you go back there and stick by Pi and keep him alive. You got this Bernie's address?'

'Yes,' said Tony.

'Write it,' said Philmill, throwing off his slippers, going to the cupboard, taking out his shoes, putting them on.

'But why?' Tony bewildered, writing on a piece of paper Judith quietly put in front of him.

'I go and get the dame,' said Philmill.

'You can't do it,' said Tony.

'Oh no,' said Philmill. 'Impossible production. This is the U.S., boy. Ever hear about them inventing the aeroplane? Listen, Judith' – he was putting on a coat. 'You wire the dame.

Tell her to be at the airport to meet the plane. All right?'

'All right,' said Judith.

'Matter of life and death,' said Philmill. 'Then sit down at the 'phone, girl, and think. All Sullivan's friends. All Mary Berry's friends. People who might know about them. Ring them all. Every damn one of them. Track the son of a bitch down.'

'All right, Philmill,' said Judith calmly.

'Well, are you coming?' Philmill asks the bewildered Tony.

'But, Philmill!' said Tony.

'Suppose I miss the damn plane?' Philmill asks.

He is out of the front door. He has the garage doors opened. He is in the car. The car is backing out almost before Tony is sitting in it. He is speeding. He drops Tony at the first cab-rank. He has to go the other way. He throws bills at him.

'But, Philmill,' Tony is protesting. 'How will we repay you? This is madness. What will we do?'

'What will you do?' Philmill asks. 'Go and keep that Pi alive. I like Pi. And while you are praying, pray that this girl will have a passport. If she hasn't a passport, that's the only possible thing that would goose me. The only possible thing!' he added firmly and swung away, and Tony stood there, bemused, bewildered, and watched the twin tail-lights growing smaller and smaller, and thought: Well, Pi and I are no longer alone, that's one sure thing.

31

'But you are not happy,' she said. 'Do I make you unhappy?'

'No, no,' he said. 'Not you.'

'We seem to be in a terrible mess, Sullivan.'

He looked at her and at the littered lounge. There were many ashtrays overflowing. There were many dirty glasses. It was disordered, untidy. There was a sort of half-brick wall behind her, cutting off the kitchen of the place. It was a nice place. He liked it. The people were nice. They were very pleasant, very hospitable, but they couldn't stay up all the morning to keep up with Sullivan's restlessness. It was five o'clock. Outside the windows, there was a pale suspicion of dawn in the sky.

'I was born unhappy,' he said. 'It spreads from me. Contagious.'

'No,' she said. 'You can be happy. You can spread a lot of things around. You can make people argue. You don't jump down their necks. They like you.'

She was in an evening dress, leaning back in the settee. She looked tired.

'I could sleep for a week,' she said.

'Go to bed,' said Sullivan. 'You go on up to bed. This is Monday morning. My God, so few hours and we will be back again. The tide will be flowing east.'

'At least you are content with that, aren't you?' she asked. 'You enjoy that, don't you?'

'Yes, but it's palling,' he said. 'It's palling.'

'Am I palling?' she asked. 'Is that what's wrong?'

'No, no,' he said. He was on his knee beside her, rubbing her hair, flattening it to her head, making the bones stand out on her small face.

'You treat me like a pet, Sullivan. You pat me and you kiss me and you fondle me, but you can't make a decision about me. Why is it? You will have to face up to it. What are you going to do? We can't go on like this forever. We will go mad. I'll go mad.'

'Pity you ever met me,' he said. 'That's the pity. You don't know me. What do you know about me? We don't know anything about each other. I can't see you when you were young. Your background. You can't see me. We're alien. You can't know what I'd be like, living with me. Terrible.'

'I don't care,' she said.

'You would have been fine,' he said, 'if you hadn't seen me. I think of that. The things I have spoiled for you.'

'I met you,' she said. 'That's all that's in it. Let's face it, Sullivan. I cannot be this way. I am with you or I am not with you. I have you or I haven't got you. If I haven't got you, please make up your mind and let me go. I will go, if you want me to go.'

'That's what I'm afraid of,' he said, 'that you would do just that. And I can't bear it.'

'Is it your heart or your pride that would be hurt?' she said.

He kissed her.

'I don't know,' he said. 'It would tear my heart out.'

She rubbed her hand on his face.

'You're rough,' she said. 'It's very easy to solve it, Sullivan. Come on with me and commit yourself. Come on with me, Sullivan, and we'll drown together. Then you won't go back on me. Your old Bernie or no, you won't go back on me. Wouldn't you like that, Sullivan? You haven't given me anything at all, except patting. I want more. So that we will be one then and I will have you.'

Sullivan's head was on her breast. He felt suffocated with emotion. The sight of Pi's pale face, the wavering wisp of a vanishing Bernie, holding out her hand on a distant shore while the ship went away, went away.

'Come on,' she said softly, kissing him. 'Resolve yourself, Sullivan. Resolve me and then we will know.'

He got to his feet. Pulled her up close to him. Looked avidly at her face.

'Not fair to you,' he said. 'You have been good. No recriminations because I am struggling with wraiths. That's what they are now at this moment, like wisps of mist rising up from the floor of the valley.'

They walked together towards the stairs. Sullivan's head was muzzy with wine and lack of sleep and love. He felt the barricades which he had erected inside himself begin to melt away. It would be such a relief too, to get it over with. To cut away once and for all, if that was what must be. He owed her loyalty, having given in when he did, and then going like a swimmer to the edge of a pool. Diving in or not diving in. Afterwards he could see great loneliness and great pain, his heart forever cut away from a far shore, but if that was what was to be, let it be. He couldn't dither and dooder, like this. He wasn't like this at one time.

They were at the top of the stairs when the telephone rang below.

They paused.

'It's for some of them,' said Mary. 'Let them come and answer it.'

They waited.

'They are all fast asleep,' said Sullivan. 'I'll have to go. It might be urgent. You go. I will come after you.'

He sent her on her way and came down into the lounge. He passed it and went into the library, where the phone was ringing as consistently as an alarm clock. He lifted it, shut off the ringing and listened.

Yes, he was Sullivan. Surprised. Nobody knew where he was. The hosts weren't even known to him before the other day. Friends of friends of friends of Mary's who had been to the play. Who was that? For God's sake he didn't know Philmill had a wife. Yes. Yes. This was really Sullivan. He listened. He couldn't answer. His hand started to shake. His knees became weak as he listened to her words, telling, authentic. Pi! Oh God, yes. He would go. He didn't know. About two or three hours. He didn't know, but he would go. Don't let them. Do something. Don't let anything happen until I get there.

He went out into the lounge. He shook his head, tried to gather his thoughts.

He went into her room. She was almost undressed. He was looking at her without seeing her. The brightness went out of her face.

He told her about Pi.

'I must go,' he said. 'I must go now.'

'What good would it do?' she asked him.

What good? Great God! Pi! Pi dying! Did she know that? Pi was dying. He would have to go to him. 'Listen. There are cars outside. I will take the first convenient one. Tell them in the morning. You hear?'

'All right.'

He turned to go.

'Goodbye,' she said, 'Sullivan.'

He turned back. He went over to her. Held her arms.

274

'Yes,' he said. 'Goodbye. I haven't what it takes. To be a great lover. Have I, Mary? See? Can't help thinking about Pi. The way he looked, the scar standing out on his face. I never told you how he got that scar. Some day I will, and you will know. He is so bound up with me. And she too. Forgive me. I tried hard to keep away from you. I didn't succeed. I wish I had succeeded. I made you unhappy. It's my fault. I don't know. Press me out of your life. Like squeezing a lemon. When the lemon is squeezed, I'm what's left. You think of Pi; what I did to Pi. I'd do the same to you too, some way. Nothing but unhappiness for you. You'll see in the future. You will rejoice. No happiness. Misery I would bring you. No misery like the misery brought by the Irish. They are full of it. Too much history, masochism, introspection, conscience. Goodbye.'

It was really goodbye. He was gone. She heard him going down the stairs in great leaps. She heard the door opening and closing. She heard the car door slamming and the sound of the starter and the crunch of the wheels on the gravel of the drive and then he was gone.

She pressed her nostrils with her fingers to try to keep from crying. But it didn't work.

Sullivan couldn't see the view below him as he turned and twisted down the winding dirt road. The house was up on a hill. It was like a bird perched over the great valley. A wooded valley, where lakes gleamed greyly in the dawn. Most of the hillsides were covered in pine trees and larch. The new green shoots were appearing on the larch trees. The road went down and down, twisting, turning. Sullivan drove the car recklessly. He just knew where he was going. He was about six miles from the house when the engine went dead on him. He couldn't believe it, but the gauge told him no engine would run without petrol. The road went down and down for another three miles and then unfortunately it started to go up and up. Sullivan was frantic, but there was nothing he could do. The hill finally stopped the car. It started to go back. He put on the brakes.

He got out of the car. Oh, Pi, he thought, what in the name

275

of God will I do? There was nothing he could do. It was far back to the house. Uphill. He looked below into the valley. He could see, far off, the lights on the main highway. The lights of the trucks. They were very pale stars competing with the dawn. The road was long. It went all round. The other way was through the woods, but it was downhill.

He flung himself off the road and started downhill. He flew. Sometimes he helped himself swinging onto a tree. The barks were rough. They bit into his hands. Sometimes he fell and rolled, and was painfully stopped by the trunk of a tree. But he kept running. Each time he looked the highway seemed to be getting further and further away. So he stopped looking and he kept running.

Away away in a great distance. You have dreamed of this. That you are on a great plain with no features. Just a plain. You and the sky that is without stars, limitless. That if you fell off this plain you would be falling and falling for ever, while eternity lasted. And out of the void of the great plain a voice calls to you, so dimly, so distantly, and from all sides, so that you turn and turn frantically and you shout 'Here I am! Here I am!' but your voice is lost and swallowed up in the void and with all your heart and your body you listen again to hear if the voice will call your name. And the voice calls your name and it seems to be nearer. And hope springs in you and you shout out again, but no sound comes from you. You see your lips calling, but from your chest there comes no sound at all. And your head is bowed and you are going to fall off into the limitless purple space when you make out the sound of your own name: Pi! Oh, Pi! Come back! Come back!

And Pi opened his eyes.

To nothing. A white space. Like the expanse. Then he felt flesh against his cheek. And tears dropped on his face, and he could feel warmth from the face and the tears, and he slowly turned his head, very, very slowly. There were mists before his eyes, but they lifted, and he saw the face so close to his own, and he felt the burning palm that was holding his.

'Hello, Bernie,' said Pi.

'Oh, Pi!' she said. 'Oh, Pi! You came back. I thought you would never come back.'

'Hello, hello, hello,' he said. 'I can hear. I couldn't hear. I kept calling and I couldn't hear. It's good to be home, Bernie. I wanted to be home. Listen. I failed. You hear that? So sorry. So sorry.'

'No, no, Pi,' she said. 'Don't say that. You hear? Everything is fine. Oh, I swear to you everything is fine. I'm here. You see me. I am here.'

'Sullivan, oh, Sullivan, Bernie,' he said. 'Gee, I couldn't help it, Bernie. I tried. So mixed up. Not his fault. I don't know.'

He was gone again. This time the enclosed place was full of tears. His own. He was crying. He knew no peace. Wailing he was, like the sound of the wind in a forest of leafless thorn trees. Joe there, in his wheel chair, with his two hands over his face. Joe crying too. What you crying for, Joe? What have you got to cry about? Look at me. I can't go anywhere. Just to fall away and be turning over and over forever. Pi! said the voice to him. Pi! Do you hear me, Pi! Pi! Pi! Pi! Like short blasts on a trumpet that you wanted to raise your hands and stop your ears so that you wouldn't hear it. But it went on, and on, and on, until there was something familiar about it.

Pi opened his eyes again to the sound of it.

'That's Sullivan,' said Pi.

It was Sullivan. Sullivan with his hair all tossed, bloody scratches on his face. Sullivan was crying too, like Joe. Sullivan put down his face and rubbed it on Pi's face. Pi felt that. Pi felt that, very much. Pi protested.

'Gee, you want a shave, Sullivan,' said Pi.

What's this? Sullivan is laughing. That's good. Sullivan is laughing.

'Bernie,' Pi called. She came into his vision.

'Oh, Pi!' she said.

'Everything is fine, Bernie,' said Pi. 'Sullivan is laughing.'

Pi was drowsy.

'What?' the two doctors said as they hurried in with the Mother. 'Still alive? Impossible!' They bent over him. They examined him.

'What's impossible?' Sullivan asked them. 'What do you know about it? Nothing is impossible. Pi is fine. I'm not a doctor. I tell you that. Pi is fine. You hear?' Persuading himself.

'Mother,' one of them said. 'Get them away. Get them out of here.'

'Please,' she urged them. 'Just for a few minutes. You'll see. God is good. God has fixed it. Now let man work on him. I know. I have seen so many. I can tell. I can see the change in his face.'

She almost had to push Sullivan out of the room. Two covered trolleys had followed the doctors.

Sullivan had a last look at Pi, very pale with his eyes closed, a man bending over him, and then the door was shut.

He caught the Reverend Mother's arms. She was a small plump woman with a cheerful face, rosy cheeks.

'You're sure, aren't you?' he asked. 'He came back, didn't he? He spoke. You heard him? He will be all right, won't he?'

'Yes, yes, yes,' she said. 'Trust in God. Trust in God. Soon I will let you back. You'll see. When they have finished. I will let you back.'

She adroitly opened the door behind her and was gone. Sullivan leaned against the lintel, the wood cool to his hot head. And then it slowly percolated to him what had happened in that room. Who had been in that room. This wasn't true, he said, this couldn't have been true. I was sure I saw Bernie in that dim room. It was all that rushing. The smell of oil in the diesel truck. The urging of the man on. Wanting to get out and push at every hill. All that has me demented. Or was Pi so closely on the verge of eternity that he could, by permission, call the shade of Bernie to his side? Shade, if she was dead. But she wasn't dead too. The whole world couldn't have been dead. And if she wasn't dead, her shade couldn't be in a room, and if her shade wasn't in a room, it had to be herself.

Sullivan turned round, wildly.

There was a waiting-room opposite. It had no door. There was an open arch into it. The light was shining on her. It was she, Bernie. Shining on her short hair. Philmill was standing one side of her and Tony was standing on the other. Talk about away on a far shore, a small figure going further and further away. This was the reverse of it. A small figure on a far shore, aye, but you on a very fast boat coming closer and closer to the figure on the shore.

Sullivan walked slowly through the arch. Looked at her.

'Hello, Sullivan,' said Bernie.

Sullivan waited. His mind was racing. His heart was pumping so much blood into his head that he was almost blind. Now wait for her to waver away and disappear. A wraith. Like I said. But she didn't. She became clearer. As real as yesterday. More real than a picture in a frame. Clearer and more beautiful to the sight than the imagination. Oh my God, thought Sullivan as he went close to her.

Bernie nearly cried looking at him. His trousers were torn in several places. They were dirty with dried mud. One sleeve was almost ripped off his jacket. His face was black with beard and the dried blood of many scratches. She could just look at his eyes, and she knew everything was all right again. The sun was shining. Pi would see the sun shining too.

'Bernie,' Sullivan said, and he raised a dirty hand and placed his fingers against her cheek. 'You're real,' he said. 'Really real. You're here for sure?'

'Yes, I am, Sullivan,' she said. 'I am here.'

The muscles were standing out on his jaws. His face was pale. He looked very haggard. Now, here is a message for you, his eyes said. I love you. I always knew that, no matter what. Just this secret. Success is ashes. Not success. The things you dream about, if they are not people. These things are ashes. I wouldn't believe this. Kept trying to light fires in the ashes. Searching them for live coals. My poor Mary! You don't know about her. But you will, for I will tell you. She was a live coal. But I blew her out.

'Sullivan,' she said, 'don't look so sad. Please don't look so sad.' She was close to him. Her hand was on his chest. Those clear eyes were looking at him, worried.

'Bernie,' he said. 'All things have meaning. I was like a clock with a poor mainspring. You can fix mainsprings, very well, from the deeps of your own nature. You know that?'

'Whatever you say, Sullivan,' Bernie said.

What is that elusive scent about her? You smell and you think: That's Bernie, and waves and waves of memories come flooding back on top of you. Shores and seas and grass and wheeling gulls.

'You are like a pair of spectacles to me,' said Sullivan. 'I can see with you. All sorts of things. Even the *Street of Anger*. I can see it to a finish. On account of now, and on account of how false I have been to so many people. I wouldn't know a lot of things if I hadn't been false.'

'Oh, please, Sullivan, please don't talk like that,' she said. 'Think of Pi, think of poor Pi.'

She buried her head in his chest. He put his arms around her shoulders, his face on her hair.

And over her head he saw Philmill and Tony looking at him. Philmill's eyes were wide, the intelligent look beaming out of them. He wanted a shave, but there was triumph in his eyes. Sullivan knew that look well.

'You did it, Philmill,' he said. 'I don't know how, but you did it.'

'Ach,' said Philmill.

'He did it all right, Sullivan,' said Tony, 'and so did you.'

The door behind them opened. Sullivan turned his head, tensed, his fingers biting deeply into Bernie.

They looked at the Reverend Mother.

She whispered. As you would when a baby is asleep in another room. You don't want to waken him.

'Come now,' she said, 'the two of you. Only for a second. Don't talk. He wants you. He should sleep. Doctors! Against the books, they said. Who wrote the only book? I said. God wrote the only book that matters, I said, and Pi's name is not in it yet. Weren't all the sisters praying in the chapel for him?'

Bernie's hand found Sullivan's and they walked, almost on tip-toe, to the door.

280

The other two watched them.

'See what you did, Philmill,' said Tony. 'What a marvellous man you are, Philmill!'

'Nuts,' said Philmill, affected by the whispering. 'You said it was impossible. That's why. And only thirty-six hours. Challenge. See, Tony? Startled the poor girl. First thing I said to her. Didn't even know me. Who I was. I knew her. Walked out of a photograph. Have you a bloody passport, tell me quick, I say. She had. I would have been goosed else, Tony. Not even I could do it. But she had. The impossible! That's why I did it. Also to protect an investment. Sullivan; Mary Berry. Complications in the cast. Bad performances. Had to protect investment.'

'Philmill the man of stone! Philmill the cynic!' Tony jeered.

'Judith the one,' said Philmill. 'What a girl! Mine was easy. On that phone nearly two whole days. What a girl!'

'You are blessed with your wife,' said Tony. 'Lucky to get her.'

'Not lucky,' whispered Philmill. 'Good investment. Always noted for good casting. You my only failure. You would have been terrific as *Chobel*. I know. Only disappointment to me in the whole play. Pity.'

Sullivan and Bernie were still at the door. Then the Reverend Mother, at an indication from within, beckoned to them and they went in and the door closed on them.

' 'Fraid you'll lose that investment, Philmill,' said Tony.

'Oh no,' said Philmill. 'You must pray. Not until I get my money back. After that to hell with Sullivan. You hear?'

'I hear and obey,' said Tony.

The grim green was gone from Pi's face. It was just pale. They bent over him. Their heads were close together. Pi saw them. Pi smiled. Like home, he thought. My life's work. In a way.

Bernie was thinking: It was my fault. I sent him into this.

Sullivan was thinking: It was my fault. I sent him into this.

Pi said: 'Sullivan, Joe. They mustn't hurt Joe. Joe didn't mean. You'll see to that, Sullivan?'

'Sure, Pi,' said Sullivan.

'Hey, Bo,' said Pi. 'Can go back to Bo. No barrel though. Hear?'

'No barrel, Pi,' said Sullivan. 'We all go home together. No barrel. No long limousine either.' He felt the squeezing of her hand.

'Bernie,' said Pi. 'Know something?'

'What, Pi, what?' Bernie asked.

'You brought them with you,' said Pi.

'What, Pi? What did I bring?'

They had to bend closely over him to hear him. Pi was falling into a long sleep.

'The apple blossoms,' said Pi. 'The scent of the apple blossoms.'

That's it, thought Sullivan. That is exactly what it is.

Other Pan books that may interest you
are listed on the following pages

Walter Macken

One of Ireland's greatest novelists. 'Where the writer knows and loves his country as Walter Macken does, there is warmth and life.'

Brown Lord of the Mountain 50p

Donn Donnschleibhe returns to his home village bringing new life, marvellous changes — and revenge . . .

Rain on the Wind 50p

A rich, racy story of the fisherfolk of Galway — of fighting and drinking, of hurling and poaching, of weddings and wakes.

The Bogman 50p

Tricked into marriage to the sexless, middle-aged Julia, Cahal's heart is lost to the wanton Maire, and his rebellion grows . . .

Macken's famous trilogy of the dark years in Irish history.

Seek the Fair Land 50p

Cromwell's armies ravage the land in an orgy of death and destruction.

'An explosive segment of history . . . action-packed entertainment'
NEW YORK HERALD TRIBUNE

The Silent People 50p

Ireland, 1826 — when millions knew only famine, oppression and degradation.

'Written with all the power of pity and suppressed rage'
LIVERPOOL DAILY POST

The Scorching Wind 50p

The bitter fight for independence from 1915 to the end of the Civil War.

'That rare thing, a really great novel' BOOKS AND BOOKMEN

Sean O'Casey
Autobiography in six volumes

Volume One: I Knock at the Door 30p

In this volume, Sean O'Casey tells of the days of his Dublin
childhood.

Volume Two: Pictures in the Hallway 30p

Sean O'Casey recalls his coming to manhood, including episodes
later used by the playwright in *Red Roses for Me*.

Volume Three: Drums Under the Windows 40p

A nationalist's views of his country and countrymen from 1906 to
that 'rare time of death in Ireland' — Easter, 1916. From his stay in
hospital came people and incidents for *The Silver Tassie*, and out of
his personal experience of Dublin during the Rising rose *The
Plough and the Stars*.

Volume Four: Inishfallen, Fare Thee Well 40p

The memorable days of Ireland's Independence and Civil War —
the background to *Juno and the Paycock* and *The Plough and the
Stars* — heralded O'Casey's early triumphs at the Abbey Theatre.
This fourth volume vividly recreates the personalities of the era and
lists the grievances which made him leave Dublin for England in
1926.

Volume Five: Rose and Crown 40p

In 1926 O'Casey came to London to receive the Hawthornden
Prize for *Juno and the Paycock*, and he never returned to Ireland.
The crowded years that followed saw his marriage to the lovely
young actress, Eileen Carey, the mounting controversy over *The
Silver Tassie*, and his eventful visit to America for the staging of
Within the Gates.

Volume Six: Sunset and Evening Star 40p

In this final volume, reminiscences of his friendship with Shaw and
of life in Devon during World War II mingle with rebellious
indignation at organized religion and true concern for the people of
Ireland.

Picador fiction

Flann O'Brien
The Third Policeman 60p

This novel is comparable only to *Alice in Wonderland* as an allegory of the absurd. It is a murder thriller, a hilarious comic satire about an archetypal village police force, a surrealistic vision of eternity, and a tender, brief, erotic story about the unrequited love affair between a man and his bicycle.

'Even with *Ulysses* and *Finnegans Wake* behind him, James Joyce might have been envious'
OBSERVER

The Poor Mouth 75p
illustrated by Ralph Steadman

Flann O'Brien's hilarious Gaelic novel now appears in paperback for the first time, translated into English by Patrick C. Power.

'A devastating and hilarious send-up of Irishry'
TIMES LITERARY SUPPLEMENT

'Wildly funny, but there is at the same time always a deep sense of black evil. Only O'Brien's genius, of all the writers I can think of, was capable of that mixture of qualities. Ralph Steadman's drawings mirror it exactly' EVENING STANDARD

'Sooner or later he gets at most of us, not forgetting himself; all the while tickling the numbest of ribs with his lithe and lusty humour'
BRENDA LEHANE, DAILY TELEGRAPH MAGAZINE

'It grows like a hard little star' WILLIAM TREVOR, GUARDIAN

Selected bestsellers

- ☐ **Eagle in the Sky** Wilbur Smith 60p
- ☐ **Gone with the Wind** Margaret Mitchell £1.50
- ☐ **Jaws** Peter Benchley 70p
- ☐ **The Tower** Richard Martin Stern 60p
  (filmed as *The Towering Inferno*)
- ☐ **Mandingo** Kyle Onstott 75p
- ☐ **Alive : The Story of the Andes Survivors** (illus)
  Piers Paul Read 75p
- ☐ **Tinker Tailor Soldier Spy** John le Carré 75p
- ☐ **East of Eden** John Steinbeck 75p
- ☐ **The Adventures of Sherlock Holmes** Sir Arthur Conan
  Doyle 75p
- ☐ **Nicholas and Alexandra** (illus) Robert K. Massie £1.25
- ☐ **Knock Down** Dick Francis 60p
- ☐ **Penmarric** Susan Howatch 95p
- ☐ **Cashelmara** Susan Howatch 95p
- ☐ **The Poseidon Adventure** Paul Gallico 70p
- ☐ **Flashman** George MacDonald Fraser 70p
- ☐ **Airport** Arthur Hailey 80p
- ☐ **Onward Virgin Soldiers** Leslie Thomas 70p
- ☐ **The Doctor's Quick Weight Loss Diet** Stillman and Baker 60p
- ☐ **Vet in Harness** James Herriot 60p

All these books are available at your bookshop or newsagent:
or can be obtained direct from the publisher
Just tick the titles you want and fill in the form below
Prices quoted are applicable in UK

Pan Books Cavaye Place London SW10 9PG
Send purchase price plus 15p for the first book and 5p for each
additional book, to allow for postage and packing

Name (block letters) _____

Address_____

_____

While every effort is made to keep prices low, it is sometimes
necessary to increase prices at short notice. Pan Books reserve the
right to show on covers new retail prices which may differ from
those advertised in the text or elsewhere